Wild Raspberries

Connie Chappell

BLACK ROSE writing™

First printing

ISBN: 978-1-61296-512-3

PUBLISHED BY BLACK ROSE WRITING

www.blackrosewriting.com

Printed in the United States of America

Suggested retail price $17.95

Wild Raspberries is printed in Traditional Arabic

For Dick and his enduring love…

If you are not too long, I will wait here for you all my life.
—Oscar Wilde

Acknowledgements

Writing quietly entered my life eight years ago. The process of writing is such a unique and fascinating metamorphosis that it takes friends with similar qualities to support a writer.

LaDonna Lowe's highly tuned insight guided me toward nearby Antioch Writers' Workshop. She pointed me toward building blocks. Of course, she did.

Both mysteriously and miraculously, Robin Wilson reentered my life. This warm and humorous fellow writer waited in the workshop's meeting room to receive me. Her encouragement never wavered.

Angela Ward, talented and creative, actually tricked me into producing short videos for the government-access channel. And don't you know, imagining a scene playing out on video enhanced that same concept when I put the words together that bring characters to life.

Then the whirlwind that is Kathie Giorgio bolted forward with the full force of AllWriters' Workplace and Workshop behind her. She added challenge and unyielding belief.

I must not forget one more fine and worthy friend. Writing is my friend. We are inseparable.

My thanks to all of you for everything.

Wild Raspberries

Unraveled

Callie MacCallum looked up a split second before a black sedan, careening out of control, plowed through her street-side flowerbed. The front radial squashed daylilies flat and the bumper mowed plumed prairie grass down before the car stopped. A woman jumped out. She left the door open and the car running. It was Arnett Oldstone Sebring. When Jack Sebring, Callie's lover for twenty-two years, died eighteen months ago, it seemed reasonable to assume Callie was done with his wife. But she was there, red-faced, and charging across her front lawn. Instinctively, Callie tightened her grip on the banded newspaper she stepped out of the house to retrieve.

"Hey! What is this?" She thrust a fistful of quilt forward. "More handiwork from the Scottish Tart?"

Clearly, nothing about the older woman changed. Arnett hadn't missed the driveway; she never intended to use it. This was not the time to admit it, but Callie found Arnett's nickname for her clever and amusing. In a combo title, Arnett referred to Callie and Jack as the Tart and Tartan.

"First, you ruin my marriage," Arnett said. The curls arranged in her coarse gray hair shook with her voice. "Now, your fingerprints are all over my son's death. Why can't you stay the hell out of my life?"

"Dan? Those were Dan's clothes?" Callie was the quilt maker; no point in denying that. The quilt Arnett held was one of a pair, actually. Her revelation meant the clothing used to complete both belonged to Dan Sebring, Jack's younger son.

Weeks ago, Callie cut squares from half a dozen Hawaiian shirts, a stained football jersey, and a collection of worn jeans where the color supplied came from paint splatter. The squares were patched into a simple quilt pattern of six rows with six squares each. Its size would cover lap and legs. All of Callie's quilts were sewed anonymously for those who grieved the loss of a loved one; each was constructed from clothes the dear departed wore in life.

Callie's first quilt was sewed with Jack's clothes. Tears and pain competed fiercely with each other when she lost him to cancer; the pain went far beyond anything tears could ever hope to drown out. Callie was a golf professional by trade, not a quilter, but quilting supplied purpose to her life and got her through sleepless nights.

The incredulity Callie showed Arnett was genuine. She would not have recognized Dan's clothing. Jack's last three years were lived in Callie's house, but his two sons never accepted her in their father's life. The seething woman in the beige pantsuit hadn't allowed it. Three months ago, Callie was shocked to read Dan Sebring's obituary. Had Jack been living, his son's death would have destroyed him.

"Honest, Arnett," Callie said, her tone sympathetic, "I didn't know."

"Honest," Arnett repeated haughtily. "That's a laugh."

"How did you figure out I was the quilter?" Callie said, suddenly baffled.

Her new friend, Beebe Walker, worked as a grief counselor and was the motivation behind the therapeutic quilting. She and Beebe formulated a plan to maintain the privacy practiced in Beebe's counseling classes. Beebe reached out to certain class members with the idea of a quilt, but never mentioned Callie's name as quilt maker. This plan collapsed rather soundly in the hour since Beebe picked up the twin quilts for delivery.

"The pictures. The pictures in that album Lizbeth's counselor showed me." Arnett drew herself up to full height, a fearsome five-three. "I know my husband's clothing when I see it."

Callie's memory flashed on the day Beebe came to the house with her camera. Just as Arnett described, Beebe wanted photographs depicting the detail sewn into Jack's quilt for the purpose of showing future prospects.

Out on the street, Arnett's trailing entourage arrived. Callie closed her eyes, trying to blot out the sight of Beebe's car pulling to a quick stop behind a silver Tahoe. Callie never confessed that the man she lived with and told Beebe stories about, the man she loved so completely, never divorced his wife.

What did it matter that her lost love was someone else's husband? What mattered was that Beebe realized the quality of Callie's love for Jack was equal to the depth of her grief. Now Callie feared the belated truth would ruin their friendship.

Lizbeth Sebring stepped out of the SUV and jogged across the drive. The tall brunette was Dan's widow. Behind her, Beebe sidled up to Arnett's car, turned off the engine, and closed the door. Beebe was forty-six to Callie's forty-four, brunette to Callie's blonde, brown-eyed to Callie's blue, and rather doughy compared to Callie's streamlined build.

"Arnett," Lizbeth breathed through clenched teeth when she was close enough. "What's wrong with you, coming over here like this?"

"Why do you even need to ask that?" Arnett said accusingly, then a thought registered on her face. "You were in on this, you and that woman!" She pointed in the general direction of an approaching Beebe.

Callie's moment of confusion cleared when she remembered a tidbit of information Beebe shared when she placed the twin quilt order: The dear departed's widow attended sessions; his mother adamantly declined.

"I didn't know Callie would sew the quilts," Lizbeth complained. "I didn't know Beebe even knew her. I didn't know any of it until I looked at the album to see what caused you to race out of Beebe's office. I was just trying to do something nice. I thought you'd appreciate a quilt when I saw the finished one Beebe showed during class. I never saw that album."

Despite her daughter-in-law's denial, Arnett shook her head. "Makes no difference. I will not have this thing in my house. I never want to see it again." Arnett winged the quilt at Lizbeth.

Callie watched Lizbeth fumble it. The quilt's bottom corner, where Callie's hand-embroidered raspberry logo was stitched, nearly scraped the ground.

"Lizbeth? Callie?" Beebe said, squinting up at them. "I don't understand."

Callie's face was hot when she and Beebe finally made eye contact. A scathing exposure of Callie's carefully tended secrets came next.

"Let me explain it to you," Arnett said to Beebe. "This woman and my husband screwed around for nineteen years before they screwed up and I kicked John out."

"Callie and John?" Beebe said, emphasizing the man's name.

"The son-of-a-bitch who was John to me was Jack to her." To Callie, Arnett said, "I've dreamed of this opportunity a long time. It's the minimum you deserve."

Lizbeth, quick and agile, caught Arnett's hand before it struck Callie's cheek and, in one motion, whirled her mother-in-law around to face her. "No. Not anymore." Lizbeth drilled the words.

Her grip surely hurt Arnett's arm, but neither woman broke off her glare. Finally, Arnett pushed the taller woman back with her captured arm, then twisted it free. Lips pressed tight, she turned on her heel. The other three women watched as she shifted the sedan into reverse. With dirt and sod flying, she whipped the car around and gunned it up the street.

After Arnett disappeared from view, Lizbeth sighed audibly. "I'm so sorry about this, Callie, but I need to go after her. We've got to talk."

Beebe touched her arm. "Should I go with you?"

Lizbeth shook her head. "Thanks, but I'll handle it, and fill you in tomorrow." She strode purposefully away, folding the quilt as she went.

Before Lizbeth reached her vehicle, Callie turned her back, eager to escape the public arena. From a shady garage across the street, three neighborhood men seated in lawn chairs stared, transfixed.

Inside, she stopped short. Two paper grocery bags greeted her. They were stuffed with articles of clothing for her next quilt. Beebe dropped them off earlier when she collected the Sebring quilts. Callie tossed the newspaper on the foyer table, wound past the staircase, and ducked through the first doorway.

She was leaning against the dining room table, her palms flat on the floral cloth that covered it, reliving the nightmare, when she heard Beebe's shuffle stop behind her. She imagined the look of betrayal etched into Beebe's face.

At long last, Beebe's voice invaded the silence. "That was an ugly scene. Are you all right?"

Shoulders hunched, Callie nodded.

The quiet swelled and was again punctured by Beebe. "Are we going to talk, or do you want me to leave?"

Callie folded her arms as if to ward off a chill. "I don't know what to say."

"I bet not."

Callie never heard Beebe speak in this superior tone. She spun, her arms falling to her sides, her blue eyes latching onto the other woman. The rationale behind her deception spewed from her mouth. "I couldn't tell you, Beebe. I couldn't. No one would want to hear my story about Jack if they knew he was married, and not to me. If I told that, who would want to help? I was hurting when I came to you. I still am. But I'm not asking for forgiveness. I loved him. Jack and I protected that part of our lives. After he moved in with me, sure, people knew. They saw us together. But after he died, my instinct switched over to protection mode again. That's where I am," Callie said, patting her heart. "That's where I'll always be."

Beebe listened without releasing a glimmer of understanding, then her eyes narrowed. "How could you do that?"

Callie looked away under the weight of Beebe's condemnation.

Beebe moved a step closer. "No," she said. "Not how, on a moral level? How, on a survival level? What a deep love. Where did you find that kind of strength?"

The question surprised Callie. She stumbled around for an answer. "In Jack, I guess. In loving Jack."

Beebe's head shook the response away. "That kind of strength doesn't come from another person. I'm a bit envious of that quality in you, of its sheer concentration."

Callie absorbed Beebe's comment while her friend moved closer still.

"Let's go talk about Jack. I'd like to hear how he came into your life, again." Beebe winked. "Now that I know the full story."

Beebe's unflagging insight spoke to Callie's needs at this moment. The string that unraveled her secret about Jack now dangled. Another jerk, and it would be free.

. . .

Callie's twenty-four year love affair with Jack Sebring mimicked a three-act play. She and Jack successfully hid their affair for nineteen years; they lived together for three after he was diagnosed and while his illness progressed; during the last eighteen months, Callie coped with his death.

The two women filed through Callie's kitchen to the rear deck of her Cassel, Maryland, home. By late afternoon, the deck with its oval table and four cushioned chairs stood in solid shade created by the two-story house. Her secluded patch of yard was wedged between an unattached garage, its opposing raspberry arbor, and the woods that separated her home from Chesterfield Park Country Club. She worked at the club, managing the pro shop and hiring out for golf lessons.

Jack also kept an office at Chesterfield. He was the consummate overachiever, completely at home with larger-than-life projects. He poured his talent and creativity into golf course design.

Beebe pulled the nearest chair away from the glass-topped table, then angled it for a view of the wooded border. She brushed a brittle leaf from the cushion and sat.

Callie looked up to the wide August sky where birds chased sunshine and shadows, then walked to the wooden banister where Noodle's treat tin sat on the flat top rail. Noodle, her neighbor's English setter, routinely begged biscuits. In a cedar at the woods' edge, she watched a pair of bluebirds hop from branch to branch in a follow-the-leader game. Next to the cedar, a wide path entered the woods. Her golf cart was parked behind the garage, only its rear bumper visible. Callie's mode of transport to and from the country club was a winding cart ride through the woods.

Many said Callie was born to golf. Her greatest weapon was an assurance form-fitted to her skill. Out on the links, her focus closed around the shape of the fairway and the slope of the green. Yet it had been so easy to lay her life open to Jack: A glance said he read her thoughts; his touch absorbed her feelings. Every day, she ached to feel him touching her again.

Callie turned around when Beebe jump-started the story.

"I remember you met Jack during your junior year at Duke when you came home to play in a golf tournament." Beebe crossed her legs. "April, right?"

"Good memory, Beebe. It was the club's charity tournament. In the two prior classics, Mark and I were partners." Callie said, speaking of her older brother and propping a hip on the railing. "But that year, I pulled into the driveway to another surprise. This house was posted for sale."

"This house?" A surprised Beebe pointed a finger toward the decking. "Another detail I didn't know. You lived here as a child?"

Callie nodded. "This was my parents' house. Mark was being transferred. I got that news in January. His house over in Bremerton sold, so his company moved everything up. When I arrived home, Mark, Cheryl, and the kids were gone. My parents decided to follow Mark later that summer."

"I forget. Where did Mark move?"

"Macon."

"That's right. Then club officials substituted Jack."

Callie nodded. At the time, Mark told the former golf pro, Bill Franks, about his change in plans, but she always suspected Bill asked Mark not to tell her. Bill didn't want her to back out. She was the draw for the event. Having more members coming out meant more money pledged for the children's home. The club's roster of members knew she owned quite a few wins in junior tournaments and was ranked first at Duke. Around town, she was considered Chesterfield's protégé.

Callie wandered through the woods and onto the course when she was ten. The MacCallums weren't members, but Bill saw her interest, then her talent. He talked to club directors and received permission to give her lessons. He sold them on his dream that she'd become big in the game and that would bring attention to the club.

"Was it love at first sight when you were teamed with Jack?" Beebe asked.

The tone and sincerity of Beebe's question touched Callie's heart. "Honestly, it wasn't quite love. It was a strong connection, though. We became instant friends." She remembered everything about that first day with Jack. His athleticism and humor melded with hers as deliciously as warm syrup and butter settled comfortably in the wells of Sunday morning waffles.

"There were two occasions in May when Jack turned up on Duke's home course during matches. He didn't announce his intentions. I simply sensed his presence, perhaps due to the fact that he was wandering through my mind with increasing frequency."

"And obviously, you were wandering through his."

Callie smiled. Her spirit drifted back to the college course, finding Jack in the crowd, his blue eyes lighting a path between them. "He claimed his presence had been job-related coincidences." She gave Beebe a devilish look. "Neither one of us believed that."

"Did the relationship progress at that point?"

Now that Beebe knew Jack was married, she wanted to pinpoint precisely when sex entered the picture. Callie left off the introductory phrase, "Sorry to disappoint you," and said instead, "No, just dinner and conversation. I didn't see Jack again until my golf obligations for Duke ended in early August and I came home." Still, no sale pended on the house.

"That was the fateful summer you fell of the bike and broke your wrist."

Callie's left wrist went up. "This one. Fixing it required the insertion of four stainless-steel pins, followed by seven weeks of inactivity, and three months more given to physical therapy."

"Ouch. Didn't need to hear that again."

"My parents knew all that would predictably install me in this house for the duration. So the week after surgery, they trailed off to Macon, pining for the grandchildren. They said the real estate agent would deal with any nibbles and never looked back. Never came back either."

Beebe sat expectant, an elbow pinned to the armrest, one finger pressed to her lips. Beebe knew Callie well enough, now. This time, Callie pulled the string that unraveled her change in mood.

"You know, throughout my entire childhood, I felt neglected. I went on winning one golf tournament after another, being written up on the sports page, and Mark got all the attention. I never understood that. But in the end, my family's estrangement worked out." She curled a lip. "After Chesterfield hired me, I bought the house. Jack had private access through the woods, and family didn't show up at odd times. My family's disregard played an important role." Her gaze dropped. "It allowed me to realize the greatest love I will ever know." She gave herself a moment, then blinked back to Beebe. "That summer, I decided not to turn pro and let the world think the reason was the wrist injury."

"Thought you'd live life inside a huge glass golf ball, huh?" Beebe smiled. "With television coverage, the onset of social media, and cameras everywhere, questions would naturally rise about that one particular guy always in the crowd. You couldn't give up Jack."

Callie matched Beebe's affirmative statement with another. "So I gave up pro golf. I never regretted it." She raised an eyebrow. "My coach did. After the surgery, I notified him of my—well, mishap. Duke issued a press release. An account of the accident was reported in Sunday's sports section, so Jack was aware of my injury when, insanely bored, I trolled over to the club the next day." Beebe's eyes flicked to the golf cart and path. Callie continued her retelling. "Jack was just coming off the course. He showed concern and invited me to lunch at the club's restaurant, I think more to lift my spirits than anything. We lunched there every day that week and had plans to meet again on Friday. That morning, I was out here with the hose, watering Mother's orphaned geraniums."

Beebe's eyes sidestepped Callie to an oval patch out in the yard that grew the same red flowers. Before her gaze returned, Callie went inside herself.

"I will always remember how my heart suddenly pumped hard. I waited a half-second, then turned." She smiled. "Jack stood there, looking tanned, broad shouldered, his soul bared. I distinctly remember the want in his eyes. It pulled me inescapably into love with a man who was twenty-two years older, twice my age. I never felt too young. I'd been relying on my own instincts for years on the golf course. I took risks." Callie's eyes aligned with Beebe's. "Jack Sebring was a risk to take. I don't know how my heart contained our love. It was all fire and wind. Any man deserves to have the woman who loves him like that at his bedside when…" She swallowed the rest. Starting again, she said, "Caring for Jack after he got sick, that was the first time I made a difference. That was the first time I did something that mattered."

"The first time?" Beebe said soothingly. "Surely that's an exaggeration. You were what, forty, forty-one when Jack got sick?"

Callie understood Beebe's intention. She thought Callie was undervaluing herself. Callie shook her head and pressed her point. "No. Nothing compares. Not when you look at the full picture." Callie tugged at her sports skirt, then kicked up a golf shoe. "I played a game my whole life. Jack's illness, terminal cancer, the care he needed— I promised to provide that care to keep him at home. That was not a game. That was a blind promise. I didn't know what was coming. Yes, hospice nurses came and went. They gave me hands-on, during-the-crisis training. He was bedridden. That meant bedsores. One, I swear, as big as a grapefruit."

Beebe winced.

"I dispensed narcotics. Tens of thousands of dollars' worth of drugs ran through this house. His pain was severe. His medication was given every two hours. That meant no sleep for me. For weeks, no real sleep. I set an alarm to keep the schedule, to wake me up. Then the coma came. He died in our bed. I watched the funeral director carry his body out. It had stiffened." Her voice was barely a whisper. "Caring for Jack was something that mattered. It's been the only thing that's mattered."

For no reason, Callie reached for Noodle's treat tin. Her hand shook; she felt herself sway. She had yet to learn how to talk about

Jack's death without reliving it.

"Here, Callie. Sit down." As Beebe scooted a chair away from the table, the doorbell rang.

Beebe looked around. Callie set the tin down. She welcomed the interruption. It would give her the opportunity to walk off the emotional threads that still clung. "I'll see who that is, then, why don't you stay for dinner?"

Callie hoped she would. Earlier in the day, she arranged to spend a week at Heatherwood, the West Virginia cabin she and Jack visited as often as possible. There was a magic about Heatherwood. Callie's last promise to Jack pledged her return. In recent months, the unfulfilled promise became as haunting as the grief. Beebe knew the story. She understood the magic and the promise. Callie was sure she would back her decision with words of encouragement. Perhaps a kernel of that encouragement would ride in the car with her to fight the pain of returning alone.

No Small Measure

Callie's hurried steps slowed to a stop when the open front door came within view. Lizbeth Sebring stood on the other side of the screen. She was angled away, her head turned toward the lawn. In the three years Jack lived in Callie's house, Lizbeth never stopped by. Now she made the drive twice in one day. Callie blew out the breath she held, steeled herself, and then pushed her feet into motion again.

"Lizbeth," she said pleasantly, capturing her visitor's attention.

The younger woman wore a rueful expression. She gestured toward the mangled flowerbed. "Arnett certainly made a mess of your yard. I'm sorry."

"Don't worry. I can fix it." Callie turned the door handle. "Come in."

Lizbeth did. "After I left Arnett's, I went by Beebe's house..." Her voice trailed off.

"Figured she was still here, huh?"

"Took a chance."

"Have you eaten? I just asked Beebe to stay. I thought I'd cook spaghetti." Callie's chin was tipped up to Jack's tall, willowy daughter-in-law with her pale complexion and russet eyes.

Lizbeth shook her head. A curl of tawny hair slipped from her shoulder. "I shouldn't impose."

"Not at all. Join us. Believe me, it won't be anything fancy."

"Well, since Chad's at my brother's for an overnight—" Lizbeth said of her four-year old son. "Okay. Thanks."

"Beebe's out back," Callie said, walking her guest that direction.

Lizbeth dropped her purse on the window seat just inside the kitchen. Callie crossed the oak floor. She announced Lizbeth's arrival to Beebe, who sprang to her feet and rushed in from the deck.

"Is everything all right?" she asked. "How did things go with Arnett?"

Callie jumped in front of Lizbeth's response, retreating toward the back door. "Maybe I should…"

"No. Privacy issues aren't important. I want you to hear this," Lizbeth said. "I've had a thought. I want to be fair."

"That's a good premise," Beebe said. "Let's talk."

The small quantity of knowledge that trickled Callie's way concerning Lizbeth and Dan Sebring wouldn't have filled a golf scorecard. The tragedy of Dan's death at forty-two left Lizbeth to finish raising their two sons alone.

Older son, Geoff, attended the University of Florida as a sophomore. He and his mother shared a treasured closeness that Jack observed, admired, and spoke of to Callie. Lizbeth, pregnant again at thirty-seven, referred to the baby as an unplanned blessing. "Mostly to convince herself, I think," Jack reported at the time. Now Callie felt Chad's tugging presence must keep Lizbeth from drifting away in her grief.

While the three women worked to prepare the spaghetti dinner, Lizbeth talked and Callie listened. The story Lizbeth told amounted to the first and last chapters of her life with Dan.

Lizbeth's love for Dan stirred into being on a spring day in May. She found the business major seated before an easel, painting a picturesque scene on Salisbury University's campus. After they married, Lizbeth encouraged Dan to pursue his artistic talent. On Saturday mornings, he found a place in rural Maryland, sat under a shady canopy, and copied the countryside onto canvas. When a cross storm rolled in behind him on another spring day in May, he didn't test his luck. His paints, canvas, and utensils were all in hand, but he didn't escape the sycamore's domain before lightning split the tree that crushed him.

The women migrated to the dining room. Beebe sat in the chair across from Lizbeth. Callie looked on from the head of the table. She faced a crosshatched bay window and the dogwood tree beyond. Years ago, the tree was a birthday present from Jack.

"So your plan before tonight was that Arnett would babysit Chad when you return to work," Beebe said.

Callie listened, confused. Perhaps Beebe was confused, too. Her words accurately summarized Lizbeth's stance. But how does anything about Arnett's behavior toward me, Callie thought, connect with babysitting Chad? Why drag Chad into this? He didn't witness his grandmother's meltdown.

"Oh please," Lizbeth laughed, pushing her plate away, "Arnett doesn't babysit. Others babysit. Arnett grandsits." Her fingers flipped quotation marks in the air with an attitude rating of plus-one-hundred. The act sent her bangle bracelets a-chattering. "Arnett spawned the exalted term to magnify her importance."

Callie never heard Jack repeat the coined word. He must have thought it mirrored Arnett's pesky character flaws. Callie smiled to herself. Proud Arnett created an image only another control-freak could adequately envy.

"So she doesn't grandsit," Beebe said, unimpressed. "You find a daycare."

"Why not use Debbie?" Callie wondered. Lizbeth mentioned her brother's wife in passing while she tore lettuce into salad bowls. Chad would spend the night at his aunt's and uncle's house.

"She's helped me out this summer, but Debbie's a teacher. School starts in three weeks." Lizbeth's eyes lost their hold on Callie's. "I'm ashamed to admit Dan and I didn't save enough. We both knew better, but still." She grimaced a smile. "So, I'm not well positioned for the loss of his salary. It will take most of Dan's life insurance to keep Geoff in school these next three years. I just can't take him out. He's a bright kid, a good kid. He studied hard all through high school. Chad and I will have to make it on what I earn. I'm not sure what I'll find. The job market's slippery, and I haven't worked since Chad was born."

"And Arnett's services are free," Beebe concluded.

Lizbeth sighed. "They are."

"And you want to be fair?"

Callie saw Beebe's tack. She was backing into Lizbeth's posturing from the other side.

"In Arnett's world, grandsitting is steeped in tradition. To not let her keep a Sebring grandson would be tantamount to breaking a commandment."

"A Sebring grandson?" Beebe tilted her head.

"The fact that Arnett bore sons and they gave her grandsons seems to be the allure. I can't explain it. And since there are no daughters or granddaughters, there's no true comparison."

Out in the living room, the telephone rang. Callie excused herself and followed the hall around the stairs. She walked briskly past the couch. At the lamp table, she grabbed the phone in mid-ring.

"Callie? That you?" the female caller inquired.

The voice was full of vitality and Callie knew instantly to whom it belonged. "Sarah," she exclaimed. Caught up in the situation emanating from the twin quilts, she forgot her early-afternoon call to Sarah Prosser, the property manager for Heatherwood.

"I nearly cried," Sarah said, "when I saw your name on the call slip."

Earlier in the day, Callie confirmed the details of her trip to Heatherwood with Sarah's assistant and left a message that Sarah call when she could.

The friendship between Callie MacCallum and Sarah Prosser hit the ground running, due in no small measure to Jack Sebring. He searched for a long-term center of operations when his work took him into northern West Virginia to design two golf courses. That search led to property manager Sarah Prosser and ended at Heatherwood.

On that first morning when an Eden-like newness dawned over the riverfront cabin, he decided that when Callie joined him, Baron, West Virginia, was the place where they would forsake their Maryland lives. In Baron, they'd push their secrets so far into oblivion that they could, without guilt or fear of discovery, hold hands in public. Such a simple pleasure was not too much to ask. Sarah stopped by daily to deliver the newspaper and tend to cleaning. She had, by pinches and tugs, drawn Jack's love for Callie out into the mountain air.

Ten days lagged before Callie found a break in her schedule and could drive south. Jack's directions sent her first to the property office on the outskirts of Baron to pick up a second key. Sarah had grown a fondness for the golf course architect that her words of greeting revealed. To the woman she heard so much about, Sarah said, "So you're the Callie of Jack's heart."

Callie was overcome by Sarah's certainty and equally stunned by the deduction that enough personal detail passed from Jack to Sarah to support the older woman's conclusion. Despite the closeness Callie felt for Sarah, she always thought of Sarah as Jack's friend first. Something awakened in Jack during those initial ten days and a large part of the benefit was owed to Sarah. At first, Callie envied the kinship between Jack and Sarah, then quickly came to treasure it. Those events took place a dozen years ago. During Jack's illness, Sarah stayed in touch. Something told her to make contact the morning after he died.

With Lizbeth and Beebe in the other room, Callie stood at the picture window, telephone pressed to her ear. Outside, dusk was gathering.

"So, you're finally coming for a visit," Sarah said.

Callie visualized the perpetually bushytailed senior, her emerald eyes alight, and mimicked her upbeat tone. "Yes. Saturday."

"God, the place has missed you," Sarah said. "God, Heatherwood, and me."

Callie threw back her head and laughed. A great relief funneled through her. "I can't wait to see you."

"We'll have a nice long talk when you get here. You promise you'll come?"

"I promise. You've helped, Sarah."

"What do you mean? How?"

"Just talking with you. I wasn't sure I was completely ready. I told people I was, but…"

"I understand."

"You being there," Callie shrugged, "it'll help."

"I'll give you the hug Jack would want you to have."

Callie pictured Sarah's eyes crinkling with her warm words. Soon, they said their goodbyes, then Callie laid the handset against her chest and whispered a belated thank-you to Sarah Prosser.

The realization that she would not be totally alone in West Virginia boosted her spirits. An immediate deflation came before she reached the dining room's doorway. The tenor of the conversation within changed in her absence.

"Why are you so upset over this?" Beebe asked. "Callie and Arnett will probably never see each other again. You should tell Arnett you understand and forgive her, just go on from here. Consider this a fluke."

"This was a blatant reminder that Arnett will not change unless she's coerced into it. She didn't need to charge across town, drive through the flowers, and attempt assault and battery." Callie heard Lizbeth's bracelets bangle and pictured her animation. "If Arnett was handling things well, she would have expressed herself calmly in your office. She could have politely declined the quilt, explained her reasons, got in her car, and drove home. But she didn't. This is what I worry about. What if Chad sees something like this? In my opinion, she's overly influenced by Gary and Stella, her son and sister-in-law. Grandsitting was different with the other grandsons: John was living. Bless him, he had a way with her."

Callie smiled at Lizbeth's expressed affection for Jack. Her words confirmed what Callie suspected was true concerning his abilities and the need to control Arnett.

"I think you're trying too hard to change something that will settle down in a week. And if you can't afford daycare..."

"I want to improve the situation."

"With threats?"

"With whatever it takes."

Conversation stopped, and so did Callie's breathing. Callie imagined two sets of eyes locked on each other across the dining room table. She heard silverware rattled against china, then Lizbeth broke the silence.

"Okay," she acquiesced. "I planned to manipulate the grandsitting situation with Chad to get her into counseling."

Callie stiffened. Chad, again.

"At the risk of repeating myself, you don't have any control there if you can't afford daycare. If you threaten to take Chad away and Arnett doesn't agree to counseling, then you have to run back with your tail between your legs for her free daycare—which I understand is feeling less and less free." Beebe sighed. "I'm sorry. There's just no teeth in that plan."

From out in the kitchen, a muffled version of the *1812 Overture* began to play. The ringtone pushed Callie free of her eavesdropping position and into the doorway.

Lizbeth quickly slipped off her chair. "That's my brother. Where's my purse?"

"Window seat in the kitchen," Callie said, pointing and stepping back so Lizbeth could pass. She jogged away.

Once Callie reclaimed her place at the table, she looked at Beebe inquiringly. "Handful?"

"She's not giving me specifics, but she seems fixated on using counseling to win some war with Arnett. She's worried about family members getting in the way. She sat there and let everything come down on her."

"That experience didn't just happen here."

"What?" Beebe expressed surprise.

"Remember out front when she grabbed Arnett's arm. She said, 'No. Not anymore.' She blurted that out. No pause for thought."

"You think subconsciously, Lizbeth's been building with something before today?"

"I heard what you told her, but this situation is not the first. And Lizbeth's right about family influence."

Beebe closed one eye. "How long were you listening?"

Callie's raised hands said guilty as charged. "This time, Arnett's actions were heated and spontaneous. But she goes out of her way; she plans. She found out the date Jack was taking a chemo treatment and knew I'd be sitting with him. She came to the hospital with Stella for the sole purpose of picking a fight with me. She grabbed the TV remote off the bed table and made moves to hit me with it. Stella waited until the last minute, then pulled her away. Jack was helpless with tubes in his arm. I was not going to show aggression; I asked her to back off. Then after Jack moved in, she came over with an armload of his clothes."

Beebe's worried frown appeared.

"It was early one morning. She hung the clothes in the tree." Callie pointed out the window at the dogwood. "And, I never told you that on the anniversary of his death, she called to harass me. There'd been other calls. In the background, I heard what I'm sure was Stella's voice of encouragement."

"Hmm. Well? So today was not isolated. What about Gary?"

"I have no details there, but if Lizbeth's casting a shadow, perhaps it's justified. Gary never did anything but give me dirty looks." Callie fiddled with her dinner napkin. "I'm concerned she's putting Chad in the middle. I will never forget one of the things Jack said when he found out the cancer had returned. He was so sad that he wouldn't see Chad grow up, that he'd miss that." Callie remembered Jack's troubled eyes turned toward her from the deck chair, the way he took her hand and held it tight. "I feel a duty to do something. I should help. It's my fault."

"It's no one's fault. This is grief. Dan's death is not your fault."

"The affair was my fault. And I'm worried about Chad."

Beebe pulled folded hands up to her mouth and exhaled long and deep. "I guess my first concern is Lizbeth. Helping her helps the boy. I see her letting this fester. She wants to get Arnett into personalized counseling. I've got to move quick on that. My hiatus is this week and next. If Gary and Stella are hindrances, then we'll get away. A hotel, I suppose. No, a state park would be nice. Serene. The bigger ones have lodges, if it's not too late in the season to get reservations. But that would be an expense for Lizbeth."

Callie turned her head toward the room's bay window. Buttons of light flickered on and off as fireflies danced through the night. She thought how Beebe's description of her ideal counseling location felt eerily close to sounding like her getaway cabin in the mountains.

"Wow. You just disappeared from view. Where'd you go?"

Callie blinked back at Beebe. She answered honestly. "I was thinking about Heatherwood. I leave Saturday."

"You made the arrangements. That's great. I'm pleased." In the next second, the eeriness Callie experienced showed up on Beebe's face. She cleared her throat. "Boy, I hate asking this, but could we use the cabin?"

"Arnett at Heatherwood? I don't think so."

Moonlight

Lizbeth breezed into the dining room on the heels of Callie's declaration removing Heatherwood from consideration as a counseling retreat.

"Heatherwood? What's that?" Lizbeth asked casually.

Callie froze. Her second nature took over. She was debating wildly, wondering how best to protect the secret world she and Jack shared in Baron, when Beebe leaped in front, turning the conversation to let Callie breathe.

"Everything good with Chad?" Beebe's tone was upbeat.

"Brushed his teeth without complaint—which he never does for me—hopped in bed on command, and will see *me* in the morning." Lizbeth reclaimed her seat. "So, where were we before my brother called?" As soon as the question was out, she stiffened, sensing the dome of strain hovering above the table. Her eyes slid from one woman to the other. "I'm interrupting, aren't I?"

She started to get up, but Callie waved a hand. "No. Stay. We're good."

And initially, Callie thought they were.

Beebe shifted in her seat to face Lizbeth. She thoughtfully tapped a finger to her lips. "Was it Gilbert and Sullivan's *The Pirates of Penzance* that was all about duty, or was it *H.M.S. Pinafore*?"

"If memory serves, all of Gilbert and Sullivan's operas are about duty."

"That's what I thought."

"What brought that up?" Lizbeth wanted to know.

"Callie was just talking about duty."

Throughout, Callie's focus remained pinned to Beebe. From the corner of her eye, she saw Lizbeth's look of confusion pass from Beebe to her. Beebe's expression said she was mildly pleased with the covert challenge she'd levied. Callie responded with a stony-faced glare, despite the fact that inside her head, bold music played. Clipped phrases from the operas mentioned sang out. Yes, they struck chords of duty, loyalty to a cause. She wondered, given the circumstances, what would Jack do in this situation, to what lengths would he go for Chad? She thought how Beebe had never given her bad advice in the past. She was tempted to accept Beebe's challenge, but strong feelings of betrayal to Jack about Heatherwood snatched the temptation away.

Beebe smiled at Lizbeth. With one finger, she looped several chin-length strands of hair behind an ear. "What if we established some kind of truce with Arnett? Would you be satisfied if she could sit in a room for counseling with Callie—"

Callie jerked to attention. "Sit in a room *with* me!" Beebe took her from merely providing the boxing ring to sparring inside the ropes.

Beebe ignored Callie and went on conversing with Lizbeth. "Would you be satisfied if Arnett could sit there and not reach down Callie's throat and rip out her heart? Well, maybe she'd want to, but she'd restrain herself. Would you be satisfied with that?"

While a speechless Callie gaped at Beebe, Lizbeth gave a hapless shrug. "Yes, probably. But what are we talking about?"

"I think Arnett needs to step up to counseling, show she wants to change, and is hopefully willing to do the work. Counseling gives her tools to use, something to reach back for on difficult days. You're right,

Lizbeth, Chad should not see what we saw in Callie's front yard. If Jack were here, I'm sure he'd agree, don't you?"

"Well, yes." Lizbeth's words stumbled out.

"Arnett could easily be counseled right here, right now, in Cassel," Callie argued. "You wouldn't need to wait until Saturday."

Beebe shook her head. "No, I definitely want to set up a separation from family members. We need to get Arnett away from those certain Sebrings who might impede our progress. Lizbeth wants to see true change on Arnett's part. That's where the quilt comes in, and you. Arnett accepts the quilt—

Lizbeth interrupted. "Wait. Away where?"

Beebe didn't wait. She kept Callie in her crosshairs. "Lizbeth knows progress is made when Arnett accepts the quilt, and you come home without a scratch."

"Well, that sentiment is not exactly swaying me," Callie said on a breath of bitter laughter. "And why would I do this? It feels like there's a carrot and stick involved in your scenario. Both losing propositions for me. I either get beaten up or eaten." Callie folded her arms. "Arnett will never agree because—"

"Oh, I think she will. She'll work hard to regain Chad. At week's end, you're the test, her interaction with you."

"And the reason she'll never agree is, this cabin, Heatherwood," Callie nodded toward Lizbeth, finally nailing down an answer to her repeated question, "is where Jack and I met for long weekends. Arnett's bound to remember Jack spent a lot of time designing two West Virginia courses. She'll never consent if she knows, and she'd have to be told. That's the first hump. Hump number two: I own Heatherwood. It was a gift from Jack."

Lizbeth leaned forward. "This plan, this cabin sounds great. Please, Callie, let me try to convince her."

Callie was startled. She just explained why use of the cabin was inappropriate, but Lizbeth forged ahead eagerly.

"I'll get her over these humps. It's quick, I know—" Suddenly, Lizbeth frowned; her face clouded over. Her voice came back burdened. "It's quick like Dan's death. Some days, I think the rest of my life will be filled with snap decisions." She looked up. "I need to have this little bit of confidence restored in Arnett. It feels like I've slipped a few rungs today. Then there's the job uncertainty. I have so much to decide, and I don't know the possibilities at Heatherwood." She swallowed. "Please, Callie, would you consider playing a part in this?"

Beebe followed on the heels of Lizbeth's appeal. "This can be the way you help, Callie. I'll be there. You'll have support. More importantly, you'll be support. If family members undo a day's work, then that's detrimental to our cause. Getting away will set the stage for the best possible outcome, and that's a good first step." Her hands rested on the table edge. "I can imagine what Heatherwood means. I recognize the strength it takes just to decide to return, let alone make the trip without Jack. But imagine that Arnett agrees; you and she are there."

Beebe, a compelling speaker, caused that very picture to materialize in Callie's head. It was vivid, despite the shiver prickling her spine.

"What's your role?" Beebe continued. "More than a carrot, or a test. You'll speak for Jack, as Lizbeth will speak for Dan. This dynamic feels vital to me."

Callie groaned and sat back in the chair.

"Their voices shouldn't be missing from these discussions. Jack's grandson deserves a grandmother and mother without tension between them. Grief's a tough battle; you've made progress. Arranging to visit Heatherwood is proof. Can we count on your help? Because, Callie, this is something that matters."

That last sentence, Callie's own words, dismantled her stacked defenses.

. . .

Callie closed the door behind Beebe and Lizbeth. She switched off the foyer light and switched on the small lamp she burned as a night light. Its blush fell across the corner of the sofa where Jack's folded quilt lay. The golf course emblems she'd cut from his golf shirts were distinctive. They were stitched alongside other squares so uniquely Jack. He had a love for pockets. All kinds. Worked into the design were hip pockets, flapped pockets, buttoned and snapped pockets, riveted, watch, and cargo pockets.

Her gaze slid to a small hand-embroidery. Along the edge of the quilt where an artist would sign a painting, Callie stitched two raspberries growing from a curved vine with just-sprouted yellow leaves. Between the two berries, the connecting vine formed a heart. She added this detail to each of her quilts.

Feeling restless and reminiscent, she wandered out back. The yard was bathed in the champagne glow of moonlight. She smiled at Noodle's treat tin sitting on the deck rail.

Whenever Jack witnessed her feeding the setter, he made the same comment, usually spoken from his favorite chair on the deck: "You like spoiling that dog."

Studying his tanned face and that wayward curl of sandy hair perpetually pitched forward on his forehead, she offered her standard reply: "One treat a day doesn't spoil. Besides, you like spoiling me."

By then, they'd have linked pinkie fingers. With his unique blend of tease and sincerity, he replied, "None of this would be worth it if I couldn't spoil you."

How many times had she heard those words, brushed back that stray curl? How many times had his loving eyes watched her with intimate familiarity?

Memories drew her down the deck steps. She crossed the yard to reach the small seventeen-year old arbor. The two wild raspberry bushes that grew hip-high on either side of an arched boardwalk-styled bridge thrived. Their yield earlier that summer was particularly prolific.

She stepped up onto the bridge and allowed a leafy sprig to rest in her palm. Callie's love for Jack lived seven years the summer he planted the bushes. They were a touchstone. Hence, her signature on the quilts.

On her way into the house, she passed his chair. Her hand skimmed the top of the cushion. She paused to crook her little finger.

. . .

The next morning, Beebe slipped her wide feet into comfortable pink clogs. Earlier, she pulled on a striped shirt and lightweight slacks. On her bed lay the sage-green no-waist dress and matching jacket she intended to wear for her luncheon engagement with Callie at Chesterfield Park. Their plans were made a week ago.

Beebe's thoughts traipsed farther back. They arrived at the day she met Callie. Beebe stood looking out the window of her new office at Trydestone Lutheran. She watched the church's custodian kneeling on the lawn in front of a stone-and-glass monument sign. He was posting her name in white letters with the title: Interim pastor. Out in the street, a SUV slowed. Like Beebe, the driver studied the custodian's work. Brake lights flashed the driver's indecision, then the SUV pulled into the church's lot.

Misery and grief over Jack's loss forced Callie inside the church that day. From their one-on-one sessions, a friendship grew. When Beebe didn't get the nod for full pastorship, she gravitated toward grief counseling.

"How do you feel about being passed over by the board of deacons?" Callie asked at the time.

"Honestly, I think those boys were struck with divine inspiration. On high, there must have been a rushed effort to get me the hell out of that church because God was about to recall me as a minister." Eyes wide, Beebe rattled on. "Like after my ordination, a defect was observed in my spiritual inner workings, like numbers somewhere along the line had been transposed, and I was not the one actually chosen."

Callie laughed. "Oh, Beebe, none of that is true. But were you passed over because you're a woman?"

Beebe thought her reference to the deacons as "those boys" struck Callie as suspicious. She cocked her hands toward the quite-large chest she thrust out. "Look at these puppies. I'm obviously a woman. Seriously," she said, "I'd like to think I was given equal consideration."

"Are you angry? A little depressed?"

Beebe closed one lid and eyeballed Callie. "Ah, the student becomes the teacher. You think I'm grieving."

Fear, anger, and depression were grief's second-stage hurdles. Callie hadn't mentioned fear. In truth, that hurdle was handled quickly. Now, anger and depression were behind her.

Beebe scuffed down the short hallway that joined her cozily cluttered living room. She was ready to meet her day—well, ready to meet the coffeemaker anyway. She angled past an occasional table and lamp. Her gaze traveled to the piled desk, and she gathered speed. The telephone console's red message light winked through a stray sheet of paper tented over the device. A picture of Lizbeth lunged forward in her mind. Had she missed a call while the shower or hair dryer ran?

At the desk, she swept a newspaper renewal notice aside and punched the button that brought the voicemail attendant to life. She recited the date and time associated with one stored message. The call came in last evening before her return from Callie's.

"Beebe, where are you?" the message began. The voice belonged to Beebe's long-lost, ex-fiancé Vincent Bostick. "The decision's been made. The assistant's job is officially yours. The employment contract will come out of Ron Smith's office. He's an attorney and one of my board members. Monday after next is the start date as planned." Beebe winced and sat down hard in the desk chair. "Call me between twelve and one tomorrow. Other than that, my schedule's full. Anyway, congratulations. I'm just as happy as you are. Can't wait to talk."

By the time Vincent Bostick signed off, Beebe stared openmouthed at the ceiling.

Vincent's message would have served her well as the conversation-starter needed for the last two months. Her new job would soon have a contract to solidify it, and she'd yet to find the words to tell Callie what Vincent spit out so easily—not as eloquently as Beebe would have liked—but oh so easily. The new job was not in Maryland, but several states away in Michigan.

Until the doo-doo hit the fan and Arnett hightailed it out of her office, Beebe's "fadeout" plan made good progress. The two Sebring quilts were completed with time to spare. Beebe definitely wanted them delivered before she turned her group sessions over to a new counselor, who would also tend to the delivery of Callie's next quilt.

The bushwhacking of her fadeout plan took place in Callie's front yard. Today, her sense of urgency was somewhat calmed by Callie's reluctant agreement to offer Heatherwood as a counseling retreat. That represented an expedient resolution to her dwindling time frame.

"Less than two weeks," Beebe said to herself. She lowered her chin and spoke to the desktop cactus in its terra cotta pot. "Maybe I'll call Callie over, replay the message, and let Vincent spit out the plan. Then I'll invite Lizbeth and do the same."

Several seasons back, God came to earth in the form of Vincent Bostick. He rang her doorbell and invited her to come home. He hadn't meant the heavenly assent. He meant Larkspur, Michigan, where she was raised.

Beebe gazed back at the tall, kind, scholarly man on her porch that frosty morning with the Maryland sun rising over his shoulder and knew somewhere, a large stone was rolled away from a tomb. Most of the time, his glasses rode on top of his head, easily lost in the beautiful crop of chestnut hair Beebe envied since high school.

Vincent acted as an activities director of sorts for a hospice (slash) bingo hall (slash) homeless shelter (slash) senior center in their one-size-fits-all hometown. He ran the menagerie enthusiastically and pretty much single-handedly. On the other hand, Beebe's confidence was shaken after her separation from the church. With her spirit-filled bosom drained, she declined his offer, but he hadn't given up. He pestered her good-naturedly in the weeks that followed. Soon, she was considering the move.

During the tussle in Callie MacCallum's front yard, something astounding happened. She felt a slow return of faith, an itching at the corners of her soul. It came with a sort of premonition. An odd foreboding might better describe it.

She watched Arnett Sebring raise her hand to slap Callie, and for the first time in months, she prayed. It was reflex, training, shock, definitely a plea for help. She prayed for God's intervention. But His intervention, she now realized, came when He led her into employment as a grief counselor. God put her in the company of these three women, and with a grief quilt folded into the mix because there was something to learn from this entangled situation.

She went to lie down on her afghan-covered couch, to indulge in some personal analytical exploration. In other words, self-counseling. She gave the requisite fifty minutes. Her head and pillow were propped against one armrest while she focused on her pink clogs laid open in a V on the distant armrest.

When the session ended, Beebe rose to erase Vincent's recorded message. The symbolic measure meant Beebe would not reveal her relocation plans to Callie nor Lizbeth quite so soon. The dilemma between Arnett and Lizbeth concerning the child must be resolved first. Only when Lizbeth's future rested on a solid foundation would Beebe share her need to return to Michigan—where she hoped to reconnect with her father.

. . .

Since she agreed to meet Callie shortly after twelve and she abhorred tardiness, especially in herself, Beebe had no choice but to don her Bluetooth and return Vincent's call from the car. He answered promptly.

"Vincent, hi." Beebe steered onto country club property and past the sign dating Chesterfield Park's origins back to 1919. The rolling front lawn was cut by a winding tree-lined entrance road.

"Beebs," Vincent said in a comfortable way that made her relish old times. "Perfect timing. I just hung up from Ron. He expects to have the employment agreement ready to mail Monday, but he'd rather email it."

Beebe remembered Ron Smith as the community center's board member and legal counsel. "Vincent, maybe we should back up a minute."

"Back up? You mean you're not taking the job." Vincent sounded nervous. In her mind, she pictured his rather large Adam's apple bobbing.

"No, I mean, back up to: Good afternoon, Beebs. How's your day? Busy, Vincent. How's yours?"

His laughter warmed her. "Okay, okay," he said. "It's just that I'm excited you're coming home to work in this crazy world of mine. How about you?"

"I was thrilled to get the news."

"It still seems right?"

"It does. The center's work. Back home. All good." A beat passed. "So how's my father?"

"I sat with Cliff at church Sunday. He's fine."

"And you, Vincent. My manners lesson aside, how are you?"

"Much better now that I know you're coming. Worried a bit. Knowing about your mother, and keeping what I know from Cliff. It's going to hit him hard when we tell him, but you'll be here, back in town to stay. That'll help."

Clifford Walker, Beebe's father, stepped into the role of single parent when mother and wife deserted him and his daughter the year Beebe turned sixteen. To support his family, he split his time between the local hardware store and caring for the cemetery on the outskirts of Larkspur. In exchange for his devotion to the latter, his family lived rent-free in the caretaker's house next door. Beebe knew her father as a steady, hard worker and a good friend to Vincent. She trained herself not to think of her mother at all. Doing so now created a twist of tension, so she was glad when Vincent moved the conversation to smoother waters.

"Can I have Ron email the employment agreement? The board wants your signature before the start date."

"Hmm. My two weeks off have just filled up with a...counseling emergency."

"A counseling emergency?"

"Hard to explain, what with confidentiality and all."

"Still, email ought to work Monday, right?"

"Sure. Go ahead and email it," Beebe said, giving Vincent the easy response. Monday was too far away and the situation with the three women too jumbled to make a prediction. She would figure out the logistics later.

Peace Summit

Callie sat on the bench near the pro shop. She watched Beebe's car wind around the oval of evergreen trees, yellow mums, and cardinal red geraniums that shielded the country club's main entrance from the parking lot. Beebe angled the sedan into a parking space, and Callie went out to meet her. Beebe got out, dropping Bluetooth, ignition key, and cell phone into a sagging leather purse.

"Good news," Callie said. "The chef has your chicken salad on the menu."

"Raisins, nuts, and grapes?"

"Raisins, nuts, and grapes."

"I'd like to give that man a smooch before I leave."

"I'll happily lead you to him."

Beebe's gaze hung on Callie a split second too long. No doubt she spied the dark circles under Callie's puffy eyes. Overnight, sleep evaded her. A deep, sorrowful longing for Jack took its place. For hours, the tears flowed.

The two women strolled into the concourse between the pro shop and clubhouse, both built of large, dark rectangular stones. A perpetual breeze lived between the two buildings. It swept up from the course and swirled their hair.

"It's a beautiful day," Callie said. "We might as well eat on the terrace."

The terrace adjoined the club's dining room. The land's natural contours placed the terrace on a level above the course. Either inside or out, diners could survey the beauty that was Chesterfield Park.

The women were heading toward the terrace's outside stairs when a ringing emitted from Beebe's shoulder bag. She retrieved and answered her phone. "Yes, Lizbeth?"

Callie eagerly listened to Beebe's truncated conversation.

"No. No, you shouldn't—we'll talk—" Beebe rolled her eyes. "Lizbeth—Lizbeth! Go straight to my office. I'll meet you there. I'm fifteen minutes away." Ending the call, she turned to Callie. "I'll have to kiss the chef another day."

"What happened?"

"Lizbeth's talk with Arnett was an abysmal failure. I was worried about that. Now, she's tossed everything over the side. She says she's going to pack up essentials and move to Florida."

Callie straightened. "Florida!"

"She apparently has family there."

"It's too soon after Dan's death to make a decision like that."

"What you and I know has still eluded Lizbeth. She's got anger issues out the wazoo." Beebe touched Callie's arm. "Listen, I've got to run."

"Call me. Let me know."

"Give it a few hours. I believe I'll be drilling through one rock-solid head." With that, Beebe hustled toward the asphalt lot.

Callie watched Beebe's exodus, then wandered over to the bench, her thoughts awhirl. With Lizbeth's family counseling idea a failure, the possibility that Callie might travel alone to Heatherwood on Saturday should have brightened her outlook. But damn that Beebe, she planted the notion that Callie could and should speak vicariously for Jack. It surprised her how quickly the concept sprouted roots in her heart.

She let herself drift with memories of Jack. She was a bird with a wounded wing when they dropped the pretense in the shelter of her back yard. He opened his arms. Something in her chest rose and took flight. She walked willingly into his embrace, and their commitment sealed around them.

In the beginning, though, love could not dissuade certain doubt. She looked up one day to find him watching, the difference in their ages heavy on his mind. "When I walk into a room," he asked, "is it your father that you see?"

Her father? Never her father. There was no comparison. Her father raised a son and left a daughter wanting.

On another occasion, Jack turned a light moment serious with a whisper close to her ear. "There's no cure for me, you know."

Before she drew her next breath, she realized it was heartbreak that he feared. He imagined her bolting one day, telling him she simply changed her mind. Left alone, he would never get over loving her. For that, she loved him more.

Another memory welled, and she was bent over his bed, quietly asking for a kiss. Their last kiss. Within hours, he was comatose. Hers were the last eyes he ever saw.

Nearby, car doors closed. Club members and their guests arrived for lunch. Callie realized her face, contorted by grief, was on public display. Jumping up, she fled from the bustling parking lot. She reached the pitted concrete path that curled around to the back of the pro shop and stopped in a patch of shade. Her arms dropped to her sides. Face raised to the overhanging branches of basswood trees, she saw glimpses of blue sky through the leaves. She pulled in long calming breaths. Soon, the song of the birds replaced the rushing in her ears, and she was back in motion.

. . .

A few minutes before two-thirty, Callie stood on the patio between the clubhouse and pro shop, having just closed Chef Gillis Jones's back kitchen door. She'd eaten a serving of his famous chicken salad at her desk and just returned the dish and fork. Her cell phone rang. She dug the device out of her skirt pocket. The caller was Beebe.

"How'd it go with Lizbeth?" No matter which task Callie attempted to complete during the intervening two hours, each was sabotaged by thoughts of the other three women recently crowded into her life.

"She's ratcheted up the stakes concerning her mother-in-law and the quilt," Beebe said, "but I moved her back to the position of peace summit—her name for the West Virginia trip. Despite that, she's still holding Florida out as her alternative if Arnett is uncooperative. Lizbeth wants things her way. She says she's tired of Arnett's heavy-handed rule over the family."

Considering what Callie knew about the Sebring family, the weight of Arnett's rule was probably an apt description. "What's next?" she asked.

"She went to pick up Chad from her brother's house. She thinks if she lets Arnett stew long enough over Florida, she'll consent to the peace summit."

"You think she's serious about Florida?" Callie wandered slowly alongside the clubhouse, her eyes on the patio's irregular flagstones.

"I think Lizbeth is exhibiting nothing less than coercion tactics to dethrone her mother-in-law's heavy-handed rule, to borrow her words."

Callie pulled to an abrupt stop, surprised by Beebe's defense of Arnett Oldstone Sebring.

Beebe went on. "Of greater concern is that Lizbeth seems married to both of her tactical strategies: Arnett's turnaround, and the Florida proposition. She's completely satisfied to let Arnett decide the next major step in her life. She did build in a delay for professional consultation. But she's is so damn angry. Mostly with Arnett. After the last few hours, possibly with me." Beebe's voice softened. "She hurts, Callie. She won't let time pass so she can heal. She wants *to do* something."

"She's fighting. That's good."

"Some women have been known to roll over and follow their husbands into the grave," Beebe said matter-of-factly.

"She can't. She's got Chad."

"Exactly. She left Arnett with an ultimatum: She wants Arnett to attend the peace summit. After her abominable behavior yesterday—again, I borrow Lizbeth's words—she must agree to accept the quilt as an outward expression of true change. Only then will Lizbeth share Chad and allow the Arnett Sebring grandsitting tradition to continue." Beebe took a breath. "What do you think?"

Grinning, Callie said, "I'm still hung up on the picture of Arnett stewing and some chant about toil and trouble."

"A serious answer, please."

"Sounds like Lizbeth has spread her newly found confidence over a layer of second-stage anger straight out of the grief sufferer's textbook."

"Thank you," Beebe said emphatically. "And by the way, A-plus." She promised to call if another salvo was launched from either side.

Callie put her phone away and went inside. Chesterfield Park's pro shop was built in the late nineteen-twenties. Seventeen years ago, Chesterfield's executive board financed a renovation, more than doubling the building's footprint. Callie walked under the wide archway that joined the original section with expanded retail space. She cut between tables displaying a new line of wind jackets and proceeded under a second archway that led to a hallway and her office. She stopped short. The weird route her life was taking turned her around. She knew what she needed. She needed a closer connection to Jack.

Back outside, she let herself in the clubhouse's side door. She traversed the interior concourse until she reached the mouth to an intersecting passage that was just deep enough for light from the main aisle way to bleed off into shadow at Jack's office door. It wasn't locked. Hallway light zipped into the room ahead of her, swirling the air inside. She inhaled a reminiscent whiff of Jack's musky cologne with paralyzing effect.

She wanted to reach for the light switch, but found she couldn't turn loose of the brass doorknob. She used it as an anchor against a thousand memories rushing past her. She just wanted to stand in the room and absorb him again. She didn't expect memories to seep in and around all the cracks in her emotions. When the moment weakened, she closed the door and flipped the switch.

The short-weave carpeting that spread to the corners of the roomy office masked Callie's footsteps. The large topography maps and paintings depicting unnamed golf courses hung on three walls and brought the high ceiling down. Venetian blinds shuttered two windows on the fourth. Beyond the blinds lay a breathtaking eighteen-hole course.

Stepping around the desk, she leaned against the credenza. Last winter, the club almost leased the office to a new tenant, but the deal fell through. At some point, the office would become occupied. She was prepared, she thought. At least all his personal items were carried home shortly after his death. The last time she escaped to Jack's office was over a year ago. That last visit was categorized as an escape because, like Lizbeth, Callie fought second-stage anger herself.

Before Jack became bedbound, news about his terminal cancer and his move to her home seemed afloat around the club. She sensed people knew. A few sent her looks of outright contempt at her decision to allow a married man to live with her. In that regard, she was defenseless.

After Jack's death, Callie didn't direct her anger at those coworkers who subscribed to the belief that the God who could create such beauty as the country club surroundings would also send disease as punishment for adultery.

It was the doctor in whom Callie vested her anger.

The oncologist promised he could control Jack's pain, but Jack suffered unbearably with every hour near the end, and she blamed the doctor. Fortunately, when her grief struck, his path had not crossed Callie's as Arnett blocked Lizbeth's. Callie's anger ran its course and subsided.

Somewhere during her reminiscences, she adapted her fight with anger to Lizbeth's fight. Callie worried that Arnett—merely by being Arnett—was pushing Lizbeth toward Florida. The two mule-headed Sebring women needed guidance, and Jack was gone. More than custody of a quilt was at risk.

In her mind's eye, she saw Chad lifted off the ground by a parachute operating in reverse. Lizbeth and Arnett cut off their incessant arguing and rushed to him, but he floated first out of Arnett's reach, then his shoe slipped from his mother's grasp. Callie shuddered at the imagined scene and was suddenly, obstinately committed to stand in for Jack. Lizbeth's comment about Jack and Arnett at her dinner table came racing back: "Bless him, he had a way with her."

Callie must find a way with Arnett, too. No, she *would* find a way. Her positive energy flowed, and she pictured the child's gentle descent, until his glow-in-the-dark Nikes touched the solid earth.

Without warning, the weird route she followed took a jog, and she knew the approach to take with Arnett.

I will simply march up and knock on her door. The thought, when she formed it, was crisp with determination.

Conflicting Opinions

Callie drove down Billingsley Drive. Up ahead was Brahms Way. Arnett Sebring lived in a two-story Tudor on the corner of the two streets. Callie looked around. The upper-class neighborhood was quiet; its landscaped yards painstakingly maintained.

She eased her blue Santa Fe over to the curb. The SUV crept forward another few feet, then she braked abruptly: Arnett just walked out from the side yard with a watering can in hand. Callie watched and waited from the opposite corner while Arnett tended to what distantly appeared to be pink begonias tucked between box-shaped shrubberies.

After a moment, Callie switched the engine off and stepped down to the concrete street. She took a few steps, willing a strengthening agent into her legs, one that would bond with rubbery bones. The determination she projected in Jack's office fled by the time she arrived home to get the Santa Fe.

Before she backed the SUV down the driveway, her pluck returned. She issued herself a stern lecture. Her cause was just. She could not stand by and let Lizbeth, in the throes of grief, make life-altering decisions. Even the contemplation of uprooting Chad and moving to Florida was a mistake. Lizbeth needed time to heal. Chad needed as much normalcy in his world as possible. They both needed stability.

On the other side of the conflict, Arnett needed to understand the stages of grief, then she could rally with Beebe and Callie and slow Lizbeth down. Callie was willing to beg for Arnett's cooperation. Was it too much to accept the quilt if that concession brought Chad back into her home?

Despite all the assertions made in her bedroom while changing clothes before driving over, Callie's stomach was knotted. She felt the fear of confrontation. She expected to find Arnett inside the house at a level removed. But across the way, Arnett was giving a medley of dusty miller and petunias growing around a lamppost a long drink. Callie kept Arnett in her sights and crossed the street. Arnett emptied the spouted jug, then turned away and disappeared back around the house.

Callie thought her luck was ripening. A tall, solid redwood fence surrounded the backyard and the pool, she knew, was there. If Arnett went around back, the fence would contain their conversation. Callie pushed on. At the top of the drive, she stepped off into grass.

In the shady side yard, she found a lone garden glove on the ground. It was green and pink with a strip of elastic at the wrist. She carried it to the redwood gate. It stood open several inches. Callie peeked through the narrow crack to the low wooden deck attached to the house. She shifted her gaze and found Arnett. She aimed a hose nozzle at a thigh-high concrete planter. A shower of water jiggled plantings in the same theme Callie noted out front: upright dusty miller and droopy petunias. Four planters in total marked the corners of the rectangular in-ground pool. Four lampposts were stationed along the pool's length, two on each side.

Callie swung the gate toward her enough to improve her view. Along the fence line, she saw a blue and white striped canvas changing room, lilac bushes, and a gold-fringed freestanding umbrella protecting two cushioned chairs from the sun. Beyond Arnett, a white trellis of yellow roses was set against the redwood planks. But it was the child's sandbox in the grass with its blue and white canvas roof that pulled her through the gate opening.

Seeing the sandbox dislodged a memory of Jack. He sat across the table from her in a restaurant. The man who was a near genius at golf course planning frequently delighted her with funny and unique phrasing. The glint in his eye teased. "Will you visit the sandbox before we leave?" Over the years, Callie never tired of the question. She would look in the direction of the ladies' room and answer one way or the other.

The scene flashed by and Callie found herself several steps inside the backyard fortress. The gate closed silently. Callie's greeting snagged the older woman's attention. "Hello, Arnett." Callie took off her sunglasses and pushed up the bill on the cap she wore. "You dropped this." She held out the glove.

Arnett, bewildered and speechless, automatically patted the pocket of knee-length shorts with her free hand. When she rounded up words, she spat them. "What are you doing here? Get out." She squeezed the hose nozzle, sending a spray of water Callie's way, treating her no better than a trespassing cat.

Callie backed out of the stream's path. "Arnett, stop," she ordered.

An indignant Arnett shot another squirt of water from the hose. "How dare you!"

Callie danced away from the spray. "I'm not leaving until we talk about Lizbeth." That brought her another frigid blast. "Will you, please, stop." When Arnett took aim again, Callie raced for the turn-off valve at the house.

"No. Leave that alone!" Arnett's last arching stream, before pressure was lost, located the stationary target. The soaking was limited to Callie's nylon jacket, which shed most of it, and one spot on her Levis. "I can't believe you walked straight into my back yard."

"You had to expect someone would come to reason with you about Lizbeth."

"Reason?" Arnett shook her head like a frustrated billy goat. "As if

I'm not reasonable. As if not wanting to spend a week in West Virginia in my husband's love nest with my husband's lover is unreasonable."

Callie slipped out of the jacket and shook off the wet. She moved toward Arnett at poolside to hang the jacket over a chair back to dry in the sun. She laid the glove and her sunglasses on the seat.

"It's hot," Arnett said, suddenly incredulous. "Why are you dressed in that getup?"

"I wore this so your neighbors wouldn't recognize me." Callie pulled at the damp spot on her jeans, trying to break the suction on her leg.

The idea surfaced while Callie was home. She thought she could save Arnett the embarrassment of having the woman Jack left her for show up, park out front, then boldly ring the bell. The alternative tack might prove advantageous, especially since Callie was trying to woo Arnett toward an amiable frame of mind with regard to Lizbeth. Disguised, Callie thought she'd be less noticeable in case anyone on Brahms knew of her existence, her frequent appearance in the sports pages, and made the connection.

At home, Callie hooked her short blonde hair behind her ears, then added Jack's favorite cap. She hoped the sunglasses, jacket, white tee, faded Levis, dirty sneakers, and general sloppy appearance with her slight build would, at a glance, imitate a teenage boy's wardrobe.

"You mean you wanted to save yourself from recognition," Arnett fired back.

Callie's head came up. Her finger jabbed the air. "No. To save you. So you wouldn't need to answer questions about my visit."

Arnett's eyes blazed. She emitted a deep scream that scraped violently over windpipe and vocal cords on its way up from her gut.

Callie's expression turned to one of exaggerated patience. "But if you don't stop screaming, your neighbors will figure it out anyway. I couldn't be sure how much they knew or what was said, but if they knew my description, well— I thought I'd come in disguise. And I parked around the corner for another degree of separation."

Arnett raised the hose nozzle and depressed the lever repeatedly, mimicking the firing of a pistol empty of bullets. "Go," she said. "Get your bony behind off my property."

"Not until we talk."

"We don't need to talk."

"Yes, we do. You need to understand what Lizbeth is going through." Callie's hands were in motion. "She's grieving. She's angry, and she shouldn't make monumental decisions now. Beebe and I don't want her to move to Florida with Chad any more than you. That would be a mistake." She laced empathy into her tone. "She's hit the anger stage of grief. Hit it pretty hard. There truly is a grieving process. You're a strong woman, Arnett, but I see Lizbeth flailing, swinging wildly. She's looking for a handhold, for someone to grab. Surely the best someone for the job is you."

"This is a crock of bull, coming from you."

"This same speech could come from Beebe. I can get her over here. She's the expert. Don't be the one to make Lizbeth angry. Cooperate. Trade in a fraction of your pride."

Arnett's stubborn chin came up, but she held her tongue.

"No matter our relationship," Callie said, gesturing, "I can't stand by and not help when Lizbeth is about to make a huge error." She waited for a reply; Arnett's face only reddened. "Beebe and I have got Chad in mind." Callie thought she tacked on a positive statement, but Arnett blew.

"She will not take my grandson to Florida!"

"If you'll consent to this week to sort things out, we can probably guarantee that. Lizbeth needs to pass through these stages of grief. Beebe can explain them best." Callie saw no chink in Arnett's body armor, yet she persisted. "It's a two-year process. I'm not there yet, either. Neither are you."

"Don't tell me where I am in the process. If Lizbeth would just leave everything alone, she'd be fine. Chad would be fine. He needs to spend time with his grandmother while his mother works. That's the way it's been with all the boys; that's the way it should be for him."

"After next week, if you'll agree, that may be the outcome. I have faith in Beebe."

"You're the one putting these ideas in Lizbeth's head. You'd do anything to hurt me. Again!"

"No, it's not the two of us against you. It's really three against one: you, Beebe, and me. We need to team up against Lizbeth, to keep her from making a bad decision at the worst time in her life. She needs to give herself more time." Callie delivered her words on a steady plane, but her mind was throwing out memories of the horrible, lost feeling that walked alongside her after Jack's death. "Please, Arnett, call Lizbeth. Tell her you'll participate. You take the credit. No need to mention my visit."

"She doesn't know? She didn't put you up to this?" Her sweeping hand took in the cap sitting back on Callie's head and the jacket draped on a lounge chair.

"No one knows but you and me."

Arnett wandered a step. "So this is a secret rendezvous then. You're so good at that."

Callie shifted position. "You're getting off the subject."

"No, between you and me," Arnett said, indicating the space between them, "that will always be the subject. There is no other."

Callie noticed a gleam lighting Arnett's dark eyes and a smirk tugging at her face. A stirring breeze fluttered by, trailing the smell of chorine. Arnett had gotten Callie's back to the pool. She was one good shove from the edge. Callie popped up an eyebrow and glanced over her shoulder to the shallow water, showing Arnett she read her drenching thoughts. Arnett wore a satisfied smile anyway. Callie could plot too. She spoke, and the smile disappeared.

"You need to think back to the last time you saw Chad because that may very well be the last time you'll ever see him. Etch that picture in your mind." She anchored her thumbs in her jeans pockets to hamper the finger-pointing urge. Callie moved to leave, then paused before she stepped past Arnett. "Call Lizbeth. She has a certain quilt she wants you to accept."

Arnett rounded on her, her anger reborn. "Why are you doing this?"

Callie's brief answer pressed the connection they made nearly five years before. "Why? You know why." She watched a shadow of understanding cross Arnett's face. Back then, Jack was ill, and it was Arnett who reached out to contact Callie. The purpose behind that contact changed everything. Callie closed her eyes. She pushed the rest of the story away. Today, herding Arnett toward a better path was the least she could do.

She lifted her jacket and sunglasses off the chair and scuffed through the grass toward the gate. Outside the solid eight-foot fence, she stopped to don her costume. She took a half-dozen steps, then large drops of icy-cold water rained down. Arnett Oldstone Sebring was agile, stealthy, and owned amazing blind aim.

Callie turned the Santa Fe around and drove straight to the small house at the end of Morris Lane. Petey lived there. Adeline "Petey" Peterson Sebring was Jack's stepmother. During her twenties, she played baseball in the All-American Girls Professional Baseball League founded by Philip K. Wrigley and was tagged "Petey" by her Rockford Peaches teammates.

In sharp contrast to being ignored by Jack's sons throughout the entire three years Callie and he lived together, Petey insisted upon an introduction the moment Callie's existence became known. Petey was charming. A spitfire. And she took no guff from anyone, including Arnett Oldstone Sebring. She put a stop to Arnett's harassing phone calls. That act effectively carved Petey out of the Sebring family. A widow twice over, Petey was watched over by the granddaughter,

Nora, who lived next door, and by Callie.

"I may have lost Jack," Petey said to Callie the first time she visited after his death, "but I love him for leaving me you." Petey made the exchange sound both treasured and even.

During one afternoon visit, Petey gave Callie an impish smile, then sat forward in her cushioned rocker. "I remember sitting at that kitchen table with Jack's father. Avery, Jack, and I just finished one of our famously long coffee breaks. After Jack left, Avery and I looked at each other. 'Something's up with Jack,' he said. 'He's happier. He smiles more.' That coffee break was twenty years ago." Her eyes lit. "We didn't know, then, that you were in the bushes."

Callie let herself inside the house. She left the disguise portion of her wardrobe behind. She found Petey seated in the rocker with the sports page tipped toward the window to catch the afternoon light. Quietly, not wanting to startle her good friend and confidant, Callie spoke her name twice. The second time, she folded one corner of the newsprint down and looked out. Grinning, Callie waved.

"Well, hello," Petey said. Her wavy white hair was wound into its usual knot at her nape, setting off a gleaming pair of blue eyes. "This is fabulous. What a surprise. I wasn't expecting you." The newspaper lay across her lap now, her wire glasses atop the paper. "I wasn't expecting you, was I?"

Callie kissed her cheek, then backed up to a nearby chair. "No, you weren't, and you're not the only person who didn't expect a visit from me this afternoon. I just came from Arnett's."

Petey's reaction was a full two seconds of flabbergasted silence, then words burst forth. "Save us all, Callie, why did you go there?"

Sitting forward, Callie answered that question. An astonished Petey listened carefully to the story that began with Arnett's arrival at Callie's house and closed with Callie's rationale for offering Heatherwood for counseling sessions. "Jack seemed to brood about Chad more than anything. He would want him happy and safe. I can speak for Jack. This is something I can do. And Beebe thinks it's best to get away."

Petey shook her head. "It saddens me to think of Jack brooding about that little boy. And now, a ruckus with Chad dead center." Then her eyes drilled Callie's. "You go," she said. "You take a stand for Jack's grandson. You'll come shining through. You always do. Stop here first thing when you get back and tell me all about it."

That promise was easily made.

. . .

The wrought-iron entrance gate to Shaker Ridge Cemetery stood open for Lizbeth Sebring the next morning. She drove her Tahoe onto the grounds and immediately let her gaze roll out to the southwest. The sky was blue with a thin cotton-candy layer that would melt as the day grew warmer. She was pleased to see no evidence of groundskeepers along the ridge. Although those groundskeepers meticulously maintained the cemetery, she preferred a wide measure of privacy during her visits.

An asphalt labyrinth curled through the cemetery's gently rolling slopes. Lizbeth passed a pair of marble fountains, then steered the passenger-side tires off the narrow road. With the transmission in park, she swung her long, lean body off the driver's seat. Quickly, she retrieved a short stool kept in the SUV's cargo area.

Lizbeth didn't know how others left behind after a death handled cemetery visits, but with her first visit to her husband's grave, and with the many since, she talked to him. Today, Lizbeth owed Dan an explanation.

The Lizbeth who marched into her mother-in-law's home the morning before possessed a newfound daring. Her springboard of strength over Arnett Sebring was made sweeter because that strength was a long time coming.

Arnett was accustomed to working every situation in life around to her way of thinking. Lizbeth wanted to change that. Arnett shouted a resounding no at the mention of weeklong counseling sessions in the West Virginia cabin. That refusal bolstered Lizbeth's defenses. Not only would she remove Chad from within grandsitting range, she'd move him a thousand miles away.

In truth, she didn't want to sever their relationship with Arnett. She honestly felt Arnett would benefit from counseling. Arnett's life had been rocked in the last few years by the disintegration of her marriage and her son's death. With Beebe's wise words and a sincere effort on Arnett's part, Lizbeth thought she and her mother-in-law could go forward together.

Reality was, Lizbeth knew Arnett too well. She didn't want fluff from her. Arnett must exhibit concrete proof of sincerity. Agreeing to overlook the location and Callie's presence to reap the benefits of counseling and the reward of her grandson were strides in the right direction.

Benefit and reward were precisely what Arnett refused.

After their bickering in Arnett's living room, a resilient Lizbeth asserted herself once more. "Think about what I've said."

Hands on hips and toe to toe with Lizbeth, Arnett snarled back. "There's nothing to think about. I won't do it. My mind's made up."

"No, it's not." Lizbeth, a head taller, loomed hawk-like over Arnett. "And you will think about it. I guarantee, you won't be able to stop thinking about it." Mentally, Lizbeth tossed a little dirt on that seed, then saw herself out.

So far, only silence grew. Consequently, the fluttering in her chest suggested impending failure.

Lizbeth set off behind a row of tombstones. Her steps through the grass were high and hurried. On this morning, she felt drawn to the cemetery, to Dan's unique insight, his ability to strike harmony with his mother.

Coming around her husband's upright grave marker to the chiseled side, Lizbeth kissed her hand, then placed it atop the arched width of marble. "Hi, sweetie, I'm here."

She set the square stool down. The stone marking Dan's grave faced Shaker Ridge with its view of evening sunsets. She lowered her slender figure to the seat and tossed a thick honey-brown curl off her shoulder before her crossed arms settled down on denim-clad thighs. The scene could have been plucked from her family room. It had been commonplace to see Lizbeth hunched on the footstool in front of Dan leaning forward from his favorite easy chair, four knees and hands in close quarters.

"Well, the last few days were not what I'd hoped, but I'll get to that in a minute. I want you to know the quilts are gorgeous. Chad loves them. He recognized your clothing instantly. That made me so happy because he must always remember his daddy." The sentiment caused her voice to falter while a multitude of memories snagged on the sharply etched letters of her husband's name. She waited while the tightness in her throat eased. "As usual, Chad woke early today. Debbie said she'd take him for an hour, so I dropped him off." She laughed. "He's named all the fish in Deb and Pat's aquarium."

Just then, she heard a car door slam. Her privacy breached, she stretched her neck to look over the garden of stones. A familiar sports car was parked behind her SUV. "Oh lord, your brother's here."

She stood and watched Gary Sebring stomp her way. He owned a full head of dark hair and an untidy mustache. His open-collared dress shirt was tucked into belted khakis. Lizbeth took in the large belt buckle, mentally rolling her eyes. As intended, his cowboy boots added height. Most times, Lizbeth considered Gary a man of both short stature and enormous ego. This Thursday morning didn't disappoint.

Still en route, Gary spoke. "A cabin? Really? A cabin in West Virginia with that MacCallum woman? That's your idea. The cabin they cheated on Mom in."

Image of Someone Else

Lizbeth glared at her brother-in-law. Gary Sebring drank coffee at Arnett's house every morning before work. There, he got the latest news: world, national, local, and the Sebring-slant. Arnett worked the family like Gary's jaws worked the gum he chewed: hard and fast. Neither was Lizbeth surprised by his unmasked fury: The same wrath flared in Arnett's eyes the morning before. The acorn didn't fall far from the mother tree.

"My idea was counseling," Lizbeth said firmly. "And yes, the cabin works. It does two things, in fact. If Arnett agrees, it tells me she wants to achieve real change. It also gets her away from you." She crossed her arms. "Too bad, though. For a week, you'll have to get your morning coffee somewhere else, baby boy."

"Baby boy! Away from me! At least I spend my mornings with people who are still alive."

Lizbeth absorbed his hurtful intentions with an impassive face. Even as a child, anger kept her tears at bay. The ongoing situation with Gary and Arnett might dry up her tear ducts entirely. She scooped up her stool. "Gary," she began, her tone said listen up, "I issued my ultimatum to Arnett after seeing her embarrassing display in that poor woman's front yard. As I told her, I will not have an impressionable youngster around her kind of self-indulgent anger, witnessing her wailings and tantrums."

"I think that's a little strong."

Her start for the car ground to a halt. "She was ready to strike that woman. Did she tell you that?" His expression said Arnett shared that morsel of information and he reveled in the telling. "If I hadn't stopped her, you could be bailing her out of jail right now."

"You're still reeling from Dan's death. You exaggerate things."

They were moving again. She ignored the excuse he made for her. "If she's unable to make this concession about a quilt—first and foremost, a treasure made of her son's clothes—then I can only assume that her bad behavior will continue, that she's either unwilling or unable to practice restraint."

"I can see the sentiment of the quilts. I can. But why don't you keep them. Let's quiet this whole situation down. There's no reason Chad should learn Mom objects to them."

"Chad already knows."

"What?" He jerked to a stop at the Miata's bumper.

"Chad knows one of the quilts is a present for his grandmother. Chad understands presents. And Arnett needs to understand that I'm not backing down about the cabin. She needs to think for herself, by herself, without the Oldstone-Sebring clan around her. Thank God Dan could stay away for more than fifteen minutes." She returned the stool to the Tahoe, then chose her next few words intentionally. She put a smile on them to taunt her brother-in-law. "Her acceptance of the quilt will weigh heavily in my decision."

He stowed the gum in his cheek. "What decision?"

"She told you about Florida, didn't she?"

A moment passed while the moustache over his one visible lip twitched. "I didn't believe you were serious."

"Well, I am. Very."

"That's irrational." He ran a hand through his hair. "Oh, that's a bad decision, Lizbeth. You've got to think."

"I have family there. With one call, I'd have a job waiting. It would be good for Chad to live closer to his brother."

She watched Gary's face fall. Immediately, he was back on track. "Fine. Make your plans. Ruin Chad's life. Because Mom's not going to that cabin. That will never happen."

Lizbeth's mouth opened. Her ringing phone interrupted her response. She dug it out of her pocket and read Arnett's name and home number on the display.

"Go ahead," Gary said. "Answer. I'll wait."

The whole scene felt staged to Lizbeth. Her shoulders slumped under his contemptuous look and the heaping dose of defeat she felt coming. She mumbled into the phone.

"Lizbeth?" Arnett's voice said.

"Yes."

"It's me. I, huh..." Arnett paused, then started again, stronger. "Well, I've given things a great deal of thought. You're treating me shabbily, but you really leave me no choice. So..." A second ticked by. "I'll go."

"You will?" Elation rose in Lizbeth's tone.

"Yes."

"To the cabin?" Lizbeth eyeballed Gary. His jaw stopped mid-chew. Green gum fell stiffly to his tongue.

"Yes. That's all I agree to at this point. Don't read anything else into this."

"I'm pleased, Arnett. I'll be back in touch."

Lizbeth lowered the phone. She used it to point to the knotted fists at the end of Gary's poker-straight arms. "Wow. Didn't see that one coming, did you?" she said mockingly.

. . .

Beebe Walker carried her dry cleaning high so the bag enclosing her gray suit didn't drag the parking lot. Dow's Dry Cleaner was the last stop on her list of errands. When Lizbeth's call came in, Beebe activated her Bluetooth, then went back to fumbling with the hanger and the hook above the backseat's window. From Lizbeth's enthused tone, Beebe pictured her dancing a snappy jig.

"Arnett called fifteen minutes ago. She's willing to go to the cabin."

Beebe's mouth fell open. "You're sure?"

"Yes, Beebe, yes. I can't believe I talked her into it."

Beebe pushed the trailing cellophane bag inside and closed the door. She thought it best to pat down the celebratory mood. "Lizbeth, I want you to listen to me. This week in West Virginia is going to represent a lot of hard work for all of us, you included. I'm not going to let you skate. I don't see Arnett as the only one who needs an attitude adjustment."

"Sure," Lizbeth said too quickly. "I understand."

"I hope you do. And have a little sympathy for both Arnett and Callie. That cabin means very different things to them." Beebe settled herself behind the wheel. Nothing came back. "Are you listening to me?"

Beebe's sharp tone jolted out an answer. "Yes, I'm listening."

"Good. There's no need to feel self-glorified. We won't have pulled off any great coup by just getting them there. Be humble. Keep your clay feet on the ground."

"But I'm justified in my actions," Lizbeth said, arguing her side.

The tug Beebe gave her seatbelt halted midway. "Young lady, I'll come down hard on you if you gloat or taunt Arnett in any way, and you know I've got the waistline to inflict some pain. Now, I need to talk to Callie. I'll call you later." The car gave her a bit of resistance, too, but on the third try, started.

Beebe was surprised when the call she placed to Callie went relatively well. She sensed no resentment or backsliding, so there was no need to throw her weight around. Callie seemed ready to prove her mettle and dodge a few of Arnett's wild swings and speak for Jack.

Beebe slipped her front door key into the lock. She used the five-minute drive home to accept the sobering circumstances. In little more than a week, Beebe would journey back to her Michigan hometown, tackle a new job, and adapt to life with her father. Somehow before then, she must divert Lizbeth's rumble down the disastrous road she'd chosen. Her threat to move south—even contemplation of such a move—was coming way too soon in the grieving process. Dan died just three short months before. Beebe was committed to diffusing Lizbeth's churning anger toward her mother-in-law.

Twice, Beebe had been in Arnett's company: first, in her office behind Swanson funeral home, then in Callie's front yard. Both times, there'd been a show of theatrics and Arnett fled within minutes.

Beebe had a thought and checked her watch. Time crept past noon. Perhaps an impromptu visit to Arnett was in order. One on one, they could become better acquainted and build a foundation for the following week. And if Beebe went to her, that would preclude another rash exit on Arnett's part.

She walked over to the couch where her dry cleaning lay. To the suit, she said, "Looks like it's you and me and Arnett Sebring."

After changing, Beebe made a beeline from the bedroom to her living room desk. She riffled through the center drawer and several untidy stacks of paperwork before coming up with the tri-folded pamphlet she wanted. The grief counselor would not go to Arnett's empty-handed. She would welcome Arnett to the group. Standard practice. She'd hand her a pamphlet outlining the stages of grief. Standard practice. And she'd stand ready to be supportive, answer questions, or just listen. Standard practice.

Beebe couldn't imagine Arnett immediately delving into the information contained in the pamphlet, but she hoped before the trip, Arnett would find a moment to read and absorb the facts presented.

Today, Beebe wanted to touch lightly on the anger element, although it had not touched lightly on Lizbeth.

Fifteen minutes later, she stood on the wide, bricked landing at Arnett Sebring's front door. Behind her, a walkway dissected the lawn. Before her, the door stood open. Beebe rang the bell. She peered through the screen mesh to a foyer and staircase beyond. Arnett stepped into the scene from the right, initially startled when she recognized her visitor.

"Well," she said, coming over to stare through the screen, "I wondered what her next move would be."

"May I come in?" Beebe asked when the door wasn't unlatched.

Arms folded, Arnett leaned back on her heel and took more than a few seconds to consider her response. "You're not carrying a quilt, so certainly. I want to hear what she's sent you to say, anyway." The door was pushed out. After Beebe was inside, Arnett added, "If you haven't guessed, I've become exceedingly resentful of my daughter-in-law over the last few days."

"I'm truly sorry that's the case," Beebe said. "And I'm not Lizbeth's emissary. In fact, she doesn't know I'm here."

"Where have I heard that before?"

Arnett's sarcastic tone confused Beebe. "I'm sorry?"

"Never mind," Arnett said. "Go on."

"Well, it's just that with the trip ahead of us, I thought we should get better acquainted."

Arnett assessed her again for a moment, then turned and strolled toward the spacious living room. Beebe followed. Their shoes tapped lightly on Pergo flooring. Beebe's steps slowed as she crossed the threshold, her attention captured by the baby grand piano and its cushioned bench in the room's southwest corner.

"Do you play?"

There was a regal air about Arnett now. Head high, shoulders rigid, she stood back-to-back with the couch. It was stretched across the middle of the room and faced a coffee table and fireplace. Matching side chairs straddled the table. "John played," she said, one hand lay on the sofa's silky fabric. "He was quite accomplished. Mother Sebring taught him."

On the other side of the doorway, an interesting nook had been arranged in contrast with the rest of the room. A wide upholstered chair was angled in close quarters with a child's hinged toy box. Within a youngster's reach, a single book shelf hung on the wall. An array of storybooks lined the shelf. Beebe knew Grandmother Arnett came to life in that corner.

Beebe shifted her gaze. A long, cloth-covered table of framed photographs lured Beebe across the room's wheat-colored Berber. The table crowded with generations of family members was positioned in front of the picture window draped with white sheers. Beebe guessed the collection exceeded four dozen. There was a mix of ornate and plain frames, everything from aged sepia photographs to vibrant color likenesses. She scanned the faces. Jack Sebring's was missing. Beebe thought the man had certainly been excommunicated with supreme prejudice.

"This is fabulous," Beebe said, her hand sweeping the display. "I can pick out Chad and Dan, of course." They were central to the discussion she hoped to have with Arnett.

Silently, Arnett appeared at Beebe's side, her focus absorbed by a candid snapshot: Father held son. They wore matching football jerseys. Their sandy hair was tousled, their cheeks rosy from exertion.

"Chad and Dan," Arnett repeated. "Lizbeth seems to think that she's the only one who suffers through every moment of every day."

Beebe watched her closely. The wary strategist who met her at the door dissolved into a mourning mother. Well now, Beebe thought, we might just get somewhere.

Turning away from the window-front display, Arnett moved to the couch. Beebe seated herself in the adjacent armchair. She immediately noticed two odd items occupying the oval coffee table: a pipe stand and kidney-shaped ashtray. Odd because, other than the status-symbol piano, Beebe could not believe one item belonging to unfaithful Jack Sebring remained in the house. Neither could she picture Arnett puffing a pipe. The stand was constructed of a round, wooden base and central spindle around which six pipes leaned upright into cutouts. The ceramic ashtray was the color of putty and flecked with brown. It was divided into two sections: the objective to keep a resting pipe from slipping into tapped-out ashes.

"Dan's the younger of my two sons," Arnett began. "He was eternally happy as a child. Inquisitive. Rambunctious. Always ready with a smile for his mother. He grew into a kind, responsible man. He was as comfortable with computers as hand tools." Arnett's dull eyes bore into Beebe's. "A mother should never be asked to bear the loss of a child. Forty-two was too young. His sons need a father's influence. Geoff's back at college," she said of her oldest grandson. "And Chad's just four. I expect memories of his daddy will be hazy at best. The day will soon come when he'll ask why his daddy died. The honest answer is: his mother encouraged his father's pursuit of a worthless hobby."

By then, Beebe ushered her natural talent for listening into play. She didn't interrupt, but her neutral expression must have slipped. Beebe knew Arnett read surprise on her face when she heaped full blame for Dan's loss onto Lizbeth's shoulders. No accidental death. No wrong place, wrong time. Not even a dodge toward an act of God to account for the tree crushing the weekend artist.

"Gary came with the awful news that day. My son died alone, in a field, in a cold, driving rain." Arnett's strong voice was accusatory. "I refused to believe it for days. Chad is the miracle Dan left behind. The pain in my heart numbs somewhat whenever he comes to play."

Elbows anchored on the chair arms, Beebe laced her fingers. Denial was a classic symptom of grief, numbness another.

Arnett brightened. "Chad's such a delight. He possesses his father's energy. You saw the snapshots. They're interchangeable. They have the same hazel eyes. Oldstone eyes. Just like my father's." With the reference, Arnett flicked a glance toward the pipe stand, and Beebe understood. The pipes were a treasured possession of an admired father.

Then Arnett checked off one more son-like-father characteristic. "They have the same grin, what I call sweet-boy smiles." Arnett went inside herself for a moment. "Chad is the very image of his father."

Beebe's concentration broke. The image of someone else. Those words touched her. Arnett relished the idea of keeping Chad close because the grandson was a duplicate of the son she'd raised. Beebe remembered all too vividly how her father seemed to push her away for precisely the same reason. Her face was a match for her runaway mother's, identical in every respect. He could not accept the daughter who simply went off to study theology. He stared hard every time she visited. Her clerical collar made no shred of difference. He saw only the wife who left a puncture wound in his heart so profound, no amount of time could heal. In Arnett Sebring's living room, Beebe was struck by the possibility that she'd chosen the ministry so that she might wear a uniform different from her mother's nursing garb—different, to regain her father.

Arnett's voice drew Beebe back to the present.

"If I don't bend to her commands, she'll pack Chad up and move him to Florida. A branch of her family is there. And Geoff. I see the conspiracy mounting." Arnett leaned Beebe's direction, a polished pink fingernail tapped the sofa arm. "Cassel, Maryland, has always been this family's home base, and this is where she should stay."

Finally, Beebe spoke. "I agree."

Arnett's mouth gaped. "You do?"

Beebe nodded. "Lizbeth is making this decision to move to Florida while she's grieving. That's a mistake. The two of you must learn to work at being a family again. How suddenly family members can be taken from us." Beebe waited for that realization to soften Arnett's charcoal eyes; she didn't blink. Beebe put her battering-ram resolve to good use. "Arnett," she said in a prepare-yourself tone, "I need you to scrape together every bit of fortitude and grace you own. You have some work ahead of you in order to keep Cassel the family base." Beebe produced the folded pamphlet from her jacket pocket. "I have a little reading material for you. It's a roadmap of sorts. You'll find yourself there on the path you just described. Lizbeth is very nearby. Look for her." With those words, Beebe watched an intensity form in Arnett's eyes.

"Lizbeth has asked me to facilitate this peace summit, as she's called it, and it's a perfect title," Beebe said with a dollop of enthusiasm. "You can conquer your temper. You must, for Chad." She placed the pamphlet on the table, its simple heading turned Arnett's direction.

Arnett read the title: *Understanding Grief.* Her shoulders and backbone stiffened. Her gaze shifted to the pipe stand and ashtray, then rose to bounce off a variety of objects while Beebe continued.

"I won't preach about grief, but you've got to believe that you and Lizbeth are grieving, and you're lodged in the second stage: the anger stage. Neither of you should make wild, sweeping decisions this close to Dan's death. You both need time to heal."

Arnett's avoidance tactics snagged on the fireplace andirons.

"All the resentment, the recent upset between you and Lizbeth, don't you see," Beebe said, drilling the phrase with a spicy zest that drew Arnett's attention back, "we can use that. The more difficult the situation, the better the redemption in Lizbeth's eyes. I will take your part if you try." Beebe sat forward. "I'm worried about Lizbeth. So worried. You should be, too."

Beebe knew Arnett Sebring well enough by then not to expect an amenable, even a pacifying response. Beebe worked herself out of the soft chair and onto her feet. "I'll pick you up Saturday at ten. Callie says to bring a sweater."

Arnett's mouth twisted involuntarily with the mention of Callie's name, then she was quickly amused. She lifted her chin and shot her obsidian irises to Beebe. "You're a little bit nuts, lady. You know that."

"Probably so." Beebe chuckled. Arnett's judgment contained a measure of warmth that stirred with the beginnings of an understanding between them.

Honesty Pledge

Arnett Oldstone Sebring sat motionless on her living room couch for a long moment after Beebe Walker left.

Anger, drizzled with confusion, percolated inside her. She realized she didn't quite know who to blame for her troubled life. For the longest time, she blamed Callie MacCallum, first and foremost. John had always been a close second.

In the afternoon quiet, though, her heart spoke and she listened. She simply could not endure life without Chad to hold and watch grow.

Arnett set her mouth. Lizbeth was to blame. More specifically, Lizbeth's pride. Arnett's middle finger scratched the sofa arm. She willed a resurgence of the matriarchal dominance that had been hers to brandish throughout a forty-year marriage and saw Lizbeth's rising stature take a tumble.

"Wait, you'll see," Arnett said aloud.

Using the heel of her hand on the sofa arm, Arnett pushed herself up. She snapped the collar of her shirt with both hands, then marched toward the table in the front hall where she'd lain the three novels her sister-in-law Stella dropped off earlier. Arnett felt a tension burn behind her eyes. When she reached the table, she slammed her hand down hard. A china figurine of a woman sitting there teetered violently. She grabbed it. The ivory woman was tall and shapely, so like her daughter-in-law. She hurled the figurine at the open door. It struck the knob and shattered into a million satisfying shards.

In the back of her mind, Beebe's words rose up, encouraging Arnett to conquer her temper.

She pushed down Beebe's chastisement, left the mess, and returned her focus to the murder mystery atop the stack. It appeared to contain a bookmark, but what Arnett slipped from under the cover was a business card Stella wanted Arnett to have. The embossed card read: Harlow Nolan, Attorney-At-Law. Stella promised this man could write a letter certain to riddle Lizbeth with the fear of the Great Almighty himself. Arnett flicked the card and smiled.

Maryland's legislature passed a law guaranteeing grandparents the right to a relationship with their grandchildren. Arnett was willing to pursue court action to secure her relationship with Chad, if necessary.

Yes, she'd committed to the West Virginia trip. Nothing wrong, she told herself, with simultaneously operating two lines of defense.

. . .

Twenty minutes later, Arnett was returning broom and dustpan to the narrow kitchen closet when her sister-in-law's voice pealed through the house. Arnett raised hers in return, then heard Stella Oldstone's heavy footsteps closing in on the kitchen. A handful of seconds later, she stood in the long room, yellow and cheery with large paned windows at both ends.

Arnett carefully swept up all evidence of her overwrought emotions, not that she minded sharing with her best friend the events that precipitated smashing the figurine. Stella would understand. She was married to Arnett's oldest brother, Raymond. Raymond and another brother, Emmett, ran Oldstone Brothers Manufacturing and Machine Works, the company that employed Arnett's son Dan. Two more brothers were back home in Laurel County, Kentucky.

This day, the demise of the figurine would not be discussed.

"Lizbeth called," Stella said, nearly breathless, her green eyes wide.

Arnett's head whipped around. "When?" Movement of the teakwood tray she held stopped, suspended several inches above the granite countertop.

"Just now. I tried to call, but your line was busy, so I came on over."

While Stella was turned to stash keys and pocketbook on the breakfast table, Arnett lowered the tray. It had grown heavy with apprehension. "What did she say?"

"First, she wanted to be sure I knew the West Virginia trip was on, and that she planned to invoke an honesty pledge."

"An honesty pledge? What does that mean? Why would she call you?"

"To gloat, dear heart, to gloat. She said she'd bring the pledge up to the others Saturday morning. The sweet thing wanted me to break the news gently." Stella shifted her weight to the other hip. "She's changed since Dan's death."

Holding a loose fist to her chest, Arnett thought aloud, "She's still plotting against me."

"Don't go," Stella said, wagging a finger in the air. "I think it's a mistake. Let Harlow Nolan handle things."

"I called him. I have an appointment tomorrow afternoon."

"Friday," Stella said. "Good, then you can back out on the trip. I don't think this Beebe person can control Lizbeth."

Arnett nodded absently. "An honesty pledge," she mumbled.

"That's what she said."

Arnett loaded the tray with the sugar bowl, china, spoons, linen napkins, and the coffee decanter from the KitchenAid appliance. Other than the two drops of coffee that sizzled on the warm burner, the room and the women were silent. Arnett picked up the tray. She and Stella turned their backs on the countertop coffeemaker. Side by side, they stepped down to the family room. Arnett always appreciated two things about her sister-in-law: First, she owned a cackle that was purely contagious, and second, she forever remained Arnett's loyal compatriot.

The family room was another sunlit space, decorated in complementary greens and blues. The tray rested on a low table, the women on the plaid couch.

"What are you thinking?" Stella asked.

"I wonder if Callie's involved with this honesty pledge." Arnett poured coffee into a gold-rimmed cup.

"You think she's feeding Lizbeth ideas? That would mean she and Lizbeth are conspiring. I get no sense of that."

Stella's use of the word conspiring kicked Arnett into motion. She was up and fidgeting with items in the room, along the mantel, on the desk. A family member conspiring against her hadn't happened in a long, long time.

Arnett, the only daughter of Judge Cyrus Oldstone, was innately attuned to her daddy's version of judgment. As the willful daughter of the invincible judge, she learned to approach life in much the same way. Truths could be locked away in his Kentucky courthouse, files sealed, gag orders issued. She was stronger because she, too, stood in judgment before her father.

At twenty, she married secretly, without his permission, and to a man not of his choosing. The backwoods news traveled swiftly. It rolled into town to rap smartly on the courthouse door. The judge sent family to deal with family. Brother Simon found the honeymooners' cottage and, at gunpoint, rousted Arnett and her handsome groom out of bed. Arnett and Eben Collins were hauled back to Judge Oldstone's courtroom.

Arnett slid an index finger along the frame of the family room's large landscape painting, absently checking for dust. A flickering memory reminded her again how the air inside the courtroom smelled distinctly of lemony furniture polish when she was escorted inside. Completely unruffled by the judgment he was about to declare, the robed figure behind an elevated dais ordered the courtroom cleaned while he waited. When the threesome appeared, the judge's head remained angled toward an opened law book.

Unintimidated, Arnett marched forward, through a wooden, hinged gate. She heard scuffling behind her; the courtroom door opened and closed. Judge Oldstone looked up. She kept her eyes on her father. She knew Simon led Eben out.

Both father and daughter, staged as judge and defendant, were positioned beneath overhead lamps, their expressions of mutual disappointment clearly visible. Arnett's ranting proved worthless that day. He shut her down with one word: "Enough!"

Just as quickly, he annulled her marriage. Balancing glasses on his crooked nose, he scratched his ballpoint forcefully over the pre-prepared legal document laying on the dais's varnished surface. With matching efficiency, Arnett was banished to Cassel, Maryland, into the care of her two married brothers who lived there. Early on, she often wondered what happened to Eben.

Stella's voice invaded her thoughts. "I still say don't go." She patted the couch cushion. Arnett accepted the invitation, sitting down with a sigh.

"Don't you see, I must go. I have to know what Lizbeth will tell Beebe and Callie." Both Beebe and Callie promised Arnett their support. The persuasive words Callie said out by the pool seemed suddenly artificial, appropriate only for a woman wearing a disguise. In truth, Arnett feared Callie. "What if John told Callie things about me? What if she runs to Gary?"

"Spiteful," Stella said, pouring coffee for Arnett.

"She would go to Gary if she's teamed up with Lizbeth, if she wants to see Chad kept away from me, if she wants to turn Gary against me." Arnett held her cup, needing both hands to steady it.

A rhythmic chink, chink, chink broke the silence. Stella stirred her coffee. "The thought of this class in Wilderness Psychobabble is enough to make me want to spit in Lizbeth's face."

Imagining that scene grew Arnett's strength immensely. She grinned over the raised cup.

And Stella cackled.

. . .

Later, after walking Stella to the door, Arnett wandered into the living room and up to the table where the sepia photograph of her father leaned back on its stand. The frame was gilded; the judge, robed. Wiry and uncontrolled described his hair and eyebrows, but not his physique or disposition.

As her early days in Maryland passed, the bite of her father's venom-like justice eased. His banishment tactic morphed into prevailing wisdom. She came around to that way of thinking about the same time something hot and sticky was searing through her veins. Arnett yearned to marry a man named John Avery Sebring.

Arnett scuffed across the room and sat in the chair that faced the table. Her eyes skipped from one framed family member to the next, picking out those who were aware of the unspoken irony that defined her: Callie MacCallum's sin had first been Arnett Oldstone's sin. They both ached for a not-quite-available John Sebring.

When Arnett met John, he was dealing with two Mrs. Sebrings, mother and wife. Mother Sebring, although not gavel-powered, was eminently strong-willed and bent on making her then current and disliked daughter-in-law's life one of continual misery. That made her son's life one of constant and wearing mediation. Arnett wedged herself into the story at that point and raised the jealousy quotient. John exhibited a valiant effort to maintain fidelity, but appearances mattered. Appearances and back-chatter. They were the eventual undoing of the marriage.

The day John's divorce was granted, Arnett secretly hailed the usefulness of judges and courts.

Her marriage to John spun into four decades and separate bedrooms. One April morning, Arnett banged through his bedroom door, waking him up. She had evidence, proof he strayed. It seemed her husband turned out to be a risk-taker even after she set unequivocal terms: She promised him ruin, poverty, if he was ever unfaithful. He understood she had the courts on her side.

Straying, however, did not adequately describe the crime. John was embroiled in a nineteen-year affair. She damned him for hiding secrets, and she dubbed the much younger other woman the Scottish Tart, refusing to speak her name. She read the name often enough in the newspapers. Callie MacCallum won this golf trophy or that, one tournament after another. She was Chesterfield Park's glory. Without fail, each article mentioned her roots. They were traced back to Scotland, the birthplace of what Arnett deemed "a wretched sport."

The sun was just rising when she threw John out of the house. She told him the Scottish Tart should watch her back. From somewhere, her mind dredged up a backwoods cottage scene where justice was delivered over the barrel of a shotgun. There was the sense she heard it fire when she slammed the front door on John's grass-stained ass.

If one element of Arnett's life ran true, it was that she'd always been a product of her upbringing. She turned away from truth early in her twenties. Secrets were gaveled into obscurity until they did not exist. Pretense overtook reality. Now she faced nothing but uncompromising turmoil at every turn.

To herself, she admitted that she wished John were healthy and living. His calming influence made him a natural mediator in smoothing out family situations. She closed her eyes and heard his voice of reason in the silence.

Deep down though, Arnett obsessed over victory. She felt victory's addictive qualities first, when she fought for and won John. The elation of that victory had always been a feeling that, over the years, she could rejuvenate and relive, even taste. Its sweetness sustained her. She found it curious, bordering on unthinkable, that Callie MacCallum approached the same situation so differently. Where Arnett unseated her rival in short order, Callie was satisfied to let the situation ride.

Crazy, Arnett thought over and over. Why hadn't Callie taken what she obviously wanted with all her heart? She was a sportswoman. She owned a competitive spirit. John and she were deeply and undeniably in love. Arnett believed that.

A satisfied smile slid onto Arnett's face. For a time, victory lived in Callie's house because John climbed into her bed every night. But only for a very short time.

. . .

On Saturday morning, Arnett sat in the same chair, facing the picture window. Two SUVs pulled to a stop at the curb. She got up, locked the house behind her, and wheeled her suitcase down the walk. She also carried a bag of groceries. Beebe insisted each woman contribute to stocking the cabin's larder.

Lizbeth stood at the Tahoe's opened cargo door. Callie MacCallum and Beebe Walker climbed out of Callie's Santa Fe. Arnett felt like she was being escorted to a torture chamber rather than a mountain retreat. The trip felt especially tortuous since the call came from Beebe. Initially, Arnett agreed to ride with Beebe, but her car failed to start. Arnett couldn't drive. She took advantage of the week away and drove her station wagon in yesterday for routine maintenance. With the last minute change in driving arrangements, there wasn't even time to book a rental car. So, it was Lizbeth she'd ride with to West Virginia.

Out in the street, ten-year old Carson Tillman from next door rode his bike in circles, watching the proceedings.

After loading Arnett's things, Lizbeth slammed the cargo door. She turned to Beebe. "We're ready," she said.

Beebe made an arm gesture that gathered Arnett, Lizbeth, and Callie into a line at the foot of the drive. Carson's bike jumped the curb. He ground it to a stop nearby. The nosy boy might have thought the ladies were posing for a send-off photograph.

A breeze kicked up Beebe's crop of straw-colored hair so that it stood out from her head like a crayon drawing of the sun. She raised her right hand into oath-taking position, then used several upward gestures with her left to prompt the others to hoist their hands as well. Beebe recited a pledge, breaking it into five chunks, which the others repeated in unison.

"I hereby swear an oath to honesty. From this point forward, I promise to provide fully factual information and will express my feelings earnestly and without reservation."

As all the hands dropped, Carson, a respectfully polite tattletale, his broad mouth gleaming with dental hardware, announced, "Miss Arnett had her fingers crossed."

Lizbeth's mouth flew open. Her gaze jumped off the boy and landed on Arnett. "How could you?"

In a teacher-to-student tone, Beebe said, "Show me your hands." Arnett complied. "Do you swear to this honesty pledge?"

"Yes, I swear." Arnett glared at Carson. "Are you satisfied?"

He shrugged and pedaled away.

The two SUVs traveled west on Interstate 70. Vehicle-to-vehicle communication was handled via cell phone. They stopped at The Porch, a trendy restaurant just off the Morgantown exit and lunched *al fresco* on salads and iced tea. Conversation was painfully stilted: There were so many subjects to avoid.

Back on the interstate and cruising south toward Baron, West Virginia, and a cabin named Heatherwood, Arnett rode again in Lizbeth's passenger seat. Lizbeth cleared her throat. "I have something to say."

Arnett looked over. Lizbeth held her chin high. Damn, Arnett thought, what's coming now?

"If I decide to stay in Maryland and allow you to keep Chad, you must agree to not only accept the quilt, but display it."

Arnett frowned. "Now you're giving me decorating tips?"

"That's the deal. And the quilt remains out in the open, not tucked in a bedroom."

"Well, should I take it to the Vatican and have the pope bless it, or will a local priest do?"

"I'm not changing my mind, Arnett. If you want visits with Chad, then I want him to see the quilt. And I want it prominently placed."

"When are these incessant terms going to stop?"

Lizbeth's lack of response was answer enough. Arnett's fury roiled. The thought of never seeing Chad again was more than she could bear. Neither could she bow to Lizbeth's demands: They'd become a smothering membrane.

Arnett executed a mental countermove: She concentrated on Harlow Nolan's letter and the favorable outcome of her appointment with the lawyer. His letter would be comfortably tucked in Lizbeth's mailbox, awaiting her return. Stella promised Arnett that Nolan would scare the pee out of Lizbeth. That picture pleased her. When her daughter-in-law stood in a puddle of her own making, then they'd negotiate.

Hum of Paradise

August ripened sweetly in the mountains around Baron, West Virginia. Lucius Dameron considered them stocked with the fullest complement of nature and wonder. The pollinating wilderness proudly displayed its fragrant offspring. Roadside wildflowers in maize and mauve and melon bordered the narrow gravel-and-dirt trails that seemed to wind all the way down from the sky. Lapping streams, forever in motion, wore grooves, like wrinkles in weathered skin, into the mountainous terrain. The streams' clear whispers told of both timeless and innocent secrets. The mountains sustained life, Lucius's included, with the heady scent of pine, the sticky ooze from maple trees, and the hum of paradise.

Lucius hummed to himself that morning as he steered his red Ford pickup through the traffic light at Carmody and Armament, then bumped into the parking lot set aside for Baron's 1892 train depot. The passenger trains of old seemed little more than a myth. Those who visited present-day Baron turned west off the interstate, chose to stop at the Waffle House or not, then used Carmody to ease toward the town's nucleus.

Baron was old, and its citizens wanted to maintain the town's originality. That made a lot of work for a restoration carpenter with twenty-five years in the business. Back in July, the town fathers hired

Lucius to introduce the mothballed station to the new century. Baron held its Festival of Leaves in mid-October. The festival's premier event that year was the christening of the old station as Baron's new visitors welcome center. He made steady progress to that end.

Five weeks ago, he ordered globes with a retro look for the overhead lights. This morning, he was regretfully informed again by the Lowe's rep that the large, bulbous, white glass fixtures had not been on the truck, so Lucius concentrated on other tasks that inched the train depot closer to its former pride.

By noon, he finished erecting the center's outdoor sign in the grassy area behind the sidewalk. Lucius stood to admire his work. He chose an angle for the sign that gave traffic on Carmody and Armament an equal look. To finish off the job, he planted pansies around the sign posts. The sign shared its location with an ancient crabapple and a salvaged and repainted iron bench. On a whim that morning, he picked up cleaning supplies and polished up the station's two small bathrooms. There wouldn't be an official cleaning crew until the official grand opening. With Lucius Dameron, one received full service: carpentry, gardening, and a Lysol shine.

During its forced retirement, the building became a repository for everything imaginable. Once its contents were emptied, Lucius decided nothing of size should interrupt the impact of the room. Stark was best—just the surround of mullioned glass and those fourteen pillars bracing walls and ceiling.

An interior twilight existed inside the station by late afternoon. The summer breeze blowing through the leafy trees across in the park caused pinpricks of light to dance across the room. That daily shift in lighting was his cue to move outdoors. He'd been prying loose rotted and weathered sections of the raised platform and replacing them with treated lumber.

Before he headed out, he stopped to measure the platform's double doors for brass kick-plates. He was down on his knees when he heard a racket behind him. He turned. Three women slammed through the parking lot door with more billowing steam and the screech of steel against steel than any locomotive braking on the tracks could ever produce. They seemed oblivious to the carpentry motif. Fussing with each other, they wound around to the ladies' room. The bathroom door closed, sealing in their voices.

Lucius was dumbstruck—not by the invasion—but by a face he recognized through the window glass. His high school classmate Callie MacCallum crossed the parking lot to his truck, probably drawn by *Dameron Restorations* painted on the driver's door.

Smiling, Lucius rose to his feet. Through the windows, he watched Callie follow the trail of detritus left behind from his morning's work. She stood among the scattering of plastic cups, empty after he transplanted the pansies. She inspected the sign, then carefully avoided stepping on the work gloves and hand spade that lay in the grass next to the nozzle attached to a length of garden hose.

She tracked the lime-green hose through the depot's front yard and around the corner. She stopped, stymied, hands on hips. The hose terminated twenty yards down at a spigot affixed to the building. Her head jerked left, her gaze falling on a pile of lumber sprawled next to the passenger platform. Farther down in the depot's side yard, she spied an unattended wheelbarrow supporting a shovel. Together, they guarded a walk-in shed, doors wide.

She strode off on what would prove a fruitless mission. Or was it? Callie was searching the length and breadth of depot property for him. That warmed him deeply.

He turned when he heard the creak of the restroom door. The older woman emerged. He stepped forward through the gathering gloom. He knew his light green irises were an astonishing shade that lit his face and held the eye. He aimed them at the woman.

Giving her a pleasant smile, he said, "Good afternoon. I don't think you ladies saw me when you came in. You're from Cassel, aren't you?"

Her mouth flew open in surprise. "How'd you know?"

"I know Callie." He swept a finger through the air, taking her gaze to Callie at the far end of the side yard. After a beat, he added, "We were separated at birth."

Her reaction didn't disappoint. Disbelief settled on her upturned face. He had no choice but to apply the tone of a tall tale to his true story. "Yes, ma'am. We were nursery mates at Browning Regional. Born on the same day, just thirty-one minutes apart. Thirty-one." He cocked a playful eyebrow. "That's a prime number, you know. Blue ribbon. Grade A. There's strength in a prime number. It can only be divided by itself."

She cut sharply through Lucius's pack of polished bull. "You can't possibly remember Callie from the hospital."

"You're right. I don't," the storyteller acquiesced, then spun out another chapter in the truthful yarn. "But we found each other again at fourteen. We were best buds back at Cassel High. She was back from Duke and working at Chesterfield when the country club boys hired me to expand the pro shop. It's been too long since I saw Callie. Of course part of that is, I became a Baron transplant two years ago," Lucius went on. "Before that, we actually ran into each other, here, not in Cassel. Look at her. She's hot on my trail." Lucius laughed. Callie hadn't found him in the shed. She was marching full speed toward the depot.

"Callie and I enjoy one of those friendships that clicked into place simply by sitting down at desks one beside the other our first day of class. We were inseparable back then. When our lives cross now—as they inevitably do," he said, leaning close to deliver the news flash, "we pick up the conversation seamlessly."

The two of them kept an eye on Callie's progress. They witnessed how her face brightened when she saw him through the glass in a platform door.

Pulling the door open, she rushed him. "Lucius! My God!"

Lucius, appreciative of the deity reference, reached out. She threw her arms around his neck. Lifting her off the ground, he brushed her temple with a kiss.

"You've still got that terrier tenacity, kiddo," he said, setting her down. "You never stop; never give up."

She tugged on a fistful of his blue shirtsleeve. "You were watching me?"

"Every minute."

Lucius Dameron was suddenly thankful the retro globes hadn't arrived. If he'd spent the day up in the rafters, he wouldn't have posted the welcome sign. Without the sign, Callie and her group would surely have driven past.

To merely be thankful for his lifelong friendship with Callie MacCallum missed the mark entirely. She never left his side during the final months of their senior year when the chants about his sexual persuasion rang through the school, and through his ears as a high-handed awakening. At seventeen, he and Callie were naïve about things in the world. He had yet to face himself with the knowledge and was far from accepting it. He bravely clung to the opinion that his adorable humor and be-bopping energy would carry him through the dreaded high school years. It was Terrier Callie who snarled and nipped and kept the bullies away. It was Callie who encouraged him to dig deep for his inner strength.

Lucius and Callie rattled out a few strands of reminiscent chatter, then he angled for the awkwardly missing introduction. "How do you ladies know each other?" By the time his head bobbed from Callie to the other woman and back again, Callie's eyes dropped.

"Answer him," the woman said.

The slyness in her tone wasn't lost on Lucius; neither was Callie's reluctance.

"Through Jack," Callie said finally.

"Oh, Jack," he said, "Girlfriend, you two were so in love. The way you looked at each other reached moonbeam quality."

His insightfully romantic comment was followed by a moment of unearthly silence, then the woman clamped both hands to her head, her eyes bulged. Behind her, the two taller women stepped into the depot's roomy lobby in time to see the first woman stomp the time-darkened floorboards and hear her produce a long guttural sound.

She's ready to blow, Lucius thought, amused by the short woman's animation.

The words, "I can't do this. I won't," spewed from her mouth. The two women sprang forward, each grabbing one of her arms.

"What happened?" the thinner of the two women wanted to know.

Callie let the question pass unanswered. "This is Lucius Dameron," she said instead. "I've known him since high school."

Lucius stood back, grinning, taking it all in. Neither of the reinforcements actually made eye contact, let alone extended a hand. The thin woman talked over everyone, recanting rules about expected behavior. From her comments, Lucius gathered the women were on some kind of truth-or-consequences trip, and not the marijuana-induced kind. The older woman, with sudden effort, yanked free of chubby woman's grasp and lunged at Callie. Fearful, Lucius swung a protective arm, like a crossing gate, in front of Callie, shielding her.

"He was *my* husband." The woman spat the words at Callie with a ferocity that reverberated off the glass.

"Arnett, stop it."

The thin woman's shout provided the missing introduction and wiped the grin off Lucius's face.

He gave Callie a sidelong look. What in the world was she doing in Baron with Jack Sebring's widow?

Lucius met Jack Sebring seventeen summers ago during the pro shop's expansion project. Perhaps it was Lucius's special wiring that alerted him to the closeness Callie shared with Jack. Perhaps it was the matching nugget-gold diamond rings they wore, third finger, left hand. During that summer, the project and the pretense played out for a short while, then Lucius pulled Callie aside. He wasn't buying for a moment that Callie and Jack were no more than friendly, long-time coworkers. That summer, Lucius became Callie's safe ear.

As a barrage of pinpricked light washed through the station, the tall woman announced an all-encompassing decision. Barely a bump in time had been given for deliberation.

"New rule, Arnett, I'm taking Beebe with me. You and Callie will ride the rest of the way to the cabin together." The tall woman's tone blocked all rights to appeal. "If you won't try to get along with her in a civil, mature manner, then we'll force the issue. Right, Beebe?"

Talkative Lucius was now stunned into silence. Reflexively, Arnett looked to Callie with the change in travel arrangements. Callie gave a thin smile, but showed no outward objection.

"Lizbeth, please, let me—" Beebe began.

"No, this is ridiculous behavior," Lizbeth said of Arnett. "She must know better."

Arnett's hands formed fists, her arms stiffened, then her shoulders humped. With a growl, she turned on her heel and fled toward the parking lot. Lizbeth pursued Arnett out the door.

"Right. This is better," a sarcastic Beebe said, rubbing her temples. "We'll take it outside."

No, Lucius thought, no. Let's all be ridiculous right here.

But Beebe already expelled a weary sigh and took up the chase.

. . .

Callie absorbed the enveloping quiet of the old depot. She found the separation from the others soothing. Beside her, Lucius dipped his chin in an effort to level his face with hers. She knew he wanted to tap into her thoughts.

Without meeting his eyes, she reached out and patted his arm. That action would tell him she'd received his transmission of barbed worry.

She believed in the kinetic connection they possessed since birth. For thirty-one minutes, the dark-haired baby boy experienced the world alone until the blonde-headed little girl arrived to keep him company.

Callie wound a path across the lobby, around a plastic hip-high trashcan and the sawhorse supports for a length of plywood. Arms folded, she leaned into a fluted pillar beside a window with a view of the asphalt lot. Outside, Lizbeth stood apart while Beebe huddled with Arnett at the Tahoe's back bumper.

Adding herself to the mix, Callie thought Lucius must perceive the four of them a very peculiar combo. She turned. "Come over here, and I'll give you the dirt before you die of gossip-deprived curiosity right there with your work boots on." She hoped he picked up her smile in the dwindling light. "They're lovely, by the way, with the brushed leather and all."

Lucius looked down his thin frame, past his Top Dog T-shirt and denim shorts to the band of white sock rimming each of his over-the-ankle boots. He kicked one boot up onto its heel. Cocking his head, he inspected the dyed leather before pushing himself into motion. "Did you say deprived or depraved?"

She laughed at his easy nature. When he reached her, he lay the width of his gentle grip across her nape and gave a brotherly jostle that made her blunt-cut hair swing.

She slid him a sideways look. "We both know I'm right there with you in the depraved category."

"Direct and to the heart of things. That's my Callie. I'm sorry about all that, gumdrop." He hooked a thumb over his shoulder, gesturing back in time to Arnett's point of attack. "I thought I was just saying something sweet. It was true, you know. I really considered the looks between you and Jack moonbeam quality."

Despite Arnett's outburst to Lucius's declaration, Callie processed his words the first time around. They'd taken her breath.

She grinned. "You're far too sensitive for everyone's good."

"Comes with the territory, I think."

"Forgive me for not asking sooner. How's Willie? He still the good-looking one?" she said, ribbing him with an old standard.

"I shall not dignify that with an answer." His tone mocked injury, but his antics caused Callie to smile: He licked a fingertip, ran it first over one eyebrow, then the other.

Lucius referred to Willie Thorne as his beloved. The way he said the word conveyed the tease and a deeply felt emotional truth. Callie met Willie on multiple occasions. The two men owned a cabin in one of Baron's woods. A fixer-upper. Willie lived day-to-day in Cassel and made the four-hour commute to the mountain hideaway for weekends. He was their age, a financial genius, and on the fast-track to retirement.

Sporting a grin, Lucius answered. "Willie's fine. Thanks for asking."

Callie looked into Lucius's mint-green eyes. It had been over two years since Callie saw Lucius. Jack was still alive then. Sometimes it was hard to believe he'd been gone eighteen months. Callie and Lucius were unique in today's world of easy communication. Their daily contact broke when she went to Duke. Like their fourteen-year separation, they seemed destined to be distanced. They were two cogs on mismatched gearing inside the same clock. Eventually, their lives would mesh again. They left it that way. Wanting face to face. Physical meetings of their souls. Predetermined at birth.

The exceptions were Lucius's many calls from Baron during Jack's illness and after his death.

With the tedious day, pressure was mounting. Callie repeated the same words to Lucius in the depot that she cried into the phone with his first call. Lucius's grin faded when her chin started to tremble. "Jack was so very, very sick, Lucius."

Lucius didn't hesitate. He pulled Callie gently to his chest. He rocked her, and she wept. After she quieted, he scooted a covered paint tub away from the wall with the toe of his boot. The tub was footstool-height. He lowered her onto it, then repositioned another tub and perched next to her. She wiped at her eyes. They both focused on her left hand.

He pulled it out of her lap. "Now you wear both rings."

Callie struggled numbly into that first cold morning following Jack's death. The pain of his heart freshly torn from hers drove her to slip his ring on her index finger. That memory choked off any hope of verbal reply.

Meddler Extraordinaire

Lucius squeezed Callie's hand, then got up. He returned from the bathroom a moment later, clutching a fist full of two-ply and a damp paper towel. She stood at the window again, but with regained composure. The three women outside were a hodgepodge of sizes and shapes, dispositions and coloring. They'd gravitated to a cluster.

"Look at them," she said when he came alongside.

"Oh, I am."

"The animated one—that's Arnett's daughter-in-law, Lizbeth Sebring."

Lucius's translation was, "Battling relatives."

"The other woman is Beebe Walker. A grief counselor."

"Ah," he said.

"She's got something up her sleeve if she allows this change in driving arrangements."

"You trust her? I noticed you didn't say anything about riding with Arnett. Maybe you shouldn't. Because, honey, Arnett is not fond of you." He tapped her nose. "You need to keep this above water."

Callie smiled at Lucius's water reference. She remembered her too-close-to-the edge-of-the-pool conversation with Arnett. "No one knows that better than I. And, yes, I do trust Beebe. At some point,

Arnett and I must come to terms with this trip."

"You know I want more, but tend to yourself first." Callie took the tissue and towel he offered and walked back to the trashcan. When they were again elbow to elbow, he said, "The new rule still hasn't landed in the acceptance category." Resistant Arnett jabbed a finger at Lizbeth's Tahoe while adamant Lizbeth jabbed a finger at Callie's Santa Fe. "I honestly didn't think it would."

Callie rolled her eyes up to his. "Honesty. That's the link to this trip. Or retreat. I don't know what to call it. Lizbeth calls it a peace summit. She and Beebe are the organizers." Lucius lifted a foot to the nearby paint tub. "I got roped in because I had the cabin. I planned to be here, anyway, this week. We all took an honesty pledge this morning. That's why I had to answer your question truthfully. Arnett was standing right there. She'd have called me out if I skirted the issue."

Lucius threw his head back and laughed. "So I was duped by Arnett. Figures. She hoped to embarrass you into answering my nosy question, but then it backfired in her face. She knew your answer, but she didn't anticipate my response. The honesty rule," he asked, "that landed in the acceptance category?"

"Yes, if you mean Arnett." Callie decided not to describe Arnett's fingers-crossed-behind-her-back escapade. "She was in better spirits this morning. Guarded, but still better. Something must have happened between her and Lizbeth in the car."

"Another triumph for honesty, I bet."

"Who knows. It seemed like Beebe and Lizbeth were in the bathroom a long time. Maybe they were discussing the problem."

Just then, Arnett stomped past both vehicles and headed for the bench under the crabapple. The other two followed suit, but stopped short of the curbing that bordered the grassy area beyond. The curbing seemed symbolic, like a toe drawn through the dirt.

"Beebe holds her counseling sessions in the carriage house behind Swanson Funeral Home," Callie informed Lucius. "Remember it?"

Lucius stood taller. "Across from the Titus mansion?"

"Yeah."

"Man, I'd love to get my hands on the crown molding in that place."

Callie pressed on. Such segues were common for the carpenter worth his weight in woodworking tools. "Anyway, Beebe counseled Lizbeth for several weeks. Her husband Dan—Jack's younger son—died in May."

"How awful," he said with true depth of sorrow. "Kids?"

"Two, one in college, and Chad in preschool. Or he would be, except Arnett wants to provide daycare." She avoided Arnett's outlandish *grandsitting* term. "Money's tight. Lizbeth needs to work. And I guess Arnett kept Geoff before he went to school."

"Geoff? The older one?"

"Right." Callie paused. She wanted to speak of Arnett with dignity, and not appear petty or mean-spirited. On a deeper level, Callie fought through the layered protections she and Jack placed over their private life. Even though that book was open to all concerned, and then some—she thought of the neighborhood clutch of men—old habits prevailed. She closed her eyes. Jack's face materialized behind her lids. She blinked away his look of betrayal, then chose her words carefully. "Apparently, Arnett has begun to show herself."

"And that means?"

Callie expelled an incredulous laugh. "Lucius, look at her." She tapped the glass. Arnett sat at rigid attention on the bench, both hands clasping the purse in her lap, her stubborn streak nearly in lights. "And you witnessed her reaction in here."

"Yes, I did," he said, pleasantly disagreeable, "but my point is: You know more, don't you? 'Begun to show herself.' That just puts the key in the lock. Turn it, Callie. Turn it and open the door." Lucius nudged her arm with his. "Jack must have told you things."

"Not as much as you think."

"Come on, Callie. What do you know?"

Callie turned away. She looked through the windowpane. "I suspect that's what we're here to find out."

. . .

Lucius's heart and stomach turned somersaults, wanting to spend the next several days with the four women. If he couldn't be physically present, then his second choice was a hidden camera inside the cabin. The unfolding drama there would far exceed anything available on reality TV. He recently paid an obscene amount to get broadband technology run down Bullwhip Road to his and Willie's cabin in the woods. Before that, he derived his entertainment from activities around him. That sometimes meant people; sometimes it meant the simple pleasure of watching squirrels play in the clearing alongside the cabin's porch. Then there was the reality of squirrelly people. One such person was angling through the crosswalk.

"Uh-oh," he said. "Sylvia."

"What? That woman?" Callie said, inching forward.

"This is not good. That's Sylvia Stick-Up-Her-Butt Boyle."

Finally, he heard Callie's laugh, an energetic tension-reliever. "Oh, Lucius, I haven't heard that since high school."

"The stick hasn't actually penetrated yet. Just wait. Speaking of high school," Lucius said, "Sylvia is Baron's full-time hall monitor. Won't drive or can't, so walks everywhere. She's cousins with the mayor. Before she went high-tech, she just took notes. Now she has a cell phone. I'm sure he loves that."

Sylvia approached, clearly observing the scene: Lizbeth had taken center stage with Arnett.

"Okay. Sylvia's picking up the conversation," Lucius said. "Walk slowing to a crawl. Watch her. She's stopping." Lucius's eyes jumped back and forth from Sylvia to the three Maryland women while he bantered the play-by-play. "There," he announced.

Sylvia straightened, eyes and mouth wide circles. Arnett just swung her purse wildly at Lizbeth. In response, Sylvia clutched hers tightly around her middle.

Groaning, Callie grabbed Lucius's arm. "I can see where this is headed. I should go out there. Beebe'll need my help."

"Yeah, I'd better head Sylvia off."

Callie slipped out the side exit. Lucius hustled through the front doors and cut through the tiny yard. Sylvia's hand fidgeted with her purse clasp. "Miss Boyle," he called to distract her before she retrieved her phone.

Her head swiveled his way, her loose silver curls bouncing. "Are you the carpenter working here?" she asked, pointing to the depot.

"Yes, ma'am. Lucius Dameron." He stood on the sidewalk beside her.

"Who are these women? They're disturbing the peace. That's a misdemeanor." Her dentures clicking, she quoted chapter and verse from Baron's civil offenses code.

"Just a little disagreement, Miss Boyle. It's covered. Don't worry."

"But that one woman tried to assault the other."

"It's all going to take care of itself," he said, and knew it would. His confidence in Callie reigned high, and by extension, Callie's trust in Beebe.

The wispy breeze that blew between Lucius and Sylvia seemed to prompt the scene change under the crabapple. Beebe broke into the squabbling. She lifted her arms over her head and danced a flat-footed pirouette. On her second full turn, she dropped to one knee in front of Arnett, nearly tipped over, and flung her arms wide. "Please, Arnett," she said, "Ride to the cabin in Callie's car."

Arnett pressed herself against the bench's backrest, too stunned by Beebe's awkward-ballerina performance to respond.

Without missing a beat, Callie climbed to the grassy stage, gave a graceful twirl, and knelt before Arnett with a flourish. "Please, please, Arnett, ride to the cabin with me."

Arnett accepted the fun and her exalted place in it. She raised her defiant chin and fixed a look on an irked and equally shocked Lizbeth, who stared down at her companions. Arnett's expression registered as a haughty, "Well?"

Lizbeth heaved an enormous sigh, then imitated the other two, but with lackadaisical style. "Please, Arnett—" she started, but Beebe interrupted with a throat-clearing cue. Lizbeth muttered, "I can't believe I'm doing this." Then she found her mother-in-law's face and completed her line with a triple-dose of politeness. "Please. Please. Please, Arnett, ride to the cabin with Callie."

Arnett rose to the occasion. She stepped between Beebe and Callie who folded in their arms so she could pass.

Sylvia, present for the entire show, said, "Respect for one's elders. That's the way it ought to be, young man."

"Yes, ma'am." Lucius smiled, and Sylvia strutted off.

The Maryland women were in motion as well. Arnett, nose in the air, led. Callie flicked Lucius a wave. He crossed to the depot's side door while Lizbeth and Beebe traipsed to the Tahoe. He didn't go inside, but waited in the shadows, picking up on the nuances of these two trailing women. Beebe exhibited enthusiasm. She seemed pumped with energy, due to the favorable resolution to a situation spiraling downward at a rapid rate. On the other hand, Lizbeth's lips, pressed tightly together, were reduced to a thin line. Her eyes were the storyteller: They glared sharply and maliciously at her mother-in-law's back. Lucius decided he trusted Beebe, too. She'd emptied Lizbeth's blustery sails and turned her into the wind.

From his spot under the eaves, he watched the SUVs exit the lot and roll through the intersection. Every instinct he owned urged him to jump in his truck and join the convoy, but his better angels won out. Tomorrow would be soon enough. He'd visit with a pretty basket of breakfast muffins and properly introduce himself. "I'm Lucius Dameron, dear ladies, gay carpenter and meddler extraordinaire."

He gave his chin a decisive nod. They were bound to appreciate his honesty.

. . .

The two SUVs streamed along Carmody Street. The residential section doubled as one of Baron's main access roads. The town, with its name drawn down from the ranks of nobility, knew strength and cunning when time was new. Identity and purpose existed yet, but the fiber of Baron was weakened by age and struggle.

Callie and Arnett rode in the lead vehicle. From the corner of Callie's eye, she watched Arnett turn slowly and glance over the seatback. A clicking sound was all that broke the silence between them. The back seats were folded down. The enlarged cargo area held two suitcases, a large aqua and white cooler on wheels, two brown paper grocery sacks, and a golf bag. The SUV's sway caused the clubs with iron heads to tap against each other.

"You brought your clubs?" Arnett's question was sharp, her tone incredulous.

"I did," Callie responded with a short slice of self-assurance.

"That's something dear John would have done," Arnett said with none of the affection the words inferred. "There are times in one's life when the importance of an occasion dictates a week without the insipid sport."

Had Callie decided not to be bated into an argument, she would have reminded Arnett that Jack's livelihood, his talent for golf-course design, provided her a generous lifestyle.

Arnett snapped her fingers. "What's the buzzword I hear bandied about these days?" Arnett bit down on her lip, overplaying a moment of feigned reflection. "Ah, stakeholder. That's it. You don't have any real stake in the outcome of this peace summit, do you? For you, this is just another occasion to play golf. How nice."

Callie remained under Arnett's scrutiny a moment longer, then the older woman shook her head, conveying lingering disgust. Callie knew her lack of a comeback would be savored as a victory, and a victorious Arnett might be more inclined to accept her proposition.

The turn signal clicked steadily while Callie waited for traffic to clear. Within seconds of maneuvering onto the turnpike, mountains rose up on their right, large and imposing. The peaks were a natural barrier against urban sprawl. At intervals, sections of the pine-covered mountaintops had been shirred for the passage of live wires that brought energy and communication. Reaching the turnpike equaled the last leg of the trip. Heatherwood was just around the corner, relatively speaking. Nothing was as squared up as corners in the West Virginia mountains. Snaky switchbacks being prime examples.

She gave Arnett a sidelong glance. Never, never waste an opportunity, she thought. A golfer always converted opportunity into success. Hopefully, Arnett was ready to plot another victory.

"I know you find this awkward," Callie said, opening with neutral words. "I do, too. But I think we can all agree that Lizbeth needs our help."

"I don't like the way you're including yourself in this." Mocking Callie, Arnett added, " *We* can all agree that Lizbeth needs *our* help"

"Look, Arnett, Lizbeth included me. It was not my choice. I was asked to help, and I will. If you don't comply, if you don't accept me in this—based on Lizbeth's frame of mind—you're cutting your own throat, plain and simple."

"Me? I figured that's what you were here to do." Her craftiness quickly changed to anger. "My life has gone to hell because of you."

"Right here, right now," Callie said, struggling to maintain decorum, "let's not make this about you and me. We need to focus on Lizbeth. We need to help her make clear decisions. Those decisions affect you more than me. In fact, they don't affect me at all."

"My point exactly. Lizbeth wanted you along to keep me stirred up. It's sabotage. She's setting me up."

Callie held back the sigh that wanted to escape. "No, she's not. She's asking you to—"

"I know what she's asking. I don't need you to tell me. My precious daughter-in-law didn't pack that quilt in her luggage. She laid it out on the back seat as a ready reminder."

Several minutes passed while the women watched the highway disappear under the SUV and an idea dogged Callie. "Why don't you and I make a pact?"

Arnett shook her head. "No more pacts. The one with Lizbeth is enough."

"Let me explain first before you decide."

"Fine," Arnett said, glaring. "Explain."

"Why don't you and I caucus about circumstances between us first. We might resolve the issues before they're brought up in group." Callie incorporated the counseling terms Beebe used in what little conversation had taken place at lunch. "You'll appear less tense if you have time to think things through. Ruminate, as Jack always said," she added with a smile Arnett didn't return. "Lizbeth and Beebe will perceive this new attitude as improvement. And it will be. I just think no pre-warning of caucus material is only going to lead to hurt feelings and offhanded remarks. There'll be no real headway, just backpedaling and apologizing."

"Are you saying you have caucus questions for me?"

"I wouldn't dismiss it. I was thinking more of your questions for me."

A look of surprise fled onto Arnett's face, closely followed by anger. "So, your pact would give you time to prepare. Another one-sided pact. Arnett loses again."

"No. You'd be prepared for my answers, and not go off the deep end."

"Like back at the depot."

"Yes, like back at the depot. No points for you there. Chad is still out of reach."

Arnett's entire body stiffened. "Cheating is obviously something you learned well from John," she said, "but I won't be partners with you."

Callie thought Arnett made a bad decision. A partner was just what she needed, but Callie understood. The ship had sailed on Callie's integrity with Arnett. "If you change your mind, let me know."

"I won't."

Both women's gazes drifted to their respective side mirrors. Lizbeth's dusty Tahoe followed like a gray ghost.

A short time later, Old County Road A came up on the left. The two SUVs turned and proceeded up its low grade. The width of the asphalt accommodated two lanes of traffic, but was devoid of a painted centerline. On Callie's side, the road dropped off. An abundant mix of wildflowers, weeds, and brambles grew up along the edge. On Arnett's side, a solid wall of evergreens looked down on their ascent.

Farther up, a clearing appeared on the right. Callie pulled onto a small off-road parking area in front of a weathered building labeled OFFICE CHECK-IN. Lizbeth eased the Tahoe in behind. Arnett nearly jumped out of the Santa Fe, following a short struggle with the seatbelt. Callie walked between the two bumpers, her gaze fixed on the building's façade, its rough-hewn finish, the six steps up to the railed porch, the two Adirondack chairs beside the front door.

Callie was vaguely aware of Lizbeth bending at the waist, stretching her long muscles and moaning. The last door closed. Beebe commented on the general-store look. Callie smiled. She had the same thought over a decade ago on her first trip to Baron. In the next heartbeat though, she fiercely resented the women accompanying her inside and their forced replacement of Jack. She felt his loss thicken quickly until its pain choked. She desperately wished she could bewitch them with a string of charmed words that would cause them to tarry in the afternoon sun, chatting and laughing.

Beebe ambled over. "Should we wait here?" Her tone was low. She seemed tuned in to Callie's thoughts. "The first time you saw this place and walked in, it must have been with Jack."

"Actually, no. Jack gave me directions. I stopped for a second cabin key."

"But still, returning must be difficult."

She searched Beebe's brown eyes. "We took an honesty pledge."

"I understand, but it works both ways. Do you honestly want us to wait here?"

It hadn't occurred to Callie the honesty pledge could be twisted to create a benefit. "It'll be fine," Callie said, not accepting Beebe's alternative, "you all can come. This is small, considering I opened Heatherwood to this peace summit."

"I don't believe that, but okay." Then Beebe's chin came up. "No, I take that back. It's not okay. You don't have to play the complete martyr. That isn't necessary."

Callie wavered. She did prefer a private reunion with Sarah, but she didn't want to appear to be hiding something and get a row started. On the other hand, Sarah needed to know she had guests. Callie shifted her gaze to Beebe. "Let me go alone first. Then I'll wave you in. Everyone can meet Sarah."

"Fine. Much better. I'll hold them here. Take your time."

"Thanks, Beebe." On a rush of relief, she added, "Heatherwood is just up the road. I couldn't drive by without letting Sarah know I arrived. She was always wonderful to Jack and me."

Beebe's hand whisked her away. "Go ahead. Go see her."

A moment later, Callie stood inside. A large oval-shaped braided rug occupied the center of the room and led to a counter parallel with the back wall. There, a smiling Sarah Prosser waited a beat before buzzing around the counter. Her broad shoulders tapered to thin birdlike legs. The oversized white shirt she wore over gray leggings precipitated her youthful appearance, but energetic Sarah was pushing seventy. Her emerald eyes didn't stray from Callie until she was gathered into a tight embrace.

Sarah rubbed Callie's back with the same hand that, after she pulled away, cupped and raised her chin. "It is so good to see you." Standing back, she took Callie in. "A little thin, I think, but we'll see what we can't do about that."

"Don't worry about me. Good to see you. You look great," Callie said, tugging on Sarah's shirtsleeve, pinching the ironed-in crease.

Quickly, Callie looked around. The building's interior was just as she remembered. A beverage cooler took up much of the entranceway. The general-store theme expanded through the room with small quantities of personal items and food stuffs on low shelving beneath the windows that lined the front and far walls.

"How are you?" Sarah asked solemnly, then held up a hand. "No. Don't answer that. You're here; I know progress was made."

Callie appreciated Sarah's efforts to let her stay the course. Callie would talk about Jack when she was ready. Hooking Callie's elbow, Sarah walked her to the counter. A reddish-brown accordion folder lay there.

"Later in the week," Sarah said, tapping the folder, "I'll stop by, and we'll go over some paperwork. Update things. There'll be a few forms to sign. But that can wait. You had a long trip; you'll want to get settled in."

Callie's finger scratched at the folder's edge. "Sarah, I know I didn't tell you this on the phone, but I brought some ladies with me."

"Oh?" Then her face lit. "For a gab session."

"Well, something like that."

"That's a great idea."

"Anyway, I want you to meet them." Callie pointed toward the windows and her traveling companions beyond.

"By all means. Get them in here."

Callie walked back to the screen door and called Beebe's name. The three women climbed the wooden stairs, sounding as offbeat as iron-shod oxen. Callie led them to Sarah. Stepping back, she gestured toward the trio now rooted to the rug. "Sarah, these are my guests: Beebe, Lizbeth, and Arnett."

"Welcome," was all Sarah got out. A rustling sound carried through the doorway behind the counter that led to the back office where a second entrance door opened and closed.

"That's Nadia, my second in command." Sarah patted Callie's arm. "I want you to meet her. Excuse me."

An awkward silence waited with the four women until Sarah returned with Nadia. Both were giggling. Nadia was a wispy woman in her mid-twenties. Her dark blonde hair was tied back with a scarf. She trailed Sarah around the counter and smiled brightly at the group.

"Callie, this is Nadia," Sarah said, extending her hand. "She got Heatherwood ready for you. Nadia, meet Callie MacCallum. Their surnames are different, but she's Jack's wife."

There, the frivolity ended for Sarah and Nadia. Their mouths dropped. Arnett shouted over Beebe's and Lizbeth's attempts to calm her. Callie was just as stunned as her companions.

"That's not true! I was his wife. Me!" Arnett's anger gathered like a heated summer storm, then she wrenched herself free of Lizbeth's grasp and ran for the door. Beebe was two steps behind.

Ground Rules

Lizbeth whirled on Callie, hands on hips. Behind her, Beebe disappeared through Sarah Prosser's office door. Arnett could be heard thundering down the wooden steps. "I'm going to pull the honesty cord here. You'd better tell Sarah and Nadia the story, so they don't step in it again!"

Callie's heart thudded. She was caught off balance between a glaring Lizbeth and stupefied Sarah and Nadia. "I never referred to myself as Jack's wife."

"Maybe, for the ladies here, you should start a little farther back and be more specific," Lizbeth said.

But it was Sarah who spoke next. Her hand lay against the base of her throat, fingers crushing her shirt's stiff collar. "I am so sorry. Oh, my word. This isn't Callie's fault. Well, I don't know, but— Jack. Jack's the one who referred to Callie as his wife. Several times. And you know, now that I think about it, you were never with him. You two weren't married? Why, I didn't know. Callie?" Her eyes pleaded for an explanation.

"It was an affair, Sarah. We had an affair."

Sarah's next question escaped on a heavy exhale. "How long?"

"Twenty-two years when he died."

"My heavens." After a beat, Sarah asked, "You're here with his wife?" Her tone said Callie was exhibiting a twitchy kind of insanity.

Callie indicated Lizbeth. "And with his daughter-in-law." She thought she used just the right amount of cheer an insane person might. Sarah swallowed an involuntary gasp, and Nadia's expressive eyes grew owl-like. "It's a long story," Callie added.

Sarah's mouth popped open. "I remember now. He called you his wife the day I remarked on his ring. I paid attention later when you came in. You two wore matching rings."

"Fifth anniversary gift," Callie said, displaying her left hand and the diamonds in both rings.

"I'm shocked," Sarah said.

Callie immediately panicked. She pulled her hand back, closing it, but Sarah was not expressing the scandal or outrage side of shock. She went on, surprised at being fooled.

"I can't believe you weren't married. You were so sweet together, so right." Catching herself, she cast a chagrined look at Lizbeth, who stepped closer.

"Is there more about the cabin story we should know?" Lizbeth asked, her attitude abrasive.

Callie bristled, but managed to work an even tone into her reply. "I suppose I could expound some. Jack bought into the association when the cabins went from rentals to condos." Callie glanced Sarah's way. "We stayed here quite a bit, more while he designed the two courses for Brier Hills. Jack transferred the deed to me shortly after he was diagnosed."

Overall, Cheat River Estates were ten cabins. Some of the cabins were built on property that dipped down to the river. Others were perched at higher elevations on Baron Mountain.

Condo manager Sarah Prosser spoke up. "When Jack bought in, he wanted the name changed."

"The name? Heatherwood, you mean?"

"Yes," Sarah said to Lizbeth. "Jack wanted theirs changed from Big Pine to Heatherwood. You'll see. There's a sign at the drive."

"That was Dad's idea?"

"Yes, and Sarah saw to a first-class reproduction of the original," Callie said, ready to terminate the conversation before Lizbeth probed into the significance behind the name. Honesty pledge notwithstanding, Callie wasn't ready to share that very personal story. "The new sign is a match for all the others. Jack loved it, you know." Callie kissed Sarah's cheek. "We'll get together on that paperwork. Nice to meet you, Nadia. Sorry about all this."

Lizbeth followed up with a round of meekly issued pleasantries.

Callie stepped out into the pine-scented mountain air. She saw Arnett, presumably locked inside Lizbeth's Tahoe. "Guess I lost my co-pilot," she said, her descent slowing on the front steps.

"Big surprise," Lizbeth said, passing her.

Beebe stood, arms folded, leaning back against the Santa Fe's cargo door. She said nothing. Callie picked up the pace. Lizbeth's Tahoe was pumping exhaust by the time Callie and Beebe piled in her SUV, simultaneously closing the doors. As Callie wheeled her vehicle from the berm to the asphalt, Beebe broke the silence.

"This has been a rough first day. Arnett was all but ready to quit back there and stay in a motel."

Tension and fatigue took over. Callie barely absorbed Beebe's words. Events were moving too quickly with no time to sort them out. When Beebe called on her to speak for Jack, Callie committed to that. She fully expected to shoulder the blame for Jack's reference to her as his wife, but she could not stand in for him as the Sebring family's mediator. She could not control the balance scale when it tipped sharply with Arnett's wild emotional rants. Her arms weren't strong enough. She prayed Beebe didn't ask her.

"After you left," Callie said, "Sarah remembered Jack only referred to me as his wife when I wasn't around. I didn't know."

"Honestly?"

Ah, Callie thought, the honesty pledge twists again. "Well, not an outright reference. There was the occasional misconception in public. In twenty years, how could there not? Once, a maître de in a Boston restaurant asked a waiter to show 'Mr. Sebring and his wife to a table.' Jack made a reservation. It was an assumption on the maître de's part."

With the mistaken identity, Callie and Jack passed smiles back and forth. Those smiles were two parts satisfaction, three parts mischievous. She and Jack had the look of a married couple, at ease, in love—as Sarah said—so right. That evening, Jack's fingertips found the small of her back as he guided her through the dining room. If he feared that the maître de's words would put ideas in her head, it wasn't evident, not by the seductive way he moved a finger over the thin fabric of her dress causing her spine to tingle.

Beebe snapped Callie's trance. "Didn't misunderstandings like that make it easier for Jack? If he wanted you for his wife, why didn't he divorce Arnett? Why didn't you insist?"

Callie spent untold hours in self-analysis, delving into the answer to that question. The truth was, she always had mixed emotions about what divorce would do to their relationship, how it would change things. But change things, it would. That scared her. What if, after the hotly contested divorce, Jack and Callie were only good at the type of relationship they nurtured for so long?

. . .

Up ahead at a break in the trees, Beebe saw a low sign staked to the ground. It read: HEATHERWOOD. The professionally carved letters were embedded in a rectangular wood plank and inlaid with goldenrod paint. A vine with the season's last red raspberry gripped the sign's top edge. Callie eased the SUV onto a gravel drive that widened to a parking pad.

Once past the initial border of trees, the property opened up. What

Beebe saw wiped away the cozy-cabin image she allowed to form in her mind. A magazine spread reporting on tempting vacation spots would print a phrase like "ultrachic backwoods rich" under a picture of Heatherwood. It had been constructed with the same rough-hewn materials as the office. A wraparound porch encased a structure that was ten times larger than expected.

"You're thinking upscale, aren't you?" Callie said.

"Higher-end upscale. Almost rambling. Not quite the Ponderosa." Beebe looked at Callie. "Okay, that's a bit of an exaggeration."

"Back when Sarah rented the cabins, groups of hunters would come—groups who were ready for all the comforts at the end of the day. When Jack came looking, he was in a rush to find something close to the golf site. This place was. It really worked out. He stayed for months. He had room for an office, and he could spread out and review large topography plans. In fact, Jack named one of the bedrooms the map room." Callie shifted the SUV into park. "After that, it was home."

Callie's and Jack's home away from home fronted onto a grassy clearing. The lawn rolled out and down to a small dock overlooking the rippling Cheat River. On either side of the yard and across the water, evergreen and deciduous trees created one of nature's thick privacy fences. Once inside its perimeter, Heatherwood was the perfect place to hide a love affair.

Beebe climbed out of the Santa Fe and met Callie at the front bumper. The Tahoe's engine shut down. A door slammed, then Arnett's voice pierced Heatherwood's stillness.

"John took money away from his family to purchase this place." She stood in front of Callie.

"He earned the money. He did with it what he pleased. I'm not going to feel guilty, Arnett. You'd lost him long before he met me. If that's not what's eating you, it should be."

"This cabin should have been included in his estate."

Lizbeth joined them. "You mean, you should have inherited the property. Like you would have ever stayed here."

Mother-in-law glared at daughter-in-law. "I could have sold it," Arnett returned. "Or burned it down."

Beebe knew the next few seconds were given to each woman visualizing identical fiery scenes. "Ladies, let's stop sniping at each other and get moved in." Beebe stared at each woman until they felt her gaze and returned it. "Then I have something to say—to all of you." She hoped her statement carried the deeply ominous sound of an immense Chinese gong.

Having retrieved their suitcases and groceries, Beebe, Lizbeth, and Arnett followed Callie up wooden porch steps. A vase of welcoming zinnias waited on an outside table. A gift from Sarah and Nadia, Beebe thought. Inside, the great room was airy and fresh. Windows sashes were raised, a service gracious condo-living provided.

Beebe took in the great room. It housed living room, fireplace, dining area, and kitchen. A subdued Callie reported the cabin had no landline and no cable or dish. The TV on the stand was merely a receiver for the DVD player. The radio on the kitchen counter worked most of the time.

With that lead-in, Lizbeth whipped out her cell phone. "I don't have a signal. What if something happens to Chad and I need to be reached?"

"I'll give you Sarah's office number in a minute," Callie responded. "If Debbie calls, either Sarah or Nadia will deliver a message."

It seemed the only option available, yet Beebe understood Lizbeth was less than satisfied with her lack of outside-world communication. Callie continued the tour, assigning bedrooms as she went. There were four. No sharing, except for bathrooms. The Sebrings were teamed together in the bedrooms and bath closest to the kitchen. Beebe suspected at one time, those were the office and map room.

Beebe and Callie took their things into the rooms near another porch entrance. Beebe could see a hot tub through a screened window. She didn't want to be around when Arnett learned of that amenity and its implied intimacy for Jack and Callie.

Beebe found her room comfortable in size and adequately furnished. The full-sized bed was spread with a floral coverlet over an eyelet skirt. She pushed a hand against the firm mattress. She stood at the foot of the bed, unpacking, when Callie appeared. She came through an internal door in the back corner. Beebe correctly assumed their rooms adjoined via the bathroom. Callie asked permission to shower before the group gathered for opening remarks. Beebe granted her request, praying she'd emerge with a fresh attitude.

Thirty minutes later, Beebe called everyone to the two honey-and-toast-tweed couches that faced off over an oaken coffee table. A square area rug in spruce green defined the cabin's living room. Arnett sat on Beebe's left, Lizbeth and Callie on the opposing couch.

Beebe got directly to business. "What's not going to work is for any new rules to be spouted out on a whim."

Lizbeth's raised hands and lowered eyes acknowledged her guilt when she, rather spontaneously at the depot, required Arnett to ride with Callie.

"If any of you feel the rules should be expanded or relaxed, please come to me first," Beebe said. "But in my opinion, this week feels too short to spend much time legislating rules anyway. The Golden Rule really ought to suffice as we interact daily. We're here to be honest with each other, to reach new levels of understanding because there are important decisions to be made." Beebe looked at the faces around her. "Life is complicated, and while family can make it more complicated, family can also be a huge comfort. We've all experienced how loss of family feels.

"Each of you has issues, inroads into this peace summit. Come to me. We'll consult privately before topics are presented to the others. Once presented, everyone will be given an opportunity to respond."

She lifted a palm. "And I don't propose immediate responses. We should give our responses due consideration. Let's caucus twice daily. That may seem a little too sterile, too organized. I guess I'm thinking about my grief groups at home. But since we've got each other's attention every day, all day, we should take advantage of that. Is this all good so far?"

Her audience nodded. Beebe allowed her gaze to linger on Lizbeth. "The tact I took in the parking lot—"

"The song-and-dance routine?"

"Yes, I'm the amateur I proved to be." Beebe smiled, countering Lizbeth's heavy delivery. "But that was a version of compromise we all need to embrace if this week is to yield any success. We'll achieve nothing without compromise."

Lizbeth stiffened. "You can't decide compromise. I don't want compromise. I set the terms. Arnett must comply."

Arnett exhibited great restraint, only muttering under her breath.

"Ultimately, at week's end, yes, you decide," Beebe said. "Chad is your son. Until we get there, my counsel won't shy away from compromise." Beebe laced her fingers. "Now that you heard what I have to say, it's best that we sleep on it. We'll be better prepared for tomorrow." Beebe closed one eye in quick thought. "To summarize, matters directly related should not be discussed in groups of two unless I'm one of the participants. This week has got to be managed for a viable, successful outcome. That's my job. Manager, or facilitator, or moderator, foreman, Indian chief, gypsy fortuneteller—" Beebe stopped as if breathless and smiled. "The title makes very little difference. There's no point in bringing up volatile issues outside group and without my knowledge."

"I don't believe it." Lizbeth straightened her shoulders. "You're actually taking Arnett's side at the outset."

"No, Lizbeth, I'm not," Beebe said calmly. "I'm taking a stand for the process. We can't attack each other. We need to speak rationally—"

"For lack of a better word," Lizbeth inserted blithely while studying her cuticles, then popped an eye over to Arnett.

Beebe patted Arnett's leg sympathetically. "I can't stress enough," Beebe went on, "that we take time to formulate a response. Ten minutes, thirty, then come back."

"When you say, it will be presented in group, that means you, you're the presenter?"

"Yes, I think the initial subject matter should be funneled through me. I'll introduce it, perhaps limiting the context. I don't know. But we'll all have our chance to comment. The discussion cannot escalate to unmanageable, nor to anger. At all cost, we want to steer away from non-productive. We must show respect for each other's feelings. This is not going to be an easy process. The week will be wearing at best. All of us will feel picked on, our insides gutted, our bodies deboned." The faces around Beebe grimaced. "Sorry. I can't help the fishing references. When I get close to lakes or streams, my terminology shifts."

Lizbeth was not amused, and like a length of Spiderwire snagged on a runaway carp, Beebe could not unhook Lizbeth from her line of sight. Out on the turnpike, while Arnett was learning civility and maturity in Callie's company, Beebe heard about Lizbeth's added requirement that Arnett display the quilt. A protracted discussion resulted and prompted Beebe's preview of caucus procedure. Beebe's position choked Lizbeth the first time around in the Tahoe, as a fat horse pill would. Beebe knew it gagged her still.

"No one will be forced to respond." Beebe got back on track. "But I hope we don't renege on group interaction. This week must involve give and take if we're going to derive the necessary benefit."

Arnett cleared her throat. "I'd like to respond."

Beebe shifted in her seat. "Respond to what I've said?"

"Yes. In my opinion—and I feel I must speak for myself; I don't particularly want to be represented by you," Arnett said, her hands primly folded in her lap.

Wisely, Beebe let that hot potato fly by in readiness for the salvo lobbed behind it.

"I feel the way I was treated by Lizbeth at the depot was tantamount to bullying. She's adopted an imperious attitude of late, not to mention her snide remarks."

"I think a good night's sleep will allow all of us to come back with fresh attitudes. Lizbeth and I spoke about this in the car. Tomorrow, she will begin anew. Right, Lizbeth?" Lizbeth crossed her heart. "I promise."

"All well and good," Arnett said, still haughty, her dark eyes on Beebe, "but can you be critical of Callie when need be? Are you capable of conquering your favoritism there?"

"You have my word, Arnett. I will offer my counsel equally and without favoritism."

"Then what about this? What about what Callie said in the car?" She raised her eyebrows at Callie, as if telegraphing her thoughts, willing Callie to speak. Lizbeth's and Beebe's heads turned. Callie wore a puzzled expression. "Well, I guess if Callie's not going to mention it, then in all honesty, I will. She wanted to go behind your back, and Lizbeth's, to set up a pact between us. I, of course, told her no. I just thought you should know she wanted to circumvent the process at the first opportunity we were alone. Typical, really."

"In the car?" Beebe repeated. "At that point, I hadn't established any rules."

"So, you will show favoritism?"

"I don't know what you want me to do. There were no rules then. The rules are set now. Callie, you understand no two-person conversations from here on, no pacts, nothing?"

"Yes, Beebe, I understand." To Arnett: "Why would I bring up, now, a nonexistent agreement? And if we'd reached agreement, which was solely in your benefit, I might add—"

"It was not," Arnett snapped, but Callie talked over her.

"I would certainly have set it aside. You're crying foul when none was committed. And, you'd better not reopen Jack's estate and take Heatherwood through the courts."

"Just watch me."

"I'll fight it. Just watch me."

"Ladies, please."

"No, Beebe. Because of her, I got dragged into this. I agreed with Lizbeth and you to sit with a bitter—"

Gesturing toward Arnett, Callie struggled with words. Beebe thought she would finish the sentence with "old woman," which would have set off more sparks, but she didn't point out their age difference. She placed them on a common battleground.

"—with a bitter enemy for the benefit of a child. An innocent four-year old. Jack's grandson." Her voice caught and weakened. "And now I get this from his grandmother. I guess I should have expected it." Callie shot up. She hurried toward her purse and keys on the table near the front door.

"Callie, wait."

She ignored Beebe and reached for the door handle. Before Beebe could skirt the coffee table, Arnett jumped up. Lizbeth followed on her heels. They bunched through the screen door. Callie pounded toward the porch steps. "I'll be back." Her words effectively stalled those in pursuit.

Arnett, who stood out front, called after her. "You know, I get the act: You're supposed to be John in all this. This is just what he'd do. You're playing him perfectly. If I did the least little thing that cantered his precious world, he found an excuse and took off for hours. John was never home."

Callie spun and came back, eyeball to eyeball with Arnett. "Maybe you'd better think about that. Why do you run everyone away? You know, that's why we're here, to keep you," she poked Arnett's arm, "from losing Chad." Callie's gaze popped over Arnett's shoulder to

Lizbeth and Beebe. "Gotta go," she said. Her faux chirpiness died off into a solemn summary for Arnett. "It seems most people can only take you in small doses."

Lizbeth looked from Callie's retreat to Beebe. "This isn't fair. She gets to leave. She knows her way around. I want to find a phone," she whined. "And she didn't leave the office number."

Weariness more than maturity, Beebe thought, kept her from stamping a foot.

A half-second later, the tires on Callie's Santa Fe were spitting the driveway's crushed stones.

Beebe expelled a long breath. She considered the heated encounter better than a brooding, vengeful silence. After their first trying day together, Beebe would log into her journal that the line of communication was so well-oiled, she would discourage any one of them from attempting a high-wire act. The slightest loss of footing would result in a whistling descent.

Alternately, she wondered about the impact of her orientation. The minute Callie pushed off the couch, Arnett and Lizbeth fell neatly back into character. Arnett revived her criticisms of Jack, and Lizbeth reiterated her desire to phone home. She promised her son they'd talk before bedtime. A mother's promise was one to be kept. Arnett, too, would benefit from chatting with the child, so Beebe herded them back inside for purses and sweaters.

Acceptance

Strains of Modest Mussorgsky's *Night on Bald Mountain* wafted through a speaker system Lucius Dameron built into the Bullwhip Road cabin he and Willie Thorne owned. The piece, magnificently performed by Boston Pops Orchestra, was such a favorite, he had the CD player set on repeat. The volume was turned low now. Twenty minutes earlier, he received a call from his beloved. The news Willie shared seemed fated to Lucius. Not to Willie. He was a man not blessed with a morsel of spontaneity.

Willie received an offer from an older couple to buy their house in Cassel, Maryland. The couple simply knocked on the door and asked if Willie was willing to sell. The gentleman caller was wheelchair-bound. Their Maryland home was one story with easy passage from driveway to walkway to a wide front entrance. The layout inside was more of the same. Willie reported the man had no difficulty negotiating the patio doors out to the deck—straight out, straight back in. Lucius recessed the sliding-door track.

Two years ago when Willie and Lucius sat down and planned this phase of their life, August had been the month they planned to list the house. The Bullwhip cabin would be ninety percent done. Lucius looked around. It was currently pushing a strong eighty. By the time the sale was completed, the cabin with its expanded living area would be completed as well.

"Looks like I designed a house for our old-age and didn't know it. Maybe I should reconsider what I'm doing here." From his viewpoint, Lucius counted three levels. Three more existed beyond that. Five feet from the front door, the cabin's floor stepped down to the living and dining rooms. He was currently using that step as a seat.

Willie panicked. "Don't you dare rip out and start over."

Lucius smiled at Willie's reaction. "We shouldn't disregard the offer out of hand, should we?"

"Where would I live? We'd be getting into a long lease or mortgage."

That was the baritone voice of financial reason Lucius came to expect from Willie. "But it's a great price," Lucius appealed, "given the economy."

"If you and the buyers are serious, then I'll ask them for two weeks. You and I can talk about it next weekend."

"You'll be here next weekend for sure?" A note of anticipation clung to Lucius's question. Willie canceled this weekend's visit to tend to a needy client.

"I'm working on getting there Friday, instead of Saturday."

That news pleased Lucius. "Either way, you'll get to see Callie while she's here. Maybe we should invite the ladies over for dinner."

"No offense, but the place really isn't presentable."

"True. That's why I've planned an elegant affair with china and candlelight in our little wilderness camp. We'll move the table and chairs out. A dinner party on the lawn."

"The nights are beautiful this time of year."

Lucius snapped his fingers. "That's my reason for going to Heatherwood tomorrow, to issue the invitation!"

He filled Willie in on his encounter with the four ladies before giving him the opportunity to discuss real estate ventures. Willie was verbally comparison-shopping the benefits of subletting over renting when Lucius heard a noise outside. He padded the few steps to the open screen door and looked out. "Willie," he said, interrupting. "I've got company. It's Callie. I'll call you back."

"Make sure you do."

Lucius left the phone on the nearby desk and rushed out to the Santa Fe in socked feet. By the time it rolled to a stop, he had the door open and was pulling Callie out. From ten feet away, he saw she was crying. Her face was blotchy and red.

"Baby, baby, what's wrong? What happened?"

"Oh, Lucius, I miss him so much." She sobbed the words while fat tears streamed her cheeks.

"I know." Her head lay on his shoulder. He kissed her hair. "I know."

Lucius helped her inside. She kicked off her shoes, then plucked several tissues from the box he offered. The scene was reminiscent of their earlier meeting at the depot. Once Callie's face was dry, her fight was back.

"This was supposed to be my week at Heatherwood." She flung a wad of tissue into the can by the desk. It landed with a soft metallic echo. "I thought I was ready to come here for the first time without Jack. Instead, I agree to sacrifice, and all Arnett can talk about is Beebe showing me favoritism."

"The bitch!" Lucius's ready agreement elicited a smile from Callie. "Come on. Tell Lucius all about it." He led her to the couch, then backed up to sit on the edge of Willie's leather recliner. He was absolutely delirious at the prospect of hearing details.

Fingers laced together in his lap, he stared straight at Callie, his mind absorbing, his thoughts spinning. Callie started with Sarah Prosser, who unwittingly played a part with an offhanded remark. He tried to maintain control of a twitching eyebrow that wanted to arch. Hmm, he thought, Jack referred to Callie as his wife several times. Interesting. He and Sarah would definitely talk. To Sarah, Callie mentioned that the rings were a fifth anniversary gift. To Lucius, she confided how utterly dumbfounded she'd been by Jack's sentimentality and generosity.

Rubbing at tension in the base of her neck, Callie described personal attacks: First, Lizbeth grilled her in front of Sarah, then came Arnett's unwarranted complaint. Lucius could just imagine Arnett storming out of the cabin after Callie. It was his job, he reasoned, to help Callie with perspective.

"You and Jack were an exclusive, sweet cheeks. You had a once-in-a-lifetime love. Your relationship was wild and daring. I'm jealous." She looked up. "Others would be too. Take the lead. Tell your story. These women," he said, pointing an index finger heavenward, "they should hear it."

Callie's shoulders sagged. "I'm so tired of crying. I wouldn't be able to talk about Jack and me, not in that way, not without crying. I thought I'd made progress with the grief after a year and a half. With all this, it's starting over again."

"If there are a few tears, so be it. Tell them anyway."

They sat in companionable silence. With every second, the questions Lucius generated about the women grew exponentially. Selflessly though, he interjected a new subject.

"I talked with Willie earlier." He went to her with his hands out and pulled her up off the couch. "He's had an offer on the house."

"You listed it?"

"No, but we're considering it."

"Willie would move here?"

"Not right away, but soon. He's not in a position yet with the firm to leave Cassel."

"Where would he live?"

"That's the first bridge to cross." He walked her past the big-screen TV. It was bracketed to the mantel over the fireplace rather than with anchors drilled into the stone wall. He stopped her in what would eventually become a lovely dining room. Currently, the middle of the cabin was a staging area and workshop around a rectangular table and four chairs. Lucius gave the area a sheepish look. "Ever since Willie called the cabin a satellite location for Home Depot, I've tried not to overstock."

Willie's and Lucius's future would not have changed—for the better, in Lucius's opinion—if not for Jack Sebring and Callie MacCallum. A wealthy West Virginia developer in the Brier Hills region hired Jack Sebring and his talents to design two golf courses. Jack found the nearby Cheat River cabin and employed it as a temporary office and weekend hideaway for himself and Callie. On Callie's many visits, she observed the restoration possibilities for Baron's downtown buildings and encouraged Lucius to make the trip and walk Armament Street. The character of downtown Baron breathed new life into Lucius.

He proudly ushered Callie into his renovated kitchen. The work there was one job from finished. The mosaic tiles for the floor remained boxed in a pantry-sized office off the kitchen that Lucius kept for his business. Callie checked out the office while Lucius turned a couple of oven dials, then went to the refrigerator. They left the Italian bread to warm, cheese spread to soften, wine to breathe, and went up the open staircase that hugged the dining room's back wall.

Built-in shelving for Lucius's extensive music library climbed the wall along with the stairs. The shelves were stocked with albums, 45 RPMs, cassettes, and CDs, along with countless movie DVDs. Carefully hidden wires from the stereo system fed speakers throughout the cabin. They still hummed *Bald Mountain.*

Lucius and Callie crossed the loft bedroom. Lucius flipped on the light to a room sectioned off for Willie's office. It was only roughed in. When Willie finally retired, the office would be transformed to a fabulous walk-in closet with storage.

A calmer Callie descended the stairs ahead of Lucius. Between the kitchen and couch with their hands full, she began to bring him up to speed on a pair of quilts. Lucius and Callie spread out their repast on the coffee table. Both the bread and cheese were sprinkled with garlic. The basket and tub sat between two half-filled wineglasses. They shared one cloth napkin until Lucius remembered his handkerchief was clean and dug it out of a hip pocket. He was too enthralled with her story to even think of running back to the kitchen for a second napkin.

Lucius listened attentively while Callie filled him in on all the details. He perceived the tangle unalterably knotted. He offered his assistance for a related cause. Callie seemed anxious about the caucuses. She experienced one rocky caucus and expected more.

"You know," he said, "we could practice caucusing. Want to?" Callie wore a pained look, but didn't answer, so Lucius decided to play both sides of the conversation. "Yes, Lucius, let's try." He fluttered his lashes. "Really, you'd like that, Callie. Great." When his playfulness caused her to smile, his demeanor changed to genuine. He leaned close and lowered his voice to a near whisper. "You know I would do anything for you."

She tipped her head to his. "I know."

Lucius handed Callie her wineglass, then reached back for his own. "To Jack," he toasted. They clinked goblets and sipped. "You know, kiddo, it seems like you don't expect people to do nice things for you. You do wonderful things for other people. You're giving. The quilts, for example. But you don't expect it in return. Why is that?"

"No, that's not true."

"Yes, it is. I can tell. You said it yourself. You were genuinely dumbfounded that Jack put such thought into an expression of his love." He meant the rings. "There had to be other examples."

"Jack was very generous."

"Jack was thoughtful, and generous about you." He tapped her knee with the goblet's base. "That's the combo that gets you. It's not a birthday-present-given-two-days-early kind of surprise. You still feel this, just like it happened yesterday. The spirit of Jack's gift lives inside you still." He saw she was struggling with composure, so he moved on. "The offer stands. If you get a caucus question, just come to ol' Lucius here, and we'll run your lines."

Soon after, he put her in the Santa Fe, then ignored her argument and followed the wandering lamb back to the fold anyway. He just felt better about it. Darkness had descended. The cutback roads could be tricky.

On the way, Lucius turned off the radio, something he rarely did. He was alone with his thoughts or on the trail of Callie's; he didn't know which. He thought how the two of them shared a facet of life that went beyond being born on the same day. They structured their day-to-day lives so that large portions were hidden from the world: his sexuality and her lifelong love affair. Was it second nature, or first, that they would not act before a bead of caution was worked in?

The missing elements of their lives—a man openly taking her arm, a young woman clinging to his—only made people scrutinize them more.

Of all the important concepts bandied about that day, it wasn't honesty or peace that drove him down this thoughtful road. It was acceptance.

He walked Callie to the door. Someone left the light on. Beebe, he thought. He kissed Callie's temple. She squeezed his hand. Once she was inside, he turned the truck around and drove home.

Secrets and Lies

Sunday morning, Arnett Oldstone Sebring stood inside the cabin's screen door, looking down to the Cheat River. She would forever be amazed that her unfaithful husband found such an appropriately named landmark to act as a boundary line for his West Virginia love nest.

It was nearly nine and the sun had yet to climb the stands of tall, thin pines growing on both sides of the river. Bands of diffused light angled through and shone on the water and small dock. Consequently, Arnett had a well-lit view of Beebe and Callie. Their dockside conversation was silent to Arnett, only a bit of laughter made its way to the door on an errant breeze. Beebe led the discussion. Arnett assumed Beebe filled Callie in on what she missed after she went off somewhere last evening to pout.

Arnett jumped when Lizbeth opened her bedroom door. She whipped a dish towel off her shoulder and hurried to the table so her daughter-in-law wouldn't catch her spying. She made a show of wiping toast crumbs off the table. She swallowed the pleasantries she'd have spoken to Lizbeth as she strolled into the great room, carrying the quilt and several framed pictures.

Offering Arnett a cheery good morning, Lizbeth buzzed over to the table by the door. "I'm just going to set these up here," she said. "Make the cabin seem a bit homier."

Lizbeth spread the lap-sized quilt across the table like a cloth, then leaned the frames back on their stands. The first was Chad's most recent picture, taken when his curls had grown long. Lizbeth set down a five-year old photo of Dan. Arnett looked from Dan's photograph to Chad's. Their Oldstone eyes dipped at the corner and would have communicated an ever-present sadness, but for the broad grins that rounded out their faces.

Arnett was about to comment favorably on the decorating idea when Lizbeth propped up a third frame containing John's likeness. Arnett's words stuck in her throat. She knew that photo. John posed for it the Christmas Eve he decided to accept one of Lizbeth's many invitations to attend candlelight services. That morning, Arnett came down with a mild case of the flu. In her heart, she knew he accepted to get away from her. But his story was that Geoff, thirteen at the time, had a special Christmas Eve gift for him. John returned after services with the necktie he wore out of the house folded into the pocket of his navy suit. Knotted at his throat was a novelty tie: Santa, with his traditional hat and full beard, wore Bermuda shorts and stood ready to putt a golf ball.

Lizbeth's decorating idea suddenly took on the qualities of a shrine. Which, in Arnett's opinion, spoke to her shaky state of mind. "Is that absolutely necessary?" Arnett said.

"I think we need a constant reminder of the reasons why we're here. And besides, I miss these guys. I like seeing them all together."

A tear ran down Lizbeth's face as she strode purposefully back to her room. A few seconds later, Beebe zipped in the screen door and passed the shrine without taking notice. She greeted Arnett, crossed the cabin, and stuck her head in Lizbeth's door. Lizbeth waved her in.

"Now what are they hatching?" Arnett mumbled to the closed door.

She scuffed over to the kitchen counter. Her mug of cold coffee sat there. She rinsed the brown liquid down the drain, feeling sorry for herself. And why not? None of them cared about her grief. She lost a son, a grandson hung in the balance. Her life had been tossed around because of John, and now Lizbeth wanted to destroy what was left by keeping Chad out of reach. In the world Arnett enjoyed before she turned John out, he protected her. He at least cushioned the impact. Arnett couldn't trust these women. She had to protect herself.

Lizbeth's door swung open. Grabbing her trusty dish towel, Arnett turned. Beebe exited the room, wearing an expression of intense concentration. She sat down in one of the four ladder-back chairs that ringed the dining room table. Her leather portfolio already occupied the tabletop. She opened the binder and exposed yellow, lined paper.

Since Beebe talked with Callie, then Lizbeth, Arnett surmised she was the subject of the next caucus. She found that worrisome. Watching Beebe make notes, she folded and refolded the towel, then she smiled. She had a plan that would reveal Callie's pitted image and defer discussion of whatever started out on the dock.

Arnett walked straight to Beebe. "I think we need a more orderly approach," she said boldly. "If I'm supposed to accept this quilt and display it in my home to keep Lizbeth from absconding with my grandson, then I think I need Callie to answer some questions first."

Beebe laid her pen down. "Go ahead."

Arnett felt a bit of weight lift off her chest. "We should deal with the primary issues first. We all broached this last night. We were all wondering about the same things. I just think this makes sense. I think Callie needs to answer for her actions."

Behind Beebe, Lizbeth stepped through her bedroom doorway, wearing a quizzical look. "What's going on?"

Beebe's gray-brown eyes did not leave Arnett's face when she answered Lizbeth's question. "I'm going to grant Arnett a little change in plans. Lizbeth, see what's keeping Callie, would you, please?"

Arnett could almost see the gears working in Lizbeth's mind as she silently slipped around the table to do Beebe's bidding. "She's coming," Lizbeth announced, then picked up her pace. She pushed the screen door open. Callie entered, carrying two brown grocery bags bulging with clothes.

"What's all this?" Lizbeth asked.

"My next quilt."

"Really. Here?" Lizbeth said, surprised.

"I don't sleep well. This gives me something to do. And it's quiet. I won't wake anyone. I'm still planning the design and cutting squares."

Callie turned. Her intention to slide the bags under the entryway table was delayed when she noticed the quilt and photographs.

Lizbeth said, "I arranged those."

"Nice," Callie said.

Then Beebe clapped her hands. "Okay, ladies, find seats. We need to get started."

Beebe, Lizbeth, and Arnett converged on the couches; Callie headed toward the kitchen.

Beebe, seated next to Arnett, held up her leather portfolio. "You all know I'm keeping a complete accounting of our caucuses and the topics raised."

Callie joined the group with a Diet Coke can in hand. She sat on the periphery, lowered to a large, round, bone-colored ottoman.

Beebe continued. "Arnett's made a good argument not to get the cart before the horse. She's proposed that we need to get a baseline on Callie from her perspective, and I've agreed."

With pure pleasure, Arnett watched Callie's face collapse. She separated herself at the outset, dragged in late to the circle, but Arnett worked it so Callie's evil deeds would be spotlighted.

"If I might paraphrase—and I think she's right—maybe we should take things in a more orderly fashion," Beebe said. "I'm going to let Arnett introduce—well, set the scene might be more apt."

Arnett eagerly took the reins. "If I'm going to be asked to concede on my feelings, then in all fairness, you should understand my point of view."

"You're just trying to get me to relax my agenda," Lizbeth said crossly.

"I wish you'd keep an open mind. Maybe after you hear a complete accounting—to repeat Beebe's words—then yes, maybe you will relent."

Glowering, Lizbeth sat back hard against the couch.

Arnett deliberately angled herself on the cushion to face Beebe and Lizbeth. The move placed Callie in her peripheral vision, outside the discussion circle. It pressed the point that she would be talked about as if she wasn't there. Spine straight, Arnett began, addressing Beebe, providing background.

"There were two specific situations that demonstrated what I was up against. Keep in mind our family had been through hell. In April, I exposed John's affair. In late June, he was diagnosed with cancer. In early July, part of his lung was removed. For three days, my sons, their wives, and I were all at the hospital in shifts, keeping watch. John lay in intensive care. I put up a good front. I did a wife's duty, pushing aside his adultery. I took the lead in John's care. Despite everything, I was expected to sit at his bedside, and I was there. Those first few days, he had extreme pain. His ribs were spread apart to get to the lung. An incision started under his arm. He was cut all the way around to his back. On the third evening, he showed improvement, but I was exhausted. He told me to go home and get some sleep. The boys had already left. But he wasn't concerned about me. He was thinking about her." She turned to face Callie. Lizbeth and Beebe followed suit. Arnett looked down her nose at cowardly Callie who kept her head tipped to the soda can she held, her thumb playing with the can's condensation.

Arnett returned her attention to Beebe. "Before I even reached the elevator, he'd called the nurse's station. By the time I pushed the button, the nurse was carrying a phone into his room. The hospital prohibited permanent phones in ICU patient rooms," she explained. "Literally, only seconds passed since I left his bedside, and he wanted her. He had her on the phone before I even left the floor. I was angry. It felt like I'd been kicked in the stomach. Reality was right in front of me. I stewed about it, then later I called her." Arnett sent Callie a challenging look. Her next words brought Callie's chin up. She wore a defiant expression. "I told you, right? I knew he called. I told you I knew the two of you would never stop seeing each other. Never. It would never stop. I couldn't make him stop." Arnett hurled words until her chest hurt. She raised a hand to her heart. "God, every time I think of the two of you together, I can't breathe."

The room grew quiet. A window curtain fluttered.

"Arnett?" Beebe said coaxingly.

Arnett pushed hair around on her head. "Yes, there's more. Two days later, John was moved out of intensive care. I went to the hospital without fail. The boys expected it. They came, family came, but I was his mainstay. I noticed one morning, the visitor's chair was moved. I pushed it against the wall when I left the night before. But first thing the next morning, it was closer to the bed. Another bit of evidence: She'd been there. I knew it. I vacated the chair and—" Her cheeks flushed with heat, she twisted her head and shoulders to Callie. "How long did it take before you were sitting in it?" Facing the other two: "She even got around security. The hospital's doors locked at nine. That's when I left. Locked doors, security guards, nothing kept them apart." She glared at Callie who only stared back impassively. "Did you scale the walls and come in the window? I called you again, didn't I, at the club? You weren't very talkative. I still don't know how you got in. Passage into the main hospital was closed off, interior doors locked. I needed help getting out. But you and John, you got things worked out. That chair was never out of place any morning after that."

Arnett swung her knees around for a dead-on question to Callie. "What about me? I want to know, at any point, did you ever think about me when you and John were sneaking around, keeping secrets, and telling lies?"

. . .

Secrets and lies, Lizbeth wanted to scream back at her mother-in-law. She knew those had been the very ingredients hardened into the mortar around Arnett's own marriage. John had been the trowel. He worked them into the cracks for self-preservation, for some measure of happiness, but in his defense, he used them to combat her volatile mood swings and her freakish need for control. She brought an impressive amount of her present-day anguish directly on herself.

Lizbeth formulated a strategic plan for the week, but was dangerously close to tossing it to the curb in favor of immediate gratification. When she might have blurted out her oldest secret, the sound of booted footsteps on the porch prevented it.

"Yoohoo! Welcome wagon."

"Lucius!" Callie said, jumping up to let him in. He carried an oblong container by its handles. It was padded and sized for a large baking dish. Once he kissed Callie's cheek, he turned to study the three women still planted on the couches.

"You are all visions, just visions." He held up the container. "Willie, my beloved, reminded me of my manners. I brought coffeecake. It's still warm. I thought about muffins, but this seemed more civilized for a Sunday."

Meeting adjourned, Lizbeth thought. She would have said he pranced to the kitchen table where he deposited the carrier.

"Let me see if I've got these names right." He stood at the foot of the coffee table. Arnett's expression of supreme irritation at the interruption, or perhaps his persuasion, didn't faze him.

"Arnett and Lizbeth Sebring. You're sisters, right?" he said, pointing. His eyes glanced to Lizbeth's for a millisecond, then devotedly returned to Arnett's. "No, no, my bad. Mother- and daughter-in-law. You both look wonderful today." He shifted his focus. "And Miss Beebe. I'm honored. Lucius Dameron here. At your service." He added a courteous bow. When his stunned audience only mumbled responses, he straightened, wary. "Oh, no. I've intruded on a caucus, haven't I?"

"A little bit, Lucius," Beebe said.

"This really is my bad."

"No. You're here. Was it coffeecake you brought?" Beebe began rocking herself off the couch. "We'll take a break. Might do us all good."

Lucius helped pull Beebe to her feet. Once up, she motioned Arnett and Lizbeth to follow.

Callie left her soda can on the counter. She carried plates and utensils to Lucius, then linked her arm through his. "Can I have a rain check, Lucius?"

"Sure, gumball." Then Lucius added, "You angry with me?"

"No, no, just need a little air." Callie's gaze glanced off the others, then she slipped out the door, not letting it slap against the frame. A concerned Lucius watched her go.

Laying fingertips on Lucius's arm, Lizbeth said, "I'll go check on her."

Lucius nodded. Lizbeth ducked out the door. Back at the kitchen table, he must have unzipped the container. "Lordy, smell that cinnamon," Beebe said.

Callie strolled toward the quiet river, and Lizbeth traipsed after her. Callie heard. She turned and waited.

"That Lucius, he's about this much on the feminine side," Lizbeth said, measuring several inches of air between my thumb and forefinger.

"He's putting on. Don't get me wrong, he's gay, but he plays it up with the right crowd."

They moved with a sauntering pace. "How long have you known him?"

"Since high school. He's a good friend. No coffeecake?"

"Not much of an appetite these days."

"Me neither."

Lizbeth knew grief picked at one's taste for food, but she found Callie's admission worrisome. "It's been well over a year since Dad's death, I would have thought your appetite had returned. I guess that's what I can look forward to."

As they neared the weathered dock, their presence hustled a soft gray bunny, nibbling on a dandelion breakfast, back into a copse of trees. In the grass, Lizbeth saw a vine snaking through. Spaced along its length were several green raspberries that never ripened.

Lizbeth and Callie stepped up to the solid six-foot-by-ten dock. They stood there a minute. Only the river's drifting whispers kept an uncomfortable silence at bay.

"Come on," Callie said with an arm gesture. "Let's sit down."

Their footsteps on the planks sounded like hollow echoes. Lizbeth mimicked Callie's actions once they traversed the span: Her sandals came off.

"Jack and I called this the dangling dock because it's just high enough to dangle our feet," Callie said, lowering herself to the platform.

The water was cold when Lizbeth's toes tested it. "You have a lot of memories here, and we're stomping all over them. I'm sorry."

Callie waved Lizbeth's apology away. "My memories will survive."

"I have every confidence they will." Lizbeth's feet swished the water. "My guess is, you went to Lucius's house last night after you bolted out of here. I thought we'd see you or your car in town. You know, it's a small enough place. We all drove back to make calls. It's crazy how the mountains play havoc with the cell phones."

"How's Chad?" Callie asked.

"He's a trooper. Thank God I have him." A laugh bubbled up, and she related a story about her brother and sister-in-law. "Patrick and Debbie don't have any kids, but they keep fish. I had to pack Chad's

Finding Nemo video, a hand-me-down from Geoff. They'll certainly be tired of that before I get back. So anyway, I'm sure Arnett called Gary and Stella." Lizbeth rolled her eyes, conveying her adversities with the two Sebrings. She thought that might lead to common ground and a spurt of conversation, but when Callie chose not to bite, Lizbeth moved on to another subject of importance. "Patrick posted some pictures of Chad on Facebook. I have my iPad, but I need a connection. Does Baron have wireless anywhere? If you don't know, maybe Lucius will. I miss Chad pretty badly already. I really want to see the pictures. And I want to get Sarah's office number to Pat and Deb." Earlier, Callie supplied Lizbeth with the emergency number.

"I haven't needed connections myself, but I think the library's wired."

"Good. I'll show you the photos once they're downloaded. Patrick says they're a hoot. Chad can be a real ham, just like his father. Are you on Facebook?"

"No. Not me."

"Really. It's great for my family, especially the Florida crowd. Is your family in Cassel?"

Callie's answer saddened Lizbeth. Her feet fell still. Callie had no family. Both parents and one older brother Mark were deceased. They'd died before John. Her family members all moved to Macon while she attended Duke University. In Macon, each in turn died and was buried. Lizbeth tried to conceive such a fate. Callie had half her life yet to live and no family. What loneliness!

"Since we've got a minute," Callie said, "I'd like to weigh in with Beebe."

Lizbeth surmised the subject. "If you're talking about Beebe's one-leader speech from yesterday, I got my comeuppance in the car after we left the depot."

"No, I'm talking about your decision to move to Florida so closely after Dan's death. I'm in full agreement with all the grief handbooks on the subject. It's your decision, and I do give you credit for your courage, but I honestly feel it's too soon. No matter what happens with Arnett and the quilt—and that's clearly your decision, too—I'd like to see you allow more time to pass between this week and a future move."

Lizbeth managed to hold her tongue inside the cabin. She accomplished the same now. She could ill afford to let Callie or Beebe learn that she'd already decided to accept their advice, but was feigning an obstinate approach in order to solidify a power shift. Arnett *would* step down from the throne.

Back in Cassel, when Arnett refused the quilt a second time, the Florida threat just sprang from Lizbeth's mouth. Now, her fingers tightened around the edge of the dock. A move of that proportion felt too daunting to undertake without Dan. While she wouldn't back down on the requirement that Arnett accept and display the quilt, the Florida threat gave her wiggle room. With the chirp of a passing wren, Lizbeth thought how pleased Beebe would be with her nod toward compromise.

"Every time I think about you pondering this decision," Callie continued, "I remember going to the drugstore a week or two after Jack's death. I literally felt like I was living inside some kind of hazy bubble. I could only see about three feet ahead. I felt isolated from a world operating normally around me."

Lizbeth nodded her understanding. The same description illustrated how she stumbled around after Dan died.

"I went in for another jar of Noxzema," Callie said. "I simply wanted a one-for-one replacement. I wanted the small size, exactly what I'd emptied. But instead of something a little larger than a golf ball, all the store stocked was a jar the size of a softball. I stood there for twenty minutes, trying to decide what to do. I needed the product, but I didn't want a jar that large. I just wanted the smaller size. That's what I came in for. Around and around it went in my head," she said, raising her eyes to Lizbeth. "That larger jar represented months and months of living and washing my face without Jack in my life. I didn't want to perceive that far into the future. In reality, I didn't want to think about living as long as it would take to use up that jar."

Lizbeth tried to read her eyes. Was Callie telling her she considered suicide? Were those desperate thoughts what caused her to search out Beebe?

"Florida. Noxzema. Florida. Noxzema," Callie said, hands operating like a balance scale. "You're truly not applying the tenets Beebe preaches about grief if you're able to make that decision at the end of this week, so soon into the process."

A tiny splinter of guilt pierced Lizbeth's heart. Callie was baring her soul, but Lizbeth knew her game plan had to take precedence.

Seated beside Callie on Heatherwood's dock, Lizbeth avoided a direct response, but the words she spoke were truthful. "You and I sitting like this and sharing stories is probably the best medicine. I hope there's time to do more of this, and I will take your thoughts under advisement. But you have to realize, I've had years to understand Arnett. She's not going to change. She is who she is."

"You should wait. Dan's death coupled with the reality that she might lose Chad could be enough," Callie argued. "I think she's scared. She knows you're serious. You're right, I don't know Arnett like you do, but I've pieced things together over the years. Jack didn't say a lot, but I know her sons and grandsons are very precious to her. Give her a chance, give her an opening, and enough time to show you."

Dumbfounded, Lizbeth blinked at Callie. Her father-in-law was more fortunate than she realized. He had this understanding woman in his life. She bore no comparison to Arnett. "You're amazing." She hooked a thumb toward the cabin. "Arnett was ready to trash you if Lucius hadn't turned up. And she will yet, mark my words. But out here, you're taking her side."

Lizbeth watched Callie's mind engage, but she didn't share her thoughts. Instead, her gaze followed a damselfly's jagged flight into shadow. That day, avoidance was the game between them.

"So tell me," Callie said, looking across the river, "what else was said about me last night?"

Lizbeth grinned. When she wasn't avoiding it, she was a devoted fan of honesty week. "You have to know your life with Dad is fascinating to the rest of us. Beebe and me especially. I suppose it's different for Arnett. Anyone who's heard part of the story would naturally want to know the rest. There's no way not to be curious. Beebe and I did throw out some speculation while we waited for Arnett to get off the phone. It centered around divorce. Why Dad didn't divorce Arnett. Why you didn't force him. Why you stayed in the relationship without a divorce. After he moved in with you, why didn't you force a divorce then? I know Arnett thought you would insist on it. How could you accept your relationship with Dad when he didn't, wouldn't, or wasn't forced to get a divorce?"

A car door closed, and they turned. Sarah Prosser walked into view.

Callie returned her wave. "I wonder why Sarah's here? It's Sunday."

"Probably looking for Beebe." That was Lizbeth's educated guess since Sarah didn't head their way. "Beebe left a note on the office door when we went into town."

Callie frowned. "Really."

Family Connections

Lucius sat around the dining room table with Beebe and Arnett. Their coffee cups were half empty. Lucius considered the infinitesimal crumbs remaining on three small plates a tribute to his baking prowess. Beebe cut herself off midsentence when she saw Sarah Prosser appear at the door. Giving the property manager a quick flick of her hand, Beebe scraped her chair back and got to her feet.

Lucius leaned forward to be seen. "Hey, Sarah P."

"Hey, Lucius. Don't leave until I talk with you."

"You got it, honeybunch."

Beebe ushered Sarah away, and Lucius wondered why those two had their heads together. It took every molecule of willpower to keep his backside plastered to the chair. It did squirm some while he debated whether he could get a read on their discussion from the kitchen window. He heard their footsteps lead down the porch steps toward the drive.

It was then he realized Arnett's dark eyes were, in fact, watching his squirming backside. A bird in the hand, he thought. He ditched Sarah and Beebe to concentrate on Arnett. Her finger traced the lip of her coffee cup. He smiled inquiringly at her.

Smiling back, she dropped her hands to her lap. "So," she said, "you knew John."

Lucius supposed she thought he'd be fooled into thinking her statement was merely a conversation starter when, in truth, he fully expected her to nibble away here and there—now that Beebe was outside—until she consumed his knowledge of the past.

"I knew him as Jack," he said sparingly.

"His mother called him John. I always did, too. Mother Sebring is gone, but John's stepmother lives on." Arnett pulled a face as if the death of the one and the life of the other were atrocities in their own right.

"I knew Jack from the country club. Not that I was a member." He pressed splayed fingers to his chest. "But I've done work there over the years."

"But now you live here?"

"Nearly two years. Before that, I was back and forth on specialized carpentry jobs. Willie Thorne, my beloved," he added, just to watch her cringe, "is still back in Cassel. Do you know him? He's brilliant. A financial consultant."

"No, I don't believe I do."

"Too bad. He is a genuine hunk. A beautiful man." Just talking about him gave Lucius a shiver that visibly traveled from head to toes and back again. "This is what's great about being gay and talking with women: We have the love for beautiful men in common." Arnett's silence spoke volumes, which Lucius immediately challenged. "Oh come on, admit it. You may be a grandmother, but you like beautiful men. If you and your girlfriends were doing lunch and you saw Willie, you'd drop your salad forks, clatter, clatter, clatter, right to the floor. It's true. People stare when they see Willie."

Her reaction was a nervous smile.

"No, you're right. You're the kind of woman who needs to see for herself. And that's all planned. Willie will be here next weekend. We're having a dinner party for all of you at our place Friday. My beloved," he said, sighing hopelessly, "knows everything about everything."

"Sounds like John."

"Yes, I got that from him."

Rocking forward, she studied him. "Did you like John?"

"Honestly—and I know this is honesty week, so you can count on me for that—I found Jack an acquired taste. One had to learn to appreciate the bouquet, the body, the slight tartness on your tongue."

First, her face went blank, then she grinned broadly.

"And every once in a while, one got a bad bottle with Jack."

She laughed outright at that. "No one here understands my side."

"Oh, I think they do. They've just gotten a bad bottle of Arnett recently. You need to re-label yourself. Sweeten the bouquet. Give them what they want." Lucius offered straightforward advice, just as he offered Callie that first night. No betrayal of Callie was intended, nor did he think Callie would perceive any. Lucius, like Callie, chose to rally around young Chad Sebring.

"It's complicated," Arnett said without a thread of further explanation.

He narrowed suspicious eyes just as Arnett projected her wariness of him. She still did not believe Lucius understood Jack possessed a shady side. Once at the club during a renovation, when Callie thought he wouldn't hear, Lucius witnessed a fearless Callie correct a headstrong Jack, his uncompromising attitude, his discriminatory word choice. Callie did so on Lucius's behalf. The thing was, Jack stayed corrected. Lucius gave him credit for that. Callie's stern rebuke reprogrammed Jack as surely as if an updated memory chip had been implanted. Callie and Jack had that effect on each other, one could wend a better quality into the other.

It was Arnett Sebring, though, in whom Lucius needed to implant some updated programming.

"What are you holding back from Lucius?" His elbow was pinned to Heatherwood's kitchen table, his head propped in his hand. He watched Arnett stubbornly turn away. "You're a proud woman, Arnett Sebring, and a strong one. Come here."

He pushed back his chair, then helped Arnett with hers. She balked when she realized he was steering her toward the quilt and photographs on the entryway table. Lucius took a second or two to admire Callie's workmanship, but knew better than to articulate his admiration.

A wand-less magician, he waved his hand over the three photographs. "This is Chad's life, Arnett. Grandpa is gone." He turned Jack's photo down. "Daddy is gone." Dan's photo followed Jack's. "That leaves Chad and a quilt. How sad. You're needed here. Accept the quilt. Step in, lift up Chad and the quilt together."

Her eyes were trained on Chad's photo. "I could," she said finally. "I could bow, and bend, and kiss her feet, and still she could take him away. I deserve that child. I deserve him in Maryland, not Florida." She scraped a fingernail over a patchwork square of denim. "And I call this the surrender quilt. That's how I've come to think of it."

Arnett walked away. Lucius allowed his twitching brow to arch. He must try harder to pry her secrets loose. He righted the two photos and rejoined her at the table.

"Thank you for the coffeecake. It was very good. Callie should have been here, though. After all, this is her home."

"Oh, pooh Callie. I've been happy to have your company. Here, let me help." Between the two of them, they carried the dishes to the counter.

She scowled. "No dishwasher."

"Not necessary. You've got me." His emphasis on the last three words brought her eyes around to his, the dark night meeting a brilliant dawn. In that dawn, he believed she saw that he welded a long-range truth to his pronouncement.

She reached for the nearby dish towel. "What do your parents think about your..."

"Sexual orientation." He supplied the politically correct term. "It was hard for them. Willie's family's different. He has two gay uncles. His mother raised five sons. She said she knew Willie was different by the time he was two. It makes a difference, you know. Ready acceptance."

"Do you see your parents?"

"Some."

"They live in Cassel?"

"Not anymore. My brother died, and they moved to Florida."

Arnett's head snapped his way, disbelief alive on her face. He made a cross-my-heart gesture. "Honest, ma'am."

From the corner of his eye, he spotted the radio pushed against the countertop's splash board, its antenna raised to the window above the sink. He let the warm water pool in the white ceramic basin and toggled the radio on. "Hmm, let's see what we can pull in."

"The radio seems to be the most modern amenity. No cable and no phone," Arnett complained. "Are we just too far back in the woods?"

"My cabin has a landline. It is possible. Heatherwood just doesn't. Some of the other cabin owners around here have added them, but only in the last year or two, like mine. Next door." He pointed up the hill. "I'm sure that cabin does. The O'Malleys live there." He adjusted the tuning dial on the old General Electric. "I'm a music connoisseur. Did you know that? I have thousands of albums, cassettes, and CDs." Straightening, he touched index finger to chin. "I will find the perfect song for you. From that point forward, it will be known as Arnett's Song."

With a minor adjustment, the radio picked up the tag end of a newscast. He added a squirt of dish liquid to the sink and grabbed the waiting sponge. He dunked his hands into the soapy water just as the radio DJ did Lucius's job for him, and quite superbly.

Hit the Road, Jack was piped out of the oldies station.

Openmouthed, Lucius and Arnett stared at each other. Arnett chirped a gleeful, "Ha!" and gave Lucius a light whack on the arm. She twirled herself onto a makeshift dance floor, crooning out the chorus.

The amazing coincidence kept Lucius trained on Arnett's high-stepping performance. At the appropriate cues, she pointed toward the road out front, then followed up by shaking her finger in a wildly discouraging fashion. Almost too late, Lucius worried about Callie. He craned his neck around to peer through the screen. Was Callie within earshot?

"You're dripping suds!" Arnett pointed out, now marching an invisible Jack in the direction of the porch.

A short time later, after Arnett's Song concluded, the dishes were stacked in the cabinet, and he ran a thick pile of paper towels through a wet spot on the floor, Sarah called his name at the screen door. Arnett followed him out. Sarah and Lucius chatted briefly about two odd jobs needed at cabins up the mountain. Callie hurried forward from the dock with a request. She asked to borrow a chainsaw to clear out underbrush along the far side of the cabin.

"Oh, I don't know, sweetheart. Why don't I stop back in a few days and clear the brush for you?" A horror film starring four women and titled *Chainsaw Massacre at Heatherwood* flashed through his mind.

Sarah spoke. "Have a good day, ladies. Either Nadia or I will be down every day to see that you have what you need." She touched Lucius's arm. "You following me?"

"Buh-bye, my lovelies. Lucius is in great demand." He blew a kiss, but one of the women slipped away. "Buh-bye, Callie, wherever you are."

. . .

Callie was inside at the kitchen counter. The next voice she heard was Beebe's.

"Well, girls, shall we reconvene?"

She hurried across the great room and out the hot tub door, carrying a cork-lined serving tray loaded with four tumblers and a pitcher of lemonade. She allowed the door to bang closed. That unspoken-but-audible message was sent and received. There was a lull while the leather soles belonging to her three roomers no longer crossed planked wood. Her heart quickened. She stepped out from the shorter porch stub and found their questioning faces. Given the situation, she wouldn't necessarily have served a beverage, but the lemonade was made, and she needed something to occupy her hands. The loaded tray was more a barrier between her and the others than a hospitable offering.

"Beebe," Callie said, "can we sit over here? I've got my thoughts together. I really need to talk." Her voice was thankfully clear and steady.

Inquisitive looks passed between them, then Beebe led the way, prepared to overlook a serious breach of caucus protocol.

Beebe, Arnett, and Lizbeth settled themselves in the three available chairs set around the rectangular table pushed against the cabin wall shared by the hot tub. A wicker rocker waited a few steps away, but Callie thought standing was better, giving herself room to move.

Earlier, when Sarah and Lucius said their good-byes, Callie was struck with inspiration. Last night, Lucius said she really wanted to talk about Jack and—in Lucius's words—their wild and daring relationship. He said the three seated women were just the ones to hear it. Out on the dock, Lizbeth strummed the curiosity chord. She said that anyone who heard only part of her tale would naturally want to learn the rest. So when inspiration reared, Callie held on. She didn't want to pack for home, regretting that she had not bravely told her story. Jack and she were robbed of a happy and much longer future together. Instead, it was shortened by sickness and death. She would not be robbed again.

She stood before the women, arms at her side. Her thumbs rubbed the tips of her fingers. The idea of openly revealing insight into her romance with Jack was more foreign than she could describe. They spent a lifetime keeping watch over that very secret.

Arnett held the nearest chair. To keep her eyes on Callie, she turned her chair around, its back to the table. Callie couldn't bring herself to concentrate on her pinched face and accusatory eyes. Callie imagined that same expression lined her face the first time Arnett phoned for harassment's sake. It seemed unbelievably foreign to Callie to hear her refer to her husband as John. What did it say? Callie asked herself that day. It clearly said Arnett was not a welded link to her husband's world, not the world that found him genuinely likeable and was asked to call him Jack.

Callie gave her attention to Lizbeth, seated on her left. "Something you said out by the river got me thinking. The long and the short of it is this: Until Jack came into my life, I struggled with my ability to feel that I loved another person. I never truly knew love until Jack." Her gaze drifted to Beebe, so attentive. "I thought something was wrong with me. But I *did* love Jack for twenty-two years. What was more amazing was—" her speech stumbled as she looked for words, "was, I guess, *his* capacity to love. I can't imagine ever loving anyone else like I love him."

A certain strength rose with that declaration. She was able to face Arnett, who radiated barely controlled hatred that only tempered slightly with Callie's confession. "And, yes, I did think about you, and how that betrayal would feel, should you ever find out about us. What I did was wrong, but it was too late. I loved him. I couldn't give him up. I was willing to accept the conditions that needed to exist to keep us together. In many respects, that's why it worked." Her eyes left Arnett's. They scanned Beebe's face, then Lizbeth's. "You have to appreciate a commitment that didn't require a certificate to force two people to stay together. We built a life. We had memories."

Callie paused for what sounded like a stray comment. "People and marriages are indeed a tricky business. In my opinion, it's a shame to waste a lifetime in an unhappy marriage. I wonder if sometimes brides don't put guns to their grooms' heads and force them to marry."

The speculation Callie recklessly assigned to generic brides and grooms was one Callie knew actually applied to Jack and Arnett. Arnett realized it instantly. She opened her mouth to respond. Beebe, innocent of the undercurrent between them, tapped her fingernails on the table and Arnett into begrudging silence. This time, caucus rules prevailed. Callie thought Arnett savvy enough, though, not to confess her guilt to witnesses.

Lizbeth moved a filled tumbler closer to Arnett. "Try the lemonade. It's good."

While Lizbeth attempted to distract Arnett, Callie dragged the wicker rocker over to the railing. She remained stationary since she began, causing nervousness to settle into every one of her leg muscles. They groaned for relief. In the close quarters of the porch, she pulled the rocker up for an unobstructed view of Beebe, diagonally across the table, and realized the disadvantage: She sat within striking distance of Arnett on her right. It felt like Callie was cozying up to a jaguar. A penance, she supposed, due and payable.

She folded her hands in her lap and called on her sportswoman's confidence. Eye contact with the woman she wronged was unavoidable. "I admit I was disappointed when Jack let things ride. The boys were grown when we met. Later, after they married, I thought he'd decide to divorce you. He loved his sons. I know he didn't want to put them through a divorce. And let's face it, there'd be hell to pay."

Arnett fairly glowed. The hellish payment made reference to her, and she was not offended in the slightest.

"I told myself I accepted the terms of our relationship. It didn't seem fair to change them later. And what if I tried and lost him? This was the first relationship I had that meant something. He was the man I wanted. Bottom line: I never asked Jack to get a divorce." Callie's head swiveled to Lizbeth, answering the question she posed on the deck. "Everything worked the way it was. I didn't want *us* to be destroyed." Her gaze rounded the table from Lizbeth to Beebe to become fixed again on Arnett. "After a while, I stopped having thoughts about your feelings. We had the two sides of our relationship. When we traveled, we didn't need to be so cautious." Callie's eyes automatically drifted to the cabin as a prime example.

"You were afraid." Arnett leveled her point-blank charge at Callie, dodging Beebe's caucus rules. Her three-word summary transmitted her disrespect: She no longer considered Callie a worthy adversary.

Callie put up a hand, deflecting Beebe's belated interruption and met Arnett's indigo pupils. "Yes. I was afraid. I didn't want to upset things. Above all, I wanted our relationship to continue."

"Me, being his wife, got in the way of that."

Callie nodded, feeling strangely calm. "As it turned out, there was nothing to be afraid of. We weathered the storm and the disease. The way we were here, when each day seemed like make-believe, that was our life. It was real. It would have lasted. We would have made it. We both realized that. After Jack moved in, *he* asked me if I wanted him to get a divorce. He told me he would if that's what I wanted. In truth, I didn't care about a divorce. I had Jack with me." Her voice broke on his name. "He had enough on his plate already."

How quickly grief and loss took hold. Avoiding faces, she looked from point to point: wall, window, hot tub, roofline, finally closing her eyes. In the darkness behind her lids, she touched her longing for Jack. In her lap, her little finger crooked.

"Callie? Are you finished?" Beebe's tentative words edged through.

She wasn't finished. Not yet. She opened her eyes and found Beebe watching, all of them watching. Beebe's hands were clasped together at her lips.

"Just a few minutes more," Callie said. She pulled in a breath and aligned her thoughts. "After Jack moved in, after the diagnosis, he spoke of so many things close to his heart. That was a whole new side of him I never experienced. We were sitting out back one morning, and he talked about the hurt he caused. The day before, he sat with the boys. He told them none of the blame should be placed on me. It was all his fault. He loved me. He made them understand that."

Suddenly, Callie's memory of that day put a smile on her lips. "Then Jack wandered out to some fantastical realm, wondering if despite our age difference and if he hadn't married, would we still have met. It turned out, the answer was yes. We had met. When I was four."

"Surely?" Beebe said, chin dipped to her chest, hinting at the impossible.

"Let me tell the rest," Callie said, her elbows on the rocker's arms. "Months later, we were going through a box of his mother's keepsakes. Her Bible was stuffed with several church bulletins and bereavement cards. You know, the kind printed for funerals. Going through those, we found that my grandmother knew his mother. They attended the same church. Sacred Heart," she said, so Beebe would know.

"Their names were listed in the bulletins as members serving on the same committees, and she kept my grandmother's funeral card. Jack's handwriting was on the back. He'd jotted a note for his mother there. That reminded him that she asked him to escort her to the service. It was entirely possible that when he and his mother offered condolences to my parents, I was right there, a clingy four-year old. I wouldn't have given my mother much space. We laughed that I enchanted him somehow that day while our mothers reminisced about a grandmother I don't remember." Callie smiled. "After Jack and I learned of our connection to my grandmother, he renamed the cabin. It was his surprise." Callie strung a suspenseful gaze around the circle. "My grandmother was born Heather Kilgore."

"It was your fate to meet," Lizbeth said.

"Not my fate," Callie whispered. "My fortune."

A Woman Such As You

Beebe watched a solemn Callie get up. She returned her rocker to its position under the porch light. She went inside and into her room, just on the other side of the cabin wall. In Heatherwood's stillness, Beebe barely heard Callie latch her door.

Contrastingly, Arnett's departure employed a share of dramatic fluster. It was wordless, but not silent. She slapped a palm on the tabletop to hoist herself up. The chair legs scraped gratingly across the porch planks as she twisted the chair and shoved its seat under the table. She yanked the door pull and stamped inside, nose high. Two seconds passed. Her bedroom door met the jamb with a bang. The explosion's retreating force fluttered the screen door a heartbeat later.

Beebe gave Lizbeth her one-eye-closed-care-to-comment-on-that expression. Lizbeth shrugged haplessly.

The two of them spent some time with their heads together quietly romanticizing the scene Callie described at her grandmother's funeral. In the end, they decided it felt a little weird to think that Jack's twenty-six-year old heart was truly smitten by a four-year old Callie, which in turn discounted the theory that Arnett was merely filling in while Callie grew to womanhood.

Lizbeth and Beebe talked on, but Callie nor Arnett ventured forth from their self-imposed exile. Beebe made a joke about cabin fever and needing a walk. Lizbeth assured her she'd manage the home front. She brought ingredients for a tuna casserole from home and thought she'd throw that together. In a couple of hours, she'd force everyone to the table.

Beebe grabbed an apple out of the fridge, then leaned into the uphill walk. Head down, pink rounded-toe clogs entered her field of vision at regular intervals. Curtains of scented, green foliage lined the faded-tar road out front of Heatherwood. She gave the apple core an arching toss into the woods. It slapped through a thicket to be further enjoyed by any variety of God's forest creatures. Old County Road A seemed endless, a perfect match for Beebe's reflections.

Arnett must have become complacent in her life with Jack, she thought. She didn't know the joy Callie described. Callie sacrificed her professional golf career. She adjusted her lifestyle. A light burned in Callie's and Jack's hearts, one for the other. Now she was split apart with longing for him.

Beebe considered the path through the woods Callie forged as a child, heading to Chesterfield Park for lessons and practice. Years later, the beaten-dirt lane doubled as Jack's hidden tunnel to his lover. Beebe couldn't apply an inkling of Robert Frost to Callie's and Jack's wooded tale. No, Robert Frost and his two roads diverging in a yellow wood was a parable for Beebe's life. She was several stanzas short of learning if the outcome of her travels would have equivalent results to those of Robert Frost's.

It was just when she needed a place of solace to escape into her past, that she came upon a cemetery. She stopped and stared. Memories of glorious days spent in her father's company rushed at her so quickly, she feared they would run her down.

The quaint and ancient cemetery was spread out behind an archway of fancy ironworks. She pushed on the gate. It squeaked its welcome. On either side of the gate, lengths of iron fence were anchored into the good earth. She followed a cement walk that widened, then petered out after cracks gave way to concrete chips. In all other respects, the cemetery was painstakingly maintained. It was someone's passion.

The sod was worn by walking paths. She took one, observing the icons rising out of the cemetery's trisections. At the back, higher than the others, stood a marble angel. The right-hand section was marked by an open Bible on a stone podium. To her left, a cannon confirmed the presence of honored soldiers. A perfect tranquility circulated beneath the leafy canopies overhanging the perimeter.

She heard the gate creak and looked back. She saw Lucius's smiling face. Only the tailgate of his truck was visible behind him. The rest was completely camouflaged by a wild and ever-present wilderness. The truck was headed down the mountain, away from Sarah's handyman jobs, no doubt completed.

"Looks like you busted out of the joint," he called.

"Hi, Lucius. I'm out for a stroll. This cemetery is a real find."

"It's quiet here. Peaceful. But I guess that's the idea. You know, I've never stopped before. It's a nice little graveyard."

"It is nice. Who's the sexton?"

Lucius stopped short and gave her a comical look. "Beg your pardon?"

She laughed.

"Are you coming on to me, Beebe?"

"Oh, Lucius, not in your wildest dreams, but it's good to laugh. A sexton is the caretaker. My father's the sexton for a cemetery back home in Michigan. We lived on the grounds."

"Cool. Did all the kids come to your house for Halloween parties?"

"No. No parties. We didn't grow many brave young souls in Larkspur."

"Too bad. Did you go into the cemetery at night?"

"I'd go with my father. But mostly, they were daytime visits. I learned a lot from him, a lot about respect for the graves themselves, for the dead, especially for those who mourned."

Lucius snatched a pencil from his shirt pocket and held it like a microphone. "Here with us today is Cassel's finest grief counselor. A round of applause, please."

Beebe felt a weight drop on her heart. She put up a hand and looked away, toward a weathered tombstone. "No, please don't. Don't say that."

Lucius took a step. "Beebe? What's wrong?"

Her wispy hair dragged her collar with the infinitesimal shake of her head. She smiled a sad smile. It was reflected in his eyes.

"Come on, tell Lucius."

The fact was, she could not tell Lucius. "You and Callie are too close. I guess I realized how close at the depot. I was out in the parking lot with Arnett and Lizbeth. Inside, I saw you hold Callie so very gently. She was crying, for Jack, no doubt. So, I can't ask you to bear my burden. It's not fair."

This quarrel, Beebe knew, was also for God's benefit. She wasn't really on speaking terms with Him yet, but perhaps He was with her. Had He caused her to witness the scene at the depot, to feel an instant fellowship for a man so filled with tender compassion for her friend? Was God telling her to confide in Lucius because of his closeness with Callie?

"So, your burden somehow gets in the way of Callie." Lucius turned her reasoning around. "Now I have to know. I can help. Let me."

"You don't know what I've done, what I'm about to do." Beebe wondered what Lucius would think of her when the decision she made and its resulting action reached out and hurt Callie.

"I won't judge you," he argued. "I've been judged my whole life. I'm neutral. I'm Switzerland. And I can't believe you would do anything purposely malicious. Tell me the circumstances? What's happened?"

"Don't get serious on me, Lucius. That's not you, I can't take it."

"Ah, my precious angel." Grinning, he rocked back on his heels, his shoulders relaxed. "Lucius can make this all better in the twinkling of any eye."

Great! A biblical reference, Beebe thought. What was God telling Lucius?

Lucius took her hand and guided her toward a concrete bench that acted as the cemetery's hub. They sat. "Now, confide all."

Beebe's stomach fluttered with a mix of relief and anticipation. Lucius seemed to corral all his concentration to hear her first words: "I need to go home."

Although she stated her initial plea simply, Lucius seemed prepared to hear an involved story that required some backtracking at times. He didn't interrupt, not for the longest time.

She began with the explanation Clifford Walker gave his sixteen-year old daughter Beebe after her mother abandoned them. The story had actually gotten its legs when Beebe was fourteen. Her mother, Abigail, was involved in a serious car accident. In the twelve months complete recovery required, she became addicted to Percocet. Her father fully shouldered the blame. He saw the signs, but wouldn't let them register with enough force to intercede.

Eventually, Abigail returned to her nursing job at Lakeview General where she had access to medication that fed her addiction. Seasons passed. She slipped up one day and didn't cover her tracks. She got wind of a hospital investigation and panicked. She raced home to fill a suitcase. After school that day, Beebe found her parents' bedroom a wreck. The new Impala her father scrimped to buy wasn't parked in the driveway. Hospital and law enforcement authorities pieced together Abigail's downhill slide out of town to Clifford the evening of Abigail's departure. After that, nothing was ever the same. Clifford's grief turned him bitter, then numb. Beebe admitted to Lucius that her father never recovered.

"How did you do?" Kindness permeated Lucius's tone.

"It was tough. I was in high school and the whole town knew. You know how kids are. Thank goodness they jump from one disaster to the next at warp speed. Pretty soon, Kimmie Stokes got pregnant, and that bumped me to the side of the road. But then they were reminded when my father shopped with me for a prom dress."

"The worst." Lucius shook his head, then eyed her curiously. "Who'd you go with to prom?"

Despite the years, a smile burst onto her face. "Vincent Bostick."

"Did Daddy approve?" he teased.

"Actually, Vincent became a fixture at our house and a buffer between Dad and me. When I was with Vincent, I was Daddy's little girl growing up, dating, ready for college. When it was just the two of us, I was the ghost of his missing wife. That's why he can't look at me. I could be her twin," she said, feeling the haunt simply by forming the words.

"Did that fool Vincent let you get away?"

"Our parting was amicable, painful, but amicable. My life would be at the beck and call of the church. Vincent didn't want to leave Larkspur. He married. No kids. Lost his wife to a brain tumor. And remained my father's best friend." She looked down at the hands in her lap. "My visits back are hard and have slipped to infrequent."

"So why go home now?"

"There's a place for me now. I've come full circle. And several months back, Vincent came personally to ask."

"The inextinguishable flame," he said, nudging his shoulder to hers.

"No, not really. That wasn't the heart of it. You see, he was keeping a secret and it was eating him up."

His eyes widened. "Lucius loves secrets."

"I guess my mother never conquered her addiction. She contracted AIDS and came home to die under an assumed name. Instead of Abigail Walker, she used Terri Miller. Vincent's a lifelong social worker. He manages an unwieldy center in Larkspur. One of the wings is a small hospice. She swore Vincent to secrecy. She didn't want my father to know."

"She's gone?" Lucius asked.

"Somewhere in my father's cemetery, he's tending to Terri Miller's grave like all the rest. He doesn't know."

"Vincent wants to tell him," Lucius guessed accurately.

"He wants me to be there." Beebe drew in a long breath. "I wasn't ready when he sprung it on me. I needed time to absorb everything. I left the church and was unsettled. Why go back to Larkspur for a double dose of upset? Then several weeks ago, Vincent and I started communicating. I'm ready now. I'm ready to live and work in my hometown, for my hometown, for the people."

"You're going to stay permanently?" he exclaimed, stunned.

"You see my problem."

He gave his head a shake. "There's a couple of really nice ladies here who are going to fall apart."

"I realize that. I can't start a new life until I finish the old one."

His eyes narrowed. "What's the timeline on that?"

Beebe laid a cushioning hand over his. "At week's end."

They sat there for another few minutes. Beebe explained that when Sarah Prosser showed up at the cabin earlier, it was in response to a note she pinned to the office door the evening before. Sarah confirmed that the office had a fax machine and gave Beebe the number. In the next day or two, Vincent would transmit Beebe's employment contract. Sarah would receive it, fold it into an envelope, and deliver it to the cabin. After Beebe read and signed the contract, Sarah would fax the return document.

Beebe and Lucius ambled along the cemetery's walkways while she continued her story. She was fifteen days into negotiations for the new job when Lizbeth grappled with Arnett, then Callie and West Virginia entered the picture. Lucius swung the creaky gate open. His truck waited on a bare patch at roadside. Beside it, Beebe laid out plans to push the peace summit to conclusion by Thursday, so she could have Friday—Saturday at the latest—to get the ladies on firm ground before she made her announcement.

"Lizbeth thinks she'll have me for ancillary consultation, but I won't be there. In the last two-plus weeks, I haven't found the words to tell Callie. She's needed me. She's needed my counsel. I think she'll do fine, but this will be a blow. I hope not a major setback." Beebe chewed her lip.

Lucius flung an arm around her shoulders. "In your business, there's never a good time to make a move like this. If it wasn't Lizbeth and Callie, it'd be someone else. That's just the nature of things for a woman such as you."

His closing remark sounded like high praise. He pried open the passenger door. It was an awkward climb for a pudgy woman to gain a perch inside his truck. When she was there, he shut her in and came around to take his place behind the wheel. Back at the cabin, Beebe felt she needed a commitment. She didn't want to impose on him further if he was disinclined to remain her confidant. She asked him in so many words.

His answer came with a kiss for her cheek and relief for her heart. "Beebe, you are a lady to join forces with."

They jumped down from the truck to the crushed-gravel drive. When they cleared the corner of the cabin, they saw Lizbeth and Callie standing on the dock, on either side of a folding lawn chair, looking out into a rapidly coursing river.

Beebe pushed herself into a speed walk. "What's wrong?" she asked as she pounded the length of the dock. Lizbeth and Callie turned to face Beebe and Lucius.

"Arnett," Lizbeth replied, anxiously.

"She's missing," Callie added.

Immediately, Lucius crossed to the dock's edge to look downstream.

"You think she fell in?"

"We can't find her anywhere." Lizbeth pointed into the chair. "This is her magazine."

Beebe pictured the scene as it must have appeared to Arnett when she walked up behind them. A group of Norman Rockwell kids grown tall, their backsides painted on canvas with Beebe on the far right, the hand at her brow blocking the sun, peering into the distance.

Arnett's voice startled them. Beebe spun so quickly, she nearly knocked Callie into the river. Lucius made a saving catch. Arnett, all innocent-eyed, claimed she'd simply taken herself off for a walk.

. . .

Lizbeth woke and rolled onto her back. Her left arm automatically reached out, but the mattress beside her was cold. Her head came around on the pillow. By then, reality had shaken itself awake to send its daily reminder to new widows. In the darkness, a tear followed.

She correctly placed herself in Callie's cabin. The next oddity to overcome was the sound of a man's voice emanating from the living room. The bedside clock read 1:17. She crept to the door and opened it a crack. Peering through, she saw Callie on the couch. The room was dimly lit, but enough light existed to see that her knees were pulled up to her chest. Dan's quilt was draped around her legs. Lizbeth recognized the baritone voice, then an infectious laugh. Both belonged to Dan's father. She opened the door further to see John Sebring's face on the TV screen.

Callie looked up when Lizbeth padded into view. "I woke you. I'm sorry." Using the remote, Callie paused the TV's image. John Sebring's face and torso, in bright sunshine, filled the screen. The Grand Canyon in its magnificent splendor was the backdrop.

Lizbeth heard about John's and Callie's vacation trip to the southwest in a screaming fit from Arnett, no matter that John moved out months before. They made the trip during the healthy eighteen months he enjoyed after surgery. Hospice and lingering decline waited. For the girl who didn't believe she could love, the woman she grew into gave him uncompromising devotion. She had time to accept the eventualities of his illness. Lizbeth, on the other hand, was in no way prepared to have her husband's heart cleaved from hers by one slashing strike of lightning.

"You didn't wake me." Lizbeth took a seat on the opposing couch. "I'm usually up several times in the night. At home, I would check on Chad, wander the house, then lie back down for another few hours."

"You're fortunate to have Chad."

"I agree, but a full night's sleep would be appreciated, too." Lizbeth studied Callie. "Have you slept at all since we arrived?"

"Very little. I didn't think I would. That's why I brought the sacks of clothes." She gestured toward the kitchen table. Lizbeth looked over to the tabletop cluttered with folded fabric, patchwork squares, scissors, and a pincushion. "That's my routine at home. If I can't sleep, I get up and work a while. When I'm ready to try sleep again, I usually read first, but I'd like the DVD to work." Callie looked at the frozen image on the television. "Jack wanted to record this vacation. He promised me I'd be glad I had it, but I couldn't bring myself to watch it after he died. I knew seeing him, remembering how much we enjoyed each other's company, would only worsen my suffering. So it sat. Then last April, on my birthday, I started missing Jack, and I lost it. That night, the memories flooded back. Everything reminded me of Jack. I cried until I couldn't stop. I didn't want that kind of grief back. I had to fight. I thought about the DVD and Jack's promise. He saved me that night." She fingered the remote. "I'd forgotten he called me Dingdong. Watch, it's coming up."

Scenes progressed until John was behind the camera. His robust voice said, "For all you viewers out in TV land, guess where Dingdong is?"

Lizbeth laughed. His camera lens was trained on a string of four port-a-lets set on a barren patch of ground. Callie exited the third stall. Smiling broadly, she shook her head, realizing she was the butt of a potty-humor joke. "Look at her," he continued. "She is so happy." Lizbeth heard the love in his softly spoken words.

Callie stopped the video there. "If I watch the DVD at bedtime, I think it makes me dream about Jack."

Lizbeth, in the light of the television screen, felt herself recoil.

"What's wrong?" Callie dropped her feet to the floor. "What did I say?"

Lizbeth used shaky fingers to comb strands of hair off her forehead. They ran through beads of perspiration. "I have nightmares almost every night," she said.

Those words summoned Callie. In two steps, she sat on the cushion beside Lizbeth, a sympathetic arm around her shoulders.

"They're always the same. Trees crash to the ground. Angry lightning flashes," Lizbeth said, seeing the events play out in her mind. "I race toward the scene. Dan is there, but I can't get to him. There's always an ear-shattering crack of thunder that wakes me up. I sit straight up in bed, soaked with sweat, just like I'd been out in the storm. I stare at Dan's side of the bed, trying to catch my breath, then I run to Chad's room."

Callie picked up the storyline without hesitation. "And he's always there. Safe and sleeping. Jack loved that little guy. When he learned his cancer was terminal, he told me how he would especially miss watching Chad grow up." She gave Lizbeth a squeeze, then leaned toward the coffee table for the tissue box that sat there.

After Lizbeth dried her eyes and nose, she looked down at the quilt Callie haphazardly threw over their laps. It wasn't Dan's as she initially thought. Carefully, she straightened the folds. The quilt was constructed from her father-in-law's clothing, and quite cleverly. Many of the six-inch patches were embroidered emblems representing golf courses around the country.

"It occurs to me," Lizbeth said, "I haven't thanked you for my quilts. I hope you don't feel I don't appreciate them; I do." She looked at Dan's quilt spread across the entryway table. "It just seems like accepting the quilt would symbolize the perfect concession for Arnett." Of course, Lizbeth knew Callie was fully aware of the all-encompassing complexities: Dan's clothes, Lizbeth's gift, Callie's hand-stitching, that connection to John. They were all sewn into it. If Arnett could just trust that in time, the anger and grief would pass, then the quilt would become a treasured keepsake.

"I think I'll try to get a few hours. You should, too." Getting up, Callie went back to her couch. She laid the quilt over her. Inspired, Lizbeth went for Dan's quilt and curled under it on the second couch. The women smiled at each other, then with the remote, Callie doused the television's light.

Life Dreams

Lizbeth's thankfully dreamless sleep was interrupted when Beebe shook her awake. Beebe patted down a wide yawn and announced she'd take everyone to breakfast. "Snap it up, girls. Let's get ourselves in and out of the bathrooms in short order. We're goin' to town!" She pushed her generous hips into rotating motion while she shook a soulful finger toward the ceiling.

Forty-five minutes later, they were belted into Callie's Santa Fe. She managed an end-around move that got the SUV's front bumper edged toward the road. A car the size of a tank, old and spinach green, whizzed by with a long, vicious blare from the horn. Its occupants were an older couple. The driver, a woman, seemed to speed up in her downhill flight. Callie swore when the woman swerved toward the SUV. An opposite reaction made more sense if the woman thought Callie intended to pull onto the road. Seated behind Callie, Lizbeth gave her the all-clear from up above, and they set out.

In addition to breakfast, Lizbeth wanted an internet connection to see the photos her brother, Patrick, posted of Chad on Facebook. From the Country Kitchen restaurant, they piled back into the SUV and headed toward the heart of Baron. They caught a green light at the depot. Lucius's truck was not in the lot, but the town itself showed activity. It was Monday morning, and Baron was open for business.

The library sat two blocks down on Armament, just past a hole-in-the-wall diner and a storefront housing the Blue Ridge Credit Union. Callie swung into a narrow lot besides the red-bricked building and angled into a parking space. The building had a Colonial feel with its long, white-shuttered windows. Lizbeth led the way up the front steps and through the double-door entry. Ranks of shelved books occupied the left side of the main room. They zigzagged through a reading area, past study tables and the circulation desk to a computer alcove.

The ladies crowded in behind Lizbeth's chair. With familiar ease, Lizbeth accessed Patrick's page. Photos of Chad were artfully arranged. Beebe and Callie pointed and commented on each. Lizbeth's favorite photo depicted Chad cross-legged on the floor, facing the TV, his back to the camera, *Nemo* on the screen.

Of another photo, Arnett said, "That could be Dan. Just like his father, Chad was born with his thumb in his mouth."

That fact was mentioned for Beebe and Callie's benefit. Lizbeth was well aware of the remarkable similarities between father and son. Patrick's photo captured Chad curled into a couch pillow, half asleep, sucking his thumb, a curly lock twisted around his small fingers.

Lizbeth felt a hand on her shoulder. "Wait," Arnett said, "I thought Chad gave up sucking his thumb."

"He's relapsed since he lost his daddy. I haven't pushed him to break the habit again."

When Beebe spoke Arnett's name in a low, concerned tone, Lizbeth turned and saw Arnett moving toward the door. Her slumped shoulders and shuffling gait seemed to tell a story of loss and suffering, unbearable and weighty. Beebe, ever ready on a whim to counsel the grieving, hurried to catch her. Lizbeth felt true sorrow for Arnett, even responsible for a share of it. Lizbeth put a high price on this peace summit. Her compassionate thoughts were short-lived.

Callie followed Beebe and Arnett out a moment later. Lizbeth wondered if Beebe still planned to ride with Callie to fill a grocery order at a place called Godfrey's. Lizbeth signed off the computer, then scooted outside. She looked around. None of the ladies were present. She wanted to call home, but read a text first. Patrick wrote that, as predicted, he was called into the office. Starting Wednesday, his vacation request would kick in, then he'd devote all his time to Chad until her return. Lizbeth gravitated to a grassy strip next to the parking lot. She sat at a picnic table under a shady elm and called Patrick's house. Debbie answered.

She surprised Lizbeth by saying Chad, always a ball of morning energy, was still in bed at nine-thirty. Surprise drifted to wariness when Debbie told her Arnett called the afternoon before. Chad's feelings were hurt. He waited up, expecting a call from his mother that didn't come. That resulted in difficulty getting him to sleep.

While Debbie carried the phone to Chad's room, Lizbeth was up and pacing. How had Arnett managed a call home? Had she found a square foot of ground where cell phone reception leaked into the mountain range? And how Arnett-like the call was; both in completing it, then keeping silent afterwards. She used and upset Chad, and by extension, Patrick and Debbie. Lizbeth could foretell Arnett's argument: Chad needs to know Grandma loves him. If he begged and pouted for Arnett to grandsit him, then what could Lizbeth possibly do?

All hostile thoughts involving her mother-in-law cooled when Lizbeth heard her son's waking moans. She pictured his accompanying frown, knew his right thumb would bear a red mark, the imprint of his lower teeth. His left fist would scrub his eye, then both hands would reach for the phone. He gave her a sleepy hello.

"Good morning, sunshine," she cooed.

. . .

Lucius started up the library steps when he saw Lizbeth crossing the parking lot, carrying her phone, her expression tight. He jogged around the wrought-iron banister and back to the sidewalk. It was indeed his good fortune to finally find the fourth of these women alone. Lizbeth was about to receive his warm and sticky comfort for the soul.

They were ten feet apart when she saw him. "Come on." He smiled, hand on hip. "Give them up. I just saw Callie and Beebe. Callie told me you've got pictures of that beautiful child. Let me see."

Lucius gathered this information while Callie was stopped for the light at Armament and Carmody. At the time, he was watering the pansies planted around the depot's sign. She yelled Lizbeth's location out the SUV's window.

He took Lizbeth's elbow, and they strolled back the way he came. It pleased him that she showed a slim line of teeth. The tension in her pretty face released. She manipulated her phone, showing him two digital snapshots. He gushed over her adorable son and was photographically introduced to his aunt and uncle. Lizbeth used the term *scrunch* to describe the extra-tight hug Chad bestowed upon Debbie. Likewise, in the second photo, Chad's short arms were flung around Patrick. The adults were a good-looking couple, Debbie's features darker than her husband's.

"He's a lovin' on them, isn't he? You and your brother favor one another, but I don't see a speck of you in Chad."

"Oh, he's his daddy one-hundred percent."

"I find that comforting for you: reminders of Dan alive in Chad. It makes the most of a difficult situation." Softly, he said, "Something to treasure."

She gave him an emotional nod.

"And your other son, Geoff. How's he doing?"

"Back at school." Her voice was steady. "He went early this year to help with freshman orientation. I hated to see him go, but it was best. He needed the busy atmosphere, and his friends. He calls more frequently."

"He's worried about his mom."

"Some, I suppose. We've always had a connection, he and I."

"And I believe you always will."

They reached the intersection across from the old train station. Lizbeth seemed to understand the depot was their eventual destination although he hadn't said as much. They stepped out into the crosswalk far enough to see past a car parked at the curb, just in case they could jump the light. Lizbeth, walking and talking and looking at Lucius, didn't see the car coming up behind her.

Lucius made a quick calculation. His heart dropped into his stomach. The driver of the oncoming green sedan was cutting the corner much sharper than necessary. The sedan's path would pick Lizbeth off. He lunged for her in the crosswalk, grabbing her arm and yanking her back. She stumbled as he pulled her to him, and the car sped past.

"That's the same car!" Lizbeth said, breathless. Their gazes followed the sedan up Carmody.

Still rattled, Lucius hauled Lizbeth back to complete safety on the sidewalk, his mind tripping over the same horrible thought Lizbeth put into words.

"I'm a single parent. What if I'd been killed? My sons would be orphans." After the introspective moment, she waved a finger under his nose. "That car nearly creamed Callie's at the end of Heatherwood's driveway this morning."

Hearing that caused Lucius to snap other facts into place. "The O'Malleys own a car like that," he said. "They're Heatherwood's neighbors. Their place isn't visible from the road. I saw Arnett talking with them up the street when I went looking for you." A light shone brightly inside his skull. "That explains it."

Lizbeth tucked hair behind her ear. "Explains what?"

"Where Arnett's walk really took her yesterday."

Lizbeth was right behind Lucius connecting the dots. "She was next door, talking trash to Callie's neighbors about me. Probably Callie, too." She stared after the sedan again. "Old people using their cars as weapons," she complained.

"I heard that, missy," a cross voice said.

Lucius and Lizbeth spun to see Sylvia Boyle barreling toward them.

"I was right back there." Sylvia stretched out her arm and set a saggy bicep swaying. She pointed toward a dark spot in the park. "I saw you two walk against the light. Now don't go blaming Timothy."

Rocking back on his heels, Lucius said, "Eleanor was driving."

That reined Sylvia in. "Really." She gave her head a discouraged shake. "He's broken or lost his glasses again."

"Now that you mention it, I did see Eleanor and Tim standing out front of Doc Quinn's place."

"It'll take a week to get them replaced."

Lizbeth got them back on track. "Eleanor's got a lead foot," she charged.

Sylvia straightened. "But she can see fine, missy. And she's a senior. Keep that in mind." Lucius knew Sylvia. She was offended by Lizbeth's "old people" comment. She took a step to leave, then stopped. "And sometimes their cars are the only weapons they've got." With that, she stomped off.

Lucius and Lizbeth looked at each other, their eyes bright with controlled laughter. Only when the appropriate walk signal beckoned did they cross the street.

"What were we talking about? Oh, the O'Malleys—" Lucius said. "Actually, Arnett might not have just been talking trash to Eleanor and Timothy." Lucius peered over at Lizbeth's quizzical expression. "We had a moment together yesterday, and I told her the O'Malleys own a landline."

Lizbeth laid a manicured hand on Lucius's forearm, slowing their step over the curb. "That's how she called my brother's house when we hadn't come to town. She talked with Chad yesterday. I couldn't figure out how. No doubt she made contact with Stella and Gary, too. The sneak!"

Lucius inquired into the relationship those two played and was informed they were Arnett's sister-in-law and son.

Lucius gave her his best smile. "Lovely. Truly a family affair," he said. "And speaking of lovely, *your* alabaster skin in Florida? Come on?"

The two of them arrived at the train platform in the depot's side yard. They sat on the planked walkway with their backs to the street and dipped their feet into the void over the tracks. Beyond the tracks, an overgrown arborvitae hedge provided privacy. The constant breeze passing lightly under the narrow, angled roof flirted with her hair.

"You think simple vanity would keep me from going to Florida? There's product I can use, Lucius. And if Arnett doesn't come around, then I'll tell her I've got to go."

"You're making a choice," Lucius said, not buying her story. "And I have to wonder if your decision isn't driven more by an overwhelming desire to punish Arnett, rather than a conscious judgment that life for you and Chad would be better lived in Florida."

They entered healthy-debate mode; accusation nor anger were participants. "My decision is driven by an undeniable calling to follow a dream Dan and I conceived a long time ago. Since his death, I think about it more and more. I don't see Arnett coming around to my terms. And honestly, I don't plan to give an inch on my demands."

"No negotiation?"

"None."

"For a dream."

"A dream that should have been reality. Haven't you ever had a dream, Lucius? Not a vision for the completed depot. A life dream. A dream that tapped you on the shoulder one day and said, 'Fill your life up with this. This is worthwhile. Do this with the love of your life and be happy forever.' For Dan and I, that happened just after college."

"What prevented it?"

"Mother's privilege prevented it."

"Arnett?"

"Yes, Arnett." She pulled a knee up, then rested her chin and her thoughts there for a minute. "My aunt and uncle live in Tallahassee. Mildred and Ralph own Gibson Promotions. The company name would have become Gibson and Sebring. Uncle Ralph is a promoter. He got an idea one day to promote cities, businesses, and patriotism through eclectic designs. The best term would be a mural larger than a billboard. The murals would have focused on famous people born in a particular hometown, or a themed annual festival, or just history—whatever makes the heart of that city beat. For a business: maybe the progression of products. Maybe farming's the subject. Or the country: the Plains, the Midwest." A honey bee floated near. "There's a four-story canvas I see on the side of an old building every time I drive through downtown Cassel. I picture what could have been. Dan did, too. I didn't discourage his desire to paint landscapes, but Arnett couldn't see it. Dan's creativity was an integral part of his makeup."

"Artwork bigger than life," he summarized. "Then Dan would have been the artist?"

"Dan and I drove to Florida after graduation. It was all set. Yes, Dan would've been the artist, and Uncle Ralph the promoter. My job was researcher, working with Uncle Ralph and the hometown people. Then, like a bubble, the dream burst. Arnett sucked the life out of it. She had other plans for her son. Dan moved into management at Oldstone Manufacturing. Time passed. I became a mom." Her eyes dimmed. "Then a widow." She looked at Lucius. "I want to breathe life back into the dream. I hear the cautions about the grieving process and decisions made too fast, but I may just go to Florida and join forces with my uncle. We'll need to find another artist, yes, but we'll fill that wall in Cassel up with a mural." Her hands moved. "I see it overlaid with snippets of the town's history and snatches of Dan Sebring's landscapes."

The words snippets and snatches hissed inside Lucius's head. Lizbeth charged him up. She continued speaking about her dream bubble and his swelled to capacity. He knew recently lackadaisical Willie wanted the dream. He wanted less stress and more fun. He wanted T-shirts and jeans, not stiff collars and hundred-dollar ties. Lucius completed his assignment. He got broadband technology down Bullwhip for video conferencing so Willie could hold business meetings in the comfort of their living room. His clients would see him on a screen in the Cassel office. Lucius scooted around, pulling a bent leg up to rest on the platform. He must work to convince Willie to sell the house to the wheelchair-bound man. With the house sold, there would be no reason for delay, and Willie would be living in Baron before the depot's rededication in October.

Lucius's eyes never left Lizbeth. Her hands made dramatic motions. He gladly let her talk without interruption. It seemed the only thing to do when dreams were involved.

. . .

The last thing Arnett said to her temperamental daughter-in-law before she slammed the Santa Fe's rear door was, "You cannot choose my friends!"

Lizbeth's berating voice rose in tandem with the mountain's elevation as Callie drove back to the cabin. Lizbeth issued her abuse simply because Arnett took measures to introduce herself to the neighbors. Tim and Ellie O'Malley were Arnett's age, grandparents themselves, and gracious people who, when Arnett mentioned the lack of a phone at Heatherwood, offered theirs. She didn't just call Chad in the villainous way Lizbeth intimated. She put in calls to Geoff in Florida and Gary's boys, Zack and Kirk.

Beebe nor Callie weighed in on the entire trip back. Arnett gave them credit for their neutrality. Earlier, too, outside the library, Beebe showed Arnett kindness. She offered to console her, but Arnett waved her off.

"You're being unreasonable," Arnett said, chasing Lizbeth inside the cabin. "Where will it end? Am I supposed to get a written permission slip from you before I ever speak to a stranger?"

Lizbeth answered by heaving her bedroom door shut in Arnett's face.

Arnett expelled an angry breath and spun to see Callie and Beebe standing two steps inside the kitchen door. They wore sheepish expressions for a split-second before jumping apart. Beebe charged off to her room, and Callie went to stow groceries. She plucked items out of plastic bags. Beebe returned with her notebook. She knocked on Lizbeth's door and raised her voice to be heard. "Caucus in thirty, Lizbeth." She aimed her next word at Arnett who hadn't moved. "Okay?" Then she glanced Callie's way.

Arnett sensed Beebe's patience with the grieving widow was waning, but still she offered no solace for the grandmother who was forbidden contact with her grandsons. Beebe took a left out the screen door. Arnett knew she was taking herself off the premises.

Issuing another sigh, Arnett strode out the other door. She went straight to the rocker and lowered herself to the tufted cushion. She put the incident with Lizbeth behind her. A caucus was coming. She wondered about the subject matter. Arnett rocked and stopped, rocked and stopped. Realizing a unique opportunity just presented itself, she put the caucus behind her too, got to her feet, and went around the corner to the kitchen door.

The door hinges squeaked her return to Callie who arranged canned goods. She must have felt Arnett's eyes on her back. Quite casually, Callie said, "You've come to talk about the gun, haven't you?" Callie closed the cabinet door before she turned to lean against the counter.

Gospel of Jack

Arnett's thunder was stolen by Callie's uncanny anticipation. Callie seemed satisfied with herself. No, smug, Arnett thought. One fact was true: Callie lured her out yesterday when she purposefully inserted a statement into her caucus about brides putting guns to their grooms' heads, and Arnett bit.

All Arnett could do was revert to her best sneer. "Can't we talk outside?"

Technically, their talk violated caucus rules, but, amicably, Callie said, "Sure." She stored a package of chicken in the refrigerator on her way past.

Arnett moved toward two chairs on either side of a small porch table that faced the river. She wanted to assert herself instantly, but Callie grabbed the petrified zinnias out of the vase on the table. She threw greenish water from the vase into the yard, resettled the vase, and walked off to the trash container with the dead flowers. When she came back, Arnett was seated. Callie took the other chair and waited expectantly. Again, Arnett found the turn of events unsettling. In her own way, Callie was a master manipulator, shrewdly delaying while Arnett's anxiety churned.

"You called this meeting," Callie urged. "I wanted to get dinner started before Beebe called the caucus."

Arnett faced her dead on. "I want to talk about the crack you made yesterday in front of everyone."

"You're the only one who picked up on the crack—as you put it—and that's because it rang true."

At Callie's suggestion, a melodious, vibrating hum, like that produced by a tuning fork, strummed Arnett's nerves. She blurted, "What did John tell you?"

"As I've said, I only got a sentence here or there. To tell you the truth, I don't remember what prompted him to tell me the story. Oh, wait." A finger went up. "Maybe I do. He was concerned that you'd follow him when he left the house on evenings he came to see me. He always kept an eye on the rearview mirror. That was the story, wasn't it? Before you were married, you followed him one night. And you came packing a gun."

Arnett jumped in. "We were engaged. The wedding was two weeks away. His mother planned a huge ceremony. And John was still bowing out two and three nights a week, not wanting to come to my apartment. So one night, I did follow him."

"Where did he go?"

Arnett's chin came up. Well, well, well, she thought, she doesn't know either. "I don't know. He spotted me and pulled into an empty lot."

"That's where he picked up the story with me. You got out of the car. His car windows were down. From the passenger side, you leaned in and pointed a gun at him. Your words were, 'You *are* going to marry me.'"

"I was young. I couldn't control him. I never could. I wanted to know what he was doing when he wasn't with me. That's all. I had that right. But he always had secrets."

Callie tilted her head, studying Arnett so long she began to squirm. "Why did he marry you?"

"We made up," Arnett said honestly. "I could always charm him back."

"But your charms wore off eventually. That left only the drama."

Arnett fought to hold her tongue while Callie openly scrutinized her again.

"I can't get over it. Why did he marry you?" She threw up a hand that landed with a soft whack on the table. "I always thought that mistake haunted him. You came after him with a gun. You threatened him, then you must've charmed him. That must be true. Maybe it wasn't love, maybe it was charm."

Arnett found it somehow comforting that after twenty years together, Callie was right there with her, still trying to understand a complexly built John.

After sitting back in her chair, Callie pitched herself forward. "You know, I may have just figured it out. He loved the excitement. That's the common denominator. He found you exciting, your personality, the chase, the gun—but the drama wore on him. The kids came," she said, her attitude matter-of-fact. "My personality didn't match yours for excitement. The excitement for him was hiding our relationship. Perhaps a punishment for you. Something he felt you deserved."

"He had all kinds of girlfriends. You weren't the only one." Arnett wasn't sure that was true, but Callie's last comment pushed her too far.

"But I was the last one. I was the one he loved. And I believe you. He probably did have girlfriends before me. But he was trapped because you trapped him. And that caught you in the trap, too. You made the rules, and you suffered under them. You promised him poverty if there was a divorce. He didn't want that. And without damning proof, you wouldn't risk Dan's and Gary's wrath and file yourself."

"I hated him for what he did to me. For the embarrassment. The public humiliation. Your affair went on for over twenty years. And you were half his age when it started. Then when I did have proof, he went and got cancer. I couldn't divorce him then. What would the boys have said?"

Arnett's hand went to the vase on the table. Callie's eyes followed.

"Don't do it, Arnett!" she cautioned sternly.

"What?" Arnett smiled.

"Lose control. That's what Lizbeth saw at my house. That's what makes her afraid to leave Chad with you."

"Afraid? She shouldn't be afraid. That's a monstrous thing to say."

"She thinks your reactions run to extremes. You resort to physical violence, and you throw things."

"I don't throw things," Arnett said. In her mind, she remembered sweeping the ceramic shards that had once been a statue into her dustpan.

"You do."

"I don't. Is that what John told you?"

"Your jealousies and petty rivalries produce temper tantrums."

"That may be, but at least I'm not attracted to fags and old men."

Callie didn't blink. She was out of the chair in a heartbeat, giving Arnett her back, crossing to the steps. The vase was weighty in Arnett's hand. She reared it over her shoulder.

"Arnett! Don't you dare." The voice belonged to Beebe.

Arnett watched Callie swivel toward Beebe. The newcomer appeared at the foot of the porch steps.

"What the hell's going on here?" Beebe said.

In the next second, Lizbeth pushed through the screen door and held it wide. "What's happening?" she said, sending a questioning look around the porch.

Beebe answered. "I caught Arnett ready to heave that vase at Callie's head."

"Arnett! What's wrong with you?" Lizbeth said.

Running through Arnett's mind was the thought that Lizbeth would waste no time sharing this news with the family. As usual, Lizbeth wasn't present for Callie's goading, her taunting, arriving only for the finale.

"That's a good question, Lizbeth." Beebe climbed the steps. She addressed Arnett. "I don't know whether to be disgusted with you or admire you. A certain amount of anger is understandable, given Jack's infidelity with Callie. She's here, and this isn't an easy situation." She gestured to the wilderness surroundings. "I would hope you'd never produce this type of reaction in front of a child. But next week with Jack and Callie out of your life, you should be able to put your life in a groove that keeps you calm and allows you to enjoy your grandson. To gain the latter, Lizbeth insists on a concession. She asks you to accept the quilt and display it. Next week with Jack and Callie out of your life," she repeated with attitude, "I wonder if you'll continue to allow your anger to fester. Or is it fear? Or pride? I could almost admire pride. What's it going to be, Arnett? Are you willing to accept the quilt and move on to next week?"

In response, Arnett set the vase on the table with a loud thud.

Lizbeth sidestepped and let the door slap closed. "I think we should just pack and go home. This is useless."

"No," Beebe said firmly, "we're sticking it out. But the kid gloves come off. I'm asking the questions. And they're going to be nosy to a fault. I want the dirt, the grime, and the baked-on crud. I want honest answers and deep-down secrets. I want to understand this mess if it takes all night." Her gaze passed over each woman in turn. "Ten minutes. Living room. Don't be late."

Beebe and Lizbeth went inside. Callie stamped off to the dock. Arnett tested the weight of the vase again.

. . .

Time expired. Callie sat across from Lizbeth, each to her own couch. A stubborn Arnett was still planted on the porch.

"Arnett, you're late. Get in here." Beebe, bent at the waist, spoke through the window screen, but Arnett's obstinate posture persisted.

"I might have been on time," she said, "if your invitation had been more cordially deliv—"

Mowing through her attempted protest, Beebe said, "Do I smell a butt coming? Why, yes, I do. It's yours, Arnett. Get it in here."

Callie grinned at a wide-eyed Lizbeth. Beebe was still miffed, but Arnett did come scraping through the door. She marched to the vacant seat next to Lizbeth and, with precision of movement and a straight back, claimed it.

Beebe already moved a tall side chair to the head of the coffee table. By accident or design, her place of prominence allowed her to look down on the other three. The construction of the chair seated her marginally higher than the cushioned couches.

"New ground rules," Beebe announced, then sailed them Callie's way. "I ask the questions, and you answer them."

"Me?" Callie tapped her breastbone with two fingertips. "You're directing everything at me?"

Beebe's eyes rolled heavenward, telegraphing mock thought. "I guess so. My questions are for you. I'm sure Arnett will want to give input, and that's fine. But we will remain civil, not argumentative. We're having a discussion between adults, the worst that could possibly happen already has. We can't change that. I don't even want to talk about Chad. He's off limits. He's the future. I want to dwell in the past. I want to write the Gospel of Jack. Sorry, Arnett, John has been taken." She laid a finger across her lips, considering her course. "You know, in biblical times, Jack could have had two wives, or ten. He wouldn't have been scorned. In ancient Mesopotamia, you two would have had to learn to live together. We know the wives didn't. There were jealousies." She paused. "And petty rivalries."

Beebe just made Callie and Arnett aware of exactly when she came within earshot of their previous conversation. If she heard Callie's comment, she also heard Arnett's pointedly hurtful one that insulted

Lucius and Jack.

"I want to stick my nose in a place that's closer to present day. Lives have been lived in obscurity, loves hidden, and I'll be damned if I can figure out how it could have possibly been managed." Beebe crossed her legs and addressed Callie. "Didn't you worry that Arnett could show up at the club at any time, without warning? After all, her husband worked there. I picture her coming for lunch with Jack or dropping in unexpectedly with a girlfriend for drinks. She could easily have caught you and Jack playing around."

On a bet, Callie couldn't have prevented her eyes from darting to Arnett. The older woman remained taciturn, quite pleased Callie shone in the spotlight. "First of all," Callie said, indignant, "Jack and I didn't play around at the club."

"But he had an office there," a contentious Beebe replied. "She could have easily walked in on an embrace or a kiss."

"I thought we were going to be civil."

"You're right. Forgive me. You may lead the charge on civility." Beebe sat back and laced her fingers together. It seemed to Callie she sounded seriously peeved. Or was it an act? And to what end?

"You don't understand if you think Arnett was the only one with whom Jack and I had to be concerned. We couldn't demonstrate a show of affection in front of anyone. At the club, we had to exhibit a friendly, working relationship."

"So Arnett would never have been the wiser when she stopped by?"

"She never stopped by."

"Not once." Beebe's arched brows expressed her amazement.

"Not since I was hired."

"Before that? Never?" Beebe asked Arnett, who shook her head. "I would think country club membership a perk. You didn't take advantage of it?"

"John worked from the club," Arnett said. "I couldn't just show up. I could call him, and I did, but we weren't members. John never paid a membership. I'd have known."

"I guess I assumed there'd been a membership. In fact, I find it quite odd there wasn't." Beebe aimed her puzzled expression at Callie. "Can you clear that up? Are you a member?"

"There was a difference between Jack and me in the club's eyes. I'm an employee who's expected to cater to club members and participate in functions when invited. Jack had an agreement with the club. He didn't pay for office space, and he didn't pay membership dues. I think they were both in exchange for his ability to bring well-known golfers to the club. He was public relations when he was out designing or modifying courses. That had a certain value for the club, a prestige the board members took in exchange for his membership." Callie took a moment. She'd reached the crux of the matter. "I think the membership extended to Arnett, but I don't think he bothered to tell her."

"Obviously he didn't," Beebe said, aggrieved on Arnett's behalf. "The club was out of bounds: a place for Jack without Arnett."

"That's the way it was before I became the pro there. It wasn't done to accommodate me," Callie clarified.

"He thought it through, and he established a place of seclusion early in his marriage. That's telling." Beebe looked at Lizbeth. "You're awfully quiet. What are you thinking? Are you surprised?

"Not really. That was Dad's way."

"Secluded? Unapproachable? A man of boundaries?" Beebe suggested.

"I wouldn't say secluded. He was definitely approachable. It wasn't so much that he had boundaries. I knew him as a man very deliberate in his actions. I understood he had under-the-table control of Arnett."

"Did you get that understanding from Dan?" Arnett asked, defensive.

"No, it was first-hand. From Dad."

Beebe sank into the chair back. "Well, under-the-table control. That was delicately stated." With a flourish, she made a notation on her tablet. "I'm going to remember to ask you to explain that later. I'm honestly not as interested in your explanation as I am in my next snoopy question." Her eyes turned toward Callie. "By your interpretation, you two never let your guard down. Jack marked the club as his own. You two had the surrounding grounds, a path through the woods, a protected world. What happened? There were nineteen successful years. How did Arnett catch on? Did you throw caution to the wind?"

"Jack never said, but I think it was my fault."

Beebe's mouth gaped. "Jack never said! And you didn't ask him?"

"I didn't push him to tell me things—"

Beebe cut Callie off with an accusation. "He kept secrets."

"No. Not secrets," Callie said, working to keep a civil tongue. "I respected his privacy. His marriage was his business. He controlled what crossed over into our relationship. But in this case, I think he was sparing my feelings because I caused it."

"What happened? What did you do?"

Beebe's words and eyes bore into Callie until the memory from her first night in Baron was triggered. She heard Lucius's prodding voice: "Tell your story." She did, in the simplest of terms.

"I fell in love with Jack all over again. That's all."

For several seconds, the world around Callie seemed to hold its breath while it decided the worth of her words. The quiet in the cabin was so complete, it worked to amplify the buzzing of a fly against the window screen. She continued her story in the same soft tone she used for its introduction.

"I was always deeply in love with Jack, but there was a specific instance one December when I felt that miraculous feeling of falling in love. Instantaneous. Irreversible. Out of my hands. It wasn't until the next April that Arnett tossed him out."

"First things first," Beebe said. "Tell me about December."

Callie complied. "The weather hadn't turned, so Jack and I set a time to meet at a driving range in town. He arrived first and was inside, talking with the man managing the range. It seemed to me they were acquaintances. I realized later—much later—Jack was trying to clue me in to the situation. He acted surprised to see me, but I didn't catch on. We each grabbed a bucket of balls and went through the connecting door to the stalls. We pulled drivers out of our bags. Jack was telling a story. I don't even remember how it went, but I remember everything else about him."

The scene painted in her mind was as vivid as the day she lived it. She remembered every detail: Jack's relaxed stance. The golf club at his side. His other hand slipped in a pants pocket. His broad shoulders. The golf jacket that brought out his eyes, more blue than gray.

"He was happy," Callie said. "Laughing. He amused himself with his own story. And I couldn't take my eyes off him. The next thing I knew, I took two steps and kissed him."

"What did he do?" Beebe's question dissolved Callie's memory.

"Nothing. He didn't say not here, be careful. He seemed genuinely overcome. Words failed him. Which was a novelty because Jack was never at a loss for words." Callie smiled. "He just tipped his head the way he did. I saw a softness come into his eyes. He said, 'I love you too, little girl.' That endearment has always touched my heart." Callie thought Lucius would be proud that she didn't hold back her true feelings. "Maybe ten, fifteen minutes later, Arnett showed up. Jack took an attitude with her, wanting to know why she was there. She turned the question to me."

Arnett sat, tightlipped, hands clenched. She was forced to listen to the telling of a romantic moment between her husband and his lover. If body language meant anything, Arnett's blustery reaction waited in the breech. If it died there, she might make it through the caucus lecture-free. She already suffered one lecture from Professor Beebe.

It was then that an alarm sounded in Callie's head and Beebe's underlying motivation struck home. Beebe was questioning Callie on sensitive subject matter to test Arnett's ability to keep her temper curbed. The ladies would be astonished by Callie's next thought: Hang in there, Arnett. You're passing so far.

"What happened after Arnett arrived?" Beebe asked.

"They had words, then Jack persuaded her to go home. A few minutes later, he went home, too."

"And you thought everything that came after was your fault because you kissed him and that man saw." Beebe put two and two together.

"Either that, or the man knew Arnett, was suspicious of Jack's and my coincidental arrival, and called her. Or that was just a day she decided to follow him."

"So which was it, Arnett?"

"The man was my niece's husband. He was just filling in that weekend for the owner who had an out-of-town wedding to attend. He called. He didn't see them kiss. If I'd known that, I'd have had all I needed. I would have booted him out three days before Christmas."

Callie's mouth suddenly dried to dust, but Beebe took the news with no reaction other than to check her watch. Laying a hand on her stomach, she said, "I know you were going to cook, Callie, but I see this going a little longer and I need you here." She ran a finger through the air, indicating their wagons drawn in a circle. "I'm going to put in the lasagna. You don't mind, do you? I can feel the hungries coming."

Callie and Beebe went to the kitchen. Callie pulled the packaged lasagna from the freezer, set the oven to preheat, and filled a drinking glass with water. Beebe followed her back to the living room. She opened a package of cheese bites. "Hors d'oeuvres, ladies. Help yourselves." No one partook but Beebe.

"Lizbeth, what was the holiday like at the Sebring homestead that Christmas?"

"Dan and Gary were aware. She phoned them before Dad returned from the driving range. They discounted it. Their parents had been married forty years. To Dan and Gary, that meant everything was fine. They believed their father—that the driving range was an accidental meeting. They accused their mother of exaggerating, building things up in her mind. They told her to let it go. That was her first conniption about Callie. Mostly, they were about Dad's traveling, always being away from home. Even when he was in town, he was continually away from home. To answer your question: On Christmas Day, she was chilly toward him. He ignored it and concentrated on family, the grandsons, who were blissfully unaware."

Beebe turned to Arnett. "So everyone talked you down? You had no defenders?"

"Stella believed me. My sister-in-law."

"Stella was not a fan of Jack?"

Arnett shook her head. "She told me to get evidence, so I hid a tape recorder in his car." She paused to display a satisfied smile. "I got all I needed. The boys switched teams quickly. I'd been right all along."

"Clever Arnett," Beebe acknowledged. "A tape recorder."

"I got John's side of a phone conversation with her." Arnett pointed at Callie. "He was reminiscing about a sexual encounter on a beach somewhere."

"It was *inside* a beach house," Callie said haughtily, correcting Arnett's conveyed misconception.

"I don't think we need specifics," Beebe put in.

The oven's indicator light clicked off, and Lizbeth jumped up to tend to the lasagna.

"So after Arnett kicked Jack out, he moved in with you?"

Callie shook her head at Beebe. "No, he got an apartment. He wanted a place where Dan and Gary would visit, where Chad could come and stay overnight. His family would never come to my house, nor allow the grandkids to visit him there. He rented an apartment in April. In June, we got the lung cancer diagnosis. He had a continual cough for months, and I finally got him to see the doctor. When the surgery was scheduled to remove part of his lung and it was obvious he'd need nursing for several weeks after he was released from the hospital, the boys insisted he move back in with Arnett. He moved back the day before the surgery."

"She would nurse him?"

"Yes."

Beebe studied Arnett closely, then directed her question to Callie. "And he moved back?"

"Yes."

"That must have been horrible for you."

Callie nodded. "And for Jack. He cried when he told me what he agreed to do. That was the first time I ever saw him cry."

"When he was going to be separated from you?"

"I was banned from the hospital, too. Days passed before Jack called. I was a wreck. I couldn't sleep. I couldn't eat. For two days, I called the ICU nurses' station and got updates, but by the third day, a nurse answered who asked if I was family. I wasn't, so no update for me. The nurse must have advised Gary. He put a note on the chart forbidding phone updates."

"And then Jack found a way to call you."

"Yes."

"But you told me you nursed him." A determined Beebe was inching her way through all the muck surrounding that period in Jack's life, and Callie could see where she was headed.

"That was later," Callie said.

Lizbeth returned and started to speak, wanting to clarify. Beebe eyed her sharply, silencing her.

"What's the story, Callie? Why don't you just tell me the rest of it?"

Callie balked at answering either of those questions. She felt like the runner caught between bases. Beebe's second set of caucus rules—or was it her third?—were pressing hard against the peculiar affinity she felt for Arnett.

Callie set the tone days ago out by Arnett's pool with her parting comment. The one that caused understanding to dawn on Arnett's face. The one that referenced a bond between the two women. Callie and Arnett arrived at Heatherwood sharing a secret—a secret they kept even from Jack.

Old Promises

Pressures of conscience mounted for Callie.

"What is it with you two?" Beebe's gaze ricocheted from Arnett to Callie. "You're looking pretty conspiratorial. You two get together and cook something up?"

Callie's loyalties were torn, but she remained reticent.

"Honesty reigns, Callie. All. Week. Long." Beebe closed one eye and turned the other to penetrate Callie's defenses. "Come on. Give it up."

Old promises caved. Callie shook her head at Arnett and shrugged the hopelessness of the situation.

"Arnett called me a week after Jack got home from the hospital." Callie no sooner spoke the words than Arnett groaned and caught her head in her hands. "She asked me to call back in a half-hour and she'd take the phone to Jack. She wanted me to ask him if he still wanted to live with me. She wanted me to convince him to move to my house."

Lizbeth's whole body jerked around to face her mother-in-law seated beside her. "Arnett," she gasped.

Arnett fell back against the couch, eyes closed.

"You didn't know?" Beebe rolled her eyes at Lizbeth. "Why am I even surprised?"

"I had no idea. Dan and Gary didn't either. Arnett, why?"

Arnett's eyes were open. Her lips parted. In her panicky state, she formed no words.

Beebe brought the line of questioning back to Callie. "Why call back? She already had you on the phone."

"So Jack would hear the phone ring."

A light dawned in Beebe's eyes. "Otherwise he'd know she placed the call to you. I guess I don't know the game of deceit quite as well as you two do."

Angry, Callie defended her actions. "It had to be convincing for Jack, and I don't think you ought to call it deceit until you've heard the whole story. At that moment, I thought Arnett committed the most selfless act any wife in her position could."

"If the younger other woman is defending the bitchy wife, then this is probably the story we came for, huh, Lizbeth?" Beebe pulled one meaty leg over the other and folded both arms across her chest. "I won't interrupt again."

Callie stared down Beebe's sarcasm. She wanted to feel mutual disrespect, but Beebe's scorn was warranted. And Beebe was right. The time had come to speak the truth.

"It's understandable that Arnett gets off the rails when she's around me. What Jack and I did was wrong. I've said that. Jack and Arnett had a bad marriage. I've said that. The boys talked Jack into moving back with Arnett after the surgery. Jack and Arnett didn't want that. Given her situation, that woman picked up the phone and called me, and I will forever be grateful."

Callie faced a jaw-hanging Arnett. "I'll be upfront. Your motivations were often blurry, but there was one part of your story that convinced me your heart was directing your actions." To Beebe and Lizbeth: "I visited Jack in the hospital the night before his discharge. He surprised me with the news that Arnett suggested he call me once a day. She volunteered to leave the house every day for thirty minutes, so he could make the call. I got the first few calls at the club. But Monday came, my day off. I was home. I expected him to call the house phone. But he didn't. He called my cell. It wasn't on." The pang of guilt she always felt when she thought of Jack's disappointment that morning pierced her again. "When Arnett got back, she went to his room. She asked and he told her I didn't answer. From some other room, she called me. She asked if I still wanted him to move in. Well, of course I did. Then she told me a few things. They'd made a follow-up visit to the surgeon. Jack wasn't eating; he was depressed. Very depressed. If he didn't snap out of it—well, his recovery was at stake. When Jack told her I didn't answer, she said he just pulled the bed covers over his head. I always thought that was so she wouldn't see him cry." Callie's voice faltered. She took time before continuing. "I'd been on edge for two weeks. Now I was frantic. I burst into tears. I hurt him. He must have thought I stopped caring. But that was the turning point. Arnett told me to get hold of myself, and call back. I couldn't believe what I was hearing." Arnett didn't look up when Callie spoke to her. "I really didn't think he'd agree. He'd been so willing to do whatever the boys wanted."

Callie wiped the wet from under her eyes. Etched in her mind was the memory of standing perfectly still in the center of her kitchen. The world stopped for a few breathless moments while she braved to ask Jack two questions. "I asked him if he loved me, and he said yes. Then I asked if he wanted to move to my house, and he said yes. That was the happiest moment of my life." Callie found Arnett looking at her. "It was the concern, the real concern in your voice when you said he pulled the covers over his head that told me some part of you wanted what was best for Jack."

Lizbeth slid out to the edge of the couch for a better look at Arnett. "But you let Dan and Gary—all of us—believe moving to Callie's was Dad's idea. He took the rap for you. They blamed their father entirely. They cut him off for over a month. No calls, no contact, no grandkids.

And you said nothing!"

Callie was as disheartened as Lizbeth when Arnett answered the charge by reducing her position to two baseline strategies that summarized so much of her life.

"I didn't want to be the bad guy in their eyes. John always protected me from that."

"That's all you have to say." Lizbeth glared at Callie. "And you're defending her?" Before Callie could answer, Lizbeth said, "She just didn't want Dad to die under her care. It was all about her. While Dad recuperated in your house, Dan and Gary pouted and sulked like little boys. I tried everything to get them to relent." Then her wrath returned to Arnett. "Why didn't you say something? That was precious time lost. Time sons should have spent with their dying father. You just let them suffer. All three of them suffered while you sat back and watched!" Lizbeth rose to tower over Arnett. "No," she said, "you will never touch my son."

Lizbeth's bluster rolled over Callie. When Jack's sons arrived to hear his decision to move, she hadn't known that their parents did not present a united front. But she should have suspected. Dan and Gary turned their backs on Jack. For weeks, she did her best to keep his hopes up, always feeling unequal to the task. Over on Brahms Way, Arnett skated through unscathed. Until now.

. . .

Beebe had to admit that her unbridled nosiness set off the catastrophe that chased Lizbeth into Baron. As Beebe drove the caucus, she was now behind the wheel of Lizbeth's Tahoe. She snatched Lizbeth's keys from her hand after she flew around the cabin, full of fury and flinging the F word.

The connection Lizbeth sheared off for Arnett without a second's thought was evidently a separation Lizbeth could not endure herself. Its effects crawled over her like a flesh-eating disease: Mother was driven to speak with son; Chad was the cure.

The job ahead of Beebe was to ease Lizbeth to an emotionally stable environment where she automatically reached inside herself for the strength she needed. Even an innocent four-year old would soon begin to feel the pressure his mother transferred to his small shoulders if she continually turned to him to soothe her rattled nerves.

Lizbeth was not ready to hear any of the counselor's rationalizations. At this juncture, forgiveness and acceptance were too much to ask of the woman who sat in the passenger seat, arms folded, mumbling to herself.

Beebe had not, in her wildest dreams, suspected a prior allegiance between Callie and Arnett. But, why the hell not? That secret was out, and quite frankly, its ragged truth snapped airtight into the rough chasm, gaping open, in this incredible story. It fit so perfectly that Beebe would walk over the passage without fear of tremor or collapse.

She pulled into the library's parking lot. Not that Lizbeth would go inside for a social media link, but simply because the library had become Lizbeth's standard place for communication home. Both women got out. Lizbeth's phone immediately chirped its shortcut tones. Beebe left her alone and strolled east on Armament through a residential area of older two-story homes surrounding an elementary school on a large lot, one side loaded with gnarly, brittle trees.

Along the way, she considered how Lizbeth was a casualty of her own peace summit. From there, the theme played out through a quote she read once: In war, patience is a weapon.

Beebe definitely had the war, but not the luxury of patience. That weapon lay outside her reach. She had the deadline of her own family situation bearing down. She hoped she wasn't too battle-weary when she arrived home in Michigan.

With forty-five minutes driving time in each direction, Beebe and Lizbeth walked back through the cabin door nearly two hours after they left. Arnett sat in the living room, *Redbook* in hand. Lizbeth stiffened and stared Arnett down. Callie would have gotten the same treatment, but her door was closed, and Beebe assumed she was behind it. Lizbeth announced her plans to take a sleeping pill. The haughty comment, directed at Arnett, let her know that the assurance of sleep would sever Lizbeth's connection to her mother-in-law if only for a little while.

Beebe heard Callie in the night. Sleepless again. She made chili and cornbread. Beebe was up at seven. The kitchen was clean, and the salt shaker anchored a note to the table. Her hackles went up when she read that Callie took off to play golf on "a course that Jack built." Callie encouraged sightseeing for her cabin mates, pointing to Sarah Prosser for suggestions and directions. With nothing to do but accept Callie's unauthorized absence, Beebe sighed, then went for a walk, searching for comfort in the mountaintop cemetery.

For the last two weeks, she hoped her father would open his house to her upon her return. She remembered trundling after him into a sea-level cemetery. Her earliest memory was being five years old and holding her father's hand. Stars twinkled above his head as she looked up to his long, lean face. His voice carried a melodious quality. There was nothing to fear in the cemetery. Instead of her father releasing her hand in order to close the cemetery's back gate, it was Beebe's hand that pushed open the front gate to her West Virginia refuge. There, Beebe was infused with the same satisfying peace that filled her every Monday morning when she stepped into the empty sanctuary of whatever church had been in her charge.

She moved forward slowly, awed by the visual image before her. Except for the green grass on which dewdrops frolicked in the shafts of sunlight straining through bordering pines, it appeared as if someone photo-shopped the scene to black and white. Beebe made two passes through the small graveyard. By the time she let herself out, she thought a day of sightseeing would distract her from the waiting. She spoke with Vincent the day before, outside the grocery store while Callie shopped. The anticipated fax should arrive any day.

On her downhill plod from the cemetery, it occurred to her that there was more at stake than a day of sightseeing. There was another gash to close between mother—and daughter-in-law before either would ride in the same car, nails retracted. Beebe considered different approaches. Nothing close to standard appealed as workable. But outlandish and startling—she'd give them a try. Going that route, she'd only get one attempt. She had to play it perfectly.

Beebe stood in the kitchen. She patted her pocket. Callie's note was inside. She picked up the two pans taken from the cupboard and banged their bottoms together until the racket brought Lizbeth and Arnett out of their rooms with looks of complaint on their faces. Both still wore nightclothes.

"Callie's AWOL," Beebe announced. "She left a note. She gave herself the day off and didn't consult me. Look, her SUV is not out there." She jerked her head toward the side window, adding fact to claim.

"What?" Lizbeth frowned, taking steps to peer through the window to the drive.

Yawning, Arnett came up alongside, stretching her neck, and concluding, "She is gone."

"We're going to find her." Beebe set the pans down. "Lizbeth, let me have your keys. While you and Arnett dress, I'll go to Sarah's and get some ideas about where she might go." Beebe wanted to go alone to Sarah's for the sightseeing directions Callie suggested come from her. Inside, she winced. She couldn't imagine extending this lie to Sarah.

"She's gone golfing," Arnett spouted.

Of course, Beebe thought, leave it to Arnett to be spot on the truth in seconds. Beebe moved with it. "Excellent. I'll get directions to the nearest course."

"Dad built courses around here. She'd go there."

"Right," Beebe agreed. Jeez, she thought. Her lies were steering both of them right back to the truth. She and Arnett trailed Lizbeth into her room. Her keys lay on the dresser next to her purse. "Callie talked to you, Lizbeth," Beebe went on, flattering the other woman with a feeling of importance. "Did you hear her mention something, anywhere else she might go?"

Lizbeth shook her head. "But why go drag her back? What purpose will that serve?"

"We had a process in place. She's no better than the rest of us," Beebe said.

"That's for sure," Arnett said. "Hey! She might be with Lucius. Remember, she ran off to pout that first night things didn't go her way."

"I'll ask Sarah where Lucius lives, but don't you think Lucius and golfing might be too obvious?" Beebe evaluated her words as merely a half-lie. She knew golfing was more than obvious.

"No," Arnett argued. "It's one or the other."

"But does Lucius golf?" Lizbeth asked.

"Don't know," Beebe answered gladly. Finally, a truthful statement.

"Let's not add Lucius into the equation. We're not even sure they're together."

Beebe groaned inwardly. Lizbeth was taking competitive potshots at Arnett's theory.

"But why go find her? And besides, I'm not sure I want to ride anywhere with her." Lizbeth wrinkled her nose at Arnett, as if an odor was set adrift from her direction.

Arnett drew her brows together and her mouth to a point. Before she spoke, Beebe said, "Callie thinks she's having a good time. And you're right, we can't literally drag her back, but we can dampen her fun. Why wait until she gets back to express ourselves? She got what she wanted by then. We'll say our piece and stomp off." She gave her head a firm downbeat to emphasize her determination on that point. "You'll want to be there for that."

"Yeah," Lizbeth said, "I do want to be there for that."

Lizbeth's animosity for Callie surfaced. She was still put out with Callie for sharing a secret with Arnett. Good, Beebe thought. She would pull this sightseeing lie together.

Arnett took it from there. "Hurry, Beebe, and get back." She was already moving toward the bathroom cut-through to her room.

"You guys, hurry. She's got a head start." Beebe pushed her speed to a fast walk as she crossed the cabin floor, buzzing away from the place where she constructed lie upon lie. Sorry, Callie, she said to herself, but sacrificing you was warranted. I promise to confess when the time is right. But you did skip out, and these two need a joint cause, some reason to try teamwork. She inhaled a fortifying breath. Dear God, let them find it today.

She latched the Tahoe's seatbelt and was adjusting the rearview mirror when the two women appeared at the SUV's front bumper. The morning sun glowed through their thin, cotton nightgowns. They bore contemptuous looks, then traipsed around to the driver's door. Beebe opened it.

Lizbeth spoke. "We don't believe a damn word you said."

Beebe's confession came earlier than anticipated. She got out, fished in her pants pocket, and produced Callie's note.

Lizbeth read it, then passed it to Arnett. "So, she really did go golfing. You knew that, and you knew where. Why the performance?" Lizbeth hooked a thumb toward the cabin. "Banging pans together. Why?"

Beebe took the few seconds necessary to close the Tahoe's door before she responded. "Because a day of sightseeing sounds great. Because I need a break. You need a break, but you two can't see it for your love of bickering and would never agree, so I lied. You drove me to it. You two can't listen to each other, or listen to me, or for that matter, listen to Callie. We can explain the past, rat each other out, and sail all the Sebring dirty laundry down the Cheat River. The past isn't going to change. It's the future you can change. From this point forward." She gave one of Arnett's deep-throated groans and actually felt better. Calmer, she said, "We've only got the one car. Let's flip a coin. One of you goes with me; one of you stays."

"Well, it's my car. I should really get to go."

"What about me?"

"Go next door to the O'Malleys—"

Beebe raised both hands. "Please, don't argue. Please. Don't. Argue. Please, get dressed, and let's go sightseeing. Can you do that? Can we act like grownups for just one day?"

Thirty minutes later, the three women consulted Sarah and chose an aggressive itinerary: Seneca Rocks, Spruce Knob, and Monongahela National Forest. They made the rounds in that order. The festivities resulted in ferocious appetites, three new Australian friends, and the recommendation to check out Cheat River Steak and Spirits.

Which they did. The restaurant's dining room consisted of dark paneling and low illumination. The carpeted floor was scattered with tables and a row of booths along an expanse of windows that overlooked the spotlighted river.

In a fifth or sixth repeated performance since their arrival nearly two hours earlier, an accented hail of "Aussie that!" went up. Other assembled guests raised their fists to paw the air and returned a chorus of "Aussie, Aussie, Aussie!" The gregarious Australian men coached the receptive diners with this response. Apparently, it was a standard cheer used at Australian sporting events. And so the party atmosphere continued. Beebe sat at the bar now with her back to the room. Had she not known better, she would have thought a squadron of Alaskan sea lions gathered to bark the chant.

The noise level fell, and Lizbeth slid onto a barstool beside Beebe. Tom, the bartender and proprietor, came over. He introduced himself to Lizbeth. Beebe made his acquaintance when he served her a Sam Adams. She found him irresistibly handsome because his eyes crinkled when he smiled.

"I just gotta have the story," he said. "What's the deal with you ladies and those Australians?"

To Lizbeth, Beebe said, "I'm guessing he can tell we just hooked up with those guys, what?" She looked at her watch. "Four hours and forty-seven minutes ago."

The Maryland women met the three older men at the stone entrance to the national forest. The women stopped to take pictures. So had the men. They were supposedly hikers on holiday. The six of them trooped around together for a while, enjoying each other's company. It was Arnett who issued the invitation to dine as a group. The food had been delicious, but the day and company were wearing thin. Beebe exited the booth under the guise of a ladies' room visit. A few minutes later, Lizbeth followed suit.

"My deduction is, you gals are on a retreat away from the husbands?"

"Boy, did you read that wrong," Beebe said.

Tom's face registered surprise. "You're available?"

And since he crinkled his eyes just-so, Beebe overlooked the way he poked his nose into her business and exchanged a glance with Lizbeth. "I guess so," she said.

Tom pointed across to the booth Arnett shared with the three Australians. "Her too?"

Upon meeting the men, Arnett became flirtatious, fun-loving, and the center of the Aussies' attention.

"Widow," Lizbeth informed Tom, defining Arnett's availability status.

His finger slid Lizbeth's way, and she dittoed her answer. "Widow."

He aimed at Beebe. She claimed, "Virgin."

Laughing, Lizbeth slung an arm around her shoulders. "Oh, Beebe, we could probably rectify that tonight if you're interested."

"Only if Tom's the rectifier," Beebe said, eyeing him deliciously.

Tom pointed to himself. "Married."

"As they say, the good ones always are." Then Beebe slapped the bar's surface with her next decision. "Tom, bring my friend a nightcap."

"Vodka and orange juice," Lizbeth said. "Heavy on the O-J."

"You got it."

A few minutes later, Tom left his station with drinks on a tray for another group. He rounded the end of the bar, and Beebe heard him call Callie's name. Beebe and Lizbeth turned. He pressed Callie into a one-armed squeeze and planted a kiss on her temple. She made eye contact with her two buddies on barstools.

"I heard you were here." In a softer tone, he said, "I'm so sorry about Jack."

"Thanks, Tom."

"Can I find you a table?"

"No, not tonight. I came in looking for my houseguests. You know you're a bad hostess when you have to go round them up."

Tom followed Callie's gaze to Beebe and Lizbeth. "These ladies are with you?"

"For the week," she chirped.

He walked her toward the bar while she placed her order. "Bring me a Perrier, would you, please?"

"Sure." He smooched her again. "Good to see you."

She smiled at him, then at Beebe and Lizbeth.

"You just getting back?" Lizbeth asked.

"Uh-huh. I saw the Tahoe." Callie's words trailed off. Beebe watched her slowly scan the restaurant. Small brass light fixtures with frosted globes hung at regular intervals around the room's two windowless walls. After one reminiscent trip, she ticked back to the present. "You guys have a good day?"

Beebe answered. "We did, although I really should skin you alive for your unexcused absence." When Callie's mortification lacked a full measure of sincerity, Beebe looked her in the eye. "That's the one you get," Beebe told her, meaning there better hadn't be a second time.

"So, how was the golf?" Lizbeth lightened the conversation.

"I got in twenty-seven. Played with the pro. It was tougher than I remembered. Where's Arnett?"

Callie still stood, so Beebe grabbed her left elbow and angled her toward the windows. "There, in that booth with the three men. She's wearing a baseball cap." On closer observation, she could've read the stitching on the hat. Bold, slanted letters formed AUSSIE THAT.

"That's Arnett? I can't believe it. The hat looks cute on her. She's laughing. She's a different person. I can't believe it," Callie repeated. "Who're the guys?"

"Australians from Sydney," Beebe supplied. "We met them at Monongahela State Park."

"National Forest." Lizbeth tweaked the name.

"I think both are correct," Callie said.

"They've taken a shine to Arnett," Lizbeth said. "We can't explain it."

"She's charmed them. We had a talk about Jack. She said she could always charm him back into her clutches."

Beebe popped her eyes at Callie.

"Well, clutches is my word, not hers."

"She's demonstrated her charm."

"Of course they are her age, not ours."

"Exactly." Lizbeth and Beebe bantered back and forth.

"I don't even think they've noticed we're gone."

"She hasn't stopped smiling since Mick put his hat on her head."

"Which one's Mick?" Callie asked.

"Gray hair. Across from her."

"You've got pictures?" Callie raised the question as if concrete evidence was an imperative.

Lizbeth snapped her fingers, simulating the many opportunities lost, then pointed at Callie and grinned. "Dozens," she said.

One of the Aussies motioned for Tom.

"That's Owen. Sportsman. Owned a fleet of ships. Resort fishing. Retired."

"How many drinks has she had?" Callie asked.

"Let's just say, she'll feel this tomorrow," Beebe said.

Tom swung by the threesome on his way behind the bar. "After this, I'm cutting them off. I've watered down the last two."

"We've got to get her home," Callie said, sounding concerned.

"Oh, Callie, you're just a potty pooper."

Two seconds of realization were followed by unrepressed giggles.

"Oops," Lizbeth said. "I meant party pooper."

"You're not driving," Callie said, decidedly.

When that round of giggles died off, Beebe said, "My mother always said, 'Laugh before breakfast, cry before supper.'"

Callie gave her a quizzical look. "You haven't even gone to bed yet. You're not driving."

Beebe shook her head. "I meant in the broader sense, taking the entire week into consideration. In that sense, we are still relatively close to breakfast." She counted the remaining time span on her fingers. "Five days to go."

"Hang on to the philosophical side," Callie said, then asked Tom for two orders of mozzarella sticks. "Some for here and the Aussies. My compliments." Her blue eyes passed from Beebe to Lizbeth. "I want you two sobered up. I'm going to need help with Arnett."

Callie's words sounded decades away. Beebe returned to the days of her youth. She hadn't thought of her mother's favorite ditty since she ran away. Now, her mother's memory was chipping its way back into Beebe's consciousness.

. . .

Callie pinned the heavily stocked brown grocery sack against her ribcage with one arm. With the other, she twisted the knob that got her back inside the cabin. Lizbeth stood in the doorway of Arnett's room, coffee cup in hand. Since Callie's departure for Cheat River General Store, Lizbeth had dressed and was ready to retrieve the Tahoe. It spent a sobering night parked in the steakhouse's lot.

Arnett's social evening provoked a black-bear hangover. Black bears were indigenous to the West Virginia wilderness, and they were killers.

Lizbeth pushed herself into motion toward the kitchen. Beebe, clothed in her striped nightshirt and terry robe, appeared next in the doorway. From somewhere in her past, Beebe learned how to concoct a Bloody Mary. It was her list of supplies Callie purchased from the overpriced general store a mile past Old County Road A.

Loudly so her words would carry, Lizbeth said, "Thanks for going, Callie. I doubt you'll get a thank-you out of Arnett."

"You're right. She won't," sailed out of the sick room.

Lizbeth gave Callie a gleefully mischievous look. "I never heard Dan speak of his mother as ever being tipsy."

Immediately, Beebe cut into Lizbeth's fun. "Now don't you two start anything that will ruin the progress we made yesterday."

"Ruin?" Arnett called in a worried voice. "Are they trying to ruin my hat?"

"No, Arnett," Beebe said consolingly, "your hat's right there on the bedpost."

"I know Jack never drank to excess," Callie said, "not since his college days, anyway. He claimed his lips got numb."

Callie watched Beebe working hers for a moment. "Numb lips," she said. "I'm trying to imagine that."

Lizbeth and Beebe pulled up on either side of Callie at the counter where she deposited the sack. "Here's the tomato juice, vodka, lemon juice." She extracted the items. "The store had Worcestershire sauce. I've already got pepper sauce." Lizbeth leaned her head back so Callie could open the cabinet door and pluck out the Tabasco brand. "There's celery in the fridge if a garnish is required." Callie dragged a loaf of bread and a box of teabags onto the countertop. "For toast if she feels better, and an herbal brew if that sounds good." She tipped the bag up. The last box slid out. "And saltines if she's pregnant."

Arnett was not amused. "I heard that. I am not pregnant. You're a couple of assholes."

Callie figured the last remark was intended for her and Lizbeth. On track with her accent, Lizbeth cheered, "Aussie that!"

"You two get out of here," Beebe said, pushing said assholes toward the door.

The words, "Stop messin'," rolled off Callie's tongue, surprising her. That's exactly what Jack would have said, she thought. With each additional day, he seemed to press closer and closer. She could feel him, in the cabin, at the restaurant the night before. Especially at the golf course. There, he seemed to walk in her shadow.

Peacekeeper

Callie and Lizbeth buckled themselves into the Santa Fe. When the road forked just past Sarah Prosser's condo office, Callie steered left. For all their high jinks back at Heatherwood, Callie and Lizbeth fell into an uncomfortable silence. Remnants of their last caucus rode in the space between them.

When Jack's post-surgical depression worsened and Arnett worked up the courage to telephone Callie, Callie was caught in a swirling updraft of quick-firing thoughts and feelings that day: her unbearable separation from Jack, Jack facing his mortality, the aggressive disease, its debilitating nature. She ached with his pain, and his fear. Pelted by such an emotional blitz, she uttered words into the receiver that seemed beaten into oversimplification. "Jack is such a special man."

"Yes. Yes, he is." Strangely enough, the tone of Arnett's response spoke volumes. Her voice listed toward a distant place in time, where more than a caring concern existed between Jack and Arnett. Where once, Callie thought, there had been love.

Lizbeth cleared her throat, interrupting Callie's reverie. "Since our last caucus, where I badly misbehaved," she admitted, "I keep returning to one thought: What if Dan died in the accident before he made up with his father? All these things Arnett does—manipulating people, protecting her image—can have real consequence." She shook her head. "I'm sorry Gary and Dan had to go through their parents' marital troubles. I am. But I look at Chad, and I'd rather he suffered his parents' divorce than his father's death. And Geoff. He still needs his father's influence. What gets me is that Gary, Dan, and I had this conversation. We knew after Dad recovered, he'd go right back to his old ways. Meaning you." She turned toward Callie. "While I was ready to accept it when Dad announced he would move in with you, Dan and Gary wouldn't. I was disappointed in Dan for that. He let Gary talk him into showing solidarity. Gary was arrogant enough to think Dad would stop seeing you if he asked him to stop. He wouldn't understand that you and Dad weren't having a fling. Twenty years is not a fling. He always got what he wanted out of his father; he would never stop asking. And of course, Gary thought he could convince Dad to live at home with Arnett because he convinced him to move back prior to surgery. So it was a blow when Dad chose you. God, he was angry. It took him a solid month to recover, and Dan hung with him."

Lizbeth fell silent for a moment. All Callie heard was the hum of tires on asphalt.

"I've seen a lot with the Sebring family, but Dad," Lizbeth said, "Dad was the peacekeeper."

Callie swung off the road onto the restaurant's gravel lot and rolled to a stop next to the Tahoe. Lizbeth's conclusion reminded Callie of her duty as Jack's stand-in.

"If I might step into the peacekeeper's role," she wondered politely. "You've acquired quite a bit of evidence against Arnett, evidence she won't want Gary to learn. You could probably keep her on track if you promised to keep those secrets, provided she followed your guidelines, quilt and all."

Lizbeth flipped her attention away. For a time, she studied her knees. Callie's strategic compromise required her to play the Sebring secrets game. Lizbeth was adamantly opposed to the game on general principle, Callie knew, but, in the short run, during this first year of grief, she and Chad would cope better with fewer changes in their life. Callie could attest to the wave of sorrow that would overtake her when the first anniversary of Dan's death approached. Progress would be lost, but Lizbeth would recoup and wade through a second year. There, Callie's prediction ended. She'd yet to complete her own journey. She didn't feel she ever would.

Without comment one way or the other, Lizbeth opened the car door and got out. She moved her purse from the floorboard to the seat and fished in an external compartment for her cell phone. She read the screen. "Damn this place with no reception."

"Use the restaurant's phone. It's not open yet, but Tom's in there. Let's knock." Callie jumped out of the SUV and came around.

"But the call's long distance."

"Leave him a couple bucks."

At the back door, they raised Tom easily. He gave them a cheery, "G'day, mates." Clearly, Australians make a lasting impression.

"Can we bribe you into letting us use the phone?" Beside Callie, Lizbeth snapped a five-dollar bill taut.

"Keep it," he said. "Car problems?" They dispelled that concern as he walked them to an alcove and pointed to a wall phone. "Be my guest."

"You calling Patrick?" Callie assumed.

Lizbeth lifted the receiver. "No, Maryland State Senator Amos Emerson," she said, the official's title tripping easily off her tongue. "I managed his local office in Cassel until Chad was born. There's a job waiting for me when I get back if I want it."

"You like politics, girl?" Tom exclaimed.

Lizbeth gave him a genuine laugh. "A steady dose, yes, I do. Back in college, I was a fast study. I crammed finance and investment, poli-sci, and American history into four years. Working for the senator, I have to admit I drew on every course taken." Callie and Tom exchanged looks that said each was a little more than impressed with Lizbeth Sebring. "But I haven't accepted the position yet."

That last sentence was added for Callie's benefit. Lizbeth wanted Callie to know Florida remained a clear-cut option. Callie managed to eavesdrop during Tom's recitation of his minestrone soup recipe. The soup headed the day's lunch menu. Lizbeth hung up after arranging an appointment with Senator Emerson for early next week.

The two ladies and the restaurateur made small talk for a few minutes around a butcher-block table overlaid with individual mounds of chopped celery, onion, and carrots. Cans of dark kidney beans waited at one corner beside a stainless steel bowl filled with curly macaroni.

Back outside, the women headed for the front lot.

"It was nice of Tom to let me use the phone."

"That's the first thing I'm going to do," Callie said. "Add a landline."

"Why? You rarely come—" A sharp intake of air sliced through her words. "Callie, are you staying?"

"Just wishful thinking," Callie said, waving away the thought she spoke aloud. "I was offered a job yesterday at Brier Hills." All bragging aside, Brier Hills Golf Course was the flagship of Jack's designs.

"Golf pro?"

"Uh-huh. And I'd need to learn the ski resort business."

"Sounds like fun."

"Yeah. But I can't accept it. I couldn't leave Petey," Callie said of Jack's stepmother.

"You and she have grown close?"

"We have a few things in common. Jack, of course, and sports. Her baseball. My golf. She's had a tremendously uncommon life. Her stories are fabulous. In her younger days, she was acquainted with baseball greats, old-time gangsters, and celebrities coming off vaudeville's heyday. I felt drawn to her after Jack died. I needed someone to talk to, someone who knew Jack. My family was gone. His family, well, you guys—"

"Did not receive you well." Lizbeth finished Callie's fledging sentence.

Callie shot her a look, surprised by how neatly she admitted a family shortcoming and, with the same words, reduced it to sounding like nothing more than a minor social blunder.

The two women arrived back at the SUVs. "The Brier Hills' offer is a pipe dream," Callie said. "Life will proceed in Cassel, the town with the Sebrings, in the house where I've lived my entire life." Shaking off a wave of melancholy, she said, "Anyway, I can't leave Petey. That would break her heart."

"Maybe I should take Chad to meet Petey," Lizbeth said in a transparently pot-stirring way. "He might enjoy her baseball stories."

When Arnett pronounced Petey severed from the family after she stood up against Arnett's harassing phone calls to Callie, that edict applied to all of Arnett's offspring and all of theirs. While a visit would have no repercussions on Petey, it would serve to further alienate Arnett.

Peacekeeping was one tough gig, Callie thought. Jack's ability to hold his family together gained her utmost respect. "Making contact with Petey might put a wedge between you and the family," she cautioned.

Lizbeth stood at the Tahoe's bumper. Red patches appeared on her cheeks. "When this week is through, Arnett isn't going to have control of my life, who I visit, or where I work or live. Arnett will be aware I have power and position over her." She squared her shoulders. "I'm feeling a group session coming on. The cheer for today: Caucus that!"

Five seconds later, she had the SUV fired up and in reverse.

. . .

Arnett waited to hear Beebe start her shower, then ran quickly through one in her own bathroom. Thanks to Beebe's nursing skills, she felt better. It had been decades and decades since she consumed too much alcohol. At the steakhouse last night, she became convinced of her immunity to a hangover. Age should count for something. That was probably the whiskey talking.

She hurriedly dressed, but did dally over brushing a woolen layer from her mouth. Arnett retrieved the Aussie cap and giggled out loud as she tugged it on. A picture of handsome Mick and his gold-flecked green eyes stepped forward in her mind. In her haste to sneak away, his small gift proved useful. It covered a rowdy group of lopsided curls. She picked and pulled at a few to give the navy hat a light-colored fringe. Only seconds were spared.

Almost an afterthought, she snatched her sunglasses from the dresser as she passed. When that first glimpse of nearly debilitating sunlight hit her irises on the porch, she was overjoyed to have them. She crossed to the steps. Inside, the sound of Beebe's hair dryer masked the creaks and squeaks of her unsupervised departure.

Riversong, the cabin next door, was her intended destination. Out on the road, she climbed the hill between Callie's cabin and the O'Malleys'. A posted sign near a narrow lane boasted the property's name. A thick curtain of trees, deciduous and evergreen, shrouded Riversong from the road—and a telephone line ran through them.

Lizbeth, given the opportunity to roam, would be sorely tempted to contact Gary and malign Arnett by detailing her conspiracy with Callie to extricate John from the family home. "Don't tell John we talked," Arnett said the morning she called Callie.

Gary and Dan asked too much after John's infidelity. They expected Arnett to nurse him to good health and inevitably right back into the Scottish Tart's arms. Initially, she wanted their adulation, but she couldn't keep up the pretense. So Arnett, the injured wife, walked her sons to their father's room, where John's sutured body took their blows. He could have Callie, she told John before their arrival, but he must deliver the news and be solely responsible for the decision. He kept that bargain.

Arnett felt her earlier nausea return as she strode from the cool tunnel of scented trees into the brilliant sunshine soaking the O'Malley's front yard. It was altogether possible that Lizbeth and Gary concluded their conversation. Gary might, at this very moment, be stewing over his mother's trail of secrets. Arnett could have possibly prevented that outcome more than once yesterday during the sightseeing tour. Lizbeth's demeanor, light and airy throughout, made her approachable, but Arnett chose not to drop to one knee and plead for mercy. She simply couldn't, not while a viable recourse remained open.

Arnett set that recourse into motion before she left for West Virginia. Back home, her attorney, Harlow Nolan, was preparing to petition the courts for her rightful involvement in Chad's life. If the summit's result was not to her liking, then the petition would be filed. In finest Oldstone tradition, her claim would be upheld, and the judge's verdict would not come wrapped in a quilt. Gary was unaware of her consultation with Nolan. Perhaps now was the time, especially if Lizbeth informed Gary of Arnett's previous infractions, to smooth that over somewhat by making a call to her son and sharing her legal plan of attack.

A series of concrete steps was cut into Riversong's mounded yard, each with a long run and a short rise, making the climb comfortable, no different than her success at the courthouse. Of that, she remained confident.

Riversong's front door stood open. Arnett knocked on the stained wood frame of the cabin's screen door. Through the mesh, she saw Timothy O'Malley striding her way. He had the appearance of a leprechaun. He was a slight sixty-year old with a fringe of reddish hair around his pink and liver-spotted bald dome.

"Good morning, Arnett," he said, pushing the door open. She stepped inside and was met by the tantalizing aroma of coffee and baked goods. "Eleanor was just wondering about you. I see you have a cap." He held his eyeglasses in his hand and pointed to the hat with a curved earpiece. The second earpiece was missing.

Arnett fingered the cap's bill. "I met some Australians yesterday."

"Aussies. Yes. Enjoyable people, I've always heard." His eyes were expressive, a pale blue under thin red eyebrows.

She followed him from the hardwood entryway to the carpeted living room stuffed with oversized furniture. Humungous lampshades hung over large bulbous glass bases on square tables squeezed into corners between a long sofa and upholstered chairs. Throw pillows in deep blue and rawhide tan picked up the room's colors.

Eleanor O'Malley, thick and buxom, rushed in from the next room. She stood nearly a head taller than her husband. "Arnett, I'm glad you've come. How are you?"

"I have a bit of a headache," Arnett said without supplying the alcoholic detail, "but I thought it would do me good to get out."

"I just picture you a prisoner over there. No car, strange place, and every one of them plotting against you. It must be intolerable."

"Oh, Ellie, she came for a visit," Timothy said. "Let's talk about pleasant things."

"Tim, look at her," Eleanor said, gesturing with an open palm. "She had to come in disguise."

With that reminder, Arnett removed her sunglasses, but left the hat in place.

"Oh, pooh," Timothy said to Arnett. "Tell Ellie she's exaggerating."

"Hush, Tim." Eleanor gave her guest a mournful look. "Are you missing that grandson? Do you want to check in? I swear our generation may have been the last sane group when it came to rearing children."

"That's not true," Timothy rebuffed.

"Well, it seems like it to me," Eleanor snapped, then revived a courteous tone for Arnett. "I've got fresh nut bread and coffee brewing. And some of those flavored creamers. We'll go all out."

Motioning Arnett to follow, Eleanor guided her into a bright kitchen where again the décor bordered on overcrowded. Against the wall sat a square cloth-covered table where the bread cooled on a wire rack. "The phone is still on the sun porch," she said, speaking over the coffeemaker's hiss. "Help yourself."

"I appreciate this," Arnett said. "You know what it's like to just need a small tether to someone at home."

"Home strings. That's what I call it. Join us in the front room when you're finished."

The O'Malleys' enclosed sun porch with its additional glass panels overhead seemed more like a greenhouse. The room boasted wicker furniture and a surround of window screens. Arnett winced at the swathe of sunshine and repositioned her sunglasses across her face. The old-fashioned black desk phone rested on its telephone bench just inside the room.

With her first look at the device, her heart beat wildly. Initially, she intended to phone Gary to see what stories Lizbeth might have put into his head, but at Eleanor O'Malley's suggestion, she thought she would try to speak with Chad first. That would settle her nerves. On the other hand, Chad's Aunt Debbie might have orders from Lizbeth not to let her calls through.

Arnett sat, punched in the Gibson's home number, and waited for Debbie to answer. She did not. Arnett lowered the receiver from her ear and studied it. There was something in the incessant ringing she found worrisome. That prompted her to dial Patrick's office. After two rings, she was relieved to hear Patrick introduce himself.

"Patrick, this is—" A recorded message interrupted the rest of her sentence. It said, "I'm out of the office today. Please leave—" Arnett pushed the plunger down and felt the blood drain from her face. "This has all been a hoax," she said under her breath. She put in a call to Gary. She endured four lengthy rings before her son picked up his office line.

"Gary, it's Mom," she drilled through the mouthpiece.

"Is everything all right?"

"I don't know."

"What's wrong? You okay?"

"Yes, I'm fine, I suppose."

"You suppose? Is Lizbeth treating you badly again?"

"Gary, it's not that. It's Chad. I just called Deb at home and Pat at his office. No one answered either place. I think they've taken him to Florida. Lizbeth has gotten them to sneak him down to her uncle's."

"Mom," Gary said, dragging out the word. Arnett could just imagine the accompanying eye roll over his droopy, dark mustache. "You're worrying over nothing."

"I don't think so. I know something's wrong."

"They've probably just taken Chad to the aquarium. He loves it there. He asks to go every other day."

"No," she said firmly, "not since Dan died, he hasn't."

"Okay," her son said, using an appeasing tone, "I'll check over at Patrick's tonight after work. I'm sure they'll be there. Chad's okay, Mom. Call me again tonight, or tomorrow."

"Lizbeth hasn't called you?" The words escaped her lips before she could pull them back.

"Now, why would she call me? I told her a week ago what I thought of taking you all the way to West Virginia. Why don't you let me come get you? I could drop everything and come right now, or first thing tomorrow. You choose."

"No, honey," she said. She was thankful Lizbeth hadn't phoned, but panicked at the same time. She couldn't leave for home and not know what else would pass between Callie and Lizbeth in her absence.

"Why would you stay? Lizbeth's threat is never going to take root. She won't take Chad away. She practically lives at the cemetery. I can't imagine her leaving."

"That's your brother's grave," Arnett said, suddenly angry at his insensitivity.

"Yes, Mom. His grave. Dan's not there. Dan would want us to take care of Chad. And see to Lizbeth."

Arnett, primed to agree with his sentiment, heard a familiar voice. She rose to peek around the corner. The layout of the cabin was such that she could see straight through to the front hall. Beebe Walker stood there, shaking hands with Timothy O'Malley. Then Eleanor O'Malley entered the picture. Another introduction was made.

Jerking back from view, Arnett promised to call Gary the next day. She laid the receiver in its cradle, then sucked in a rejuvenating breath. Breezing through the open corridor, she remembered to snatch the sunglasses off her face.

In the living room, the O'Malleys maneuvered Beebe to one of the champagne-colored chairs with wide, rounded arms. Timothy occupied the other. Eleanor sat across the way at one end of a sectional couch.

"Arnett," Beebe said merrily, seeing her, "there you are. I was beginning to think the Australians planted a homing device in that hat, then came back to whisk you away."

Those seated laughed. Arnett added a lackluster chuckle. "What an imagination."

Eleanor patted the cushion beside her. Arnett took the seat and pulled a brocaded throw pillow into her lap. She fiddled with a corner. The situation felt awkward in the extreme. It was like having your mother show up to share in the fun when you're at a friend's house, skipping school.

"Are Lizbeth and Callie back?" Arnett inquired conversationally. Secretly, she wanted a reason to break up the little foursome even if it meant a caucus loomed in her future.

"No, not yet." Beebe dashed Arnett's hopes. "And since that makes a little free time, and since I saw a whittled rainbow trout hanging on the cabin's sign just now, I'm wondering if you aren't a fisherman, Tim."

"I am," he professed gladly.

"I haven't fished since I left my hometown in Michigan."

"Is the river calling you?"

"Hardest four days of my life not to walk out into that water for a little fly-fishing." Then Arnett watched Beebe proceed to overact. The only male in the room was her audience. With her chin tucked to her chest, she shyly fluttered her eyelashes at Timothy. "But I haven't any tackle." She heaved a great sigh.

"I've got enough for the both of us. Let's go," Timothy said, bounding out of the chair. "Actually, the fishing is best off Heatherwood's dock."

"Then we'll go where it's best." Beebe was on her feet. "Ladies, you don't mind, do you?"

"Of course, they don't," Timothy answered for Eleanor and Arnett. He took Beebe's elbow and led her to the door. "They have a hen party planned, anyway. Hens stay cooped up. Fishermen get out-of-doors." Arnett thought it was ludicrous how the little man paused to thump his chest. Then his tone changed to regretful. "I've been too gender-specific. What would you be? A fisherwoman?"

"How about lady-fisherman?"

"Sounds like a British title of sorts: Lady Fisherman."

"Tim. You're a funny man," Beebe said, stepping through the door he held open.

Eleanor was left dumbfounded. Arnett didn't think she had anything to worry about, but that scene was a perfect example of just how easily a husband could get stolen.

Hollowed-Out Dream

Lucius paced the Bullwhip cabin's living room. Every three seconds, his gaze shot to the working laptop, resting on the coffee table. The long-awaited message indicator finally appeared on the display. After a few keystrokes, a living, breathing bust shot of his beloved appeared on the screen. He sent the image to the cabin's forty-four-inch plasma above the stone fireplace and opposite the black leather recliner where he perched.

"Why the big screen, Lucius?" The question came in response to an earlier email requesting the video conference. The question also projected a hint of annoyance Lucius rarely heard in Willie's voice.

Willie Thorne—tall, dark, and business-class handsome—sat with his forearms on the walnut table in his Cassel conference room.

Lucius slid back into the recliner and cocked his head. "I guess I requested the big screen because I didn't get my fill of you last weekend, snookums." Inwardly, he flinched at the bogus-sounding remark. He shut down his smile, straightened his spine, and started over. "Actually, I need to see your face when I tell you this."

"Tell me what? What's wrong?" Willie asked, concerned.

"I'm worried about something: We have a life dream, don't we?" He posed the question using the term Lizbeth coined at the depot

Monday.

A look of bewilderment fled onto Willie's face. "A life dream? If you mean a commitment? Yes. Forever."

Lucius shook his head.

Narrowing his eyes, Willie repeated, "Lucius, what's wrong?"

"I'm talking about our life dream." Lucius gestured around him to the West Virginia cabin he overhauled from early hunter to classy rustic male. "I'm here. You're not."

"Oh, the cabin."

"You make it sound insignificant. It's not for me."

Willie remained absolutely still for a beat. "It's not for me, either."

"Good. Then make the move. Sell the house to that man who made the offer and get your sweet caramel butt to Baron."

"I can't. Not quite yet. Lucius—"

Lucius cut him off. "I'm here, building this for us with my own two hands."

"I help those two extremely talented hands every time I'm there."

"Oh, please, Willie, you pick color swatches." Frustrated, Lucius got up.

"Lucius, sit down. All I see is the recliner."

Lucius paced another few steps, then slid back into the picture frame. "I don't want to lose our dream before you've even arrived to live it. The best part of the dream is being here together. I don't want something to happen—to me, to you—before we have our chance. God—" Biting off the rest, he ran his hand through his hair, then jumped to his feet.

"You're out of the chair again."

"You mean, your recliner." Lucius tipped his head down within camera range. "The recliner I bought for your forty-fifth birthday last March. It's here. You're not." He came around and flopped onto the soft leather.

Suddenly, Willie sat back and propped an elbow on the chair arm.

He wore a thoroughly satisfied expression, the one that said he could read Lucius like the financial pages. Lucius found it comforting. Despite the miles, he felt their souls snuggle up close.

"Oh, Lucius, you've gotten yourself wrapped up in those women." Willie's eyes twinkled. "Tell me what's going on."

Lucius took a moment to arrange his thoughts. "I've known Callie since we were fourteen. She's always been tough. Strong-minded. She had a plan, and she held it together even though Jack was married. Then she got her chance, their dream. It lasted less than three years and part of the time, Jack was recovering from surgery and chemo, then a stretch at the end when the cancer came back. She has suffered so much with his loss." His words faltered, mired in the hopeless feeling that overcame him every time his heart went out to her.

"She loved him," Willie said in snapshot summary.

Lucius wanted to remind Willie of their love. In comparison, he waited in West Virginia nearly two years. But instead of rehashing, Lucius eased the point of his call forward.

"I can't help but think that if they had more time together, if their dream hadn't been cut short, it would have made a difference. To finally get what she wanted, then lose it so quickly. She's got her whole life ahead of her. Then, there's Lizbeth. She lost Dan in one day. They got out of the same bed one Saturday morning for the last time. She was never going to lay down beside him again. He's gone, and all she can think about is the dream they had after college that never happened and is never going to happen. Regret is tearing her up. She's trying to find a way to fulfill the dream now. It's too late. It will never be the same. Dan's not there. Someday, she's going to realize that all she's got is a hollowed-out dream."

Willie knew the particulars on Callie, but not Lizbeth. When he asked, Lucius filled him in on the idea for multi-storied murals that in Lizbeth's mind crossed over to comprise her husband's landscapes. He told Willie about the partnership Lizbeth foresaw with her Tallahassee uncle and the impression he had that money was the concern. Professional daycare would cut into her income, but her mother-in-law's free services would not. He didn't forget her older son at the University of Florida, another reason to draw a mother south.

"Willie, the point is, your business can be run from here. Your office is almost done. I can push it. Two weeks is all I need."

"You've got the depot still."

"Then you could rent an office in town for a short while, but at least you're here. By the first of the year, your office upstairs would be ready." Willie nodded agreement. Lucius allowed hope to rise.

"The first of the year is a goal I'm going to strive for. But," Willie said, shifting in his seat, "I've got a new wrinkle here."

"What now?" Lucius's hope took a nosedive.

"Isabelle. She just told me. That's why it took me so long to call. Vance is being transferred. I've got her until the end of the year. After that, they move to Seattle. To make Baron work, Lucius, I've got to have an office manager here."

Isabelle York, Willie's longtime employee, was intelligent, trusted, and well-compensated. Her husband was Vance.

"Most of my clients are here. I'll need someone in the office for a while yet." He laced his fingers. "You know, that was always the plan: someone capable and an office with a video feed."

Willie's calm festered inside Lucius until it catapulted him out of the recliner. He heard Willie's tone change. "Okay, I'm talking to the chair again. Lucius, damn it, come back."

Lucius's forehead was pressed against the cabin's front door. Eight, nine, ten. He inhaled deeply, then returned to his seat.

"I'll double-time it," Willie said. "I promise. But someone needs to be trained, and I need to get it done while Isabelle's still around to help."

"What about Fran?"

"Fran's a great assistant, but she's not a manager. She'll be an asset, but she's not the answer."

Lucius slumped in the chair, pinned his chin to his chest, stretched out his legs, and stared at his work boots.

"Look at me," Willie said. "Tell me you understand."

Lucius raised one eye to Willie. "I understand."

"I can't bungle this. Who this new person is, is critical. I can't be in Baron and not know the person running the office in Cassel. I need to advertise the position, locally, and in trade magazines. I always wade through a two-interview process with a background check in between for successful candidates. Sometimes, three interviews, then make the offer. All the while, Isabelle's departure looms and time for adequate training slips away. You know, I trust Isabelle. Yes, if Isabelle stayed, I'd make the move. You're right; I should be there. With you. But by the time my office was ready, I'd be right back here in the thick of hiring, interviewing, and training four days a week. It would be exactly as it is now. Four days in Maryland. Three days in West Virginia. On top of that, there's the house to move. We haven't talked about that. What's here is pretty much all excess. You've got the cabin furnished. We're set there."

While Willie rambled, Lucius's thoughts ran off on tangents. Two years ago, Lucius took on an assistant. Darren Engle stole nearly a thousand dollars' worth of tools the first time Lucius left him alone at a job. Lucius developed a trust for the man, was fooled, and got burned. Other people's money: that was a huge responsibility. Safeguards were crucial in Willie's profession. Lucius understood that. Willie understood it better. Lucius could almost feel the guilt creep up, just thinking about the possibility a security breach remotely associated with Willie being rushed too quickly into a move.

Typical for Willie, his ramblings were a verbalization of his thoughts jelling into a forecast for a committed strategy. That was more than half the battle with his beloved. If the house sold, the standard thirty days given to vacate the premises would coincide with the critical time

Lucius must devote to the depot's final punch list. Timing and weather were a problem. He wanted all the outside work completed before the weather turned. The platform wasn't finished. A temperature drop would prevent the very necessary application of a weather sealant to the wood.

The depot's dedication by the town fathers was just six weeks away. If Willie asked him to help arrange an auction of household goods, Lucius would feel the bind. Selling a house and training a replacement had a punch list, too. Neither could Lucius bungle the depot restoration. After that, he'd get busy and finish the cabin. It looked like Lucius's and Willie's schedules would come together the first of the year, a reality which Willie repeated right on cue.

"First of the year, it'll be you and me in Baron."

Lucius smiled. They were in absolute synch.

"I'll need to make frequent trips to Cassel, though. Don't forget about that. Gradually, it can be done. I can operate fully from the cabin. Hell, my clients retire and need to communicate from Hilton Head, Martha's Vineyard, the south of France. No reason my setup can't be in that cabin."

"It'll work fine," Lucius said with cheer he now felt.

Willie's response used a softer tone. "I'll be there, Lucius. I promise."

Lucius knew that assurance was fully underwritten with affection.

Willie grinned. "And I want a bloodhound to sit at the foot of my chair."

Lucius didn't think he was serious, but with Willie, one never knew.

"Oh, another thing: With Isabelle's bombshell and other things I need to get going, I won't pull in until Saturday."

Lucius's shoulders slumped. "Not Friday? We've got our dinner party with the ladies?"

"Tell them Saturday. Extend my apologies. I'll make it up to you, sweetness. You know I will." He gave Lucius his best naughty look, the one that made Lucius's socks roll up and down.

"Oh, Willie," he cooed, "behind closed doors."

. . .

Thirty minutes later, Lucius pulled into Heatherwood's drive and got out of the truck. Both vehicles were gone, but he took a chance someone was there to receive the change in plans for the dinner party. He cleared the corner of the cabin, ready to mount the steps, and saw Arnett angling through the yard toward the dock. Oddly enough, she wore a baseball cap. Her nose was tipped to several sheets of paper. Then he saw another odd sight planted in the river. Pleasantly plump Beebe Walker and—as he looked closer—tiny Tim O'Malley from next door were each wearing rubber waders and casting fishing lines into the shimmering water.

Lucius hustled around the porch to intercept Arnett. "What you got there, jellybean?"

She stopped short, clamped the papers to her chest, and then after a second, relaxed her hold. "A fax for Beebe. I was just taking it to her. It must have been delivered while we were out. It was there on the table, under the vase." His gaze followed hers back to the porch. "I was going inside when I saw it."

She was jabbering, trying to make her actions appear quite innocent, but she provided too much information, as a guilty party would. Lucius cut to the chase. "And you sneaked a peek, didn't you, Arnett?" He bounced on his heels. He would bet Willie's new bloodhound she found and read Beebe's anticipated employment agreement. "Where's the envelope it came in?"

"There wasn't one."

They eyed each other suspiciously, but she told the truth. The pages showed no sign of folds, even though Beebe told him in the cemetery

Sarah would fold the fax into an envelope for delivery.

"Let me take it to her." Hand out, he took a step forward. As if timed to music, she took a step back.

The grin of a Cheshire cat crossed her face, and she waved the pages. "You already knew about this employment contract in Larkspur, Michigan."

"Yes, I knew, and I'm going to be honest with you, Lizbeth and Callie do not. Beebe's worried how they'll take it. She wants to tell them herself, but not before whatever time is needed is given to fixing things between you and Lizbeth. It's to your benefit, and Chad's," he added, pointedly, "to keep it under your hat." He smiled when her eyes rolled up.

"You think I see this as ammunition?" she said.

"I think leverage might be a better word." Given the right circumstances—for instance, to get the spotlight off Arnett, Lucius thought, she would spout out Beebe's plans in front of the others. Lucius didn't think Beebe could be bribed if Arnett went to her privately to strike a deal. Beebe would just make her announcement prematurely. Arnett owned a streak of meanness. Confidences were only kept if the keeping was beneficial to Arnett. Arnett's mind had just worked out the same scenario.

"I'll keep her secret," she hissed her chosen word, "because I'm worried she'll change her mind and not go if I get in the middle. I know when to stick to the sidelines. Thanks for the info, Lucius. This has made my day." She passed the pages.

Holding them, he couldn't help but notice the large, centered type at the top of the facsimile cover sheet. Just one word. Crossroads. It aptly summarized most people's lives, and it was the name of the organization run by Vincent Bostick.

He heard tires crunching gravel and looked around. The absent SUVs returned. Callie and Lizbeth were out quickly and coming his way. Hastily, he folded the pages down and slipped them into his back pocket. Giving Arnett a wink, he touched an index finger to his lips. He knew she understood his sign language because she gave him a rebellious look.

Lizbeth caught sight of the activity in the river. A brief word passed between her and Callie. With loping strides, Lizbeth headed down to the riverbank. Lucius took up the chase. Callie and Arnett fell in behind. By then, Beebe and O'Malley were coming in.

"Don't get behind me, Tim," Beebe laughed. "If I rock backwards, I don't want to take you out." She took a few tentative steps, using her arms to maintain balance. "Boy, this was a lot easier when I was a child. Which is to say many, many pounds lighter." She laughed again.

Lucius and Lizbeth met her at the shore and hauled her in. While river water still streamed from Beebe's over-the-knee boots, Lizbeth said, "I need a conference. I've got something for today's group."

Beebe's eyes darkened to serious. She waddled around Lucius and took Lizbeth under her wing. "Scatter, everyone," she said. "Give us some space."

Lucius waited around until the huddle between Beebe and Lizbeth ended, then he got five seconds alone with Beebe on the porch. He changed the dinner invitation at Bullwhip from Friday to Saturday while he helped her pull off her waders.

When she was again in pink clogs, she said, "You can't stay for the caucus, Lucius."

"I know," he said quietly, looking around. All appeared safe, so he slipped the folded pages from his jeans pocket. "The fax arrived. Arnett had it when I got here. She read it." He watched Beebe's face show signs of concern. "She said she'd keep the contents to herself. Will she?" He shrugged. "She's Arnett." Lucius pecked her cheek and headed for his truck.

. . .

Lizbeth led Beebe to her bedroom. They stood between the bed with its yellow corduroy spread and the small dresser beneath the window. The top drawer was open. Lizbeth scooted aside nylon underpants and nightgowns. She extracted a file folder containing evidence she brought from home, evidence that would unmistakably make her case.

"This is what I was telling you about outside," Lizbeth explained. She handed the file over for Beebe's review.

"Okay. But remember this, judgment without mercy is nothing of which to be proud." Beebe put up a hand to silence Lizbeth's comeback. "I say that for guidance sake, not for response. Take a moment to reflect on that. Arnett is a person with feelings." Beebe handed the file back, then walked to the end of the bed. "I don't like seeing you this way. You booked this as a peace summit. At your behest, we all took an honesty pledge. And, yes, I think for full disclosure, this needs to come out. Just take care with how you present it. That's all I ask."

"But you saw her in Callie's front yard and with the vase." Lizbeth jabbed her finger in the general direction of the porch.

Beebe bobbed her head. "You've got the upper hand already. There's no reason to grind her into the dirt. Present the facts calmly. Wait for a response. And above all, leave an opening."

"For what?" Lizbeth said, puzzled.

"For healing. The purpose of the quilt. That was your original reason for having one sewn for Arnett." Beebe had the doorknob in her hand. She swung the door wide. Callie and Arnett waited. "Let's take seats. We're ready to begin." Beebe crossed to her chair at the head of the coffee table.

Lizbeth arranged her papers on the table behind the couch where Callie sat. Arnett occupied the other. Lizbeth remained standing, using the sofa table like a short podium, considering which of her secrets to reveal first. It made sense to follow chronological order.

"Arnett, in deference to our honesty pledges, I want to ask you a question. It just occurred to me that you may not be aware of the information I've learned." Lizbeth slid Beebe a look and received tacit approval for her cushioned approach. "I assumed from the first, you did. I may be wrong." She took a breath. "Do you know the name Ruth Parker?"

Arnett's eyes widened, her cheeks paled. Suddenly, words burst from Arnett's mouth. "Where did you hear that?"

Good, Lizbeth thought. First hurdle crossed. She didn't deny it.

Callie sat with her back to the couch arm to keep Lizbeth in view. "Who's Ruth Parker?"

Watching Arnett, Lizbeth answered Callie. "Dad's first wife." From the file folder, she passed Callie the duplicate marriage license she obtained. It represented a time when photostatic copies were white on black. "Dan knew nothing about his father being married before. Why the secret?"

"It wasn't a secret," Arnett said too quickly. "I never denied he'd been married before. Once we were married, there was just no reason to bring up the past. Why bring it up now?"

"Because it's a sin of omission, Arnett."

Arnett turned quickly to Beebe. "Are those your words?"

"No, Arnett, they're my words," Lizbeth said, drawing her mother-in-law's fire.

"How did you find out about Ruth?"

"Quite innocently. My cousin's hobby is genealogy. She was researching both sides of the family for Geoff and Chad. She found it. Of course, I claimed ignorance." Lizbeth threw open her palms. "No family keeps secrets like the Sebrings keep secrets."

Casually, Callie raised one finger in the air. Beebe called on her. Callie glanced up to Lizbeth. "Could I just jump in here?"

"Sure. Jump away." She gave Callie a double-take. "Did you know about Ruth?"

"Just a minute, Lizbeth." Callie twisted head, shoulders, and her still-pointing finger toward the other couch.

Arnett glared back defensively. "What did John tell you? He gave me his word."

"And he kept it," Callie said.

"Then who told you?" Arnett gasped, assuming. "It was that old loon, Miss Petey."

Beebe spoke Arnett's name and gave her head an infinitesimal shake, chastising her for name-calling.

Lizbeth whipped around the end of the couch and sat down next to Callie, who pressed on. "According to Petey, yes, there was Jack's divorce." She interrupted herself to scratch an ear. "And there was Arnett's annulment."

Every eye darted. Arnett should have felt as pierced as Callie's pincushion. The desperate look on her face told Lizbeth the accusation was true. She glared at the woman who was so full of bluster concerning her husband's hidden life with another woman, but who'd built her own family life on a foundation of secrets. The scheming hypocrite, Lizbeth thought.

"There's more," Callie said, fiddling absently with the ring on her index finger. "The reason Petey gave me this history lesson—and it came after Jack died—was really to make another comparison entirely." She shifted in her seat to face Arnett. "You broke up Jack's marriage with Ruth, so you could have him."

"Arnett!" Lizbeth said, stunned.

"None of this is true," Arnett argued.

"Oh, I think it is," Callie said calmly. "You stole him away and consummated your relationship by pointing a gun at his head. You called that love, and then had the nerve to fuss and fume when I committed the same act—minus the weapon. The difference now being, you, not Ruth, lost Jack. I still can't believe you didn't suspect after nineteen years. If I was the Scottish Tart, what did Ruth call you?"

Silence spun through the room. On its tail, another point registered.

"Arnett, a gun? All these years you had your grandchildren in the house with a gun?" Lizbeth's shock drove her voice down several decibels.

"What's wrong with that? I grew up with guns in the house."

"Do you still have it?"

Lizbeth watched Arnett consider her options, but it was Callie who answered.

"She still has it. Or at least she did when she caught Jack and me at the driving range. Jack mentioned it. He was worried she brought it. My concern was, he had to go home to a woman who was angry and armed."

Beebe rocked forward, her forearms crossed over her lap. "Arnett, you would be willing to dispose of the gun," she said in an affirmative tone. "I can see the suggestion coming, and I would agree that our negotiations should come to an end if you don't concede on this point, right here, right now."

In Lizbeth's mind, memories roiled. John Sebring commented offhandedly about Kentucky Oldstones, back-alley justice, and how they got things done. She opened her mouth, but Beebe waved her quiet.

"I certainly have no problem disposing of the gun. With John gone, I don't know who I'd shoot with it anyway." Her coffee-brown eyes held a mischievous glint she cast at Callie.

"Good. A decision made. Let's move on," Beebe said.

"Wait." Lizbeth, not so quick to cap the problem, said to Callie, "What's the story about Arnett pointing a gun at Dad?"

Lizbeth held one finger to her temple in disbelief while Callie filled everyone in.

"Well," Lizbeth began, "since Callie's and Dad's secrets are out in the open, and now yours, that just leaves mine." She watched surprise flutter across Arnett's face, then she reached around to pluck the next sheet of paper off the table. "Both Dan and I were married before, too."

"What are you talking about?" Arnett argued. "Of course you weren't."

Laying a marriage certificate on the coffee table, Lizbeth said, "Yes, we were. Four months before the wedding you arranged, we married *each other* in Harmony, South Carolina, on our graduation trip."

Arnett's eyes dropped to the original certificate. "Why didn't you tell me? This makes me look foolish, planning another wedding."

"Dad knew. He told us not to tell. Mother's privilege."

"Mother's privilege?" She blinked. "What's that supposed to mean?"

Lizbeth basked in the glowing confusion emanating from Arnett's face and felt the strength that came with an exchange of power. "Mother's privilege was my indoctrination into the family, although it was a concept in place long before I heard it. I suppose it was the closest thing to hypnotism I ever witnessed. Dad said the words and whatever he decided would keep peace in the family, his sons went along with. From Dad's view of the world, you being left out of your son's South Carolina wedding would *not* have been peaceful."

"You're making this up!"

"Do you think I have some kind of perverse creativity? Just say mother's privilege to Gary."

"Just a minute," Beebe intervened. She flipped back through the pages of her tablet. "Mother's privilege was something Jack set in motion? That's what you meant by 'under-the-table control'."

Lizbeth gave Beebe a satisfied smile.

"But Arnett can't be held responsible," Beebe said. "She was unaware—"

"That's the point. She was unaware because she was the cause." Lizbeth snapped her head toward Arnett. "He had to intercede and do whatever would keep you at low tide."

"That's enough, Lizbeth." Beebe's voice was stern. "Move on."

Lizbeth's mouth opened, primed to respond, when Arnett sprang to life, working her way forward on the sofa. "It wasn't right that these things were kept from me. I should have been told. Damn John. Damn him. Most of this is his fault. He's to blame."

"There's enough blame to go around," Lizbeth returned. "You'll be shocked to know that I blame you for Dan's death."

Arnett's eyes flew wide. She sucked in a long, deep breath. "How can that be true?"

"If you hadn't played on Dan's sensitive nature, he wouldn't have taken the job at Oldstone Manufacturing and we'd have spent our lives in Florida. Then Dan wouldn't have been sitting under that tree, carving out time on a Saturday to paint. We'd have been in business with Uncle Ralph, using Dan's artistic talent to make a living. We made all the arrangements that June after college. On the way back, we were married, then we had to wait for mother's privilege and a second wedding we didn't need."

"I am not to blame. You cannot blame me for Dan's death. It's not true. It's not!"

Quickly, the grief counselor lay her tablet on the coffee table and went to Arnett, whose eyes still blazed. "I think this is enough for one day," Beebe said, patting Arnett's hands, clenched in her lap.

Thoroughly satisfied with the impact her revelations had on Arnett, Lizbeth offered no objection.

Beebe rose, got Arnett on her feet, and walked her out to the porch. As the two women disappeared from the narrow view Lizbeth had through the screen door, Lizbeth processed an odd, indescribable sensation. During its short life, Lizbeth saw herself in Florida. Ruse became reality.

Face in the Window

Beebe lay in bed, staring into the darkness. Her bedroom window was open. The crickets chirred. They couldn't sleep, either. Her mind spun ever since Lucius laid the folded pages of the faxed employment agreement across her palm. Not until then had she fully embraced the reality of going home. Every moment since was either shot through with euphoria or trembling fear. Above it all, she felt a strong, sudden kinship with Jack Sebring. She thought God inserted her among these three grieving women to glean a useful message from their experiences. She listened intently, took copious notes, dissected every discussion, and yet, it was Jack who rose up in her mind, bearing inescapable parallels.

Her brain couldn't seem to shut down replay of a film clip. The scene began each time with Jack loading a scanty supply of personal belongings into a car trunk. Jack stepped out of the framed portrait on the cabin's entryway table. He accomplished his work in a white shirt and Santa tie.

The trunk lid closed, and the story jumped ahead. The road to Callie's house was not paved with unbridled elation. Beebe had omniscience enough to appreciate Jack's post-surgical movements in the garage as protective against weakness and pain. She also clearly understood his worries. He became a wanderer in his own life, jostled between two women, between home and apartment, now to reside in his lover's house. Beebe was little more than a vagabond herself, going from church pastor to grief counselor to community center spiritual assistant, her newest and longest title.

Aside from their pillar-to-post existence, Jack and Beebe also shared the fellowship of rejection by family. Surely that wound gouged Jack more than the lengthy incision or the invasive disease. His sons rejected him openly, while Beebe was never sure her father understood that his attitude, more than his actions, built the barrier between them. For both Jack and Beebe, another woman was involved. Perhaps more from Gary than Dan, his sons' rejection of him was tied to their loathing for Callie. Beebe's father's rejection of her was tied to her absent mother.

Beebe's facial features favored her mother's and fueled her father's behavior. Cliff Walker couldn't bear to look at his daughter. Every time, he saw his wife, and he hurt. He hurt, Beebe thought, because he still loved Abigail Walker. According to Vincent Bostick, Abigail's personal possessions remained closeted in Cliff's Larkspur house.

There in the dark, Beebe attested, on Jack's behalf, that a combination of rejection and change breeds a pesky form of doubt. Jack, through the sheer strength of will she knew the man possessed, fought that uncertainty.

Beebe threw the covers off and switched on the bedside light. Her portfolio rested on the nightstand. The contract was closed inside. Grabbing the portfolio, she used it, her lap, and the pen clipped to the week's notes to sign the agreement. She pressed firmly, making wide, bold strokes, wishing her signature included an *i* to dot or a *t* to cross.

She looked at the clock. At two-sixteen, she slew an attack of emerging doubt. Now there was nothing left, but to anticipate the drive to Michigan. Arrival in her hometown would launch another story.

Dousing the light, she settled back under the sheet. Sleep evaded her, still. Her mind moved on. It conjured up Jack's arrival at Callie's house. Callie met him in her driveway. He returned her smile, broad and sincere, but Callie didn't see his wince of pain when her welcoming hug came too strong for sore ribs.

Replay after replay, trip after trip with Jack, Beebe felt sufficiently girded. She would cross her emotional battle line at the outskirts of Larkspur. Everything beyond that last curve into town remained a blur.

One thing was clear: God called her home to ease truth into the light and into her father's heart. Her mother's rightful name should mark the grave in which her earthly shell lay. After the revelation of truth would come the healing. Truth and healing followed Jack into his life with Callie. Truth and healing were two ideals woven into the fabric of the West Virginia summit.

Despite the wakeful night, Beebe rose energized. She dressed and went outside to Heatherwood's porch. There was nothing else to do with Thursday's early morning view but inhale its glory. The rising sun shone as a golden outline around the distant treetops. In the foreground, the river was the only measure of haste as it flowed through the pines. She filled her lungs and stored the memory. She pulled the hood of her lightweight sweatshirt up, then headed out to faithful Old County Road A and a downhill walk to Sarah Prosser's office. There, she'd fax the signed employment contract back to Vincent.

. . .

Callie stared across the Cheat River, tears streamed her cheeks, bare feet dangled in the water beneath Heatherwood's dock. Her bout with overwhelming sorrow descended quickly. Her shoulders shuddered with her silent sobs.

"What's wrong?" Lizbeth's jarring steps vibrated through the wooden planks.

By the time Callie's two index fingers wiped the wet from her face, Lizbeth was squatted beside her and digging in her purse. Callie took the tissues Lizbeth offered and held them first against one eye, then the other. Not since the night Jack died at home in her arms, had anyone but Beebe, in her counselor personae, witnessed such a meltdown. Callie intended her grief for Jack to be a private matter as her life with him had been.

Lizbeth filled the time Callie needed to gain control by making herself comfortable against the wooden mooring post. She sat angled, her long legs stretched out behind Callie.

"Whoever coined the phrase, broken heart, certainly got it right," Lizbeth said. "All that is death, loneliness, and grief seems to emanate from right here." Callie looked over. Lizbeth raised her closed hand to her striped shirt. "I never imagined such an ache was possible."

Callie decided to tell the story that brought the tears. Lizbeth would understand. Grief was a changeling that secretly ran their world. One moment, it produced Callie's tears; the next, it took the form of Lizbeth's heartache.

An old, old Agatha Christie paperback lay beside Callie on the dock. She found the book earlier in a bedside drawer. Shifting the damp wad of tissues to her left land, she lifted the front cover and withdrew the folded piece of paper she handed to Lizbeth. She carefully opened the four-by-five sheet torn from a page-a-day calendar. An Oscar Wilde quotation had been memorialized on a Wednesday in April four years before.

Callie watched Lizbeth's eyes skip across the favored quote: "If you are not too long, I will wait here for you all my life." Lizbeth took a moment to absorb the meaning, then angled the page to read a note added in the corner. There, Jack penned: "This is me loving you."

The Oscar Wilde quote spoke to Jack, and then the two men in tandem to Callie. The quotation underscored Jack's enduring love and devotion.

Lizbeth looked up. "You used this as a bookmark?"

"Jack put it there so I'd find it. I always had a book around to read when he was working."

"And just when you were going along, trying to navigate a normal existence."

"I thought I'd sit here and try to pick up the plot again."

"Then you found the note, and it all came rushing back." Lizbeth sent her attention to the distant bank. "Dan bought my birthday present early this year."

Callie studied the woman who, in a split second, slipped from keenly perceptive to sounding lost. "When's your birthday?"

"June."

Callie waited. A blackbird up in a pine tree chattered, then Lizbeth's focus returned.

"Every year, Dan and I took a weekend trip to celebrate. Of course, that didn't happen this year. If it had, I'd have found the present where he'd hidden it." She gave Callie a wan smile. "In my suitcase."

Callie organized the timetable. With Dan's death in May, his wife's birthday in June, that meant— "Oh, Lizbeth..."

"Yes, I found it when I packed for this trip." She shifted to give Callie a better view of the gold ankle bracelet she wore continually. A charm hung from a delicate chain beneath the hem of linen pants. It was a diamond-studded dolphin.

If Callie and Lizbeth were any other women, the scene would have warranted a polite compliment. Instead, Callie said, "Did you break down?"

"I couldn't afford to. Chad was playing in the hall."

Her words rocked Callie with an immediate epiphany. Lizbeth, both widow and mommy, hadn't Callie's freedom to indulge grief. By comparison, she pandered wantonly to the emotion while Lizbeth bundled hers inside, compressing it daily for the welfare of the young child she would raise alone. That understanding opened Callie's ears to the muffled cries from Lizbeth's broken heart.

"Well," she said, cutting into Callie's thoughts. "I'm going into town. You want to come?"

Callie declined Lizbeth's offer, but picked up the book, rose with her, and slipped her sneakers back on. She suddenly itched for exercise.

Lizbeth handed the folded quote back. "Take care of this."

Callie slipped the precious keepsake into the paperback. Lizbeth veered off toward the Tahoe while Callie paused to give the cabin an appraising look. Her critical eye gravitated to the overgrown area along the hot-tub side of the cabin. She would need to remind Lucius about the chainsaw.

The cabin had an empty feel when she entered. She called out for Arnett before sticking her head in her bedroom. Arnett had vanished. Visiting the O'Malleys, no doubt. Callie deposited the book in her own room, pulled the porch door closed behind her, and set a quick pace for Sarah Prosser's office. Sarah mentioned papers Callie needed to sign now that she was Heatherwood's owner and member of the unique condo association.

The walk energized Callie. She bounded up the office's outside stairs quietly.

"The good thing about faxing is, you get your originals back." Sarah's buoyant voice floated through the screen door.

"Well, it's done," Beebe said firmly.

"Good luck in Michigan with the new job."

That dizzying news stopped Callie in her tracks, her fingers just inches away from the handle pull. Questions stammered around inside her head. She couldn't face another rip in her universe, and she couldn't face Beebe. She needed time. She wanted to escape, to hide, but where? Just on the other side of the door, Beebe expressed her gratitude for Sarah's assistance. The excitement that fringed her tone worked against Callie's fight to maintain control. Callie turned. She did not want her retreating footsteps heard making a mad dash. The best she could do was appear to just be arriving.

She tiptoed down the steps. Her stomach twisted at the prospect that if Beebe left her, she'd be truly alone. She ran to Beebe as she ran to the golf course as a child, seeking the support she never received at home. Now Beebe was fleeing, just as her parents moved to Macon, chasing their son and grandchildren. Her parents went to their graves while Mark still ranked high, prior to his eventual divorce, his plunge into alcoholism, prior to the cerebral hemorrhage brought on, the doctor said, by his chosen lifestyle. Other than keeping up with her niece and nephew through birthday and Christmas cards, Callie learning of Beebe's plans, as an outsider looking in, was equal to that long line of family hurt all rolled into one staggering punch.

"Callie. Hi. Out for a walk?"

From where Callie stood in a haze at the base of the steps, a steadying hand gripped around the banister, she jerked her head up toward Beebe.

"Is that Callie?" Sarah came into view at the screen door behind Beebe. "I had an extra *USA Today* delivered."

Again, Callie mounted the steps to the covered porch. Beebe pushed the door open and came out. Sarah caught the door and handed Callie the newspaper.

"That was nice." Callie forced some cheer. "Thanks." She tucked the rolled bundle under her arm, careful to avoid Beebe's watchful eyes. Callie noticed Beebe's hands were empty. The fax must have gone to a pocket.

"How are things at Heatherwood?" Sarah asked.

Before Callie could answer, before she could separate herself from Beebe's company with the condo-paperwork excuse, the opportunity was lost. Sarah stepped outside, pulling the door closed and checking the lock.

"You heading out?" Callie said.

"Nadia just called. She's out on rounds and needs my help." That meant Sarah's assistant was tending to housekeeping duties at cabins rented out on time-share.

Ill at ease, Callie moved with Beebe across the porch and down the stairs, following Sarah's hasty dissent to her car parked alongside the building.

"I'm glad you're here," Beebe said after Sarah drove away. "I won't notice the uphill walk so much with someone to talk to." They moved in that direction, physically and emotionally, up a hill, their heads bent to the asphalt road. After a dozen or so steps, Beebe said, "You overheard, didn't you? I was afraid of that."

Callie's burden felt immensely heavier. Beebe had always been able to read her. "You're leaving. Going to Michigan. When?"

"I'll drive up Monday."

"Monday!"

"I'm sorry you found out this way. That wasn't my intention."

"When were you going to tell me? How can you just leave like this?" Callie's questions teetered on a panic she wished she could mask.

"I planned to tell all of you tomorrow, maybe Saturday. It depended on our progress with Chad." In a softer tone, she tacked on, "And the quilt."

Beebe made a point of cutting the larger, multi-jointed problem into Callie's self-centeredness, which made little difference to Callie. Her emotional attachment to Beebe hung in tatters. An empty feeling drove her next statement. "Knowing you're leaving makes everything associated with this week seem valueless."

"Valueless? What do you mean?"

"I'm not criticizing you. It's the circumstances. Lizbeth may yet decide to move to Florida. You're going to Michigan. And I was offered a job Tuesday. I could stay at Heatherwood and work at Brier Hills. Arnett could be the only one to remain in Maryland."

"How exciting for you!" Beebe pounced on Callie's news. "Are you taking it? Are you at least considering it?"

As Beebe neatly steered the conversation away from her impending move, Callie steered her attention to the cracked earth at roadside.

"I know you, Callie," Beebe said, not bowing to Callie's avoidance tactic. "You love Jack, still. Your life keeps you in all the places you and Jack shared together. Your home, the club, out on that course. Some women, older women, when their husbands die, won't leave the old house they spent their marriage in. They don't want to leave the memories. But you, you can leave Maryland, live in West Virginia, and still have ties—strong ties—to Jack here. Heatherwood. Brier Hills. All the places where you and Jack spent time. I saw the way you looked around the steakhouse. You were remembering evenings spent there with Jack. Memories are important to you. And you'd have those here. You don't need me, Callie. Not to live in the same city. And it would be fun to visit back and forth. What about a reunion? The four of us every August at Heatherwood?" Beebe asked sarcastically.

"You can't be serious," Callie scoffed. "Makes no difference, anyway. I can't leave Cassel."

Beebe's eyes dimmed. "Why not?"

"Petey Sebring."

"Jack's stepmother?"

"We've grown very close. She praised Jack one afternoon for bringing me into her life. She said she looked behind all the sorrow of losing Jack, and there I was."

"She's family," Beebe concluded. A contemplative moment passed between them, then Beebe said, "Michigan is home, Callie. I'm going home. My mother died recently."

The news rendered Callie initially speechless, as was often the case when one hears such an announcement. Beebe's use of the word recently mixed confusion into her delayed response. "I'm sorry to hear that. How's your father handling it?"

"He doesn't know."

Beebe's matter-of-fact reply stopped Callie on the rising grade.

Now a step ahead, Beebe looked down at her. "Not all my memories of home are pleasant ones, but I'm determined to pave over those. I'm forty-six, and for a couple of years now, I've struggled with who I am. I honestly don't think I was cut out to be a minister. I got that wrong. I think God has taken me through all this, right into the trials of this week, with this decision about home ahead of me, so that I would realize my true calling. It's like someone waking up one day and realizing he's, well— Gay is the example that comes to mind."

"Like Lucius?"

"Well, no. More like Jack."

"What?" Callie said, confused.

"My point is, I haven't been truthful with myself."

Callie was still mired by Beebe's analogy. Recognizing that, Beebe came back, linked arms, and walked her through the explanation. "Lucius has always been truthful with himself. Jack and me, not so much. All sides of this week helped me decide to go home. I've battled with the decision for months. You three women and Lucius have lit the matter up nicely, but Jack—whom I wish I'd met—Jack has been a star in the heavens, bright and luminous, and there to guide me home."

Beebe's words describing Jack caused Callie's throat to tighten and Beebe to misunderstand Callie's lack of response. "Don't you see? Jack lived his life on the edge of happiness. I can just imagine his exhilaration when he was finally out of the closet," she said, carrying her original analogy through, "out of Arnett's house, open with his sons about you, and so happy. Finally, happy. It just fills my heart to think what you meant to him, what finally being together meant. I'm looking forward to feeling that in my life when I get home. God has really dragged me through it. He owes me this, and I'm going to collect."

Awed by the other woman's candor, Callie said nothing.

Laughing, Beebe jiggled their hooked arms. "Be happy for me."

"I am," Callie jerked out the words.

"I smell a but coming," Beebe said, prodding Callie to express her feelings.

Before Callie could repeat back how normal it was to grieve the loss of a face-to-face friendship, she heard the sound of a car approaching at high speed. Dropping the newspaper to use both hands, Callie heaved Beebe to the side of the road. The O'Malleys' green tank roared around the bend and passed them, fluttering the newsprint. Eleanor sat behind the wheel. Timothy rode shotgun. A face showed in the back window.

"Arnett," Callie and Beebe exclaimed together.

"If she were holding up a sign," Beebe said, "I could almost believe they'd kidnapped her."

"I've got a bad feeling about this. She's going into town after Lizbeth. Come on." Callie scooped up the paper and grabbed Beebe's elbow to drag her up the hill toward Heatherwood and the Santa Fe. After a few steps, Callie abandoned Plan A for a more expedient Plan B. She ran ahead for the SUV. She would drive back for Beebe.

. . .

Lucius Dameron crawled out from under the low-hanging crabapple and got to his feet when Lizbeth Sebring steered her SUV into the depot's lot and parked next to his truck. He tugged off a pair of rawhide work gloves and tossed them into the wheelbarrow where only splintered remnants of Black Forest mulch remained.

Coming around the truck's open tailgate, she said, "Hey, you've got this place looking nice."

"Fresh mulch always dresses things up, doesn't it?" He crossed the small yard to Lizbeth and kissed her cheek. In addition to the tree, he mulched around the new sign, the area under and around the bench, and each platform support post. A half hour ago, from the platform side of the depot, he watched unnoticed as Lizbeth drove past. He assumed the library was her intended destination.

On that assumption, he said, "Well, where are they?"

"Where are who?" she said, looking around, confused.

"Not who. What. New pictures of Chad."

Her face brightened. "You're too sweet. Of course, I've got new pictures." She dug her phone out of her shoulder bag's front pouch. "This is Chad with Maria and Gracie." She handed the device to Lucius. Four-year old Chad squatted between two girls, obviously sisters, both dishwater blondes with bangs. The older girl, maybe six, sat cross-legged on a patch of grass. The younger—around three, Lucius guessed—sat with her knees pulled up to her chin, her little hands clasped at her ankles.

"Cousins?" he inquired.

Lizbeth squinted up at the sky, thinking. "No, not really. I've always thought of them as Chad's cousins, but these are Debbie's sister's girls." With those three words, her index finger ticked off the retreating relationship. "Debbie's my sister-in-law, so Chad would not be related."

"Then they can be kissing cousins." To enhance this observation, he gave Lizbeth another peck.

She smiled up at him, then down at the phone. "They're a cute trio, aren't they?"

Lucius studied the round, innocent faces. The playground scene depicted was all denim and grass stain between ruffles and lace. "I agree. A handsome lot."

Hearing car doors slam at the curb, Lucius turned to see Arnett Sebring charging toward them. "Uh-oh. Something's up."

Arnett arrived in the O'Malleys' bulky battleship on wheels. Timothy's attempt to waylay his wife proved futile. Eleanor dodged his outstretched hand and trooped in close quarters behind Arnett. Timothy, feet dragging and head shaking, brought up the rear.

Lucius stood shoulder to shoulder with Lizbeth.

Arnett barreled up to her. She wore an ugly look. "Where's Chad, Lizbeth?"

Lucius, although confused over Arnett's demand, thought the O'Malleys and their landline had something to do with it.

"You and that brother of yours snuck around behind my back and whisked my grandson to Florida. Is that why you insisted on this nonsensical trip, to get me out of the way? I can take you to court over this, you know. Grandparents have rights!"

"How typical." Lizbeth retooled Arnett's intimidation as flippancy. "It's just like you to invent something like this." Then her eyes grew wide with understanding. "You sent Gary to spy, didn't you? Well, Patrick has not run away with Chad."

"You bitch. You're lying."

Lucius stood on the wrong side of Lizbeth's windup, and so was helpless to intercede when Lizbeth slapped Arnett hard across the face. Crying out, Arnett staggered back. Her hand reflexively covered her cheek. Lucius stepped between the two women. Timothy lunged for his wife. Eleanor tried to wriggle free of her small-but-mighty husband.

Sylvia Boyle's voice, sharp as a train whistle cutting through a sleepy dawn, blasted into the game of freeze tag. She rattled off the violation committed, reciting section title and numerical cross-reference. Lucius looked around. A police car cruised away from the spot at the curb from whence Sylvia preached. The officer lit the car's light bar. It flashed red and blue through the intersection and into the depot's lot.

Sylvia was on them before Baron's slow-moving policeman exited the black-and-white. "I witnessed the assault," she said. "It's a clear case of the young attacking the elderly."

"Shameful," Eleanor tacked on, now free of her husband's grasp.

Sylvia addressed Officer Oren Mann. He lumbered over the lot's curbed boundary and onto the grassy crime scene. "This one," Sylvia said, jabbing an angry finger at Lizbeth, "slapped this poor woman."

All heads turned to Arnett, who played the moment perfectly. Her hand couldn't have been pried from her face with lubricant and a putty knife. Lucius thought her eyes, though, bespoke her enjoyment.

"Come with me, ma'am." Officer Mann grabbed Lizbeth by the arm and walked her back the short distance to the cruiser.

Storm

"Stand right here." Six-foot-six Officer Oren Mann looked down at a shrinking Lizbeth. "Did you strike that woman?"

Lucius's worried heart tapped recklessly in his chest. He eased toward the pair to intercede on Lizbeth's behalf. "Officer Mann," he said. Mann peeled his gaze off the suspect, and Lucius began again. "Oren, let me explain something about this."

"What, Lucius? What've you got?"

"First, you've got to understand these women are under distress. Lizbeth here is Arnett's daughter-in-law." He used finger and thumb to make the introductions fore and aft. "Lizbeth's husband, Arnett's son, died recently. They're still in mourning. Emotions are high. They're trying to come to terms with it. His death was an accident. No warning. It's been difficult. Please, please, don't arrest Lizbeth." He spun to Arnett. "Tell him you won't press charges."

In Arnett's hesitation, Sylvia answered. "Makes no difference. I witnessed the altercation. It was assault. Officer Mann has his duty."

Everyone talked at once, but Lucius's attention skipped to the cavalry's arrival in the form of Beebe Walker. She got out of Callie's Santa Fe, trapped behind a red light. On foot, she cut across Carmody toward Armament on the diagonal. Beebe marched toward the outdoor drama with cheeks, boobs, and belly bouncing. She was a beautiful sight to behold.

At the corner, Lucius fell into step beside her, concern dark in her eyes.

"What happened, Lucius? What's going on?"

"Lizbeth bitch-slapped Arnett." He thought the tiny smile that flickered across her face was the result of his excited choice of words rather than the act they described.

"What for?"

"Chad's gone. Arnett says he's not in Cassel. She accused Lizbeth of arranging with her brother to get him to Florida while you were all here this week."

"No, I can't believe that." With her conclusion, she shifted into high speed, moving into the fracas like a juggernaut on parade.

Callie got through the light. Lucius saw her rushing forward from the parking lot. He crossed behind the O'Malleys and Arnett to meet her.

She asked the obvious question. Due to close proximity with the others, he wisely selected a neutral response. "Things got a little out of hand."

Sadly, his wisdom was not matched by Eleanor O'Malley. She dropped out of line and stamped within range of Callie who stood between Arnett and Lucius. "How dare you steal this poor woman's husband? You and Jack," she spat. "I knew something wasn't right about you two."

Callie's face seared with instant anger. She turned on her accuser. "I didn't steal him." Then glaring at Arnett, she said, "She gave him to me. Did she tell you that?"

Slap!

Arnett struck Callie hard. Lucius, again caught flatfooted, threw a protective arm in front of Callie. She was shaken. Arnett delighted. Eleanor retreated out of arm's reach. A siren blast bit through the caterwauling.

Everyone turned to Officer Mann. The hand that switched off the siren, now rested on his holstered sidearm. The menacing move had its effect. He strutted away from the car, full of bearing and authority. He looked at Beebe and Lizbeth huddled near the bumper. "Stay there." Then he pointed to Arnett. "On the bench." She went. "Tim, take Ellie back to your car and wait there. I'll call you if I need you. Sylvia, don't move. Lucius," he said. The restoration carpenter stiffened. "Bring that woman here."

Lucius's hand found the small of Callie's back. They stepped over the curb and up to the cop. "Are you all right, ma'am?"

Callie nodded, her cheek streaked red.

"Lucius, tell me what you know." In a commanding voice, Mann spoke to the group. "No one speaks but Lucius, or I swear, I'll haul the lot of you to jail." His cold eyes swept across everyone in turn. "Hit it, Lucius."

Lucius, surprised to be singled out, but loving it, summarized the story in as few words as possible. "Arnett thinks her grandson, Lizbeth's son, is being transported from Maryland to Florida by Lizbeth's brother, and that Lizbeth suggested this trip to Baron to hide that fact from Arnett." Tempting officer brutality, Lucius turned to Arnett. "I saw pictures just before you got here. Chad was sitting in front of a sign with Maria and Gracie. The sign said Marietta Playground. Does that make sense? Do these girls live in Marietta? Aren't they children related to Chad's Aunt Debbie?"

Before Arnett could answer, Mann waved Lizbeth over. "Let's see the picture."

Lizbeth complied. Mann took her cell phone over to Arnett, as if she occupied the witness stand, and held the phone down to eyelevel. "Do you know these girls? Is this a recent picture, not something taken a year ago?"

Arnett had the grace to look chagrined. "Yes, that's recent. I know the girls."

Mann's giant paw lifted Arnett off the bench by her elbow. He led her within a few steps of Lizbeth. "For my satisfaction, can you get your son on the phone, so his grandmother can speak with him?"

"Certainly." Lizbeth took the phone and speed-dialed.

"Put it on speaker," he ordered.

A man's congenial voice answered. "Hi, sis. What's up?"

"Pat, can you bring Chad to the phone?" Lizbeth said. "Arnett's here. She wants to talk with him."

When his response was, "You're asking a lot," Lucius thought Officer Mann would go through the phone with a chokehold for the unsuspecting brother, but patience won out. "The girls have a puppy," Patrick explained. "They're playing outside." His movements and his call to Chad carried through the phone. "Your grandmother's on the phone."

Lucius's gaze leaped to Arnett when Chad's voice radiated from the speaker. "Grandma, Grandma, Grandma," he said, high-pitched, enthusiastic, and coming closer. Arnett melted. "Hi, Grandma." He held the phone himself now.

"Hi, sweetie. Are you having fun?"

"Oh, yes. Maria has a puppy. She's the oldest, so it's her puppy, not Gracie's. She named him Buster. But she lets me and Gracie play with Buster."

"She's sharing. That's nice."

"Yeah, that is nice."

Softly, Mann said, "Ask him how long he's going to stay there?"

"Chad, how long you're going to stay at Maria and Gracie's house?"

"Well, today, we're going on a picnic. Tomorrow, we're going to spend the day on a farm seeing the animals. I don't know about the next day. When are you and Mommy coming home?"

"In a few days. Go back and play, Chad. Love you."

"Love you, too."

Patrick came on. "You still there, Arnett?"

"Thanks, Pat. Take good care of him."

"You can count on it." The connection was severed.

Mann aimed his disgust at Arnett, Callie, and Lizbeth. "Well, what the hell are we going to do about this mess? The kids appear to be playing nicely together, but the adults here, not so much. You," he said, pointing to Callie, "Are you going to press charges against this one?"

Callie glanced at Arnett. "No, I won't press charges."

The officer's head swiveled down to Arnett. "Are you going to press charges against your daughter-in-law?"

Naturally, Arnett had the nerve to consider her answer. "No, absolutely not," she said eventually.

"Okay," Mann said, pulling his shoulders back. "Now, ladies, have we gotten this bad spell out of our systems? Can I release you on your own recognizance?"

Sylvia Boyle stepped forward. Eyes wide, she argued, "Their own recognizance? Are you sure that's the wise thing, Officer Mann?"

"Objection noted, Sylvia," he said without a flinch of aggravation, "but I've got this covered. Well, ladies?"

Contrite nods bobbed around the half circle in front of him.

"All right then. Next time, the phone call will be made from the booking desk. Got that?" Mann watched another round of nods, then called over everyone's head to the O'Malleys. "Tim, it's all over here."

A drizzle began to fall from low-hanging clouds, so Timothy motioned his wife to the car.

"Sylvia," the officer said, "I'd give you a lift, but you know the rules about civilians in cruisers."

Gentleman Tim interceded. "We'll drop you, Sylvia."

Reluctantly, Baron's self-appointed hall monitor headed off. "Can Ellie keep it under twenty-five for five blocks? No reckless driving?"

"No speeding. No reckless driving," Timothy called back.

Lucius was pleased when Arnett politely declined Timothy's

invitation to return her to Heatherwood.

Beebe rejoined them. Lucius went from one woman to the next, hugging and kissing each, and repeating a prayer of rejoicing. "My lovelies are not jailbirds. Thank God."

An idea sprouted, and he clapped his hands. "This calls for a celebration. I propose homemade pizza, store-bought ice cream, and one of my favorite movies."

"Nice try, Lucius," Beebe said, "but I don't think so. You're not smoothing this atrocity over that easily. And these three are certainly not entitled to any reward until I get through with them. My God, you can't spend five minutes in public together without police intervention. Grown women. I can't get over it." Beebe rolled her eyes. "Maybe I can get you to pull on each other's hair, and with the rain coming, throw yourselves down and roll around in the mud. How about that for a show?"

Lucius looked from face to face. Not one of them looked contrite now. Somewhat apprehensive about Beebe's mud-wrestling suggestion, but not contrite.

"I'm done here," Beebe announced. She threw up her hands, took two paces, then performed an about-face. "No, I'm not."

The rain picked up.

"Lucius," she drilled, and he jumped. "Is the depot open?"

"Yes, ma'am," Lucius said, waving the group that way.

Beebe stalled them for a moment to continue her scolding. "If I was fortunate enough to have three arms, I'd grab each of you by the scruff of the neck and tow you inside. But let's walk, shall we, like ladies instead."

"What did I do?" Callie's brave complaint sparked Lizbeth and Arnett with the will to form words.

"Don't get it started again, out here," Beebe commanded, silencing them all.

Lucius held the door. He was torn. He had not been excluded, and he was, more or less, the depot's host, but his wheelbarrow and tools sat out in the wet. After the last lady filed in, he tucked his chin to his chest and ran through the huge raindrops that exploded on asphalt and concrete, praying he wouldn't miss too much of the show, to repeat Beebe's term.

. . .

Inside the 1892 train station, cluttered with Lucius's restoration paraphernalia, Beebe led the thoughtless and somewhat damp threesome to the first patch of cleared floor space. The depot offered none of Heatherwood's amenities: no comfy couches and no lights to ward off the thickening gloom. So be it, Beebe thought, and turned on Callie.

"What did you do? Plenty. Here's how I see it: You can't have it both ways."

"What do you mean?" Callie asked, throwing her shoulders back.

"I mean, Eleanor baited you, and you snagged it, like a largemouth bass," Beebe said, referring to Callie's "Arnett gave Jack to me" line. "It makes me wonder which sentiment is more important to you. To the three of us—the first time we heard it—Arnett's actions were sacred enough to be a prized and willingly kept secret, treated with reverence. Out there," Beebe said, jutting her chin toward the parking lot, "it was a snottily delivered condemnation against her."

Glaring, Callie clamped her mouth shut.

Out the corner of her eye, Beebe watched Arnett stand tall. Beebe didn't comment. Not yet. She'd get to Arnett.

"So here's the point, people. Listen up. Everything has two sides. Everything can be spun more than one way. Bottom line: we need to act with basic human kindness and a modicum of desire to make the right choices."

Beebe stepped up to Lizbeth. "I didn't see you slap Arnett, but I'm sure if I had, I would have wanted to put you in that Tahoe, point you toward Florida, and say go. Just go."

"No," Arnett cried.

Beebe knew she feared the passage south included the loss of her grandson. "And you're an angel?" Beebe snapped at Arnett. "Slipping around behind Lizbeth's back. Be friends with the O'Malleys, fine, but don't recruit them for your team. At home, you recruit your son and sister-in-law. You and Lizbeth must face each other, talk, and resolve this situation in your two hearts. No backsliding. Move your relationship forward for Chad and yourselves. Why would you want this never-ending turmoil?"

Beebe put Lizbeth in her sights. "Don't ever resort to physical attack. That was exactly how this whole thing got started. Arnett wanted to slap the living daylights out of Callie in her front yard. What were you thinking? Or more aptly, do you see how grief's anger, left unchecked, can distort things to the point of violence?"

Beebe closed her eyes and rubbed her temples, suddenly exhausted. When she spoke again, she moderated her tone. "I think, now, we can understand. We can draw the line right here and walk away, instead of continuing this circuitous route." Beebe slipped hair behind an ear. "I had a friend in high school. Tonya Fuller. Tonya had a sister. They would fight, as sisters do. Tonya's mother would make them put one arm around the other and hold hands until they kissed and made up. It was intended to be punishment, to dissuade unacceptable behavior, but it was also an important reminder of how sisters, how family, how people should act, how forgiveness is portrayed. Eventually, the sisters did it, but Tonya said it was a sham. They just complied to get away from the close quarters. We pledged honesty here, sisters." She pointed her finger at each of them in turn. "Honesty, Arnett, says you don't go next door for the purpose of spying on Chad's whereabouts. You approach Lizbeth for a simple explanation, and you approach her privately."

Arnett folded arms under ample breasts, but withheld comment.

"So," Beebe said, "we've made no progress in, oh, I don't know how many days now."

"Six, if you count today." The voice belonged to Lucius.

Beebe whirled. She forgot about him. When did he slip inside? He held a broom. A small mound of sawdust lay at his feet.

"She wants to take me to court," Lizbeth said accusingly.

"Grandparents have rights," Arnett declared.

"Oh, Arnett, no." Beebe raised her hands and let them fall, slapping her thighs. "Now you want to recruit the court system. How big of an army will it take to keep one woman and a small child in Cassel?"

"It was John who ruined everything," Arnett said, reprising her standard excuse.

Beebe's glower cut off Lizbeth's and Callie's intended remarks.

"Is that what you want to do, sit down and etch onto Chad's heart the idea that his grandfather was a villain? Maybe you could use one of those fancy cells phones with a camera," Beebe said, demonstrating, pretending to hold such a device at arm's length. "With Chad on your lap, you could record the scene for all time. Chad will definitely want to preserve *that* for posting on his Facebook page. The world should know."

Quiet rang through the depot.

Beebe's head hurt. Her chest was tight. She wanted to bring this caucus to an end. "So, my dear sweet Sebrings, where are we? A hug and a kiss?" She looked from one to the other. "Just a hug, then?"

Suddenly, Lucius was beside her. "Aw, come on, a little sugar? One of you?"

"Ride back in the same car together?" Beebe looked at Lizbeth.

"Up to her," Lizbeth said, passing the decision.

No concession came from the other Sebring.

"Everybody will feel better after pizza and ice cream," Lucius said, pushing his earlier plan.

"It's too good for them."

"Ple-e-e-ease, Beebe," Lucius begged, gripping the broom handle tightly in both fists.

"Fine, then."

"And a movie?"

"Why not?"

"Excellent. I'll meet you at Heatherwood in..." he squinted at his watch, "ninety-two minutes. Now, scoot. Lucius has to shop."

On the way out, Callie tapped Beebe on the arm. She turned and received Callie's car keys. Callie said she wanted to spend time with Lucius. Arnett heard and planted herself in the Santa Fe's passenger seat, leaving Lizbeth to drive back to Heatherwood alone.

. . .

Callie ran for Lucius's truck while he locked the depot's doors. Raindrops thudded loudly on the Ford's metal roof.

When Lucius was behind the wheel, he said, "That was grueling, but nice of you to make things easier on Arnett." His eyes shone their unusual shade of green against the stormy backdrop.

"How do you mean? I want some one-on-one time with you."

"You gave Arnett an out," he said, fitting the ignition key into the slot. "She wouldn't ride with Lizbeth, and she wasn't forced to ride with you."

"Beebe is better?"

"Better than walking." With the truck's engine purring softly, he flipped the windshield wipers into operation. "Still mad at Arnett?"

"A bit, yes, but Beebe took a lot of the sting out."

"She made a lot of sense."

"You knew she would." Then pointedly, she added, "And you knew she was moving to Michigan."

He froze, elbow out, hand gripping the gear shift.

"You knew. Now don't deny it."

"Well," he whined.

"I saw you two yesterday. Your heads together. You passed her some papers."

"She begged me to be her confidant—"

Callie turned his way, her bent left leg pulled onto the worn fabric seat. "And something's up with you and Willie."

"No." His answer was almost shrill.

"Yes," she mimicked his tone. "You moved the dinner from Friday to Saturday. Why? I want details, Lucius Dameron. Don't make me call Willie."

"You wouldn't."

"I would."

"He won't tell you."

"He'd tell me in a heartbeat."

"Isabelle."

"Isabelle won't stop my call."

"No." He took a breath. "Isabelle's the problem."

Callie sat back, satisfied. Beebe had one approach. Callie, most definitely, another.

Between the depot and Godfrey's for groceries, Lucius divested himself of detail after detail. Callie listened and felt herself stepping into Jack's shoes, becoming the masterful peacekeeper he had been. Callie thought she had a solution to the Isabelle situation. She laid it out for Lucius, then stayed in the truck and, with Lucius's encouragement, placed a call to Willie's office. Isabelle answered. While she had Isabelle on the line and before she was put through to Willie, she asked her to locate an out-of-state phone number involving a second situation on Callie's mind.

She and Willie talked through Lucius's return with his purchases, then the three of them conversed, via speakerphone, until the mountains blocked the signal. At that point, an eager Willie was making plans and grateful to Callie. Lizbeth Sebring, Callie passed along, possessed a degree in finance. She might measure up as Isabelle's replacement. Maryland State Senator Amos Emerson could provide a trusted reference on her work ethic.

At the Bullwhip cabin, so Lucius could pick up a movie on DVD, Callie used Lucius's landline and placed another call to the Michigan phone number Isabelle provided. When Vincent Bostick identified himself, she said, "You don't know me, but I'm Beebe's friend."

. . .

Arnett glanced out Heatherwood's kitchen door. A steady rain fell. She and Lucius shared one couch; Callie and Lizbeth, the other. Beebe sat, her legs crossed, in her standard chair at the end of the coffee table. She faced the TV. Everyone watched Lucius's movie selection: the 2008 musical, *Mamma Mia,* starring Pierce Bronson and Meryl Streep.

The coffee table was laden with plates, napkins, soda glasses, and the remains of two pizzas. Arnett slipped unobtrusively between the opening alongside Beebe's chair with her empty plate and glass. Her course to the kitchen took her past the quilt and the photographs of three Sebring males. In addition to everything else, the quilt still demanded their focus.

Steeling her fortitude, Arnett snapped her eyes forward and went to rinse her dishes in the sink. She dried her hands, intending to return to the group, but a handful of nearly forgotten memories peeked around the corner of her mind. She wandered back to the quilt.

If the quilt maker's identity remained anonymous, she would admit to being impressed with the workmanship patching Dan's clothing into a keepsake. Callie clipped the numeral fourteen from the front of his high school baseball jersey. How many times that dusty and stained uniform came through the wash. Arnett slid Chad's picture over a bit and off the square with the red Kool-Aid stain. A wriggling Chad, six months old and cradled in Dan's arm, kicked the glass he held. Dan's favorite weekend-around-the-house shirt would not release the stain. Neither would Dan release the shirt. He wore it anyway. The story must have been related from Lizbeth to Beebe to Callie in order for Callie to understand that the stain spoke to Dan's laid-back, unpretentious nature.

Several squares were cut from his paint-splattered Levis. She smiled as she counted another eight very colorful squares. Why Dan adored Hawaiian shirts, she didn't know, but his collection was honored nonetheless. The three patches Arnett treasured most, Callie cut to fit diagonally into the six-inch-square design. Each patch consisted of one word. Together, they read, World's Best Dad. Arnett owned a clear memory of taking Geoff, aged nine, shopping. They bought the black-on-gray imprinted sweatshirt for a Father's Day gift.

Arnett looked over to the women whose combined efforts produced the quilt. Emotionally, she was steering a path between melancholy and redemption, but she rerouted that. Her gaze zeroed in on the back of Beebe's head. It would take more than Beebe's contempt for Arnett's first line of defense to alter her strategy. The court system and the power of its judgments were both indulgences and obsessions. It seemed foreign to abandon those emotional highs now.

The movie played on. A balcony-bound Meryl Streep with a two-woman backup group sang down to a courtyard filled with young people.

Since she was up, Arnett went ahead and scooped ice cream into bowls, wondering about Lucius's thought process. He selected Rocky Road.

. . .

The rain's droning banter had not lulled Arnett to sleep, so she threw off the sheet and chenille spread, dropped her legs over the side of the bed, and pushed her feet into slippers. Standing in her bedroom doorway, she looked down the row of doors and saw that Callie's, at the far end, stood ajar. She took a few steps into the great room. As she suspected, Callie's form came into shadowy focus on the far couch. She appeared asleep. Arnett moved quietly to the kitchen door. Multiple flashes of lightning from the worsening storm lit the quilt and gave a ghastly glow to the three framed images. With care, she pried the door loose of its frame.

The air outside cooled significantly. Her summer-weight, knee-length nightgown was not much protection against the damp and dripping world. With the porch roof and towering picket fence of pine trees around the property, she had no window to the sky. Thunder rumbled closer, and when lightning ignited the heavens, it illuminated a fully saturated yard.

Arnett skirted the round table to sit in the adjacent chair. She folded her arms for added warmth and pulled her feet under the chair to avoid the backsplash of rain falling off the roof.

It was not often that sleep evaded her. Her father, the proud Judge Cyrus Oldstone, claimed that fortune as well. How appropriate that she would think about her father, dead now for years, during a lashing and howling storm. He had not mellowed with age, quite the opposite. The enraged storm was, in all likelihood, his reincarnated spirit come to order her out of bed to appear before him as he'd done once before. On that occasion, he shouted down her best arguments. Mentally, she was arranging her evidence for the current West Virginia case when an earth-rattling crack of thunder vibrated the porch. Inside, on a two-second delay, a long chilling scream sliced through the night and left her frozen to the chair.

Seconds passed before Arnett recovered her wits. She jumped to her feet just as Lizbeth slammed through the screen door. Launching herself off the porch and into the yard, she screamed her dead husband's name repeatedly. A pajama-clad Callie fled the cabin behind her, pleading for Lizbeth to stop. Callie chased her in jagged rents through the muddy yard. Drenched and stumbling, the two drifted closer and closer to the river.

Arnett waited at the break in the railing. The door banged again, and Beebe was at her side, peering into the darkness. She asked no questions. The mad scene in the yard summed it up completely.

Directly overhead, lightning and thunder strobed and crashed in a frenzied dance. Then a bolt struck a solid object so near and with such force, Arnett and Beebe cringed away, hands clapped to their ears. When Arnett opened her eyes, Callie's face was turned up, mesmerized. Arnett ducked her head out from under the overhang to see what captivated her. Rain pelted her face, but there was no mistaking the looming danger. "Oh my god," she breathed, "the tree."

Responding to the warning tone, Beebe's head and shoulders leaned past the canopy. She saw it, too. Halfway up in the evergreen, a fire flared. Its momentary life was smothered by the downpour, but the sacrifice was noted. It drew and held the eye. Staged to perfection, the tempest silenced itself to permit the sound of ripping lumber to thrill the audience. A ragged crack appeared. Quite gracefully, the top of the tree, in freefall flight, glided toward the ground.

Arnett grabbed the porch post and watched in horror.

Callie snapped into motion, desperate to outrun the falling treetop. She lunged forward to grab Lizbeth's arm, but hand and arm were slippery. The connection wasn't made, but she succeeded in pushing Lizbeth. Lizbeth staggered several yards, lost her footing, and fell. Callie tried to regain her balance and keep her momentum. The entire scene seemed to both drag in slow motion and play out rapidly to its conclusion. The Big Pine, the cabin's former namesake, tumbled down on Callie. She was swallowed up by the stormy night as the branches flapped serenely to rest against the wet earth.

Tiny Twist of Truth

Arnett and Beebe raced into the yard. Cold rain streamed their faces and plastered nightgowns to their bodies.

Beebe took charge. "Get up, Lizbeth," she yelled, "Go back to the porch."

Barefoot, Arnett went to her. Her slippers were sucked off several steps back. Lizbeth appeared unharmed. The treetop barely grazed her. She threw her arms up to shield her face. Arnett pulled her up and nearly chased her back to the porch. Behind Arnett, Beebe called Callie's name. Above Arnett, the storm continued its rant.

Beebe peeled back branches in the area where they last saw Callie. Arnett didn't know what they'd do if she were severely injured. She made it to Beebe's side just as she exposed the tail of Callie's pajamas.

"Callie!" she screamed over the storm.

Callie moaned. "I can't get up. Help me!"

The weight of the prickly branches, Beebe's and Arnett's awkward stance, and the lack of light made rescue difficult. Beebe made a herculean effort to lift an armful of branches. Callie struggled, but managed to get to her knees. She crawled out. Sticky needles caught her nightclothes and scratched her face and arms.

Arnett helped her up. "Are you hurt?"

Beebe didn't give Callie the opportunity to answer. Supporting Callie, Arnett and Beebe whisked her to the porch where they all faced a hysterical Lizbeth.

"Dan," she cried, wild-eyed. "Go back for Dan."

Arnett grabbed Lizbeth's forearms and moved her back. "Dan's not out there. Dan is not out there." The suffering widow's eyes remained glazed. Arnett gave her a shake. "It was Callie. Not Dan."

"No," she argued.

"Yes." Arnett shook her again. Her heart thumped several anxious beats before reality surfaced in Lizbeth.

"Oh," Lizbeth said, still dazed. "Oh no. Callie." Lizbeth seemed to allow the woman to come into focus. A watery stream of blood ran from a small gash at Callie's temple. Reaching out with a trembling hand, Lizbeth said, "It's all my fault. I'm so sorry."

Beebe cut in. "Arnett, get her inside and into a warm tub."

Although Lizbeth moved under her own power, Arnett would not relinquish hold on her arm. She was aware of Beebe and Callie filing in behind, of Beebe asking, "Do you hurt anywhere?" Their voices dwindled out of range. Beebe ushered Callie into her room, and soon water ran into both tubs.

Arnett could not quell her anxiety even after she changed into dry clothes and Lizbeth was wrapped in a robe with her hair rubbed dry. She hovered and cooed a continual reassurance, while marveling at Callie's heroism. In fact, she tried to linger in that vein. For if she didn't, she fought the tormenting visualization of Dan's death. She blinked back tears. No wonder Lizbeth nearly lost hold of reality.

Arnett bent over Lizbeth, now between the sheets. She moved an unruly strand of hair off Lizbeth's face as Beebe eased up to the bed. She too donned her robe. Her hair was combed straight back, and she held a glass of water. "How is she?"

The two women smiled down at Lizbeth, paler than usual, but calm, and strangely in a world of her own. If there was ever a time for Arnett to abandon her honesty pledge, this was it. "She's much, much better," she said.

"I think she should take one of her sleeping pills," Beebe said. "Sleep will cure the worst of this."

Lizbeth nodded when asked her opinion, raised up on an elbow, and downed the pill.

Beebe set the glass on the nightstand, then tipped her head sideways at Lizbeth who lay motionless in the bed. "Talk to me," she said, grinning. "Say something."

Lizbeth's eyes sparked, which Arnett took as a good sign. "Thank you," she said. "I'm fine."

"Are you cold?"

"No. I'm feeling better." Then her chocolate eyes melted and her voice retreated. "It was my nightmare."

Those words lowered Beebe to a seat on the edge of the mattress. "Yes, I know. Callie told me."

Arnett listened. It seemed she was the last to learn of Lizbeth's repetitive nightmares. A mild case of irritation and jealousy flexed their muscles. Not that mother- and daughter-in-law ever grew close, but Arnett would be happier not knowing Callie starred as Lizbeth's first confident. To her credit, she stamped those old impulses into immediate submission and searched Beebe's manner for guidance. Roiling inside Arnett was an urge to confess an awful truth.

"Listen to me, Lizbeth," Beebe said, composed and nurturing. "Arnett is going to sit right here. I want you to talk to her. Just keep talking until you feel sleepy. Okay?"

"I will." Lizbeth pulled on Beebe's arm when she started to rise. "Is Callie okay?"

"Miraculously, she's only got bumps and bruises, a few scratches. I'm going back to her. You'll see her when you wake up. Now, talk to Arnett and let that pill do its stuff."

Beebe gave Arnett's hand a reassuring squeeze before she

disappeared toward the hovel of light surrounding Callie's bedroom door. Arnett stepped forward from the doorway. Alone with Lizbeth, she felt her knees weakening. She replaced Beebe at bedside and hung onto composure.

"I must be part of your nightmare," she said, by way of introduction. Arnett tried to hold Lizbeth's eyes, but her gaze slid off to a wrinkle on the pillowslip. "You said the other day you blamed me for Dan's death. In some respects, that's true."

Lizbeth emitted a chortle of skepticism. It faded abruptly. "How is that true?"

Arnett glanced away nervously, then quickly back. "I'm glad Beebe said you should keep talking. I'm going to need you to talk me through this."

"Please, Arnett," Lizbeth drilled, impatient. "How is that true?"

Again, relying on the grief counselor's lead, Arnett took Lizbeth's hand. "Dan came to see me the morning he died, before he drove out to Mumford County." Lips parted, Lizbeth gave her a direct stare. "He told me he wanted to resign from Oldstone Manufacturing and move you and Chad to Florida."

"He told you first?" Lizbeth's words were strafed with competitiveness and disbelief.

"He was gauging my reaction, trying to see how much work was ahead of him. John used to do that. If John were alive, Dan would have gone to him first, then they'd have teamed up against me. John certainly learned the knack. Well," she said, her tone shifting, "I wasn't happy about Florida, and I told him so. But he'd done his research. He promised your new house would have a guest room with my name on it. He wanted me to come for long visits and opportunities to visit Geoff and Chad. He knew you weren't happy about that separation. We all knew Geoff's love for marine biology was not going to bring him back to Cassel. He would stay in Florida. Dan said he wanted his family together and didn't I understand that? Well, of course, I did. He had me there." She licked her lips. "He learned that kind of approach from his father. It was clear. I was being handled, and quite admirably."

Arnett took a moment for the peevishness she felt to pass. Thankfully, Lizbeth didn't fill the breach as Arnett thought she would.

"At that moment, it felt like I was hanging, swinging in the wind without a foot- or handhold in reach." Her voice felt thick in her throat when she spoke again. "I lived for the times Gary and Dan came to see their father. I didn't see them as often as I saw you and Marta. You'd come about the kids, one of their ailments, but the boys came to talk to John about house repairs, this car or that, sports, all the things that didn't involve me. When John left—when I kicked him out," she amended, "that connection was broken. Those conversations took place elsewhere. Everything was changing." Arnett surprised herself with the words that came next. "And it made me feel so very old."

She gave Lizbeth a weak smile. "So Dan got off late to paint that morning. You were right to blame me. If he hadn't come to see me, he probably would have finished earlier, before the storm hit. If I'd been a different kind of person—of mother—he wouldn't have needed..."

Her confession faltered short of full disclosure, and Lizbeth closed her eyes. Her hand went limp in Arnett's. Arnett's face grew hot. She didn't think Lizbeth slept. She wanted escape, a way to punish, of not offering forgiveness or understanding, of even pretending it.

Arnett laid Lizbeth's hand on the spread and rose. Lizbeth would be sorry to learn that if she asked, Arnett would accept the quilt. She was ready, in her mind, to relate the quilt maker to the woman who saved her daughter-in-law's life, not the woman who stole her husband. Arnett would sit with Chad and the quilt and tell him the story of the stormy night that reminded her of her father, and would never need to assume responsibility for the loss of his.

Would Lizbeth consent to this tiny twist of truth? Probably not. She was so righteous.

Arnett paused at the foot of the bed. Lizbeth's breathing was light and regular. She seemed lost in slumber. A convenience, Arnett grumbled to herself, when I made such a sacrifice.

Walking through the bathroom to her room, she gathered towels and clothes permeated with the sickening smell of wet evergreen and went to the laundry nook.

. . .

The sound of a chainsaw chiseled into Lizbeth's sleep. She pried her eyelids open. A brilliant sunshine glowed behind the white cotton curtains at the window. Rolling over and throwing off the covers, she found she slept in her bathrobe. A glass with a swallow of water sat on the bed table, her bottle of sleeping pills next to it. All at once, scenes from the night before snapped through her mind like narcotic-induced flashbacks. She dragged her legs over the mattress, then sat there for a moment while her head and stomach settled into a proper synch.

The cabin's stillness told her it was empty. She padded barefoot to the screen door. All the activity took place in the yard. A small crowd tended to the felled tree. She closed her eyes at the sight, cringing again as she had last night. She was butt-first in the mud, gazing up at a sky cleaved by lighting with an evergreen plunging out of the gash. She pulled her knees up and crossed her arms protectively over her face. The whish went by her. She was left miraculously untouched.

She studied the outdoor scene again. The thirty-foot section of tree lay in Callie's back yard like a whale belched up from the river. It dwarfed the people, especially small-of-stature Timothy O'Malley, who manned the chainsaw. His wife Eleanor, Sarah Prosser, and Lizbeth's cabin mates dragged branches sliced off the pine to an established rubble pile at the far side of the drive.

Lizbeth felt as if her actions were somehow the cause for all the intense labor, although she knew she couldn't be held responsible for the lightning strike. All she did was parade around in the storm like a crazed widow. She had vague recollections of Callie's cut and bleeding face and Beebe's comment about bumps and bruises. She pictured Callie's battered face on the dust jacket covering the many chapters of Lizbeth's recent and reckless behavior.

She shook her head. First the whale metaphor, then a roundabout way of judging a book by its cover. The senator would fire her the first day if he rehired her. "Perhaps," she said, crossing back to her room, "I won't give him the opportunity."

Twenty minutes later, showered and dressed, she leaned back against the kitchen counter, nursing a glass of orange juice.

For days, she fussed at Arnett about the idea of moving to Florida. She threw some type of reverse, or perverse psychology into the mix: specifically, that Arnett accept the quilt. That was no longer a concern. After hearing Arnett's midnight confession, Lizbeth had no option but to take the offer off the table. Dan wanted his family to live in Florida. So to Florida, Chad and she would go. Uncle Ralph and Aunt Mildred would take them in. She would join Uncle Ralph at Gibson Promotions, and Geoff would be less than three hours away. When she found her own place, she was quite sure she would renege on the guest-room promise.

Arnett selfishly kept her last conversation with Dan to herself for three months because it represented a scenario she didn't want to see enacted. Clearly, her happiness superseded everyone else's.

Lizbeth imagined Dan sitting on his mother's couch, hands folded between his knees, speaking in his quiet no-nonsense voice. Arnett would know there was no changing his mind about Florida.

She raised the juice glass and toasted her decision. The corners of her mouth curled, imagining Arnett's shock: First Dan mentioned Florida, then Lizbeth. Arnett must have thought Dan was communicating from the grave. Lizbeth froze. The nightmares. Had he been communicating from the grave?

Her gaze swept over to his photograph on the entryway table. With the glass held high in tribute, she said, "Message sent and received." She drained the glass's contents and set it firmly on the countertop. A clear, lucid, and unmistakable understanding infused her: That nightmare would never chase her again. It was ground into the sod beneath the fallen pine.

Lizbeth turned her ear toward the screened window over the sink. Sarah's voice sifted through. "Wait. We should get these SUVs moved."

Outside, Lucius's truck, tailgate headed in, was lined up to pass the Tahoe and Santa Fe on the outside. His head hung out the window. "I think I can get around." On the truck's back panel, white lights were steady, red lights tapped out caution.

Timothy stepped into view. Belatedly, Lizbeth noted the chainsaw whined no more. Callie followed him. Together, they lifted a thick, rectangular piece of plywood from the truck bed and positioned it on the ground where the truck's back wheels rolled over it and stopped. From the screen door, Lizbeth silently applauded this exercise in forethought. The wooden base prevented the truck's back wheels from sinking into the saturated earth.

Reaching over the side wall, Timothy got his hands on another chainsaw while Lucius climbed down from the cab. His expression was devoid of its usual animation. He called to Callie, and she came back. Callie needed only one look at him to know, as Lizbeth had, that something was wrong. Her pace quickened. Her lips moved, but Lizbeth couldn't hear her words. He draped an arm around Callie's shoulders and walked her a few steps closer to Lizbeth's vantage point. Neither seemed to notice her presence behind the mesh.

Lizbeth chewed her cheek with worry: Lucius was the bearer of bad news. She watched their faces in profile, their gazes locked on each other. Finally, Lucius began. With each phrase spoken, Callie's chin dropped by increments to her chest. When her shoulders drooped, he pulled her to him and, more tenderly than Lizbeth could have imagined, kissed the top of her head. A moment later, they separated, and he led her to the planked porch and eased her down.

"Do you want me to sit a minute, button nose?" he asked.

Swiping at a tear, she shook her bowed head. He departed, eyes tipped to his boots.

Lizbeth's heart ached with sympathy. She wanted desperately to learn the news, but Callie shooed Lucius away, so she respectfully held her position. Her hand flexed repeatedly against the door while Callie wept. Suddenly, Callie stopped crying. Strong, stoic Callie tilted her head back and drew in a long choppy breath. She slapped her hands resignedly against the faded knees of her Levis and rose. Instead of climbing the steps, Callie set a course through the yard to Sarah. Beebe, nearby, caught their conversation and joined them. Beebe said something, then lifted Callie's chin with her fingertips and spoke again. Of course, Beebe would drill home whatever words of encouragement were needed. Having given the perfunctory nod, Callie turned and trudged toward the cabin.

When she cleared the top porch step, Lizbeth pushed the door open, her anxiety at full billow. "What happened, Callie? What's wrong?"

Eyes red-rimmed, Callie heaved a belabored sigh. "Petey died last night."

Even after the long buildup, Lizbeth was not prepared. "Oh, Callie, I'm so sorry." Callie came inside, and Lizbeth wrapped her in a tight hug.

"She went peacefully, in her sleep. I need to get in touch with Nora. I left Petey Sarah's number, just in case. Nora found it and called."

Callie went to the kitchen sink. She pulled the long sleeves of her

T-shirt away from her wrists and washed her hands. Lizbeth spent very little time with Dan's step-grandmother, Petey Sebring, but she recognized Callie's reference to her granddaughter, Nora Dobbs. Lizbeth knew neither of them well.

Turning off the water, Callie said, "It just so happened Nora called when Lucius was down at the office."

"Did you tell Arnett?" Lizbeth asked. Petey Sebring was Arnett's mother-in-law.

Callie spun around, the terry towel still in her hands. "I didn't even think to tell Arnett."

"Don't worry about it. There'd be no display of sympathy. No love loss either. Hey, I was thinking of going into town. Your car's blocked. I'll drive you." She turned on her heel and strode into the bedroom for her purse.

Callie trailed behind. "Thanks, Lizbeth, but with all that's going on, I don't want to go that far. Sarah said I could use her office phone."

"Then I'll drive you there and back, first." The full-sized bed stood between them. Callie waited in the swath of light shining through the parted curtains at the bedroom window. It placed a long, bruised scratch and the chunk out of her cheek on display. "I'm sorry about last night, Callie. It all seems pretty hazy, but I know you probably saved my life while risking your own. Thank you doesn't seem quite adequate." She felt herself deflate. "I just don't know why I went running out there."

"It was the nightmare. It seemed real. The circumstances—well, the circumstances are understandable. It was the strange surroundings. If the storm and nightmare teamed up at home, you'd have dealt with them differently."

"It did seem real. I was sure Dan was out there."

Purse in hand, she stood with Callie. Something caused Callie to catch Lizbeth by the shoulders and walk her backwards the few steps needed to reach the bed.

"Callie, what?" she said, surprised, sitting. It felt like a coming-to-God moment, with all the energy she would expect from Beebe.

"Listen," Callie began, dropping down beside her. "I had a dream about Jack several months after he died. I woke from it, but kept my eyes closed, you know, trying to hold onto the moment, playing it over in my mind, afraid any movement would snatch it away. And I could have sworn—no, I *believe*, and I still do—Jack was there in the room. He touched my hand." In imitation, she laid her right hand over the back of her left. "I felt it. It was real. His hand touched mine."

She spoke the closing declaration with such a riveting certainty that the hairs at Lizbeth's nape rose. The testament of one woman was meant to validate the claims of the other. To Lizbeth, it felt as though they'd been inducted into an exclusive society. Given the circumstances of the day, she thought the membership rolls might have boasted one other member. "Did you tell Petey that story?"

"No, not Petey and not Beebe. Only you. Now, come on." She softened her brusque tone with a smile. "I want to make the call and get back."

Lizbeth followed Callie through the cabin. For five-five, she was a stalwart figure, carrying herself tall. Lizbeth raised her own earlier victories to a place of prominence again. She slid behind the Tahoe's wheel, buoyant, poised, her decision to relocate in Florida firmly fixed in reality. She had the example of Callie's pull-oneself-up-by-one's-bootstraps strength to thank. She witnessed Callie lifting herself out of despair over Petey's death to face that deeply felt loss head on. Sadly, she'd faced too many in her young life.

Inner strength brings a substantial measure of self-reliance, Lizbeth decided. If the situation had been different, had she not been driving Callie to make a long-distance condolence call to Petey's granddaughter, she'd share her Florida decision. But Lizbeth owned discipline enough not to intrude on Callie's grief. There was satisfaction in knowing she reached a decision and would implement it as soon as she came within bounds of cellular service. She needed no one to pat her on the shoulder. Nor, in all honesty, did she need anyone to talk her out of it.

Ragged Shreds

Down at the office, Lizbeth guided the SUV across the road's centerline and eased to a nose-to-nose stop with a truck hitched to an industrial chipper. The driver's door was open. She read Updyke Tree Service from the panel below the window. Getting out with Callie, Callie introduced her to Jimmy Updyke, Nadia's husband. He was lanky and clean shaven. Jimmy was headed up the hill to Heatherwood to join the cleanup, so he insisted he would transport Callie back after her telephone call. Lizbeth was sent on her way to Baron with an assignment to return with buckets of chicken to feed the hungry crew.

Lizbeth followed the four-lane road, which was more or less a straight line straddling the base of two mountain ranges. When she swung onto the Baron exit ramp, her phone produced an alert tone. It lay on the passenger seat. The lit screen said a text message waited. In all their wisdom, the cell-tower gods deflected their signal to the vicinity of a boarded-up gas station. She pulled across the road onto the station's lot. It was a sea of cracked asphalt.

She checked the text. It was the monthly payment reminder due her mobile carrier. Lizbeth thumbed through her contact list to the line labeled Ralph and Mildred. She pressed call. The second Aunt Mildred answered, Lizbeth realized she'd lost track of the days. It was Friday. She should have called Uncle Ralph's business number. She explained her mistake. "No, honey," Aunt Mildred said. "He's here. He's getting the RV ready."

Aunt Mildred's melodious Southern drawl loosened the gate on Lizbeth's stockpiled emotions. Everything tumbled out. She did steer around the West Virginia trip, but gave her aunt a full rundown, including Dan's conversation with Arnett the day of his death. She didn't hesitate to cast Arnett in bad light. For three long months, she held onto Dan's desire to reconstitute the mural business. She wanted to pick up the baton and carry Dan's dream through. Lizbeth enthusiastically promised that Chad and she would pull into their Tallahassee drive within a week.

There were a few seconds when Lizbeth thought the signal was lost, then out of the silence came Aunt Mildred's halting voice. "Honey, I don't quite know what to say. I'm afraid it's too late. Ralph sold the business. He signed the papers two days ago."

The impact of her words hit like a slap across the face. Lizbeth's eyes closed tight. She knew what it meant: She lost to Arnett Oldstone Sebring again.

"I'm so sorry, Lizbeth. But you and Chad, you come to us anyway, if not to stay, then for a nice long visit."

It was then that Mildred's earlier words registered. Uncle Ralph was outside tending to the RV. Lizbeth held herself together and declined the invitation issued out of pity. "No, you guys deserve a vacation. It was just a thought," she said, downplaying her earlier eagerness without a shred of believability. "I'm sorry to bother you when you're getting ready to leave. You must have a million things to do."

"Well, you hardly knew we were leaving and you're certainly never ever a bother. Now, let me get Ralph in here."

"No, he's busy."

"He'll want to talk to you. He will."

"No, tell him congratulations. You, too. Retirement. That's great.

Where you headed?" She pitched the question up, wanting to sound genial.

"Cross-country," Mildred said. "To see the sights." Her voice came back dulled with worry. She saw through Lizbeth's pretense.

Tears brimmed Lizbeth's eyes. For the last twenty years, that could have been her and Dan on their many mural-painting excursions. "That'll be fun," she breathed into the phone. "Talk to you soon." She disconnected.

With those last words, longing, thick and unbearable, closed her throat. The feeling of suffocation came next. She slapped at the door handle and stumbled out. She gulped air, but the oxygen didn't prevent the world around her from spinning. She wanted a day, just one, where change would not rip her existence into ragged shreds. She wanted a place where familiarity gleamed.

She looked down at the phone clenched in her fist. The call that began with the dawning promise of hope deteriorated quickly. Her mother-in-law delayed her confession just long enough to make its timing feel planned. Heavy chunks of disappointment and conspiracy plunged deep into her anger. The volatile ingredients exploded, and a furious rage seared through her.

For the first time, it singed Dan—and that damned mother's privilege that kept him catering to *her* first.

Lizbeth threw her head back and released an ancient groaning scream that ended in wrenching sobs and buckling knees. She fell back against the Tahoe's steel hull and sank to the ground. That crippling grief was the kind she never gave herself permission to suffer with Chad always within reach. Submitting completely to grief's power, she wailed again.

She shot a look across the crumbling, dried-out asphalt deck to the dingy, weather-beaten station that represented everything ugly about her life, and gulped a sob.

Suddenly, a shuddering panic rose within and hustled her back inside the Tahoe. She slammed the door, then threw the cell phone into the other seat. It bounced to the floor mat. She let it lay. Emotions governed her every action, so much so that she accepted reception from the cell-tower gods like candy from a stranger. They lured her to a lonely spot with the intent to do her harm.

She started the SUV. It fishtailed off the property on a layer of dirt and loose stones. By the time she entered Baron's corporate limits, she calmed. Decisions came easier. Sadly, she let all thoughts of a move to Florida fall away. That avenue was closed. She got a tight grip on the steering wheel, a passionate grip. She willed her inner strength to gather and rise up. By God, she only lost so much to her mother-in-law. Not everything. While she yet breathed, she would not concede any middle ground to Arnett. She must accept and display the quilt. Lizbeth still felt that would go a long way to soothing Arnett's loss as well.

She found the restaurant and ordered lunch. She made a right-hand turn out of the chicken place with buckets stuffed with combinations of every famous recipe available. She didn't doubt her choices for a moment. She would stay in Maryland—forced to stay, yes—but reinforced by the counseling tenet on which Beebe harped and harped. It said she should not venture too far afield too quickly.

The Tahoe rolled to a stop behind a semi needing extra room to negotiate a left-hand turn onto a narrow street. While waiting for the semi to accomplish the maneuver, Lizbeth was revisited by her earlier cry for familiarity. Familiarity seemed important. It still did.

In actuality, the murals were a fantasy shared with Dan. She wouldn't know how to live that life. That realization came as the semi belched a cloud of gray exhaust and lurched around the corner. Up ahead, the abandoned gas station appeared behind the haze. She saluted when she passed. The layover did her good.

. . .

Callie sat on the great room's ottoman. The tree-removal team's break for lunch included a sideshow. Beebe and Lucius got a bump-and-grind going when *Viva Los Vegas*, sung by Elvis Presley, was piped through the radio. They used the floor space in front of the bedroom doors as a stage. Their audience was scattered about the cabin. Counting the entertaining duo, those present numbered nine. The O'Malleys were still there. Nadia and Jimmy Updyke would probably finish the day at Heatherwood. Overflow seating went to both sofas when the chairs around the kitchen table filled.

The performance was quite well choreographed, considering its spontaneous nature. Both entertainers sang into their chicken-leg microphones. A good deal of the dancing included looks at their gyrating backsides. When the singing ended, Beebe bowed and Lucius curtsied. Laughter and well-deserved applause erupted. No one in the entertainment world had anything to worry about.

Callie enjoyed the impromptu performance because she owned one less worry. All morning, she fought the feeling that memories were slipping through her fingers. Lucius lifted that anxiety after he battled his way over the felled pine's prickly branches. The tree collapsed deep in the yard. He was lost from sight when he stooped to inspect the dock. After an unbearable wait, he shouted the good news. The dock remained structurally sound, undamaged by the fallen tree. Callie sighed and tipped her face, eyes closed, up to the warm sun.

The dock was tangible proof she and Jack built a life together. It had not existed until they sank the timbers and added the cross-members. There, they shared hours, talking, laughing, and dangling their feet in the chilly river. Callie was mad when it came to guarding the physical items she associated with memories of Jack. And mad felt like the right word. Death leaves behind an odd type of insanity. It snipped the balance chains on her heart and substituted an endless ache and a handful of treasured objects to act as a prop.

She set her lunch dishes on the countertop at Arnett's elbow. Arnett stood at the sink with Eleanor. She thanked them for taking on kitchen duties, then went out to resume the work. She crossed to the porch steps and stopped short, startled by the noticeable change in the landscape. How many times would her gaze automatically dart to the gouge in the tree line? How many times would her shoulders slump with a sad reckoning between the missing tree and the missing man?

She forced her focus to the job at hand and trundled down the steps. Instead of heading out toward the larger issue in the yard, she veered off to check on Lucius's trimming job along the cabin's sidewall. He refused to relinquish his chainsaw into her hands, but attacked the underbrush, small trees, and a healthy crop of honeysuckle himself. She told him she'd be satisfied with the result if he could walk through the shady tunnel upright without a branch brushing through his short-cropped 'do.

Hands on hips, she surveyed the cleared area. It was definitely wide and tall enough. Cuttings lay on the ground. Looking, she saw raspberry vines in the mix, surprised the basal shoots came this far. But then, the grounds had basically been left unchecked for nearly two years. She and Jack intentionally planted raspberry cane closer to the riverbank. The shoots were those supplied by the bushes in her back yard.

Those bushes with their bowed purple vines transcended the day she walked away from Jack Sebring. Even now, she remembered the awkward, embarrassing moment, seventeen summers ago, that left her sick and alone.

That summer, Jack and Callie were separated by the needs of a golf course Jack designed for a fertile area in northern Louisiana. His original three-week stint onsite stretched to five when Callie received his call from the Baton Rouge airport. He was excited and heading home, hoping to make it in time for the birth of Gary's first child. He couldn't stay, couldn't see her, just in and out.

He arrived with ninety minutes to spare. Zachery was born in the wee hours. Jack counted ten fingers and ten toes, then went home for some sleep. Callie learned all this when he checked in at dawn the next morning, speeding back toward the airport. He apologized and asked forgiveness for not being able to stop.

Callie said she understood. Nothing changed as a result of the last eight hours. Little Zack or no little Zack, in Louisiana or in Maryland, that night would pass without Callie being seen, touched, or held by Jack. She appreciated the importance. It was the birth of a grandchild. Jack possessed the wherewithal to jet back and forth at a moment's notice. Also of paramount importance was the supervision needed during the initial stages of course construction.

But still, the slight glared. It cut. It hurt for the first time. Little Zack. Another Sebring. Another life to stand between her and Jack. The airliner carrying Jack flew over her home and the woods beyond. She stood outside. Cool morning air surrounded her.

Jack's invitation to join him in Tennessee came two weeks later. Callie still chased the slight and was percolating pretty good by then. Jack agreed to meet a man named Roland Abbott. He lured Jack to Tennessee in the hopes he'd agree to design a golf resort.

Jack planned that he and Callie would stay for a few extra days. He gave her directions to Abbott's property and invited her to drive straight there. She accepted, but felt a shadow pass over their relationship, reminiscent of the plane's shadow passing over the house.

Callie and Jack stood with Abbott on the one-hundred-fifty-plus acres he owned. How strange it must have seemed to Jack that she didn't touch him upon her arrival. She would always remember how she didn't step close enough to kiss or hug hello, her fingers didn't graze his, their arms didn't brush. But what she did do that day, when their love affair was nearing its seventh anniversary, would touch them forever.

"Raspberries can succor new canes some distance from the main plant," Abbott claimed. "They're vigorous, invasive, and would require continual maintenance."

Abbott's argument in opposition came after Callie insisted he save the two most gorgeous wild raspberry bushes she ever saw and plan the resort's landscaping around them. For her, their beauty enhanced the Tennessee setting, and she worked them into her emotional state that day. The bushes grew on an emerald isle encircled by farm fields, hosting the dead remains of whacked-off, sun-bleached cornstalks, and fence lines of gnarled skeletal trees.

While her emotions roiled inside, while her heart pounded loud in her ears, while her stomach cramped, she avoided Jack's stare, and proceeded to pick a fight with the man who offered Jack a year's worth of work over—of all things—the demise of two raspberry bushes.

Having said her peace and feeling ridiculous for it, she stamped off.

Jack caught up. He turned her around and took her shoulders in his hands. "What's this about? What's wrong?"

Over time, Callie summoned the truth about Jack. He owned an irrational fear. Like those who are claustrophobic or panicky in high places, he was deathly afraid of poverty, of becoming destitute, and that fear paralyzed any effort or thought of divorce. In his mind, divorce was synonymous with poverty.

The words Jack spoke so often rang true: "None of this would be worth it if I couldn't spoil you."

She understood this, too.

An impoverished Jack could not spoil those he loved with generous gifts; the need to spoil his loved ones was integral to his makeup.

Given all this, Callie could not and would not ever ask him to file for divorce. Because what if he tried? How would his fear respond? What would happen to him when he didn't seem to realize he possessed such a fear? Whatever funds were lost to Arnett in a divorce would promptly be replenished. He operated a lucrative business, but Jack saw divorce as a no-way-back ticket.

So divorce, to answer his question, could not be what this was about.

In the same instant, something else became clear. Neither could Zack be what this was about.

How could she make reference to his birth and the realization that similar situations would arise over and over in their life that was so top-loaded with Sebring family needs? How could Jack enjoy his grandson if he had to live with the fact that he lost her over Zack's birth? The rip she caused would scar his heart forever.

Jack's eyes were intense, focused beams. His strong grip and mild shake demanded an answer. Mentally, she zipped through options. Since telling the truth served no purpose, her only choice was to endure in silence. She would make peace with the circumstances because she did love him so.

The second shake he gave her wrenched words from her throat. "Just think about it, Jack. You figure it out." With the noncommittal challenge, she pulled away.

When he arrived at her front door the next morning, she was shocked by his unkempt appearance. The results of hard work and perspiration showed on his clothes and in the dust and dried mud layering tasseled loafers. He gave her a smile that didn't quite mask the fearfulness brimming his blue eyes: They told her he was a man trying to hold on to a woman letting go.

"Where would you like these, ma'am?" he teased, adopting a deliveryman's personae. Her gaze followed the rawhide gloves he held and a forearm crisscrossed by thorny scratches. They pointed to two raspberry bushes tucked inside the bed of a pickup truck parked in her driveway.

Callie's connection with the distant past broke when the wind swirled through the tunnel alongside the cabin. A cut twig teetered off its red maple perch and toppled to the ground.

Again, she looked around at the area Lucius cleared. She could drag the larger pieces to the chipper, but the rest of the work would go quicker if the smaller pieces could be raked. She stored no rake at the cabin. Jimmy had one, but Nadia used it. Callie thought Sarah might be a good source for a rake. Sarah went back to cover the condo office after Nadia arrived with her husband.

Callie stepped back inside, filled a plate with food, then buzzed out to the driveway, and climbed into the Santa Fe. She parked the vehicle on the graveled patch in front of the condo office. Carrying the foil-covered plate, she entered the outer office and found it empty. "Sarah, are you here?" she called.

"Callie, that you?" Sarah's voice floated through the doorway of her private office. A few seconds later, she appeared, stopping behind the counter where a short stack of outgoing mail lay.

"I hope I caught you before you had lunch." Callie held out her offering. "Fried chicken, mashed potatoes, and biscuits."

"How sweet. Thanks." Sarah's eyes crinkled. "I'm starved." Callie laid the Styrofoam platter in Sarah's outstretched hands. "Are you getting that tree cleared away?"

"It's nearly done. I could rake twigs the rest of the day, but for the want of a rake." Callie let her pleading face finish out the request.

Amused, Sarah said, "I have two you can borrow."

"Great. And thanks for the lend of Nadia. She's nearly as expert as Jimmy."

"I'm fortunate to have her. She's quite capable." Sarah's brows knitted briefly, studying Callie. "Say, while you're here, why don't you take a look at the papers that need your signature? There's just a few. You can use my desk." She left the plate on the counter and motioned Callie around.

Yesterday, Callie planned to sign the necessary paperwork, but overheard Beebe's plans to move to Michigan, and a panic set in. Today, she'd take the time to complete the task.

Nothing in Sarah's office changed since the last time Callie peeked in. Sarah picked up the brownish expandable folder tagged Heatherwood from the top of the filing cabinet just inside the door. She carried it to a wooden desk angled to face a large window on the back wall. The property behind the office was small, rocky, and dropped off to a shallow ravine. Across the ravine, a forested area climbed up the mountain.

Sarah indicated the seat behind her tidy desk, and Callie sat down. A closed manila folder lay on the desk blotter. Sarah slid a pen within easy reach. "Everything's self-explanatory," she said. "Take your time."

Sarah exited the office, saying she'd eat her chicken dinner outside. A few seconds later, Callie heard the squeak of the screen door's hinges. By then, the folder's top flap lay back, exposing a dozen stacked sheets. Sarah's SIGN HERE and INITIAL HERE tags positioned on various pages acted as guides. A copy of Heatherwood's deed topped the stack. Jack transferred the cabin to Callie when his cancer returned and hope for a successful fight was lost. No further signature was needed, so Callie flipped that over to the left side of the folder. The condo association agreement came up next. She read the three pages, signed, and dated the last. She scanned the one-page fee schedule and scribbled her initials in the lower corner. She'd already mailed in her dues. Sarah xeroxed the check. That copy followed. She flipped it over.

She signed an agreement giving Sarah permission to enter the property for routine maintenance and general inspections when Callie was absent. Callie gave signed permission for Sarah to hold keys to Heatherwood, necessary in order to complete the maintenance. Callie paid the insurance premium in March and sent Sarah a copy of the statement. She turned it over and initialed a neatly typed sheet acknowledging that the contact numbers and email address listed were correct. That brought up the last sheet, but it was not any type of association form. It was a letter. The handwriting was Jack's.

She remembered Sarah studying her over the office counter. She knew the letter waited. It was the reason she afforded Callie privacy.

Dear Sarah, the letter began.

Enclosed is a copy of Heatherwood's deed. I've signed the property over to Callie. I know of your recordkeeping fetish and so have thought ahead to provide you with your very properly recorded copy.

These changes in ownership are necessary, Sarah, because I'm ill. The doctors give us no hope.

Callie promises she will continue to drive to West Virginia, to stay at the cabin, to enjoy the special world we built there. I hope she can follow through on that. In the meantime, while we're both stuck in Maryland, please continue to give Heatherwood your utmost care.

You have been such a good friend that I must ask one more favor. Look after Callie for me when she visits. I'm going to miss her so very much.

Jack Sebring

A tearful Callie greedily absorbed every word written. She read the letter twice, then noticed a stirring in the doorway and turned. Sarah entered, a sense of reverence with her and a sympathetic look on her round face.

"After knowing Jack," she said quietly, "after seeing him with you, then receiving that letter, well— It's just foreign to think of him married to anyone other than you. God, he loved you." Sarah patted Callie's back. Her fingertips lingered, and Callie looked away, her chin trembling. "And leave it to Jack to turn my perception of the hereafter on its ear."

Head bowed, Callie smiled at the other woman's amused tone, and then Sarah found a thoughtful one.

"I still can't get over it. He was going to miss you after he died, and love you even then." She patted Callie again. "Anyway, I thought you'd want the letter."

Unable to speak, Callie nodded. From somewhere, a tissue box appeared, then Sarah slipped out, closing the door. The quality of her friendship was higher than most.

On that Friday, Callie proved her mettle against grief. Public tears were the worst, but the fight was on. After a three-tissue blow, the starch was back in her backbone.

Letter in hand, she got to her feet. The office door opened quietly. Sarah was nowhere around, neither inside nor out, but two rakes leaned against the Santa Fe.

Callie reached through the open passenger window and laid the letter on the seat, then grabbed the rakes and went around to the cargo door to store them. Settling behind the wheel, she never let her gaze drift from the letter. No wonder Jack made her promise to return to the cabin. She suddenly thought of the cabin as it had always been—a rendezvous for lovers. He'd been waiting there for her for such a long time. Waiting, and missing her. How comforted he must be by her presence. She ran a fingertip across the folded sheet. Jack was just the kind who'd have the strength of will to carry himself beyond death.

Closing her eyes, she thought back to the predawn when she felt the touch of his hand, when her promise remained unfulfilled. That supreme effort was meant to convey his patient understanding. If she listened carefully that morning, she might have heard his voice in her ear. "If you are not too long, I will wait here for you all my life."

Now in a rush to return to Heatherwood, she turned the engine over and negotiated a tight U-turn. The odd twist of feelings rode with her.

Throughout the afternoon, she performed the outside work robotically. They were an exhausted group when the tree was cleared. She expressed her gratitude to the O'Malleys, Updykes, and Lucius for their time when they headed out. Callie and her cabin mates dined on leftover chicken. By sunset, a swift coolness plunged down from the northern mountain peak. Callie scurried around, finding blankets to ward off the overnight chill she knew would come. If there had been conversation among them, Callie could not have attested to its content.

Eventually, a quiet darkness engulfed Heatherwood. Callie started out between the sheets, but, as had become the rule, sleep would not claim her. On that night in particular, she didn't expect it would. She slipped out of bed, draped the blanket around her shoulders, and went into the great room. The surreal feeling that embraced her ever since she read Jack's letter walked with her.

She drifted through the cabin, letting moments with Jack fill her mind and tug at her heart. She stopped to look through the window in the kitchen door. She knew she owed him more. She owed him a successful outcome to this horrendously difficult week.

In the night sky, gauzy cloud-cover trailed away. Moonlight lit the river and served to illuminate a decision Callie wrestled with for hours. She needed one more caucus. Through her, Jack would be heard. If Beebe wanted a topic to head the next clean page in her notebook, sentimentality should be written there.

"Jack," she said to his nearby portrait, her little finger crooked, "when morning comes, I will speak for you." Staring at the gleam in his eyes, she kissed the air between them, then slipped back to their bedroom, crawled between the covers, and slept.

The Godfrey's Caper

At seven, Callie woke to a quiet cabin. She showered and dressed. She was nursing a mug of coffee and working patchwork squares into a design at the kitchen table when first Beebe, then Arnett stirred. Both went to stand under hot pulsating sprays. Lizbeth, with cartoon-like slits for eyes, shuffled out for coffee. She mumbled a good morning, which Callie merrily returned, adding that Lizbeth had thirty minutes before she served pancakes and sausage. The nod she gave Callie sent a cow-licked section of hair into a wild bob.

Callie felt for Lizbeth. After lunch yesterday, Lizbeth joined in with vigor to dismantle the tree. Last night's hard sleep allowed the body only slow, deliberate movement. Callie worked out the worst of her kinks. The others would feel better soon.

And food would help. Callie's pancake recipe, Jack's favorite, called for egg whites only in the floury mix. She measured out small amounts of lemon juice, sugar, and baking powder. She got the griddle going and paid close attention to the link sausage in the skillet. She cleared her sewing away to set the table. Beebe appeared. By the time she poured four glasses of orange juice and set the coffee carafe on the table's hot pad, Arnett and Lizbeth were seated. The cool mountain air gave everyone black-bear appetites.

When the clinking of silverware on china eased, Lizbeth announced she was considering a drive into town.

"Maybe later," Beebe said, taking charge. "Callie has reserved time for a caucus."

Arnett shrank visibly with the news.

"I thought she and I would chat about that while you two clean up. Would you mind?" Beebe sent her rhetorical question to Lizbeth and Arnett. She was already scooting her chair back.

Callie knew, as she followed her away from the table, she would not preview much more about her sentimentality story than just that. With the tree to clear, the group had not caucused the day before.

The windows and doors, closed against the overnight chill, prevented the cabin's occupants from hearing Lucius's truck pull into the drive. He simply appeared outside the kitchen door, swept through, bussed Beebe's cheek with a kiss, then Callie's. He glided over to the table where Lizbeth and Arnett still sat and pressed his lips first to a damp head, then curly locks. Between each kiss, he spoke musical and individualized hellos.

Callie wondered how long Lucius had been mainlining sugar.

"What are my precious girls up to this morning?"

"Callie and I were just going out to talk. She wants a caucus."

"No, no," Lucius said, his face a mask of horror. "Absolutely not. Lucius has his dinner party tonight. You haven't forgotten." He strode up to Beebe. "You mustn't caucus. Not today. Upset ruins the digestion."

Listening, Beebe tipped her head to one side, amused. "But Lucius—"

He cut her off. "No caucus. No upset!" Then his lips curled up at the corners. "No need," he said, smug.

"Lucius, what are you up to?" Lizbeth said, her eyes narrowed by suspicion.

"Nothing, pumpkin. It's just that I prayed you wouldn't caucus," he said, "not since my last trip to Godfrey's."

Lucius's last word caused Callie to straighten, unobtrusively, she hoped. Godfrey's was meant to clue her in. She caught and held his gaze for a nanosecond before Beebe spoke. "It's Callie's call if she wants to cancel."

Everyone focused on Callie. She had to trust that Lucius's show-stopping buildup to the evening's dinner party was more about the true resolution the two of them were conspiring to produce than a successful social gathering. They became conspirators at Godfrey's. Shortly thereafter, they maneuvered two others, Willie Thorne and Vincent Bostick, to climb onboard. She wanted to create a magic similar to the kind Jack could spark: diamond rings and a cabin's name being excellent examples. She searched the carpenter's face and made a decision.

"Okay," she said, "I won't cancel, but I will wait." She was not opposed to keeping her midnight promise to Jack at the party, in front of Willie and Lucius. Digestion be damned.

Lucius took two long strides and pulled her toward him. "Thank you, sweet knees." His next words dropped to a whisper. "We'll talk outside." Letting go, he turned to the seated pair. "Now, what was breakfast?"

"Pancakes," Arnett said, getting up, infused with new energy, the kind only a delayed caucus could produce.

"Good," Lucius said. "Pancakes will hold you. Do not eat. No caucusing, no eating. Put your heads together and come up with something else to do. If you can't think of anything, Lucius has it covered. What, you wonder?" the day-planner said. "Just wait. Lucius brought a surprise. But first, I'm two chairs short around my dinner table. Callie, my dear, dear nursery mate, may I?" He laid an arm around Callie's shoulders, then slid a covetous glance toward her kitchen furniture.

"Sure, fine. You get one. I'll get the other. A little help, please," Callie said to Beebe, who pushed through the screen door and held it wide.

They carried the chairs to the rear of his pickup and out of earshot.

"See, I told you we needed a codeword." He set the chair down to reach into the truck bed for one of the mover's blankets he brought along.

"Where are things?" Callie said, suddenly anxious.

"Willie reported in," Lucius said, still in secret-spy mode. "He made the call to Senator Emerson. He's sounding positive. He's got a plan for tonight. We'll follow his lead."

Instinct told Callie she could rely on intelligent Willie Thorne. With teamwork, they wrapped the first chair in its blanket, then moved to the second.

"What about the shipment?"

The shipment Callie referenced connected a fact learned while speaking with Vincent in Lucius's cabin to a gift for Beebe. A quilt, in fact, one Callie planned to sew from Beebe's mother's clothes. Callie's style of quilting came up during the conversation, and Vincent mentioned that the mother's clothing still resided in Clifford Walker's house.

"Vincent confirmed the shipment," Lucius said. "I think it's all going to work out." Closing the tailgate, he faced Callie and clicked his heels. "It has been my sincere pleasure to serve."

The Godfrey's Caper, Callie thought. Jack could not have done better.

Callie waited while Lucius collected a half dozen DVDs from the pickup's front seat. Of course, she thought, this was Lucius's surprise. With any amount of spare time, Lucius watched movies. She remembered the specially designed shelves his music and movies occupied in the Bullwhip cabin. Back inside, he sought out Lizbeth. She whipped a terrycloth kitchen towel over her shoulder in order to receive the DVDs in both hands.

"I've got another handful of animated movies in the truck I thought

Chad would like."

"Oh, my!" she said. "Thank you."

"I'll put them in the Tahoe." Smooching his fingertips, he tossed a measure of expressed affection into the air for everyone's benefit.

Callie walked Lucius back out. He went to the truck. She opened the Tahoe's passenger door, so Lucius could place the four retrieved Pixar DVDs on the seat. He released them, and the slippery plastic cases fanned out, becoming a collage of images and color. At the same time, Callie noticed Lizbeth's cell phone lying on the charcoal-gray floor mat. She leaned in to scoop up the phone. The device responded to her touch. With similar ease, an idea flashed through her mind.

"Lucius, be my servant one more time."

"I'm yours to command, Oh Great One." His tone was as sly as hers.

She thumbed through the stored contact list. The two numbers she wanted came up back-to-back: Patrick, Lizbeth's brother, followed by Ralph and Mildred, their Florida relatives.

"This may take some time," she said. "More than we've got before the party. But we'll put it in motion anyway. Here's what I need you to do." He grinned through her entire explanation. As Beebe would receive a special gift, so would Lizbeth. A mural.

She intended that he just take the phone numbers, but Lucius said, "I'll just borrow this, then give it back at the party." The cell phone dropped to the bottom of his jeans pocket.

Callie just crossed the cabin's threshold when she and the others heard his shout, reminiscent of a cavalry charge. "My beloved is coming!"

Beebe took a step toward the window. "Is Willie out there?"

"No," Callie said, waving Beebe to a stop. "Lucius is just giddy with anticipation."

Across the room, Lizbeth stood at the sofa table where she arranged the movie DVDs. Arnett looked on. "They're all Denzel Washington,"

Arnett observed.

"Must be a favorite of his," Lizbeth assumed.

Beebe's idea was to take the day and see the countryside with a drive to Brier Hills. She wanted her first-ever golf lesson, which Callie agreed to give. Lizbeth was game, but Arnett declined for obvious reasons. She and golf never got along.

Beebe climbed into the back seat of Callie's Santa Fe. Lizbeth belted herself into the passenger's seat. Callie motored the SUV past Sarah's office and out to the turnpike. She couldn't make out what Lizbeth muttered as she dug in her purse, but she knew the woman searched for her lifeline to the outside world. That lifeline—her cell phone—was in Lucius's possession.

"What are you looking for?" Beebe wondered. Her tone said she was exasperated on Lizbeth's behalf.

"My cell. Where is it? Oh, no." Lizbeth's chin came up. "I left it in the Tahoe. We've got to go back."

Callie, who knew the futility of that exercise, merely passed Lizbeth a glance. "I doubt there'll be service at the course or anywhere along the way. If there is, my phone is charged. You're welcome to use it, or you can call from a landline at Brier Hills." Callie pressed the gas, and the SUV sped along the shady parkway. Lizbeth seemed appeased. The Godfrey's Caper still ruled.

After stops at two overlooks to appreciate the breath-taking views, Beebe and Lizbeth glimpsed the beauty of Brier Hills. Vivid color abounded. The scent of pine cleaned the air. The flag bearing Brier Hills' dignified crest snapped with the wind, high on its flagpole.

"Look how pretty," Lizbeth said.

"This is gorgeous," Beebe added.

The curved entry road gave the visitor a long look at Brier Hill's chateau. The resort could sleep three hundred guests. Fairways of the two sister golf courses splayed out to the left. Only a few were visible from the entrance. Jack designed the rest to cut in, around, and over the foothills. Farther off in the distance, two stationary ski lifts rose to higher peaks. Abundant evergreens covered the grounds and the mountains.

Callie drove around the main building to the clubhouse and parked. The clubhouse matched the chateau's image, just a much smaller version. Jack laid out the area for the driving range next to the clubhouse. Beebe and Lizbeth received their first golf instruction there. The ladies met Eric, the young man with a thin face and stringy hair who stood inside the golf hut, behind a counter, dispensing yellow buckets of balls. With her bag of clubs over her shoulder, Callie walked her friends, each carrying a full bucket, past several groups of men warming up for their day on the course.

The lesson got underway with the basics, of course. Each lady held a club. Soon golf balls were laid at feet positioned a shoulder-width apart, and the real action began. Beebe's stance and her swing told Callie that somewhere in her past, she played softball. She swung so hard, she nearly fell down and always whiffed the ball.

Callie corrected Beebe's posture. "Keep your arms relaxed," Callie told her. "When you tighten your muscles, that shortens your reach and you miss the ball."

Beebe nodded her understanding. She rolled her shoulders and let her head loll a moment on her neck, then addressed the ball again.

"Oh," Lizbeth exclaimed from next door. "Look what I did."

Callie stepped over. Lizbeth chewed her lip. Both she and Lizbeth stared at a gash in the ground caused by Lizbeth's club head.

"Well, yes," Callie said, "that's a little more than a divot. No matter. Golfers are required to repair all divots."

She traipsed ten feet out to where the fresh rip of sod lay and picked it up. She fit it back over the brown earth and instructed Lizbeth to tap it down with her club head. She did, still gnawing her lip. Callie moved Lizbeth away from Beebe and away from the repaired divot. Lizbeth would not want to be reminded of the damage she caused. Callie knew men thought absolutely nothing of it, but it was a proven fact in Callie's book that there was something innately bred into amateur women golfers that made them not want to hurt the ground, to leave a mark. They wanted to play the course and leave it pretty and pristine. In time, they realized the divot is an important part of the game.

A pure and uninhibited "Sweet Jesus" emitted from Beebe's lips. Surprisingly, Lizbeth kept her focus on Callie. "Take some practice swings," Callie suggested. "Skim the grass with your club head when you swing through. After you do that six or seven times in a row, step up and swing at the ball." The ball was already in place on the grass.

Sweet Jesus? Callie thought, giving Lizbeth and her six iron a wide berth. Beebe straightened her shirt. It hung over capris. Momentum from her hundred-mile-an-hour swing twisted the fabric around her hips.

Callie faced Beebe. "It's a rocking motion. A weight shift." Callie demonstrated the foot movement Beebe's should imitate. "No need to swing so hard. Let the loft of the club face do the work. Watch your balance," Callie cautioned, studying Beebe's set up. "Keep your feet under you, butt out."

"Butt out?" Beebe mixed the question with a confused expression.

"Butt out," Callie repeated. She faced away from the practice range, showed perfect form in profile. "Get your rear bumper out there. It will help anchor your weight."

Beebe gave her backside a wiggle. "Well, if that's all it takes, I've got it licked."

Their neighbor from several yards away walked over and caught Callie's eye. He wore a white Titleist hat and plaid golf shirt. The yellow bucket he carried was empty.

When Callie closed within distance for a discreet conversation, he said, "Got a softballer and a tender-turf maiden there."

"'Fraid so."

"Boy, this brings back memories. Couple years ago, I taught my wife how to hit the ball."

"How'd it go?"

"She's better. A lot better, really. Dumped my teaching abilities for the pro back home. Now, she finds it necessary to remind me— Wow!"

Her back to the range, Callie heard a solid crack on the ball.

"She got all of that one," the man said, his eyes following the ball's upward flight.

Which she? an excited Callie wanted to know. Before she turned, he told her. "She nearly fell. Watch it. Whoops. Whoops. Whoa. She's down."

From the ground, Beebe turned a sheepish look on Callie. "Rear bumper out. I know."

Lizbeth rushed to help her up.

While Beebe dusted herself off, she noticed the golf cart parked next to Eric's hut. "Hey, I want to take a spin. That looks like so much fun."

"I want to call Pat and talk to Chad," Lizbeth tacked on.

"Maybe Eric will let us borrow his cart for a few minutes to drive around to the chateau." Beebe tugged on Lizbeth's arm.

"What do you think?" Lizbeth asked Callie.

"Let's ask," Beebe said.

Callie trailed along. She knew how it must have looked to Reese Norton approaching in his own cart from the first dog-leg along the creek. Reese was the pro Callie played golf with earlier in the week. He witnessed an animated conversation by three women not dressed in golf attire—in fact, one of them wore pink clogs—and young Eric who craned his neck to view the symbolic "rear bumper" of the object drawing all the attention. The backend of the cart jutted out next to the teensy structure he worked from.

The look on Eric's face clearly said he was overwhelmed. His mouth hung open even as he took the ten-dollar bill Callie offered. At the same time, Beebe climbed behind the wheel and Lizbeth jumped in the other seat. Beebe sped off, a little recklessly at first.

Eric still held the money. Callie said he should think of it as a tip.

Reese redefined the transaction.

"Taking bribes again, Eric?" Reese angled himself out of the cart. His white golf shirt billowed. His hands slipped into pants pockets.

Although Callie knew Reese teased the painfully timid young man, all the color drained from Eric's cheeks. "It'll be okay, Eric. If everything goes my way, I'll be your boss before summer is over. I can tell you now, you'll always be my favorite."

"How do you figure that?" Reese no sooner spoke the words, then astonishment registered. "You're taking the job!"

Callie and Reese stepped away from Eric. On Tuesday, Reese detailed the job when he gave Callie the sales pitch for assistant pro. That day, she resisted his persuasive efforts. So the current circumstances begged the obvious question: What changed?

Reese knew her connection to Jack Sebring, to Brier Hills, and since Tuesday, he knew her connection to the old woman who was Jack's stepmother, none other than Adeline Peterson Sebring. Petey. Today, Callie rewrote the ending. Today, Reese learned of Petey's recent and quiet death.

"It's time to start over." She spoke around the thickness she felt lodged in her throat.

Reese expressed his condolences. They set a realistic date for her first day on the job and shook hands. He took off in the cart, heading back out to the course.

Callie went over to Eric. She pressed another ten spot into his palm. "Don't say anything about what you heard to my friends."

He looked like he would rather throw up before he dared utter one word about Callie's move to West Virginia.

She forced Eric to take something other than an honest pledge. This was a sliver of the Godfrey's Caper she gave to herself. And the secret would only be a secret for a short while.

With time to spare before Beebe and Lizbeth returned, she went over to her golf bag and drew out her driver. She held the long shaft in the crook of her elbow and resting on her forearm while she worked her fingers into a leather glove. Her focus dropped past her hands, to the grass around her feet. She believed she stood on this very spot with Jack before Brier Hills existed, when the land was raw and the possibilities for created beauty lived only in Jack's mind.

She knew she stood here with Jack after the courses were complete. They made use of the practice range many times. She let her gaze out to a horizon that seemed so familiar. She would have traveled to that horizon with Jack. They would have held hands every inch of the way. Her consolation prize for that loss of companionship for that unachievable dream was Brier Hills and memories of Jack.

She set one of the range balls up on a tee. With the club head resting on the ground, she curled her fingers around the grip. Her eyes never wavered from the ball while the golfer inside her executed a perfect swing. Contact was made. When she found the ball in flight, she watched it sail long and strong and straight, on its way toward that distant horizon. While she watched, she felt the shadow of Jack step up and stand beside her.

The ladies returned to Heatherwood that afternoon on the fly. There was just time to change clothes, primp for two minutes, grab Arnett out of the middle of Denzel's *Training Day*, and race back to the Santa Fe, which Lizbeth accomplished without searching the Tahoe's floorboards for her cell phone. Callie now jumped that hurdle twice.

Callie made a left turn from Bullwhip and steered through a border of trees that shielded Lucius's and Willie's cabin from the road. Once through the entrance, she pulled in beside Lucius's red pickup and Willie's black Lexus. In a shady clearing next to the cabin, Lucius had literally constructed an open and elegant dining-room scene. The overhead timbers of a wooden tent-like framework were draped with yards of white chiffon. The gauzy fabric spilled off at the corners, where it gathered into long folds that reached down to a grassy carpeting.

Awed, Callie got out. She and Beebe rounded the rear bumper.

They joined Arnett and Lizbeth who stood motionless, their gazes running the distance to the unique and stunning setting. A light breeze lifted the chiffon and caused the flames on tapered candles to wink off water and wine goblets.

Lucius and Willie strolled gracefully out the cabin's door and down the porch steps. Tall and thin, they sported wide smiles. They wore their comfort with each other as casually as old clothes, but were in fact clothed in stiff white dress shirts, open at the neck and tucked into belted trousers.

Handsome Willie Thorne startled Arnett into a hushed comment. "Denzel Washington. I get it now."

Al Fresco

Lucius watched Willie meet the ladies under the aged sycamore. Although the newcomer to the group, Willie handled the introductions. Callie, he knew. She turned her cheek up to receive his kiss. Willie apparently formed an accurate image in his mind of the other three after a week of Lucius's nonstop stories.

Wine and cheese were served without delay on the porch. Not a soul seemed inhibited. Conversation thrived. The atmosphere was carefree, light with laughter.

Twenty minutes later, Lucius heard the kitchen timer ding. With a lady on each arm, he and Willie squired their guests to the table. The hosts went inside to put the meal on a serving tray. Lucius spent his afternoon slaving over New England pot roast and cat-head biscuits. An old, old woman in Baron supplied the biscuit recipe.

"Cat head refers to size, not ingredients," Lucius said, across the island counter, giving his beloved an ornery smile. "And we all know, size matters."

Willie's ardent brown eyes twinkled. "Lucius, don't even mention the lack of cat-head ingredients at the dinner table."

Coffee was served with dessert, a light peanut butter pie. Everyone cooed their compliments. So far, Lucius considered the *al fresco* evening a beaming success. They were an intimate group under the tissue-thin canopy. The candles danced with the laughter Willie eased out of the women clad in volumes of color.

Sitting back in his chair, Lucius watched Willie. He teased their guests good-naturedly. From the first, they knew instant rapport. The conversation was animated and bright.

For entertainment, Willie employed a version of comedic investment advice. Arnett starred as his intended patsy. With her hand layered between his brown pair, he gazed deeply into her eyes. Speaking with a French accent, he made wild financial claims. "*Madam*, you cannot lose money. No risk. None. I know this fund. For years, it has prospered."

Quickly, Lizbeth probed the financial education Lucius knew she owned. "No one, not even our handsome *Monsieur* Thorne, can make that claim, Arnett. Rates of return are based on account premiums, withdrawals, fees, and earnings." She ticked the items off on her fingers. "Tell *Monsieur* Thorne you know past performance is no guarantee of future results."

"*Monsieur* Thorne, I know past performance is no guarantee of future results," Arnett repeated dutifully.

"Now, everybody." Lizbeth looked down the table to the others. With her hands, she whipped Beebe, Callie, and Lucius into the chorus.

"*Monsieur* Thorne, past performance is no guarantee of future results," they sang out.

"*Oui*, *Madam* Sebring, *oui*, that may be, but I can show you figures. Exact figures." Willie patted his shirt's breast pocket. "I don't have them here, but trust me."

"Estimates." Lizbeth leaned into the table, talking past Willie, directly to Arnett looking so serious, taking it all in. "He can show you estimates only. The term is dollar-weighted rates. One can make assumptions for estimation purposes only. Keep that in mind with this guy." Lizbeth winked and tipped her head Willie's way, then she called on her chorus. "Again, folks—"

The trio repeated: "*Monsieur* Thorne, past performance is no guarantee of future results."

"On the other hand," Lizbeth said, "future predictions—and only predictions—are based on past results."

Willie tugged Arnett's attention his way. "With me and my company, *madam,* I will work hard for you. Daily. *Oui,* daily, I will make trades for you. Many times a day. No worries."

"I find that hard to believe," Lizbeth said, using a tsk-tsk tone. "Arnett, tell him you know *reputable* firms have excessive trading policies and monitor fund-transfer activity for the benefit of their valued clients."

Arnett perked. "Am I a valued client?" She batted dark eyes at Willie, articulating her own thought, one so like Arnett.

"Oh, *oui, oui.* What if I put you into an annuity that provided you an extra, say, fifteen hundred dollars a month? Would that meet your expenses, give you a cushion, allay your fears?"

Lucius watched Arnett actually consider that one. "Is that possible?" she wanted to know.

Lizbeth's discouraging voice answered. "First of all, that figure is pre-tax. All the taxing agencies will want their share. And it may be your responsibility to remember and pay them. Secondly, that figure may be good today. But don't bank on it for years on out. Over time, inflation will erode your spending power. *Monsieur* Thorne should be telling you about mortality tables and fine print."

"Mortality tables? I don't like the sound of that," Beebe said, frowning.

"He can make estimates now, but they're purely hypothetical," Lizbeth said.

"This financial stuff is crazy," Beebe directed her words to Callie. "Purely and hypothetical used in the same sentence."

Callie, Lucius's co-conspirator, grinned, then passed him a knowing look.

On it went, Willie's claims designed to part poor Arnett from her money; Lizbeth redirected his strategy toward safer ground.

"I can't believe you just said bullish with a French accent. What a hoot," Beebe laughed.

"Watch him," Callie said. "He's a fast-talker."

"It's all get-rich-quick scheming," Beebe decided.

"You want prudent planning," Lizbeth advised Arnett. "Remember words like: stability of principal, growth funds, and variable annuities." Lizbeth snapped her fingers at the choir and the terms flew back.

"Stability of principal, growth funds, and variable annuities." They were a little out of synch, but Lucius thoroughly enjoyed the fun.

"Listen to Lizbeth, honey," Beebe said, "*Monsieur* Thorne appears to be a charlatan of the highest degree."

It was Beebe who shot the first make-believe arrow at Willie. Then Callie picked up her imaginary bow and repeated the exercise. Neither could Lucius resist. Willie played along masterfully. His hand covered his heart, where the invisible arrows struck. Slowly, dramatically, he deflated. Lucius's gaze circled the table and his band of merry women in Nottingham Forest.

Beebe capped the performance by raising Lizbeth's arm in victory. She had no idea how great was that victory.

Lucius clinked his dinner knife against a wineglass to silence the jabbering. His gaze drifted around the table. "I am so glad we did this. Our first dinner party," he laughed, "maybe not in the cabin, but on the grounds anyway. We couldn't have asked for a more beautiful group of ladies to be our inaugural guests." The men clapped their hands, then Lucius looked at Willie. "Well, up or down?"

Four heads turned. Willie gave a thumbs-up gesture, then licked his index finger and drew an exclamation point in the air.

"Excellent," Lucius said, thrilled. "The floor is yours."

Willie shifted in his chair, turning a line of white teeth on Lizbeth.

"My dear, your entrance into Lucius's life at this moment in time is nothing less than a miracle. You're an intelligent young woman with impeccable credentials." Sitting forward, he added quietly, "I've checked."

Everyone was riveted to the scene: Lizbeth stared at Willie, open-mouthed, cheeks flushed.

Willie continued. "All the shop banter about finances and investments was a test. I listened and graded your responses. You see, I'm in need of a first lieutenant, someone to manage the Cassel office. I spoke with Senator Emerson." Lizbeth's eyes bulged and Willie's glittered. "He agrees you'd be underutilized and underpaid in his office. He gave you a glowing recommendation that when added to Lucius's high praise, and with what I've heard and seen tonight, brings me to this question: Lizbeth, will you accept a managerial position in my firm?"

Lizbeth stammered. She turned to her faithful counselor and searched Beebe's face. Consent was written there. When Lizbeth flipped her questioning gaze at Lucius, he put his hands together in prayer and mouthed, "Say yes."

After Callie's exuberant nod, Lizbeth's course around the table got hung up on Arnett. The light went out of Lizbeth's eyes, taking the night's gaiety with it.

She swallowed. "My plans to move to Florida hit a major snag yesterday. Once that sunk in, I realized I was looking for something that never truly existed."

Her explanation came without form or content. Lucius's heart went out to her. He understood the nonexistent something was the murals.

"Willie," Lizbeth smiled, "yes, I will accept the position because you come very highly recommended yourself." Boss and underling shook hands. "Or maybe I should call you Mr. Thorne?"

"Willie is preferred."

Beebe whistled. Applause and congratulations followed.

Willie said, "We'll set up a private interview next week, but only after I make a contribution to Emerson's campaign fund."

"No. He didn't." Lizbeth laughed in disbelief: She'd been traded like a football star. A quizzical look came over her, and she wagged a finger from Willie to Lucius. "Wait, how did you guys know I had a finance degree? Lucius, we never spoke about my college studies."

"Callie," Lucius said. "She put it together. She knew Willie had a position to fill."

Still Lizbeth appeared stupefied.

"Don't you remember?" Callie said. "You gave Tom your resume when we asked to use the restaurant's phone."

Lizbeth bestowed Callie with a fond look. "Thank you so much."

Callie nodded. "You'll do well."

Lucius scooted his plate forward. "Now, my lovely ladies, more good news. You are also present to hear about the next chapter of our life, Willie's and mine." He paused for effect. "We're selling the house in Cassel next week. Come January, Willie and I will be here under the same roof. Our good friend, Lizbeth, will be efficiently managing the business by then, and I'll see her and her alabaster skin daily by video feed. It will be a delight."

Willie chirped up. "Very quickly, though, I need to find temporary accommodations through the end of the year. I don't want to be living in the office."

"You've got them. My house." The speaker was Callie.

"Move in with you?"

"No, you'd have the place to yourself. I took a job offer at Brier Hills."

Lucius was up-and-out-of-the-chair ecstatic. He gave Callie multiple and loud kisses on the top of her head. "My Callie with me in Baron. And Willie, too." He skipped around, smooched Willie's head, and was rewarded with a whiff of sexy cologne.

"Apparently, Lucius didn't know."

Willie's comment stopped Lucius in his tracks behind Lizbeth and Beebe. "Ah!" He pointed at Callie. "You, girlfriend, kept a secret from Lucius."

He reseated himself just as Beebe cleared her throat. She pulled her napkin from her lap and laid it on the table. As her weeklong confidant, Lucius knew what was coming and covered her hand with his. When he took it away, she turned her chair to face Lizbeth.

"This appears to be the evening to speak of new beginnings."

Lizbeth's face went slack. She seemed to sense the arrival of something ominous in the night air. Even the birds and crickets oddly ceased their chatter.

"I've been in a state of flux for a while. Months ago, my mother died, and I need to reestablish a closer relationship with my father. I've agreed to join forces with an old and dear friend and take on some social work."

"Where?" Lizbeth asked, hesitant.

"My hometown. Larkspur, Michigan. I leave next week."

Lizbeth stiffened. She drew in a long breath, then let it escape. "First Callie, now you. Here, I'm staying in Maryland, and you're both leaving."

"But you'll survive." Beebe patted Lizbeth's shoulder.

Lizbeth raised her chin. "Yes. Yes, I will." She lifted both arms to Beebe.

When the embrace ended, Beebe said, "You're all invited up. If not this fall, then next spring." She smiled. "After winter's thaw."

"Fine, because we're all coming." To Callie, Lucius said, "May I?" She tipped her head, granting permission. "We'll trek north," he announced, "and we'll come bearing a quilt."

At the notion of a visit, Beebe's expressive eyebrows climbed her forehead. Slowly, they slipped back into place. "A quilt? I don't understand."

"I called Vincent yesterday from Lucius's cabin," Callie said.

"You found Vincent? How?"

"Lucius remembered the agency's name from the fax," Callie answered. "With the name, a phone number was easy to find, and I needed to know that you'd be all right back home." Callie tapped her chest hard. "I needed someone to provide that comfort. And I wanted to know a little about Vincent as well, and whatever part of the story he'd tell me. But he got me talking about how I met you. That led to talking about the quilts. He told me your mother's clothes were still there, in the house."

Beebe's hands found the discarded napkin. She twisted it.

So very gently, Callie said, "Vincent talked with your father. He talked him out of the clothes."

The expression on Beebe's face deteriorated to dread. "No, Callie, no," she said, shaking her head repeatedly.

Lucius scooted to the edge of his chair. In his best soft-as-combed-cotton voice, he said, "Look, kitten, we all want Arnett to accept her quilt, but I'm asking you first. Accept yours."

Beebe flung off his proposal. "No. It's not possible."

Lucius's eyes never left the woman struggling with the weight of the years, the abandonment, perhaps some strong feelings bordering on hatred, the taunting of schoolmates, a teenager's crumbled life. She saw its rocky remains piled at her mother's feet. Or was she picturing her grave?

"Are you saying you won't accept a healing quilt made of your mother's clothes?" Lucius said. "You've been urging Arnett to accept hers, given the circumstances, but you won't accept yours?"

"But my mother's clothes—"

"Have already been shipped to Callie's house." Lucius revealed that confirmation to Callie at Heatherwood after the pancake breakfast. He hunched over the corner of the table. "Now, Beebe, in front of all of us, by next spring, will you accept the quilt?" Lucius could almost hear Arnett's mind chirp, "And display it."

Final Caucus

Lucius asked again. "Please, Beebe, accept the quilt?"

For the longest time, she didn't move or speak or breathe. No one did. Finally, she dragged her eyes around the dining room scene, from Lucius to Callie, then to Arnett. There, they stayed. "I hope to be living at home with Dad. He and I can share the quilt and heal together."

Lizbeth patted Beebe's back. Willie applauded. Lucius watched Callie. She wore a satisfied smile. He wished he'd lain fine linen place cards at each chair, so at this moment, he could instruct everyone to turn the card over. Fancy calligraphy, graceful, yet with bold lines, would hand-letter the week's true ending. By candlelight, each guest would read: Life repackaged by Callie.

The woman on the road to golf stardom met and fell irreversibly in love with Jack Sebring. Lucius didn't doubt that Callie, with her many strengths, experienced vulnerability with Jack, and he with her. A giddiness preceded Lucius through every moment since he drove Callie to Godfrey's the day before. Along the way, she conceived the plan to lift Lizbeth and Beebe over the hump, and she enlisted his willing assistance. He went to sleep last night tingling to greet the dawn. He fully expected to tingle with every dawn greeted thereafter. Callie gave Willie sanctuary and eased Lucius's loneliness. Those were priceless gifts.

Lucius stared down the table to transparent Arnett. She felt the pressure to drop her defenses, follow Beebe's lead, and accept her quilt. She squirmed nervously as though she sat on a quilt in progress, straight pins and all.

"One more piece of information before I ask the question of the week." Lucius drew Arnett's pained gaze. "What Lizbeth doesn't know—because it would be crass to discuss salary in public—is that Willie's job pays enough to send Chad to a fancy pre-school. Paycheck-Saver Arnett won't be needed for that reason any longer. You've lost some ground there, gummy bear. I hope you can let go of some pride, too."

Callie tugged his shirtsleeve. "Wait! My caucus."

At the interruption, an anticipation-stiffened Arnett went absolutely rigid.

Beebe frowned. "From earlier?"

"I said I'd put it off, but I didn't agree to abandon it altogether. What I have to say must be said now."

Beebe quickly studied faces. "Okay. Begin when you're ready."

For all her urgency, Callie hesitated. She tipped her head back, her eyes closed. She was steeling herself. That worried Lucius.

She began the caucus with a dedication. "I miss Jack so much, and what I have to say, I want to say right. For the most part, these are his words. Without realizing it, he allowed me a glimpse of Arnett. Two glimpses, really. Miniscule as they were, I meshed them together. Before you all showed up in my front yard, I'd already formed an image of Arnett in my mind. All week long—with everything that's happened, with everything that's been said—I've been unable to blot that image out. And we have Jack to thank."

Callie looked dead on at Lizbeth. "I know what Jack would do if he were here. You know it, too. He would never permit this treatment of Arnett. You may not understand his motivations, but I do. He would not want his family torn apart further. If he were here, if Chad were here, he would sit that little boy in his grandmother's lap, and then he'd stand guard in front of them." Callie wired determination through her words and pointed one finger in the grandmother's direction. "He would dare you to take him away. He'd be the first to admit to Arnett's faults, yes; but he would never allow this."

Night had fallen. The canopy blocked what little benefit the moon and stars might have provided. For a moment, Callie stared at the dwindling dinner candles. When she spoke, Lucius knew she found memories in the candlelight.

"One afternoon, I caught Jack lost in thought. He stopped at Arnett's earlier to get more of his things. When I asked, he told me he was thinking about the hurt he caused. Then for some reason, he added, 'Arnett is so sentimental, especially about family.' I tucked that away. Months later, I learned about Arnett's grandmother's chair."

There, Lucius departed briefly from Callie's presentation to smile down at his own memory. Grandma Hannah and he spent many mornings reading storybooks in her grandmother's chair, wingbacked and sized for two.

"Over the course of four grandsons, I guess the chair required recovering," Callie said. "Jack went to settle the bill with the upholsterer and see to its delivery. So now, I've got two things contradicting my prior impression of Arnett: sentimentalities and a grandmother's chair. This is the image I can't force from my mind. No matter what I've heard, that image sticks. I can't stop seeing Arnett and Chad sitting in that chair. It may be Jack's influence." Callie leaned onto the chair arm to face Arnett. "You may discount everything I've said on that argument alone, but he would not wish you any more heartache. He would want you to bend just this little bit, for the sake of family peace, and accept the quilt."

Callie painted a nice picture of Arnett, Lucius thought, only to be struck by the irony of taking Callie out of the equation. What if Jack's life had proceeded without Callie? Would he have died on the same day? Would Dan have? Would Lizbeth's feelings for her mother-in-law have been any different? Probably not. But without Callie, there'd be no quilt to accept. This trip would never have happened. In all likelihood, Arnett would have done something else to royally piss Lizbeth off, and the fight over Arnett's involvement in Chad's life would have shot off from the starting gate anyway. Given the general animosities between wives and their husbands' girlfriends, Callie had every reason to side with Lizbeth, but she chose to stand with Arnett.

"If you don't accept the quilt on my terms, Arnett, you can't ride home with me," Lizbeth said, reviving her ultimatum. "Your only option is to ride with Callie. I'm going straight to Marietta to get Chad. The prohibition starts tomorrow. We're out of time. Decide now."

"You can ride back with us," soft-hearted Willie said, reaching out a hand to Arnett. "We've got real estate matters to tend to."

Willie's brief interruption was no deterrent. "I have rights to that child," Arnett blasted Lizbeth. "Maryland grants rights to grandparents. It's the law. I can win in court—"

"Court again, Arnett. No," Beebe rebutted. "We've been through this."

"You've been through it. Why would I agree to compromise when I can get temporary visitation—"

Lucius tapped a knife against his wineglass. "Shhh, Arnett. You don't have to decide right now."

"Hey," Lizbeth argued.

"It's my party, and I say she can wait." After the firm words, Lucius released a sigh and some tension with it. "Look, we're all sitting on some pretty nice rewards this week. Our benefactor," he indicated Callie, "gets a new start in West Virginia. Lizbeth gets a to-die-for position in Willie's firm. My beloved has been offered a home while in flux. This wild one gets a memory quilt she will treasure, and our promise to visit." Beebe returned his smile. "And my precious, over-the-top-stubborn Arnett, you, my pet, get one minute and thirty seconds."

The gazes of four women bounced off each other like so many billiard balls smacked with a wooden cue.

Lucius leaned over on a hip and pulled Lizbeth's cell phone from his pocket. "Lucius has a secret weapon."

"That looks like mine," Lizbeth said.

"It is yours," he said. In total darkness, Lucius believed Lizbeth would recognize her precious phone.

"How'd you get it?"

"Forgive us, peaches. Callie and I found it on the floor mat when I put Chad's videos in the Tahoe."

"Callie." Eyes wide, Lizbeth shot the name across the table to the owner. "You knew all along."

Lucius responded. "Of course, she did. This very helpful device gave me access to Brother Pat and Uncle Ralph."

"You didn't!" Lizbeth sputtered.

"I'm glad I did because it also gave me access to Arnett's minute and a half." He cut his eyes to Arnett. "That can be a lifetime, darlin'."

With that, Lucius ushered everyone into the living room and Arnett to the seat of honor, Willie's recliner. Beebe and Lizbeth sat on the couch. Lucius turned the desk chair around for Callie, so it faced the flat-screen above the fireplace. Willie controlled the laptop. Lucius nodded, and he activated the electronics. A stilled picture appeared on the wide screen.

Chad, in a red and navy striped shirt and faded jeans, sat cross-legged in grass. Behind the camera, his Uncle Pat sat at ground level too, his legs stretched out.

"How did you get this?" Lizbeth flung at Lucius.

"Pat posted it. Sent the link to your phone. Need I say more?" He had no choice, really, but to peek at the linked video, what with the coveted reputation of meddler extraordinaire to protect.

Lucius stood off to the side for a view of the television and the women. Willie, next to him, tapped the laptop's touchpad, and the picture moved forward.

Patrick's voice asked, "What did you like best about Wednesday, the day we arrived to visit Maria and Gracie?" Occasionally, one or the other of his worn running shoes drifted into the picture. Chad was stationed just beyond. The filming took place at dusk. Fireflies dotted the background.

Chad's response was immediate. "Maria got Buster that day."

"What did you like about Thursday?"

"On Thursday, we went on the picnic."

"What did you like best about today?"

"We saw farm animals. And I rode a pony." His fists came up to accentuate his accomplishment.

"What will you like best about tomorrow?"

The boy's face brightened. "Tomorrow, you promised I could sail remote boats in the pond."

"Remote-control boats," Uncle Patrick helped.

"Right, remote-control boats."

"And what will be best about Sunday?" Patrick posed enthusiastically.

"On Sunday, Mommy and Grandma will pick me up. I can't wait to see them."

Willie paused the screen's image. Throughout the elapsed one minute and thirty seconds, the steady camera lens captured the four-year old's excitement for puppies, picnics, and ponies, but that dulled by comparison with his wiggling expectation of a joyful reunion.

Lucius went to stand by the boy frozen on the plasma, the downturned shape of his eyes a match for his father's. "You've heard how much Chad wants to see you, Arnett. And you've heard Lizbeth's final decision. No quilt, no Chad, starting tomorrow. Time is running out. Will you accept the quilt?"

Bless her. She withstood ten piercing eyeballs, an even dozen if Chad's were counted. Arnett Oldstone Sebring was tough as rebar.

. . .

Lizbeth woke Sunday morning with the same thought wedged inside her head from the night before. She stared up at the cabin's ceiling. A sheet and thin spread were the only weight on her, but the combination felt as heavy as being pinned under a truck. "Please, Arnett," she prayed, "please, don't make me explain to Chad why you didn't come with me."

On the silent ride home from Bullwhip, Arnett would not speak, so no one spoke. Lizbeth thought her hold on the situation slipped. The removal of Florida from the equation left Arnett feeling victorious. Given enough time, Arnett assumed she could chip away until Lizbeth lost her grip altogether.

After watching the video, everyone appealed to Arnett. Everyone asked her to decide. Then each, in turn, recognized the futility of his or her efforts. Simply said, that was Arnett. She sapped every ounce of energy out of a person, every last breath, then she merely stepped over the misshapen lump for her seemingly effortless win.

It went without saying, the gentlemen walked the ladies out to the SUV, saw them settled inside, and closed the doors. As Callie steered the Santa Fe through the tree-lined entrance, Lizbeth looked back. In the distance, behind the two men, stood Lucius's moonlit outdoor dining room. The moonlight was bright enough for Lizbeth to witness Lucius's chin drop and his shoulders sag. Willie rubbed his back. What a disappointment for Lucius, she thought. After all his sweet intentions, his enchanted evening ended on an Arnett-soured note. The others all faced forward in their seats, so this memory was solely fixed in her mind and strung to her heart.

Lizbeth noticed Arnett spent some time searching Chad's eyes on the TV screen. In a few short hours, though, when Lizbeth pulled the Tahoe into Maria's and Gracie's Marietta driveway alone and Chad came racing out the front door, his eyes would be hers to search. His loss, hers to console again.

All week long, Lizbeth swaggered and lorded her position of authority over Arnett. But until she turned out the bedside lamp last evening, Lizbeth hadn't once considered that ultimately, she was the person taking a grandmother away from the boy who'd lost so much already. Arnett knew. She walked the situation through. Quite the artful dodger, she devoted a lifetime to manipulating people and situations so that she was never the one dispensing unpleasant news. No words could undo the visual for her young son: his mother occupied the SUV; his grandmother did not. That would be tantamount to rejection. Lizbeth expected gigantic hot tears from both of them.

Lethargically, she crawled out from under the covers. Once dressed, she stood over her suitcase at the foot of the bed, packing her belongings. The anticipation of seeing her son should have overwhelmed as deliciously as waiting to sample a three-layer chocolate cake. The day now came to partake, but she found the icing slid off in the warm weather.

The new job would help, she told herself, and Chad would make friends at daycare. While it was months away, they would make plans for the holidays, when Geoff came home from school.

Lizbeth looked around the room for anything she missed. A corner of something stuck out behind her purse on the dresser. Going over, she saw the three photographs from the entryway table lay there. Frowning, she picked them up. Where was the quilt?

"Arnett! If you've done anything to that quilt, I swear—"

She yanked the bedroom door open and blustered through.

The first thing she saw was Arnett standing at the screen door, looking out. Her suitcase sat at her feet. The sounds Lizbeth's heels made on the hardwood echoed through the eerily quiet great room. She stopped after four steps and looked down to the other bedroom doors. Beebe's was closed, Callie's cracked open a few inches.

She swung her attention back to Arnett, waiting on Lucius's and Willie's arrival for the promised ride home. Since she hadn't announced her decision last night, they had no alternative but to make the trip over this morning to hear her answer.

And her answer was clear: She couldn't be bothered to understand Lizbeth's side and do what was best for Chad. Lizbeth's anger flared, forcing her mouth open. Charged words of frustration and defeat were forming on her tongue when Arnett pushed her shoulders back and turned. Folded across one arm was the quilt. She held it tight against her. Lizbeth glanced right. The entryway tabletop was empty.

With her head tipped to the quilt, Arnett ran a reminiscent hand over one of the Hawaiian shirt patches. Lifting her chin, she said, "My father never issued his verdict on the same day the case was given him. Sufficient time for thought was required. The parties were due just and thorough consideration. That was his rule."

Lizbeth put a smirk on her face. So, this was to be Arnett's high-handed verdict from the bench. Thankfully, Lizbeth resisted the urge to roll her eyes heavenward in disgust; that put Arnett dead center in her crosshairs when the transformation occurred. Lizbeth watched the woman soften by degrees. When Arnett spoke again, the formal, black-robed Judge Oldstone was no longer in the room.

"To tell you the truth," she said sheepishly, "I always sort of waited for John to brave my bucking temper and defend the other side. Then, just like he had some innate understanding of Oldstone custom, he gave me overnight. The next morning, I was ready to go along. The only difference between him then and you now is, I never acknowledged openly that I accepted his position. He would see me standing here and know there'd be no way I'd give up that little boy."

A wave of unbridled relief flooded into Lizbeth's heart, snapping bands of tension. She started forward.

"No, wait." Arnett threw up a hand. "I have more, and I have to say it now." Her eyes never left Lizbeth. "I was ready to accept your demands after the storm."

Lizbeth shook her head. "Two days ago?"

Arnett nodded. "That night, I gave myself the talk John would have." She paused. "You know, now that I think about it, those words weren't John's rationale. They were mine, with a tiny twist of truth tacked on." She smiled. "Typical for me. But I was so grateful you weren't hurt, and overwhelmed by Callie's heroism. It's hard for me to admit when I'm wrong. I guess that doesn't come as a surprise. I hope as time passes, you and I operate more in tandem. I waited for you to ask me to accept the quilt that night, but you were too upset because I held back my last conversation with Dan. The next day, when you were up and around, then yesterday, too, I sensed something changed in you. I compensated with my best serving of stubbornness and anger because I was so scared."

Arnett's gaze dropped to the floor. "I thought that because John worked so hard to keep peace in the family, to negotiate truces, that he still loved me, and would love me, no matter what. That turned out to be a smokescreen. He found happiness elsewhere." Lizbeth watched Arnett disappear inside herself. "In the end, he found it hard to say he'd given all he had to give." Arnett patted the quilt. "Thank you. This was awfully nice of you."

"You're very welcome," Lizbeth said, touching her arm. She eased over a moment before, just about the time Arnett became her scared mother-in-law.

"I'm ready to go get that boy," Arnett declared.

Beebe's celebratory whistle punctuated the announcement. She and Callie swung through the latter's bedroom door, clapping. They'd been listening. Beebe rushed forward for a group hug. Callie hung back. A coolness still existed between the wife who once loved, and the other woman who always would love Jack Sebring.

Beebe tugged Arnett into a little dance. The joy was intoxicating. The jig ended with Beebe red-faced and flapping the front of her shirt.

Lizbeth had no illusions about Arnett. She would slide into Cassel, head high. She'd carry the quilt over her arm, walk with her grandson hand in hand, and be practiced with the angle she'd add to the Florida story. Lizbeth's decision to remain in Maryland would become the victory Arnett gleaned from her time at Heatherwood.

Lucius and Willie arrived a few minutes later, saw Arnett with the quilt, and leaped forward to plant a kiss on each cheek. The men, then, surprised Lizbeth by lavishing their attention on her. Lucius led her to the kitchen chair Willie pulled away from the table and turned toward the group.

Lucius looked to Callie. "It's all arranged. Can I tell her?"

She inclined her head. "Be my guest."

On his knees in front of Lizbeth, Lucius took her hands and told her about the mini mural to be created from one of Dan's landscapes. The mural would be hung like wallpaper on her dining room wall. His coordinating partners helped. Uncle Ralph had the business contacts to enlarge the painting and see to its printing; Brother Patrick, a frequent visitor in Lizbeth's home, provided the wall dimensions.

As Lucius spoke, Lizbeth's eyes welled. Speechless, she expressed her gratitude by throwing her arms around Lucius's neck. She released him after a tight, tight hug.

Lucius rose and went to slip an arm around his nursery mate. "Life repackaged by Callie," he said. "This was her idea."

Lizbeth worried no further about being short on words. Everyone talked at once.

Once the Tahoe was packed, Lizbeth and Arnett headed to Marietta. At destination's end, when Lizbeth's hand gripped the knob to shift into park, Arnett's fingers overlapped her daughter-in-law's.

"When you get home, there's going to be a letter in your mailbox from Harlow Nolan. Promise me you'll throw it away unopened."

Immediately, Arnett jumped out. She still held the quilt.

Up at the house, Chad slammed out the front door. His short legs, sticking out of cutoffs, carried him straight to his grandmother, who swept him up in the wide-open quilt. Arnett puckered and landed one of Chad's sweet kisses. When Chad reached out to his mother, the patches around his grinning face were Dan's number fourteen baseball jersey and his Kool-Aid-stained Saturday shirt.

While the scene unfolded, Lizbeth counted her blessings. They included Beebe, Callie, Lucius, and Willie. Protectors all. She would survive the loss of a love.

One Black Glove and A White Lace Hanky

A few weeks later, Callie and Lucius, via video feed, learned that Lizbeth and Arnett worked out another compromise. It whittled back Arnett's grandsitting time. They agreed Chad should be enrolled in preschool. He needed to see faces other than his mother's and grandmother's. He needed to play and learn and grow and laugh, and they needed him to come home enthusiastic with stories of his day. Arnett picked him up at three every afternoon, and Lizbeth got him from her house after work, where she thrived. Occasionally, Chad and Lizbeth stayed on with Arnett for supper.

Lizbeth reported the quilt made of Dan's clothes lay across the back of Arnett's grandmother's chair. She never saw Arnett and Chad sit there. That was not a picture Arnett permitted. Dan sat with them, Callie thought. For Lizbeth, that was enough.

In early October, a workman hung the mural. Lizbeth told Callie and Lucius she would find herself leaning against the room's doorframe, daydreaming about walking with Dan hand in hand through the field of tall grasses and colorful wildflowers depicted in the mural toward a centuries-old barn and silo in the distance and purple-peaked mountains beyond. In a moment of honesty, she confessed there were days when she could not face the mural, when she couldn't bear to lose herself in the meadow again, and kept her eyes averted. On those evenings, she sat with her back to the field of memories and let her son's jabbering at mealtime keep her grounded in reality.

Lucius's big night came on the third Saturday in October. Baron celebrated its Festival of Leaves and the town fathers dedicated the new visitor's center that inhabited the shell of the 1892 train depot. Lizbeth and Willie drove down together for the dressy affair. Lucius's fabulous restoration work brought him accolades all evening long.

During the last week of March, Callie sent an email to Lizbeth. The short message read: Beebe's quilt is finished.

Lizbeth took on the coordination of schedules. A plan was made to gather at Beebe's house for dinner the second Saturday in April. During the intervening two weeks, Beebe reported her father, Clifford Walker, was eager to receive both the quilt and Beebe's friends in their home, seamstress Callie in particular.

Beebe's first two months in Michigan were filled with strain and grief for the two Walkers. Callie noticed her conversations and texts reflected improvement soon after Abigail Walker's grave was moved to the family plot and a new headstone erected. Forgiveness played a part as well.

The distance between Maryland and Michigan was broken into a two-day trip for Lizbeth, Arnett, and Chad. They were the first to arrive. Lucius and Willie would be the last. Willie wanted to keep an appointment with a client in Pittsburgh, just a jog off Interstate 79.

Callie checked in with Beebe when she passed the new school campus at the city limits. Beebe told her the women's gabfest was on. Her father and Chad were taking a walk to the back gate. Callie understood that meant they escaped to stroll the neighboring cemetery.

At first blush, Larkspur put Callie in mind of a fishing village. She drove the main drag to the outskirts on the north side, then a bit farther to Larkspur Cemetery and the caretaker's house. The house was as old as the cemetery, the cemetery as old as the town.

Callie motored her Santa Fe into the drive. She no sooner stopped behind the Tahoe than Lizbeth rushed out the door and down the porch steps. She gave Callie a long hug, disproportional to the amount of time they spent in each other's company, but Callie understood the origin for the fondness.

Lizbeth expressed her feelings to Callie the week before in an email. Callie was pleased to read a small remembrance of Jack woven into Lizbeth's opening sentence: *I ruminated for several days before composing this message.* Ruminated, Callie thought, Jack would have said that.

The message continued:

I feel a closeness for you, that until recently, I could not adequately explain. At first, I thought I pumped you up in my mind when Arnett tended to be Arnett, but the epiphany arrived with your last email. When I read that Beebe's quilt was ready, the news lured me to Chad's room.

I had to smile at my sleeping son, curled in a tight ball and covered by a uniquely crafted quilt. It was then I understood the source of the bond. Every night when I put Chad to bed, I pulled you closer and closer. Every night when I brushed curls from his forehead, I silently thanked God for the quilt maker and the quilt maker's gift. That quilt symbolizes a father's love: It cushions, and warms, and protects.

Thank you, Callie. In your grief, you not only touched Chad and me, but you touched others who grieve. I pray it lessens the burden on both sides.

The sentiment moved Callie deeply.

From the rear of the SUV, she lifted out a large, sturdy gift box. Lizbeth closed the cargo door, then hurried to open the wide mahogany door with black iron accents that gave them entrance into the caretaker's house.

It was late afternoon, and the sun swept in through the west window and across the living room, making dramatic contrasts of bright light and deep shadow. The walls looked freshly painted, but other than the butter yellow, all the furnishings came from another age.

Callie set the box on the coffee table. She was still taking in the room when Beebe and Arnett appeared under the dining room's archway, carrying trays of cookies and fruit. Beebe's face lit. Lizbeth went to take Beebe's tray.

When Callie and Beebe separated, Beebe was transfixed on the box. Lizbeth and Arnett left the trays on the dining room table and returned. Callie and Arnett nodded silent hellos while Beebe went to sit on the couch. The remaining three gathered around the low table. A quiet no one wanted to disturb filled the room. Just to let Callie know the world was still out there and operating, she felt refracted sun warm the backs of her legs and superimpose her image on the wall.

Finally, after excruciatingly long seconds, Beebe reached out with both hands and lifted the lid. As soon as it was free, Arnett stepped in to hold it. The box was lined with white tissue paper. Through it, like a dissolving morning mist, squares of color took shape. Beebe folded the tissue back with trembling hands. Very delicately, she lifted an exposed corner of the quilt, then her movements froze.

A sad, almost tragic smile lengthened her face. Tears were close, memories closer. Callie felt the heat of tears herself. Her stomach clenched. There was a contagiousness to Beebe's hesitancy that fed her fear. What if Beebe wasn't emotionally ready to face her mother? What if the quilt was less of a cure-all and more of a setback? Callie thought back to recent telephone conversations with Beebe. She spoke of her father's eagerness to see the quilt, his readiness, never her own. Callie was nearly ready to grab the lid out of Arnett's hand and slam it down on the box when Beebe's chin rose. She looked into the faces around her. Her lips parted.

"Help me."

Lizbeth and Callie each took a corner of the quilt. It tumbled open. Hands were placed at four points across the top edge to prevent sagging. The quilt was draped at an angle over the coffee table. Beebe pulled it into her lap and straightened the lower half. Arnett sat on the edge of the couch and held up a corner.

Callie watched three speechless women study the quilt, their attention skipping from patch to patch. For Beebe, though, each square must port her back in time, and the burden Lizbeth mentioned in her email stepped forward in Callie's mind. Beebe seemed to gaze right through the cloth, reliving scenes with her mother. Snippets of life would overlap, like flipping through pages in a photograph album. Callie desperately wanted her to view them with an open, forgiving heart.

Nursing uniforms in white, pastels, and prints, cut to size, were scattered throughout the quilt, alongside squares clipped from dresses, blouses, and skirts.

Callie devoted time to several unique patches. One patch included the two-inch waistband from a black-and-white hound's-tooth pleated skirt and four inches of perfectly aligned pleats. Beebe ran her finger under a clipping of an eyelet lapel and collar folded back at their proper angle. The eyelet was used as decorative trim on mint green summer pajamas. Then, her hand went to a square sewn in high and right of the quilt's center. The patch was taken from a heavy cream-colored tablecloth with a tapestry look. Stitched to the square was a knotted bow made from downsized apron strings. The apron fabric was a rose organdy. Beebe peeked at the quilt's underside. The rest of the tablecloth doubled as backing.

Callie carried her pocket theme into this quilt as well. She tacked three fingers of a black glove so they jutted from a slanted pocket cut from a dove-gray, lightweight jacket. Several squares over, the corner of a white lace hanky hung listlessly over a welted pocket in navy. Callie found the glove and hanky in the pockets. By exposing them, Callie hoped to convey a sense that Abigail Walker never planned to abandon her daughter. When it came, the desire to flee was quick and intense, exactly the way addiction preys upon need.

From deep in the house, a door opened and closed. Clifford Walker called out. "We're back."

Her father's voice interrupted Beebe's concentration on the quilt. Her head jerked toward the sound. "Oh, Daddy, hurry," she said. "She's here."

. . .

It was dark when Callie unlocked Heatherwood's door and let herself inside. She enjoyed her time in Michigan, but the drive back was a long and tiring one. She set her suitcase next to the entryway table and looked around. During the past seven months, she adapted well to life in the cabin. Heatherwood, more than the house back in Cassel, felt like her true home because, from the first, it belonged to her and Jack.

Callie turned on a few lamps. Her thoughts drifted back to Beebe and her father with the new quilt. In all honesty, Callie felt like she intruded on the emotional reunion. The seamstress in her, though, was heartened to see her labors bloom and bear fruit. The quilt was, indeed, a presence in the room. The presence was Abigail Walker.

Jack's quilt, tugged off the back of the couch, fell into Callie's lap. Her finger traced the chain-stitch embroidery along the bottom edge. The curling vines of her traditional raspberry logo formed a heart.

Without much inducement, faraway memories of Tennessee settled in beside her.

Back then, she hadn't wanted to retain any portion of that chapter in her life. She hoped she would never again come within miles of Eastern Tennessee and be reminded of that awful scene with Jack. Of course, even now, the memory remained clearly preserved in her mind.

Jack arrived at her door in Cassel at nine the next morning, disheveled, with two bushes in the back of a pickup.

"What brought that on?" he asked after she shyly let him into the house.

Callie couldn't explain her behavior in Tennessee, but she promised the raspberry bushes made everything all right.

"Okay then. I still don't know specifically what this was about, but I know it was about us," Jack said, lifting her chin so her eyes met his. "Now, it has to be about whatever I can do to insure that the raspberry bushes have truly saved us."

Zack, Tennessee, the raspberry bushes, they represented the first real hurdle Callie faced in her lifelong relationship with Jack. She stumbled badly; Jack helped her up. He took it on faith that she loved him still. Her commitment was real. He figured that much out.

That day, Callie combined Jack's two longtime fears: poverty and losing her. Those two challengers were steeped in battle against each other.

Long after midnight, when he was gone, the bushes planted, and she lay in bed, too tired to sleep, questions popped up in her head. Some things didn't make sense, timing-wise. Why hadn't he showered and dressed in clean clothes before leaving the Tennessee motel? She assumed that with Roland Abbott's permission, he called a local nurseryman for advice and assistance in digging out the bushes. But he arrived at her door at nine? If it was a six-hour trip from Tennessee to

Maryland, then...

"Oh my God," she breathed, "he stole the bushes in the middle of the night."

Callie smiled down at the memory as she pulled Jack's quilt up to cover chilly arms.

Love, larceny, and wild raspberries, they made a heady, heady brew.

CPSIA information can be obtained
at www.ICGtesting.com
Printed in the USA
FFOW03n1032010216
20856FF

9 781612 965123